Chicago China Blue
By Michael Collins

PublishAmerica
Baltimore

© 2003 by Michael Collins.
All rights reserved. No part of this book may be reproduced, stored in a retrieval system, or transmitted in any form or by any means without the prior written permission of the publishers, except by a reviewer who may quote brief passages in a review to be printed in a newspaper, magazine, or journal.

First printing

ISBN: 1-4137-0641-X
PUBLISHED BY PUBLISHAMERICA, LLLP
www.publishamerica.com
Baltimore

Printed in the United States of America

To my wife, "Sam," for her encouragement,
her dogged belief in me and this novel,
and her unwillingness to give up,

and

To Francis Collins,
the man whose real life inspired this story,
and the uncle I never had the opportunity to know.

Prologue

Japan annexes Korea in 1910.

With the start of hostilities in Europe in 1914, Japan begins to assume control over many former German island possessions in the Central Pacific. Japan's occupation is validated in 1919 by the Treaty of Versailles, which seeks to penalize Germany for its actions in the Great War and mandates that Japan govern the Pacific islands it already occupies.

Using Korea as a staging area, Japan occupies limited portions of northern China in 1918. Over the next two years, it slowly expands the area of its tenuous control.

In 1920, Captain Andrew Long becomes Director of the Office of Naval Intelligence, ushering in a new and vigorous era for military intelligence. But in 1929, U.S. military intelligence suffers a major setback when Secretary of State Henry L. Stimson disbands the U.S. Army's special "Black Chamber" cryptanalysis operation.

On Tuesday, October 29, 1929, the New York Stock Exchange suffers a precipitous decline, initiating the "Great Depression." Thousands of Americans suffer financial ruin. Impacts spread worldwide. In Japan, widespread economic hardship enables the military to increase its political power. Militants look to Manchuria in the northern reaches of China to expand Japan's possessions beyond Korea.

On September 18, 1931, secret agents of the out-of-control militant officers of the Japanese Kwantung Army blow up the Southern Manchurian Railway near Muken. Blame is placed upon Chinese bandits. Japan uses the contrived incident as justification to invade Manchuria. By March of 1932, the Kwantung Army has occupied virtually all of Manchuria and established the puppet state of Manchukuo.

Franklin Delano Roosevelt is elected the thirty-second president of the United States on November 8, 1932.

MICHAEL COLLINS

Japan withdraws from the League of Nations on March 27, 1933, after being condemned for its occupation of Manchuria.

The Chicago Cubs open their 1934 season on April 17 with a 6-to-0 win over the Cincinnati Reds. "Lanky" Lon Warneke allows only one hit.

I

FRANCIS

1

SEAMAN, FIRST CLASS, FRANCIS MARIAN looked at the large, round clock high on the wall above the door to Captain Bates' office. Francis had been ordered by Chief Holmsley to report to Bates at fifteen-hundred hours and it was almost that now. Francis could feel the sweat—nervous, smelly sweat—running down his back. He was worried—damn worried. Rumor had it that Bates, the commandant of the Navy's training school at San Diego, was an old navy sea dog that could chew you up and spit you out before you knew what hit you. And the reason Holmsley had ordered him to see Bates had to be—it couldn't be anything else—because Holmsley didn't believe Francis.

Francis thought that after nearly four weeks in the communications course, he and Holmsley, the course instructor, were on pretty good terms. Sure, Holmsley had accused Francis of cheating after the first week of classes, but that was not surprising, nor the first time someone had drawn that conclusion. Francis finished his exams quickly and got everything almost always right—all the time. But once Francis explained to Holmsley why the exams were so easy for him, he thought Holmsley was satisfied. But apparently that wasn't the case. Holmsley's obvious smirk of satisfaction when he told Francis to report to Captain Bates seemed to say it all. Being ordered to see Bates could only mean trouble.

Then, as the hands on the clock moved to precisely three o'clock, a voice boomed through the intercom on the yeoman's desk by Bates' door. "Is Marian out there?"

The yeoman looked up from the sports page he was reading—the Chicago Cubs had given up only one hit in beating the Reds in the opening game of the season—and flipped the intercom switch. "Yes sir," he answered.

"Send him in," the voice commanded.

"Aye aye."

The yeoman looked nonchalantly at Francis and cocked his thumb toward Bates' door. "You heard the man."

Francis opened the door slowly, cautiously, and stepped into Bates' office. Bates, a large hulk of a man, sat behind a wide, shiny wooden desk—the scratches from long use readily apparent despite frequent waxing. Approaching the desk, Francis saw a thin brown folder in the middle of the desk amidst a stack of papers there, and it had the name "Marian, Francis S." on the tab. The sweat began to stream down his back.

"Seaman Marian, reporting as ordered, sir."

Francis stood at attention several long—at least so it seemed to Francis—moments, waiting for Bates to say something.

Then, finally, in a rasping but firm voice, Bates said, "At ease, Marian."

Francis assumed a rest position—hands clasped behind his back and his legs slightly spread—but he felt as taut as a stretched string.

"Chief Holmsley talked to me yesterday—seems he's worried that you might be cheating on your examinations."

Damn! I knew it. Holmsley doesn't believe me, Francis said to himself. Francis started to open his mouth to speak. "Sir, I told—"

Bates held up his hand, stopping Francis from saying anything else. "He explained what you told him, and I'm interested in that. Is it true? The chief says you told him you have quite a knack for remembering things you read—that you can remember all the things you read in your instruction manuals, even the wiring diagrams. Is that right?"

Francis' tense muscles relaxed. Maybe Holmsley did believe him. But Francis had told Holmsley about what he could do only to get Holmsley off his back, not to be cross-examined by a noisy captain. He had tried to leave questions like that back home in Chicago when he left to join the Navy.

"Well, Marian, what about it?" Bates asked, with obvious annoyance at having to prompt Francis to speak.

Francis bit his lip, a feeling of desperation taking hold of him, trying to delay the apparently enviable.

"Well ... I guess I do, maybe, sir. I do pretty well remembering what I read ... at least for awhile." Francis stopped, not wanting to say more.

"What do you mean, 'at least for awhile'?" Bates growled.

Francis let out a sigh of surrender. "Well, I can read something, and if I pay attention to what I am reading, I can remember what I read for a couple of days."

"What do you mean, 'a couple of days'?" You mean if you read something—carefully—something in a book, something you never read before, you can repeat what you read, word for word, several days later?"

Francis hesitated.

"Speak up, Marian. I want to know," demanded Bates.

"Yes sir. For the first few days, I can remember the words really easily. After a few days, things become disconnected. Some of the phrases I remember—and some I don't. The longer I don't try to repeat what I read, the less and less I remember—at least word for word."

Francis stopped talking, hoping Bates was satisfied. Francis looked silently at Bates for a few moments, as Bates rubbed his chin. Then Bates twisted in his chair.

"Marian, see that bookcase in the corner?" Bates asked as he pointed to a small bookcase with some well worn books in it and a photograph of an old single-piper steamer on the top of it. The steamer was moving in a strong wind, with a large flag—but not U.S. flag—stretched out from the ship's bow.

Francis turned his head to look. "Yes sir."

"Pull out that thick gray book—the one with the title *Harbor Equipment and Structures*. Turn to... uh... page two-forty-four, and read out loud until I say to stop," Bates ordered.

Francis took three steps to the bookcase and then paused as he looked at the photograph of the steamer, struck by the strange looking flag. Then he pulled out the book and turned back to face the captain. Turning to page 244, he looked up at the captain and asked, "It doesn't start out with a new sentence at the top of the page, sir. Should I still start at the top of the page?"

"Yes, yes," Bates responded, as he motioned impatiently with his hand for Francis to start.

Francis started, his voice shaky. "And other utilities are handled following normal practice, except at rail and vehicular traffic crossings. Loads are severe at crossings, with both static and dynamic loads of importance. Cast iron and steel pipe materials are subject to rust. Waterlogged soils are conducive to development of rust...." Francis continued for several minutes, turning page after page as he worked his way through the complicated text.

Then, as Francis started to turn yet another page, Bates cut in. "That's enough, Marian. Put the book down on my desk here and go sit in the other office until I call you."

Francis did a wobbly about-face and exited the office, closing the door as he did. He sat down in the chair in front of the yeoman's desk.

FRANCIS GRIMACED, his emotions in turmoil. Francis knew what would be next—he would return to the captain's office and be asked to recite what he had read. And he knew he could do it. But if he did, what would happen? Old memories of being made to look the fool when he was a kid because he could remember so many things so easily—everyone thinking he was pulling some trick all the time—began to flood his mind. And mixed in with all the mockery was the painful derision of his stepfather, who could see no use for such a talent. "Successful businessmen don't rely on memory; they have secretaries!" he would always say. Now Bates—he obviously was not ridiculing Francis, but Francis didn't like the questioning, or where it might lead.

But if Francis pretended he couldn't remember, he was sure to be accused of lying to Holmsley and somehow cheating on Holmsley's exams. And that was something Francis did not want to happen. He really liked the Navy. He didn't want to be kicked out of the communications school—or maybe even the Navy—for cheating.

"What the hell's wrong with you, Marian?" asked the yeoman as he stared at Francis.

Francis looked at the yeoman and said nothing.

BATES MULLED over what to do next. Obviously, if Marian had any smarts he would know that he would be asked to repeat what he had just read. But could he do it? And was there anything else he could check that Marian might not expect? Ah, the photograph! Bates rose from his chair and stepped over to the bookcase, picked up the photograph, smiling a bit at the memories it brought back, and then returned to his seat, placing the photograph face down on his desk.

As he waited before calling Marian back, Bates looked at Marian's file again: Marian, Francis Soong. Serial No. 30-0215. *Strange middle name—has to be Oriental, like his eyes*, Bates surmised. It had been a long time since he had seen deep, narrow black eyes like that. And the hair, thick and dark—like most Orientals he had known. But his complexion was light, and he was slim with broad shoulders—not the build of an Oriental. Maybe he had mixed blood in him. Bates' mind drifted off—back to the years spent plying the China coast when he was only an ensign, and the many women he had known there. Mixed-blood match-ups—and their consequence—were not uncommon out there.

Bates returned to Marian's file. Rank: Seaman, first class. *And*, Bates thought, *if he successfully completes his training here, petty officer, third.*

And unless Holmsley is shittin' me, that won't be a problem. Born San Francisco, Cal., 29 Feb. 1910; Graduated James Madison High School, Chicago, Ill., June 1929; Entered Univ. Chicago, Chicago, Ill., Sept. 1929; Enlisted USN, Chicago, 15 Aug. 1930. *Why did he quit college? Maybe it was money. Times were really tough about then—not that they were getting any better now, of course. Roosevelt's election a year and half ago, despite all the promises, hadn't changed much of anything yet. Marian probably joined the Navy to survive, like so many were trying to do now.*

Bates continued studying Marian's record. After basic training at the Great Lakes Naval Training Station, sea duty on the *San Juan*, a cruiser stationed just up the coast at Long Beach. Nearly three years of sea duty, with assignment after six months to communications work on the ship. Nothing unusual in his fitness reports, except that they were all quite good. In 1933 he applied for communications school—nothing strange about that either. Marian seemed to be a real go-getter. *But,* Bates mused, *the captain of the cruiser had added his personal recommendation to the request for communications school. Usually a cruiser captain wouldn't say much except to approve the request, if he were so inclined. Maybe he saw or heard something.*

Then Bates turned in his chair, pulled a key out of his pocket, and unlocked the file cabinet behind his desk. He thumbed through the files in the second drawer, finally extracting the one labeled, "Office of Naval Intelligence." Bates opened the file and turned several sheets until he found the document he wanted. He read it again—with much greater interest than the first time when it had arrived a year ago.

11-MAR-33
FROM: JAMES MALCOLM-WILSON, ASSISTANT SECRETARY OF THE NAVY, OFFICE OF NAVAL COMMUNICATIONS, OFFICE OF THE SECRETARY OF THE NAVY
TO: COMMANDERS OF ELECTRICAL AND COMMUNICATIONS TRAINING SCHOOLS AND PROGRAMS/ U.S. NAVAL YARDS AND STATIONS
SUBJECT: IDENTIFICATION OF PERSONNEL
REPORT TO CAPT. C. A. MCDONALD, COMMANDER, SPECIAL PROJECTS GROUP, OFFICE OF NAVAL INTELLIGENCE, PEARL HARBOR, HAWAII, ANY TRAINEES UNDER YOUR COMMAND WHO COME TO YOUR ATTENTION WHO APPEAR TO HAVE THE FOLLOWING QUALIFICATIONS:

OUTSTANDING TECHNICAL CAPABILITIES;
WELL-DEVELOPED MEMORY CAPABILITIES;
HIGH APTITUDE FOR RECALL OF GRAPHICS AND DRAWINGS.
DO NOT INFORM THE TRAINEE OF THIS IDENTIFICATION UNLESS DIRECTED TO DO SO BY CAPT. MCDONALD. COPY THIS OFFICE ON ANY RECOMMENDATIONS TO MCDONALD.

It was obviously to Bates some hocus-pocus was going on, but as to exactly what, he had no idea. But it was not his job to know why McDonald wanted people like that; it was just his job to help find the people. And from the little he knew about "Cam" McDonald's exploits in some of the little-known backwaters of the World War—if McDonald wanted people like that, it was important.

Bates looked at his watch. Nearly twenty minutes had passed. He rose from his desk and walked to his office door. He opened it.

"Come back in here, Marian."

As Francis entered Bates' office, Bates sat down and picked up the gray-covered book.

"All right, Marian, repeat what you read a few minutes ago," Bates ordered as he opened the book to page 244.

Bates watched the serious-looking man standing in front of him, watching him hesitate, biting his lip, as if he didn't know what to say, or maybe wasn't sure he wanted to say it.

"Well, Marian?" Bates asked, beginning to wonder whether Marian might have been lying, saying anything to get out of trouble.

Then Francis straightened and began to speak, without hesitation, his voice strong. "And other utilities are handled following normal practice, except at rail and vehicular traffic crossings. Loads are severe at crossings, with both static and dynamic loads of importance. Cast iron and steel pipe...." Bates tracked every word in the book as Marian continued his recitation. Not a single word was in error! "... emergency repair operations on ships possibly requiring service after battle operations. Subway-like access tunnels are frequently used to cope with this problem. Such access tunnels can." Francis stopped.

"Well, go on," Bates said as he automatically turned to the next page.

Francis looked sheepishly at the captain. "But that's all you had me read, sir."

"Oh, yes, that's right." Then Bates asked, "Are you sure you repeated what you read correctly?"

"Pretty sure, sir," Francis answered, but Bates could tell that Marian knew damn well that he had gotten it exactly correct, word for word. There had been no hesitation, no stumbling. Marian's voice had been firm and unequivocal.

"Interesting," Bates mused. "Haven't other people quizzed you like this before, Marian?"

"Not too often, sir. Mostly, when somebody said something about it, they thought I was pulling some trick. After awhile I got tired of being asked to do tricks like a magician, so I didn't say much about what I could do," Francis said apologetically.

Bates reflected a moment, wondering what to tell Marian—if anything—and Holmsley, who would be likely hotfooting it up to Bates' office tomorrow to "know what to do with that Marian." Making his decision, Bates abruptly said, "All right, Marian, return to your duties."

"Aye aye, sir." Francis saluted and then turned and walked toward the office door.

"Oh, just a moment, Marian," Bates said casually.

Francis stopped and turned.

Bates picked up the picture from his desk, with the back of the picture frame toward Francis. "Marian, do you remember seeing this picture on the bookcase?"

"Yes sir."

"Describe it," Bates said softly.

Francis began to stare, almost trance-like, as if he were looking at something, except there was nothing at which to look. "It is a picture of a single-piper steamer, moving in a strong wind, I guess, because the smoke is blowing laid back. The steamer is painted white topside but black below the deck line. The ship's water line is showing above the water level. There are ten cabin doors to the deck. The deck door by the stern is open, the others are closed. The ship's name is painted out—there is a block of lighter paint where the name would usually be on the bow. There are some large crates—three—on the deck in front of the cabin area. There is a group of sailors—offices and enlisted—fifteen to twenty, hard to tell—next to the biggest crate. There is a large, white house on a low cliff in the far distance. There are lots of clouds in the sky, maybe rain clouds. A large flag is flying from the bow of the ship."

"Describe the flag," Bates broke in.

"The flag has five horizontal stripes, with a triangle at the end of the stripes pointing toward them. The second and fourth stripes are very narrow; the others are wide. There is some type of symbol in the middle of the triangle, but I can't see what the symbol really is." Bates saw Francis' body relax. "That's all I can remember, sir."

Bates said nothing, not letting his astonishment show. Marian had seen things that Bates had forgotten were in the picture, despite the number of years that the picture had been with him, wherever he had been stationed. And the number of men on the deck—exactly eighteen. And he knew, because he was one of them. Finally, he said, "All right, Marian, return to your duties."

Bates' eyes followed Francis as he turned and left the office. *Hot damn. Hot damn!* Bates said to himself.

2

FRANCIS LOOKED GLUMLY out of the rain-pelted window of the train as it rumbled through Chicago's south side, thinking about all that had occurred the last few days. He thought visiting his family in Chicago—he hadn't seen them in over a year—on the way to his new duty station would work out okay, particularly since he had gotten a promotion after finishing his training in San Diego.

After that afternoon with Bates, things had gone pretty smoothly. Holmsley had seemed to lay off Francis after that day. Francis had finished at the top of his class and been promoted to petty officer, third. Now he was on his way to joining a communications repair facility at the Brooklyn Navy Yard—a great assignment. There would be lots of things to do in New York; and the list of telephone numbers a classmate from New York had given him—real hot numbers so the classmate had said—might lead to some interesting things as well. Taking a couple of days leave in Chicago had seemed like a good idea—at least before he left San Diego.

But only Ma had seemed impressed by his promotion. Marge, his sister, was more interested in her boyfriend, some dumb-ass guy named Marty who worked for the Chicago Transit Authority supervising bus drivers and handling rider complaints. That guy had the nerve, to Pa's obvious delight, to ask Francis when he was going to quit the Navy so he could help Francis get a *decent* job—maybe like his—with the CTA. Just thinking about working for the CTA wanted to make Francis puke.

And then there was Hal—or, rather, Hal's absence. Hal, Francis' younger half-brother, was off traveling in Mexico with his friend, Bill. The last time any news had been heard from Hal was nearly four weeks ago when a post card arrived from Laredo saying he and Bill were having a great time and, if their car didn't break down, they would be reaching Monterrey, Mexico, in a week or so.

Hal's trip didn't surprise Francis. Hal was always doing fool things, and usually getting into trouble in the process. And Francis had usually been the one to get him out of trouble, and hide the details from Ma and Pa. But, despite all Hal's failings, Francis still loved his half-brother deeply. The fact that Hal hadn't written for nearly four weeks didn't surprise Francis either—Hal seldom worried about anybody else's feelings except his own. But what did surprise Francis was Pa. Pa, uncharacteristically, had laughed when he told Francis about the post card. Pa was obviously proud that Hal seemed to be taking after him. Of course, Pa boasting about Hal was no surprise; Hal was always his favorite. Francis could feel Pa's unsaid accusation that Francis never had the courage to go out on his own—like Hal. Pa said being down there in Mexico on his own was good for Hal—built up his self reliance, like he had to when he had his business in the Orient and traveled all across the Philippines and up and down the China coast drumming up sales.

Francis had heard Pa talk about his travels in the Orient so many times that he could describe them better than Pa. Pa had this great business, or so Pa said, in the Philippines, until that "damn Democrat Wilson" got the U.S. into the War with Germany and Pa had to come to the U.S., where he met Ma in San Francisco and decided to marry her, "even if she already had a son from a previous marriage," the son, of course, being Francis. Francis had always had the suspicion, something he never voiced because he was sure it would really hurt Ma, that Pa had gotten Ma pregnant so that Ma would marry Pa and Pa could easily become a naturalized citizen. Ma didn't know it, but Francis had once seen Ma and Pa's marriage license—and its date—and had made the connection to Hal's birthday. Marrying Ma, a U.S. citizen, made it easy for Pa to not only become a U.S. citizen, but, so conveniently Francis thought, also shorten his name from Marianninski—Pa was born in Serbia—to Marian, in the process giving Francis the Marian name as well. Pa always said he changed his name to make it sound more American—to make it easier to do business—but Francis had long ago convinced himself that Pa's real purpose was to escape the consequences of some past mistakes in his life.

"Ticket. Ticket, please," the conductor asked as he reached Francis' seat. Francis handed his ticket to the conductor.

The conductor looked at the ticket, and then asked, "Going all the way to New York? This ticket is good only for the seating car. It doesn't let you use the sleeper. You know that?"

"Yeah, I do. Left Chicago earlier than I thought I would. All the sleeper berths were taken when I got my ticket." Francis had left home two days earlier than necessary to get to New York. Things had gotten so intolerable that he had decided to leave early. He made up the excuse—actually, thought he hated to admit it because Ma cried when he left, it was a lie, and Ma probably knew it was a lie—that he had to report to the Yard on Tuesday, rather than Thursday.

As Francis continued staring out the window, the smoke stacks of Gary, Indiana, came into view. God, he was glad he had been able to join the Navy—and get out from under Pa's thumb. His only regret in joining the Navy was not being able to continue at the University of Chicago. But, with Ma's savings being used to replace the cutback in Pa's pension money—a common occurrence after the Crash—Francis didn't have the money to continue, despite his part-time job. Being able to join the Navy—something Francis felt damn lucky to be able to do—was an ideal way for Francis to deal with the money problem—and get away from Pa.

THREE HOURS LATER Francis stood in the growing line of people in the slowly rocking, crowded dining car, waiting to be seated for dinner, as the train sped across the farmlands of Indiana. Damn, he was hungry—the fact that he was having to wait just made it worse.

The line of people moved forward sporadically as the headwaiter seated people. "I have a table for a party of four," he said to the family standing behind Francis. "Are you ready, sir?"

"Yes," the husband said as he squeezed his family past Francis with a sheepish look on his face. "Excuse us. I'm sorry. Excuse us."

A moment later, the headwaiter returned and spoke to the woman immediately in front of Francis and at the head of the line. "I'm sorry, ma'am, but we can only seat a minimum of two in a party for awhile," he said as he looked at the long line behind Francis. "Perhaps you would like to join someone?"

The woman turned to Francis, a look of minor exasperation on her face—a very lovely face Francis thought. "Would you care to?" she asked.

"Care to? Oh... yes, that would be great," Francis answered.

"Fine, just fine. Follow me, please," the headwaiter said as he walked briskly down the length of the dining car.

As they were seated, menus were thrust into their hands. A busboy arrived and filled their water glasses.

"Hi. My name is Elaine. Thank you for rescuing me," the woman said as she gave a friendly smile to Francis.

"My name is Francis. Don't thank me. You're the one who rescued me," Francis said as he returned the smile. "My stomach has been growling for the last hour. Traveling makes me hungry as a bear."

"You too? I really don't understand it, but it always happens," Elaine said.

Embarrassed because he didn't know what else to say, Francis bent his head to look at his menu. A smile came to Elaine's lips and she too began to look at her menu. But as she studied her menu, Francis began giving her fleeting glances. The more he sneaked a look at her, the more attractive she looked. Full, rich lips, beneath smooth cheeks with a sprinkling of freckles her makeup didn't quite hide. And above the freckles, penetrating but mellow green eyes that had an aura of healing and strength. He guessed she was a few years older than he, but he was a real sucker for brunettes. And from what he could see of her, her lovely face was matched by a very lovely body. Then he saw the wedding ring on her finger.

The waiter arrived at that moment and took their order.

Another lag. Then both started. "What are you—" They both stopped. Elaine gave a little laugh. Francis smiled.

"You first. What brings you on this trip?" Elaine asked.

"Not much to say. I just finished a communications repair and facility operations course in San Diego. I've been assigned to the Brooklyn Navy Yard. Have to report in on Thursday."

"Communications repair and facility operations course—that sounds interesting. What is it?" Elaine asked with what seemed to Francis to be real interest.

"You learn about the different types of radio gear that are used on ships and shore bases—how to repair and keep it in working order. That's the repair part. The operations part is learning how to run a program of maintenance for them, sort of like a car repair shop," Francis said.

"Oh, that sounds important," Elaine said.

"Just another Navy job. No more important than any other job. The Navy is just one big machine with a lot of parts—people, ships, equipment—that have to be kept in working order," Francis said, surprised—and a little embarrassed—at how authoritatively he had answered her.

"Well... how did you get into this... radio and communications work?" Elaine asked as she sipped from her water glass. Francis could see the red lipstick left on the glass—the color contrasted sharply with Elaine's girl-next-door looks.

"Oh, I just sort of gravitated to it during my first couple of years of sea duty. Then I applied for radio communications training school in San Diego. And as they say, the rest is history. How about you? Why are you on this trip?" Francis asked, inclining his head forward, wanting to show his interest in what she had to say.

"My sister and I went to visit my mother in Denver. Mom and Dad moved to a small ranch near there after Dad retired from his business in Fort Wayne—that's where I grew up. But Dad died last year. We tried to talk Mom into moving in with one of us—she's getting up in years—but she said she would never leave. Can't say that I blame her. Beautiful out there. And she seems to be getting along okay, at least for now." Elaine paused, then continued. "Where are you from?"

"Oh, I was born in San Francisco," Francis responded. "We eventually moved to Chicago. My family still lives there." Not wanting to describe the complexities of his family's blood line, Francis didn't say more. He changed the subject.

"You said you and your sister went to visit your mother. Where is your sister?"

"Oh, my sister got off the train in Fort Wayne. That's where she lives now with her husband—they got married last spring. She had planned to come back home with me for awhile," Elaine hesitated, as if debating something in her mind, "to see... meet... my husband's relatives. She... was in Europe when I got married... has been there for several years. She had hopes of becoming the great American female novelist, until reality set in last year—when her money ran out."

"I know that feeling," Francis said with a slight laugh.

Francis saw Elaine's questioning look. "Had to drop out of college when my family's money ran out—after the Crash. That's when I decided to join the Navy," Francis said.

"Oh. Well, it looks like you did the right thing," Elaine said.

"I think so, more and more every day," Francis said with a smile. "But—about your sister?"

"I was hoping she could... uh... get to know him—my husband's family, that is—a bit. We had even gotten a private compartment for both of us. But she changed her mind after we left Chicago... she... just decided to go home... not to go with me. No problem at all... just a little lonely for her husband... I guess," Elaine said.

Francis wondered why Elaine was so hesitant, and was about to ask more, but the waiter arrived with their meal. Francis and Elaine turned to their eating, but soon were talking again. As their conversation continued, it became more relaxed, more comfortable to Francis. Francis became more animated, more engrossed as he talked about life in the Navy, feeling more and more attracted to the woman across the table—even if she was married. And, so it seemed to Francis, she was enjoying the conversation as much as he. In fact, he felt like she was warming to him—and, *maybe*, he thought, *just maybe—a little more than that*. It wasn't as if he were trying to put the make on her. He just really liked being with her.

By the time they had finished their meal—and their talking—it was dark. The twinkling lights of the farmhouses in the distance could be seen through the dining car window as they got up to leave. They walked down the aisle to exit the dining car and entered the first of the string of general seating cars. Francis' seat was in the next car, so he continued walking behind Elaine. When they reached the seat with Francis' white canvas sea bag in the rack above it, Francis stopped, trying, unsuccessfully, to figure a way not to have to say good bye to Elaine.

"Well, I guess I'll be saying good night to you. This is my seat," Francis said as he pointed to the sea bag.

Elaine turned, her eyes following Francis' pointing finger. "You mean you don't have a Pullman berth? You're going to spend the night in here?" she asked.

" 'fraid so. I left Chicago a couple of days early and I couldn't get a sleeper ticket. So it's curling up on a seat for me tonight."

"That's too bad. Well, perhaps we could have breakfast together in the morning—my treat," Elaine offered. "It's the least I can do if you're going to be on that hard seat all night. I'll come by in the morning and get you."

"I'd like that. See you in the morning then," Francis responded, glad that she had made an offer to see him again. He didn't know whether he would have had the courage to ask to see her again, despite how much he wanted to see her again.

"Yes... in the morning," Elaine said as she turned to walk away.

Francis watched her as she swayed back and forth with the rocking train, working her way down the aisle, toward the next railcar—savoring the way her hips and trim legs moved. He watched her until she reached the end of the car, where she slowed her weaving steps and then unexpectedly turned. She took a step back toward Francis, but then stopped. A frown came momentarily to her face, but was quickly replaced with a smile—an embarrassed smile, so it seemed to Francis. She gave a little wave. Francis smiled and waved back. She turned and left the car.

Francis sat down and stretched his legs across the space between the seats. He looked out the window. Damn, she was a fine-looking woman. And, boy, did he feel comfortable with her—something that was unusual for him. Talking with her was a real delight—it wasn't like most conversations with the girls he had dated. He really liked her. He didn't know if he had ever had such a warm feeling about a woman as he had about Elaine. It was strange, but there was just something about her that, well, he couldn't quite explain it, except that he liked the way it made him feel.

His eyelids became heavy.

FRANCIS FELT A HAND on his shoulder. His body jumped. He looked up. It was Elaine.

"I'm sorry. I didn't mean to startle you," Elaine said.

"That's all right," Francis answered, as he turned to look out the window. The sun was just starting to come up. "Boy, you are up bright and early," Francis said with a yawn.

"I thought all you sailors got up at the break of dawn," Elaine said with a light laugh.

"Not if we can help it," Francis replied, mirroring her laugh.

"Actually, I thought you might like to freshen up before breakfast—you can use my compartment, if you like," Elaine offered. "Come down to the dining car when you finish. I'll get a table for us," Elaine said as she handed Francis her compartment key.

TWENTY MINUTES LATER, Francis entered the dining car and looked down the row of tables. Elaine waved from the other end of the car. He walked toward her, still feeling heady from the sweet smell of her that had filled her compartment. As he reached the table, she asked, "Feel better now?"

"Sure do. Could I have some of that coffee?" Francis answered.

Elaine smiled and picked up the small, steaming pot of coffee on the corner of the table. Francis looked at Elaine as she poured the black liquid into Francis' cup, more enamored than ever by her earthy but sensual looks. *God, she looks beautiful*, Francis thought.

Setting down the coffee pot, she asked, "I hope you don't mind me ordering for you—I had to keep the headwaiter happy. Scrambled eggs, bacon, and toast—a sailor has to like that!"

"That's perfect," Francis said with a wide smile, just as the waiter brought two plates of food to the table. Francis' plate was full. Elaine's plate held only some sliced fruit and toast.

Then Francis' voice became serious. "Last night, when you went to your compartment, you started to come back—but didn't. Why?"

Elaine looked at Francis a moment before answering. "I thought, for a moment, that maybe you might want to use the spare bunk in my compartment—the one my sister was going to use. But then I realized it wouldn't be a good idea—things might get out of hand, despite all best intentions."

Embarrassed by her answer, Francis tried to make light of what she had said. "I would have behaved—if you wanted me to."

A frown came to Elaine face. "That's the problem, Francis. I don't think I would have wanted you to."

Francis leaned back in surprise. "You what? ... wouldn't have wanted me to. What do you mean?"

"Just what you think I mean. Listen to me, Francis. I have to be honest with you. I enjoyed—enormously—being with you yesterday. I am glad we can talk a few moments again this morning too. It's been a long time since I have been able to speak to a man so freely—and to one as warm as you. If we had met at a different time, maybe we ... could have gotten to know each other better ... more. I am ... attracted—very attracted—to you. I just want you to know how much our short time together ... meant so much ... I don't know how else to say it, other than it was very special. It was special enough—you are special enough—that I couldn't trust myself last night. I hope you can understand what I am trying to say, even if I am not saying it very well."

Damn, she feels like I do, Francis thought. "Elaine, I have never met a woman like you. It was special to me too—you're special. I want to see you more—a lot more," Francis said with a sudden surge of courage.

"Francis, if things were different ... if you only understood ... my situation."

Francis broke in. "I know you're married."

"I know you do—I wasn't trying to hide it. But that's not really what I mean. If only we had more time, I might be able to explain—let you know ... about ... . But now ... there is just no time ... it won't work."

Francis broke in again. "What do you mean, 'just no time'?" Francis demanded.

"Philadelphia. Philadelphia in fifteen minutes. Philadelphia," came the conductor's call as he walked down the aisle.

"That's what I mean. I have to get off the train at Philadelphia," Elaine said.

"What?" Francis asked in surprise.

"I have to change trains in Philadelphia," Elaine said. "This train goes to New York and your life there, not Washington, where I live—and where my life is."

AS THE TRAIN CAME to a grinding halt in the station, Francis tried to reason with Elaine, trying to tell her how he felt about her, trying to find out how he could contact her.

She adamantly refused to give him any information—and just as adamantly refused his pleadings. "Francis, we are just two ships—you know the cliché as well as I. You're wonderful. Perhaps if things were different ... but they aren't."

"Elaine, this can't be the end. I have to see you again," Francis said in desperation as Elaine started toward the end of the car where the porter was waiting.

"No, Francis, no," Elaine said.

"But why? Washington isn't that far from New York," Francis asked with a pleading voice.

"It is in terms of our lives. I have commitments. More—much more—than you know," Elaine said.

"Let me go with you. Tell me how I can reach you. I don't even know your last name."

"No! Absolutely not. Please, Francis, no. Don't try to contact me. Let me go—now. I can't deal with this," Elaine said with finality.

With that, she took the hand of the waiting porter and stepped down from the train. She took one more look at Francis, his face in dismay. Then she turned and walked quickly toward the door to the ticket lobby. The tears streamed down her face.

3

TWO DAYS LATER, Thursday, Francis reported to the officer-of-the-day at the main gate of the Navy Yard on Sands Street in Brooklyn. Francis was directed to room 202 in what was called—euphemistically in Francis' mind—the Yard Communications Building. The dilapidated structure obviously had once been a machine repair shop—it looked now like a puff of wind would blow it over.

Francis climbed the noisy wooden stairs to the second floor. The title on the door of room 202 said, "COMREPHQ" in big letters, and beneath in smaller letters, "Communication Repair Facility Headquarters." The lettering looked newly painted. The door squeaked as Francis opened it.

"I'm looking for Ensign Gray," Francis said to the skinny young sailor at a desk. The guts of a radio were spread across the desk and atop a Navy manual entitled *Basic Communications Equipment Repair*. Francis knew it well from his training at San Diego. The young sailor looked lost in what was spread out before him on the desk.

"He's in the next room. Are you the new guy?" the sailor asked as he pointed to a door.

"Yes, I guess so," Francis answered.

"I'm Jimmy—Jimmy Stevens."

"Well, my name is Petty Officer Marian, sailor," Francis responded tartly, thinking, *What kind of outfit is this—"I'm Jimmy." God.*

Stevens jumped to his feet. "Sorry. Seaman Stevens."

That's better, thought Francis as he went to the door and knocked.

"Come on in, Jimmy," was the reply. Francis looked back at Jimmy with a disgusted scowl. Jimmy smiled dumbly and shrugged his shoulders.

Francis opened the door and walked in. Ensign Gray was sitting with his feet propped on his desk, reading a book.

"Petty Officer Marian, reporting as ordered to Ensign Gray. Are you he?" Francis asked.

Gray dropped his feet to the floor. "Guilty," he said as he swung his chair around, dog-earing a page in the book as he did so. "Are you the guy from San Diego who's supposed to be coming in? Sit down and take a load off."

Francis wasn't quite sure what to do. This was not quite what he had expected, to say the least. First "Jimmy" and now this guy. *Is he really in charge of this place?* Francis asked himself. Francis decided he had better stand until he knew more about what was going on. He assumed an "at ease" position, trying to look casual for the benefit of Gray, but sufficiently military just in case another officer, Francis hoped, walked in.

"That a copy of your orders?" Gray asked as Francis handed him a large envelope.

Gray looked briefly at the orders, then shoved them back into their envelope, opened a desk drawer, and threw the envelope into it.

"Well, let me tell you what's going on around here," Gray said. "We opened shop, so to speak, a few weeks ago. Our job is to repair equipment that comes in off ships or is sent from other yards or stations. We look it over; figure out what's wrong; fix it if we can. Once we get the thing fixed—whatever the thing is—we send it back to the ship or wherever it came from. Simple as that," Gray said with a twirl of his finger.

"Where do we work on the equipment? Where are the work and equipment storage rooms, sir?" Francis asked innocently.

"Right in there, Chief," Gray said as he pointed out his open office door to another door in the room where Jimmy was. The door had "Repairs" stenciled in black on it. "Take a look."

Francis walked from Gray's office and to the door. He opened it. The blood drained from his face. Chaos. All sorts of electrical communications equipment were spread out across several work benches, much of the equipment already disassembled with the interior parts of the equipment exposed. Various pieces of testing apparatus were set up with wires hanging from them, looking as if someone had tried to use them but didn't quite know how to connect them to anything.

Francis turned to look back at Gray. "Mr. Gray, who works in here?" Francis asked, hoping not to hear what he expected to hear.

"Why we do—Jimmy and I. And now you, of course. Who else is there?" Gray answered, as if surprised that Francis would even ask.

"You mean you, Jimmy, and I are the only ones assigned to work here… sir?" asked Francis as his optimism for his new assignment began to fade.

"Sure, at least for now. Isn't that great? We can do our work totally undisturbed," Gray said as he reached over to pick up his book.

Francis turned to look at Jimmy, who had walked over to where Francis was standing. Jimmy had a look of deliverance on his face. "I could sure use some help, Chief," Jimmy said in a whisper.

"Oh, Francis—you don't mind if I call you that, do you?" Gray asked from his office. Without waiting for Francis' answer, he continued, "A Captain McDonald, over in the main administration building, wants you to drop by next Tuesday to see him. His office called earlier this morning and told me," Gray said.

"You wouldn't remember what time I'm supposed to report, would you, sir?" Francis asked.

"I think, yes... I'm pretty sure... yeah. They said to be there at eight o'clock," Gray answered.

"Is there any particular item you would like me to start on this afternoon, Mr. Gray?" Francis asked.

"No. But maybe... what you could do first—make a list of things that need to be done. Why don't you do that, Francis."

God, thought Francis, *what is happening to this Navy?*

4

FRANCIS GOT TO THE ADMINISTRATION BUILDING at 7:30 just to be on the safe side. After a bit of confusion at the main desk—the building directory apparently had not been updated yet to include McDonald's office—Francis was directed to an office on the third floor. The sign on the door merely said, "Captain C. A. McDonald."

Francis looked at his watch; it read 7:50. Francis figured it probably wouldn't hurt to be a few minutes early, so he knocked on the door. From inside the door he heard, "Come."

Francis opened the door and entered McDonald's office.

"Petty Officer Marian reporting, as ordered, sir," Francis said as he drew to attention. McDonald was short and big, not fat, just solid—like a rock.

McDonald said, "At ease."

A long moment of silence followed. Francis could see McDonald studying him, looking him over.

"Are you settled in over at the repair facility, Marian?" McDonald finally asked.

"Sort of, I guess… yes sir, I am," answered Francis, not knowing quite how to answer in view of the utter confusion that existed at COMREPHQ.

"Good, because you're not going to be spending all your time over there. Starting next Tuesday for the next six weeks, you will report to me in room three-thirty-three next door at thirteen-thirty hours every Tuesday and Thursday for some testing activities. When not engaged in the testing activities, you will carry out your regular duties at the repair facility under Ensign Gray's direction. Any questions?" McDonald asked.

"Well, yes sir. The testing—what kind of equipment am I supposed to be testing, sir?" Francis asked.

"It's not equipment testing. It's testing of you," McDonald answered.

"Me? I mean, why am I to be tested… sir?" Francis asked in surprise.

"At this point in time, it's none of your business," McDonald said.

None of my business! Francis thought. *What's going on here. Why won't McDonald tell me? Okay, if that's the way McDonald wants to play it, so be it.* But Francis knew something was going on. First Bates, with his little memory test, and now McDonald, with his orders to undergo some type of testing—for reasons he wouldn't explain. It had to be something to do with his memory abilities, and he wasn't sure he liked that idea at all.

"Any other questions?" McDonald asked, as if daring Francis to ask anything more.

"None, sir," Francis said coldly.

"All right, Marian, return to your duties," McDonald ordered.

Francis did a stiff about-face and started to leave.

"And one more thing, Marian," McDonald said. Francis stopped. "Get that knuckle-head Gray straightened out, and get that goddamn repair facility shipshape, will you?"

"Aye aye," Francis said as he smiled and left McDonald's office, thinking maybe McDonald was okay.

IT WAS TUESDAY, EXACTLY 1330 HOURS. McDonald entered room 333. Francis and the three other men in the room—none of whom knew each other—all drew to attention. "Be seated—each of you at a corner of the room," McDonald said as he walked to the front of the room. "The order doesn't matter. Just maximize the space between you. You do not need to get to know each other for what we are going to do here." The men did as they were told.

"Each Tuesday and Thursday, as per my orders, report here for testing. The type of testing will generally be different each day." Then McDonald paused, as if to give emphasis to what he was going to say, "You are not to discuss what goes on in this room with anyone else—including each other. Got that?"

There was no answer. "I said you are not to discuss what goes on in here. Do you understand?" McDonald asked with a stern, commanding voice.

A mixed chorus of "Yes sir's" and "Aye aye's" rang out.

"And, one more thing. No going to the head once the testing for the day starts, so pee before you get here. Any questions?" McDonald asked in a belligerent tone.

There were none.

"Good," McDonald said as he started handing out pencils and examination materials. "Keep the exam sheets face down until I say 'begin.' The instructions are at the top of the first page. Do not ask me to explain the instructions. You have three hours. If you finish before the three hours, just sit there until the three hours are up. At the end of the three hours, return the exam to me."

McDonald looked at his watch. "Begin."

BY THE END OF THE MONTH, Francis had started to make some progress at COMREPHQ. An equipment inventory was completed and Francis had shown Jimmy how to use the test equipment to identify some of the simpler radio problems. Francis got the paperwork in order for the equipment that came in for repair and saw to it that Gray began to sign off on the repair work. Order slowly began to emerge from the chaos.

On the other hand, McDonald's examinations, while simple at first, rapidly grew more difficult. They obviously were some type of IQ tests—matching words with words, symbols with symbols, sequences of numbers with other sequences, sequences with symbols, words with symbols, numbers with symbols, numbers with words, sequences with words—and then trying to figure out what things didn't match. The interweaving of words, thoughts, symbols, and sequences grew more and more convoluted, more intricate.

Francis continued to wonder why the Navy—McDonald—was making him take these tests. Every time Francis thought about marching up to McDonald and demanding to know what was going on—what the Navy was planning to do with him—he would see McDonald staring at him from the front of the classroom and Francis would lose his courage.

But Francis was not going to give up that easily. He was going to find out just who this McDonald was. Francis did some nosing around the administration building, talking to some of the enlisted men who worked there, asking what they knew about McDonald. But Francis was stymied. Nobody knew much about him, except that he wasn't permanently stationed at the Yard, that he was probably connected with some communication outfit, that he would come and go pretty regularly, and that... maybe... he was stationed on the West Coast at Treasure Island in San Francisco, or... maybe... at Pearl Harbor, or... maybe... in D.C., or... maybe....

IN THE THIRD WEEK, the tests took a new twist. Tuesday's examination was a memory test—on the exams they had taken the previous week. Some portions of the previous week's exams had to be repeated, word for word. Even the answers that had been given had to be put down. Francis did reasonably well, he thought, although he was not absolutely sure he had gotten everything correct.

On Thursday, more memory tests, but this time on diagrams that McDonald zipped through on a flip chart that had to be reproduced or described from memory.

During the fourth week, the memory tests became even more difficult. Various written reports, short and long, but military in content, were read and had to be rewritten from memory. McDonald threw a surprise into the process by asking that some of the reports read on Tuesday be rewritten on Thursday.

During the last two weeks of testing, Francis and the others got a real shock. The exam questions were in a foreign language. "No. I told you not to ask questions. There is no mistake. Just do the best you can—and no more questions!" McDonald had retorted when one of the men in the class asked if a mistake had been made.

Francis realized as he got into the actual examination that it was sort of like a puzzle. A question had to be guessed at and then an answer selected from the listed answers—answers sometimes given in English, and sometimes in a foreign language. Francis began to see some patterns in the questions and similarity of words from one question to another that he used as keys to help him. When graphics or symbols were part of the questions, it only made the questions easier.

During the two weeks, questions were given in at least five different languages, as best as Francis could tell. Francis had recognized some of the Chinese. The Japanese was less recognizable, but he was able to make some comparisons to Chinese to help him guess what the Japanese might be. The Middle East languages, however, were total gibberish to Francis.

On the Tuesday following the last of the tests, McDonald spoke to each man privately. Francis was the last to whom McDonald spoke.

"Marian, you seem to have what some people call a photographic memory—not perfect, but damn good, based on the tests of the last several weeks." McDonald looked at Francis, as if expecting a reply.

Francis didn't know what he should say, so he said nothing. But he sure hoped that McDonald would explain what the hell had been going on the last couple of months—why McDonald was so damn interested in his memory capabilities.

McDonald continued. "Not only do you have an excellent—no, extraordinary—memory, but you also seem to have a good aptitude for sorting things out, particularly in Oriental languages. Any suggestions as to why that might be?" McDonald pointedly asked Francis.

"Well maybe, sir. My natural father was part Chinese. He died when I was young, a few years after he came to the U.S. with my mother—on some type of trade mission. I can remember him talking to me in Chinese and playing games with me in Chinese. And too, I have always been pretty good with graphics, so the pictograph and ideograph characters don't immediately throw me for a loop."

"Umm... interesting—father part of a Chinese trade mission." McDonald paused momentarily. "Well, maybe that's part of the reason. Anyway, your testing with me is complete."

Thank God, Francis thought.

"Starting in September for several months, you are going to be on detached duty in Washington, D.C., so you can take a Chinese language course. It's run by the State Department for their up-and-coming diplomats, but we made special arrangements for you to get into the course. You have any problems with that?" McDonald asked.

Damn, is that what McDonald wanted to know—could I learn to speak Chinese? Jesus Christ, Francis thought, *all that testing just to figure that out*. Francis thought about McDonald's question for a moment longer. Then he summoned up his courage. "I... was wondering, sir... why I am to learn Chinese?"

"Like I told you before, it's none of your business—at least for now. You just learn how to speak Chinese—real good—and I might just tell you then. Now, I'm asking you again, do you have any problems with taking this Chinese course?" McDonald said.

Damn, Francis thought. *More fucking stonewalling. But, learning Chinese might be fun—and he could get away from that flake Gray.*

"I... suppose not... sir," Francis answered, as he wondered why, if McDonald was regularly stationed somewhere on the West Coast, he couldn't get some Chinese-Americans from there for whatever reason he needed for somebody to speak Chinese. There were plenty of Chinese out there. Something was not quite right. McDonald was not telling him the whole story—that was for sure.

"Good. You leave for Washington next week, so rap up everything around here by the end of the week. And one more thing. While you are there in Washington, you are to undergo some special evaluation by a civilian psychologist. His name and address are in your orders here," McDonald said as he handed Francis a large envelope. "When you get to D.C., call his office for an appointment; they are expecting you. You will see him several times, until he decides he's done. Any questions?"

"Uh… yes sir." *For crying out loud, more evaluation—more damn tests more than likely,* Francis thought. *McDonald didn't say anything about more tests when he said I would learn Chinese. What the hell is going on?* He started to ask McDonald why more tests, but then he looked McDonald in the eye—and lost his courage again.

Francis sighed with resignation. "What about the repair facility … and Ensign Gray?"

"You've done your job over there. You got Gray reasonably organized," McDonald answered.

Francis was surprised. He started to ask McDonald how he knew, but McDonald cut him off.

"Yeah, I've been checking on you. Gray knows what he is supposed to do now. It's just up to him to keep on doing what you started. He'll be getting some more permanent help soon. My plans for you are more important than repairing radios."

5

FRANCIS SHOOK THE BEADS of the September rain off his coat after he got inside the office building on C Street in downtown Washington. He looked at the building directory, and then stepped to the elevator. "Third floor," Francis said to the attendant.

Francis exited the elevator and walked a short distance down the hall. The sign on the door said, "Lewis Franklin, Ph.D., Fellow AAP, Experimental Psychology" *Experimental psychology? What the hell?* Francis said to himself as he entered the office.

The office reception room was empty, but a small sign on the receptionist's desk said, "Please be seated." As Francis turned toward a chair, the receptionist, in a slightly rumpled nurse's uniform, came from an interior office door. She was young, plump but not fat, and rather voluptuous.

"Oh, I am sorry. We... I didn't hear you come in. May I help you?" the receptionist asked as she self-consciously brought her hand to the top of her uniform and the two unhooked buttons there.

"Yes. I have an appointment with Dr. Franklin at one-thirty," Francis said.

"Oh, yes, you are..." she said as she glanced down at the appointment book, "...Mr. Marian." She pushed the intercom button. "Doctor, your one-thirty is here—Mr. Marian."

"Oh, yes, Chief Marian. I have been looking forward to meeting him. Give me a moment," came back the voice from the intercom.

Several minutes later Francis entered Dr. Franklin's inner office.

"ALL RIGHT, CHIEF MARIAN, what I will be doing is testing your cognitive and mental constructive and recall capabilities. I will be giving you various tests, which I in part will be devising as we go through the evaluations. Everything I have seen from your preliminary testing indicates you are a very interesting case, a real challenge," Dr. Lewis Franklin said.

Case? thought Francis. *Does he think I'm a nut?*

"What I would like to do today is have you do what I call a constrained multi-potential constructive language capabilities test," Franklin said.

Francis was bewildered. *What is this guy talking about?*

"This is a rather new type of test, something I devised myself. You can read the article I wrote that describes it. It appeared in *American Psychologist* last year. Would you like a copy of the paper? I have reprints."

"Uh… I guess… oh, sure, I would like that," Francis responded, wondering whether declining the offer would offend Franklin.

"Fine. Make sure Angelica gives you a copy before you leave. Now, here's what I want you to do. I am going to give you four construct elements. Each is of equal length. I want you to try to construct a new alphabet by forming letters using the four elements. I want you to lay out each letter, as you form it, right here on this mat," Franklin said as he put his hand on a black rubber mat.

"The rules for forming each letter of the alphabet are, one, you may use one or as many as you want of the elements. Two, the letter must be no larger than the box formed by a square made from the four elements. Three, when you put two elements parallel to each other, they must be at least one-quarter of an element length apart—that is, you can't put them side by side touching each other," Franklin said as he lay two of the elements side-by-side on the mat in illustration. "Four, intersections of elements must be at zero, forty-five, or ninety degrees. I will record the letters you form on my note pad, and time you as we go along—there is no time limit, but timing helps in my evaluation of you. So, that's it. Any questions?"

"No sir," Francis answered, thinking the "construct elements" looked like oversized tooth picks.

"Fine," Franklin said as he picked up a stop watch from the table. "You can start… now."

Francis picked up the "construct elements" and began. Francis formed his first four "letters" by merely orienting a single construct element in a different direction—horizontal, vertical, slanted to the right, slanted to the left. Then he added another construct element, also oriented in different directions relative to each of his first four letters, to form sixteen new letters. He kept building, systematically adding new elements with different orientations, different points of connection to other elements. As each letter was formed, Franklin sketched it on his pad, keeping a running track of the letters being formed. Within a minute, Francis had developed twenty-five different "letters."

"Keep going, Chief, keep going," Franklin kept urging. Francis formed 512 letters before he ran out of ideas.

6

THE CHINESE LANGUAGE instruction course, which began in mid-September, was given at Georgetown University. Francis attended a lengthy class every morning with a Professor Chi and, on days when he didn't have to be at Franklin's office, afternoon tutoring sessions with one of Chi's assistants.

At first, Francis had some difficulty catching onto the language, but then as the structure of the language began to take hold in his subconscious, his mind began to integrate the effects of intonation on the meanings of individual characters and the sequences formed from them to build logical thought. *Ma* meant, for example, "mother" in a high level monotone, but became "hemp" when spoken in a rising high tone—and then became "horse" when spoken in a low-downward dipping tone. Rather than being stymied by the typically limited correspondence between the characters on the written page and the spoken word, he was soon able to almost effortlessly sort through the potential combinations of meanings that spoken characters might mean and identify the intended meaning of a string of potentially senseless written characters. And the more difficult struggle that the student of the Chinese language would have in distinguishing between even the more common dialects—Mandarin, Wu, and Cantonese—seemed to pose no problem for Francis.

As the days passed, the language and the multiplicity of its subtleties began to make sense to Francis. Not that he didn't have to study—he did, extremely hard. But the language became almost second nature to him. And, as the weeks passed, his growing understanding began to show.

"Chief, may I speak to you before you leave?" Professor Chi asked one early November day after the close of class.

"What's up, Professor?" Francis answered as the other members of the class began to leave the room.

"Chief, you have been doing very well in this class. Relatively speaking, you are leaving most of the other students behind," Chi said.

"Thanks. It's hard work, but it seems to make sense to me. I mean, it sort of flows naturally to me," Francis said.

"Yes, I can see that. And that's why I want you to consider attending events at the Chinese embassy here in Washington. Speaking with the people there would be of enormous benefit to you," Chi said.

"Well, I guess I have no objections. But how do I get invited to the embassy?" Francis asked.

"That is no problem," Chi answered. "I know some of the people there. I have already spoken to them about you. They would be pleased to have you come. In fact, if you are free tonight, you can attend a reception—for some refugees from Manchuria. They will be talking about the Japanese occupation of Manchuria. I think you may be surprised by what you may hear. Not many people in the United States really understand how terrible the occupation is."

FRANCIS ARRIVED at seven-thirty as instructed by Professor Chi. The professor took Francis in tow, introducing him to various people. Everything was in Chinese. Francis struggled, picking up perhaps a fourth of what was being said. The professor would lean over to him every once in awhile and say in English, "Hang in there, Chief, you are doing just fine."

What Francis was able to glean from the evening's activities was limited, but he did understand that most of the discussion dealt with the Japanese occupation that had taken place in 1931. The refugees had only recently escaped from Manchuria, or Manchukuo as the Japanese had renamed it, and had come with the support of the Nationalist Chinese government to tell their horrific story—what was really happening in Manchuria: the seizure of homes and land with kangaroo courts making everything legal—at least in the eyes of the Japanese. Torture and murder were commonplace—no one dare oppose their new masters. Francis was appalled—it was the first time he had ever heard the likes of it, except in the adventure stories he had read when he was a boy—but now it wasn't fiction.

AFTER THAT EVENING, Francis began receiving frequent—almost weekly—invitations to the embassy, directly from the embassy. He struggled through each evening, sometimes having more difficulty and sometimes less. Sometimes the professor would be there and sometimes not. But it didn't make any difference to Francis. He was intrigued by what he was learning about the tumultuous times in China: sporadic clashes with the Japanese, disgruntled warlords fighting among themselves, and the disruptive Communist influence amid the struggling Nationalist movement under Chiang Kai-shek. And as Francis' knowledge of the Chinese language grew, so did his understanding of the Oriental mind.

MCDONALD PUT DOWN THE PHONE. He was very pleased with this week's report from Professor Chi. Francis seemed to be living up to the potential shown by his testing. His attendance at Chinese embassy functions was going very well. Francis was making outstanding progress from what Chi said. McDonald concluded that it was time to add another piece to the complex puzzle he was building for Francis Marian.

McDonald picked up the phone again and had the long distance operator get a Washington number—the Office of Naval Intelligence, Security Clearance Branch.

"You remember my discussion with you a few months ago about running a complete background check on one of the people in my program?" McDonald asked the man on the other end of the line.

"Sure do, Cam. Wasn't the fellow's name… Marian?" came the question.

"Yes, Francis S. Marian. I will ship his complete file to you tomorrow along with a formal request for the background check, but I wanted to give you a heads-up—and a little more insight into what I want."

"Shoot," came the response.

"Well, I want more than the usual check on where he was born, where he grew up, where he went to school, who he knows, and so forth. Marian apparently has relatives that came from China—he says his natural father was part Chinese. I want a complete rundown, not only of his relatives in the United States, but also as much as you can find out about his relatives in China or other parts of the Orient," McDonald said.

"Boy, you are asking a lot, Cam. Getting information about people in China is never easy—and with conditions the way they are now, what with Chiang Kai-shek trying to keep Mao and the Communists under control while fighting the Japs at the same time, it's going to be doubly hard. It's going to chew up a lot of time of some of my best people," the voice over the phone complained.

"It's important," McDonald shot back. "Something Marian said to me about his father being on a trade mission to the U.S. when he died—I have a gut feeling that Marian's relatives are not just run-of-the-mill Chinese peasants," McDonald said.

7

TODAY WOULD MAKE THE SEVENTH VISIT with Dr. Franklin. Francis was beginning to feel like a guinea pig. And he still hadn't gotten a word out of McDonald. The last time Francis had seen McDonald was about two weeks ago; he seemed to come to town every several weeks or so. And true to form, when Francis tried to do some digging on McDonald at the Navy offices downtown, he still couldn't find out much about McDonald, except what he already knew—that McDonald was probably stationed on the West Coast, or maybe even at Pearl Harbor.

And when he did come to town, all McDonald did was to ask Francis how things were going and remind him to keep his mouth shut about the testing Francis was undergoing. Francis was doing that—and hoping he would be finished with Franklin's tests soon. Maybe when they were over McDonald would let him in on what the hell the Navy was trying to accomplish—he knew that it had to be for something pretty important. At least Francis wanted to think so. He didn't want to be going through all this crap with Franklin for nothing.

Francis opened the door of Dr. Franklin's office, pulling off his overcoat as he did so. Then his eyes became riveted on the person in the nurse's uniform standing by a filing cabinet, thumbing through a file drawer. *My God, I can't believe it. It's Elaine!* "Elaine, Elaine!"

Elaine turned and looked at Francis. The blood drained from her face. "Oh, my Lord. Why are you here?"

"I'm here to see Dr. Franklin. What are you doing here?" Francis asked in return, moving toward Elaine, staring to extend his arms.

Elaine put up her hands to ward Francis off, keeping him at arm's length. "I... work here. I'm... I'm filling in for Angelica. My God, Francis, you can't come here. You mustn't be here."

"Why the hell not?" Francis demanded, his eyes opening wide.

"I can't explain... not now, Francis. Just don't say you know me, please, I—"

Lewis Franklin walked into the waiting room. "Ah, there you are, Chief Marian. Are you ready to get started? Elaine, have you met my star patient here, Chief Francis Marian? He and I are doing some really unusual testing."

"Yes, we just met. He was introducing himself to me," Elaine said with a clearing of her throat as she quickly dropped her hands.

"Good. Come along, Marian. We have lots to do today," Franklin said as he turned back to his office.

As Francis followed Franklin into his office, he looked back at Elaine. Elaine was shaking her head slightly, as if to say no.

Francis approached the table where the testing always took place. "Your receptionist seems rather nice. Is she taking the place of Angelica?" Francis asked.

"Oh, Elaine. No—Elaine is more than a receptionist. She is really a registered nurse, although she hasn't done actual hospital work for some time. She is just filling in for Angelica for a while. Angelica has some sickness in her family. Elaine does this for me from time to time when I am without a receptionist or need some special nursing assistance," Franklin answered.

"Oh. How long has she been working for you?" Francis asked with an attempt at nonchalance as he started to pull a chair from under the table.

"Oh, I think Elaine started helping out... let's see... about a year or so after I opened the office here in downtown D.C. Had to be about then. Elaine and I had gotten married only two months before, so—that would be about right—yes. She's been helping out about five years now," Franklin answered.

Francis' knee crashed into the chair. *Married to Franklin. Jesus H Christ.*

"You didn't hurt yourself, Chief Marian, did you," a solicitous Franklin asked.

"Hurt myself? What do... oh... no, no, it's all right." *Damn!* Elaine married to Franklin. Francis was dumbfounded. But maybe, just maybe, he and Elaine could pick things up where they left off—on that miserable morning nearly six months ago in Philadelphia. Maybe what had seemed to be starting between them—and had been defused so quickly—was possible after all.

"Chief, Chief. Are you with me? Did you hear what I said? Do you understand the instructions for the test?" Franklin asked.

"Not all of them, Doc. Sorry. Maybe you could go over the last part again," Francis said, still not paying much attention to Franklin.

"All right, Chief Marian. Maybe we had better call it a day. You don't seem quite focused enough to handle what I wanted you to do today. Just make an appointment for next week sometime, and I'll see if you're ready then," Franklin said.

"Yes sir. I'll do that," Francis answered.

Francis stood and left the room. Franklin walked out behind him. "Elaine, make Chief Marian an appointment for next week." Franklin turned to Marian and spoke with an irritated tone. "See if you can get focused for next week. We will have a lot to catch up on." With that, Franklin went back into his office.

"Elaine, you're married to him?" Francis whispered as two newly arrived patients stared at him as he stood in front of Elaine's desk.

"Yes, but we can't talk now—here—you have to leave," Elaine answered in a hushed voice.

"I'm damn well not going to let you get away—again. And I don't give a damn who the hell knows," Francis said, trying to keep his voice in control.

Elaine looked at him, her eyes wide in desperation. "All right... all right, Francis. Oh God, Francis... I can't let this happen... you win—you win." She took an appointment pad and wrote something on it. Then she tired to return to her normal voice, but it cracked. "And what time... would you like... that appointment next week, Chief Marian? Would Tuesday at three work?" Francis could see tears welling up in her eyes as she tore the top sheet from the appointment pad and slid her note across the table to him.

"Yes, that will work. Anything will be okay—now," Francis said, as he pocketed the note, his heart pounding.

Outside in the hallway, he opened the note. It read: "6:30 Columbus Sea Bar, Ave C & 1st."

8

THREE HOURS LATER, Francis sat at a booth in the Columbus Sea Restaurant & Bar, watching everyone who came in. When Elaine walked in, it was like a thousand rockets had exploded. Francis had never seen a woman so beautiful. She had changed from her nurse's uniform into a light blue dress that seemed to caress her body. Matching blue high heels with light tan stockings accented her slim legs. A subdued red lipstick set off her eyes and dark hair. God, she looked beautiful.

Elaine looked around for a moment, then walked quickly over to the booth as Francis stood up. Francis took Elaine's hands in his, looking at her. Then he leaned toward her, but she backed gently away. "No, Francis… that's not why I came here."

Francis said nothing. He helped Elaine take off her coat and she slid into the booth.

Then Francis spoke, trying to ease the tension that Elaine's words had created. "It's wonderful to see you again, Elaine. I don't know quite what to say, except that I can't believe I've found you. I never thought I would see you again."

"Seeing you was a bit of a surprise to me too, Francis,"

"But Jesus, Elaine, married to him—that's hard for me to believe," Francis said, without thinking about how Elaine might respond to his undisguised scorn.

"Why not? You knew I was married. Lewis and I have been married for nearly six years. I don't know that I should even be meeting you here," Elaine said defensively.

"Then why did you come?" Francis responded sharply.

"You didn't leave me much choice," Elaine retorted.

"I'm sorry about that, but I had to talk to you, Elaine," Francis said gently, realizing things were getting off to a bad start. "When you left the train, it… it really tore me up. I haven't forgotten about the time—as little as it was—

that we spent together. You made me feel like I've never felt before. Some people might say it's impossible, but I think I fell—"

"No, Francis, don't say it. Don't say it. It will just make things worse, just more difficult. When I said we had different lives, that was the truth. We have different responsibilities. They just won't let us... be together... no matter how much we... you... may want it," Elaine said, struggling with her words.

"Different lives, different responsibilities? You don't even know why I'm here in Washington. The last thing you knew, I was on my way to New York," Francis snapped back, unable to control his frustration.

"You're right, Francis, I don't. But something must have happened, or the Navy wouldn't have Lewis giving you all those tests. I looked at your file. Lewis may be a bit of a bore, but if there is one thing Lewis isn't, it's inexpensive. The Navy's racking up quite a bill for you," Elaine said.

Francis hesitated, knowing he might get in big trouble with McDonald if he started talking about the details of what had been going on the last several months.

"Cat got your tongue, Francis?" Elaine asked caustically.

"No, it's just something ... I can't talk about, for now. Besides, that's not what I want to talk about, and you know it. I want to talk about you ... and us," Francis responded.

"There is no *us*, Francis. I said that on the train, and I'll say it again." But Elaine's voice became less strong, less sure as she continued, "There is just... no... possibility... for... us."

"The hell you say. There was a reason we met on that train. I know what you did to me—and I think I did the same to you," Francis said with conviction.

"Oh, Francis, please don't make this difficult for us ... for me ... please," Elaine pleaded.

"Why should it be difficult? If you have your life and I have mine—like you seem to want to believe—it should be no problem," Francis countered. "You can just go your way and I'll go mine—if that's the way you really feel. Do you really feel that way, Elaine? Do you really want that?" Francis asked, hoping he had not pushed too hard.

Elaine said nothing for a long, long moment. Then she let out a big sigh, as if in anguish. "No, Francis, that's not the way I feel. I... God help me... I... have been praying for the day I would find you again. But this won't work—it can't." Elaine's eyes began to glisten with tears. She buried her face in Francis' arms.

THEY MET AGAIN at the Columbus Sea the next Tuesday, as they had planned. This night they would have more time together. She had told Lewis she would be shopping at some downtown stores before coming home.

When Francis told the waiter they would like a booth near the back of the restaurant, he led them to an alcove recessed deeply into a fake wall, with a façade of rustic looking bricks framing its entrance. Strings of cheap colored beads hung down from the bricks to fill the opening, giving the booth a false sense of privacy.

They sat and held each other's hands for a long while, talking and listening to each other, sipping their drinks, behind the intimacy of the colored beads. An hour passed, then another. Then Elaine said she had to go. Francis let her go, but only with the promise they would meet again next week.

A WEEK PASSED. Elaine and Francis hid again behind the intimacy of the colored beads at the Columbus Sea. Francis had finally built up his courage.

"Elaine, I have to tell you something, and I don't want you to stop me," Francis said.

Elaine looked at him with a questioning look. "All right, I won't," she answered.

"I am in love with you." Elaine started to say something. "Don't," Francis said. "You said you wouldn't interrupt me. I may not get the courage to say this again. You are the most wonderful woman I have ever met. I want to be with you—forever. I want to marry you—if I could. Will you marry me?"

"Oh, Francis. You know that's impossible. I… to divorce… I can't do that… it just isn't possible," Elaine said.

"Why not?" Francis demanded, "Don't you love me?"

"You just don't understand…. Oh, Francis, you know I love you. How could you not know I love you," Elaine said as she brought her hand to Francis' cheek.

"But… I don't understand… if you love me…."

"Francis, just don't ask me why any more," Elaine said with gentle finality. Then Elaine took a deep breath. "But, Francis, I do want to be with you—in a way we have never been."

For a moment Francis didn't understand what Elaine meant. Then he realized. "Tonight?" Francis asked.

"Lewis is attending a convention in Philadelphia. He won't be home until tomorrow night," Elaine answered.

Francis paused a moment, looking at Elaine. Then he said, "Let me make a phone call."

Francis left the booth and went to the phone at the back of the bar. He dialed the number of the landlady of his apartment. When she answered, he said, "This is Francis Marian. Could I speak to Chief Scott?"

In a moment, Scott, Francis' roommate, came to the phone. "Scottie, you wouldn't be able to stay at the barracks tonight, would you?" Francis asked.

A long pause followed, then Scott spoke, "So you finally broke her down, Francis. Congratulations."

"It's not like that, Scottie," Francis said.

"I know—it never is. Yeah, no problem. I'll be out of here in twenty minutes. I hope you know what you are getting into," Scott said.

Francis returned to the booth, paying the check as he passed the bar. He leaned over to Elaine and kissed her gently on the lips. "Scottie won't be at the apartment. Are you ready to go?"

Elaine looked back at Francis, a blush coming to her cheeks. "Yes, Francis, I am… I am."

FRANCIS AND ELAINE continued to see each other as often as they could, even after Angelica returned. After that first night, they would sometimes just be together, eating dinner and perhaps going to a movie or an art exhibit—or just talking. But other times, when Scott wasn't in town or could be convinced to spend the night somewhere other than the apartment, they would go to the apartment to spend their available hours there together, in each other's arms. As they spent more time together, Francis began opening up to Elaine, telling her about what he was doing in Washington. Francis could tell Elaine, so he rationalized, because she was already privy to Franklin's files.

"It's something I don't quite understand, Elaine. I know it's this memory thing with me. All those damn tests in New York—most were aimed at testing my memory," Francis said as he sat on the edge of his bed in the apartment.

"I was wondering what all those test were about. I saw their results in your file at the office. Lewis has said from time to time that you have some remarkable capabilities," Elaine said.

"Well, maybe so. But why the Chinese lessons? If we were at war with them, or something like that, I could believe they wanted me to be some type of translator. But we're not at war with them—and I don't see any prospect for that happening," Francis said.

"Won't that Navy officer—that, what's his name, Captain McDonald—won't he tell you what's going on?" Elaine asked.

"You gotta be kidding. That guy's mouth is tight as a drum. He acts like what I'm doing is a matter of national security. I've tried to do some checking on him—and I can't seem to find out squat about him. All I know is that he keeps saying it's none of my business," Francis said with resignation.

"Well, I know what business I'm interested in right now, sweetheart," Elaine said as she leaned over to kiss Francis. Francis returned the kiss, and pulled her down onto the bed. He began to unbutton Elaine's blouse. In a moment it was open, and then on the floor. Her remaining clothes soon followed.

NEW YEAR'S DAY CAME and went. Scott left, on to another assignment—to do other things, in other places. Francis, at least temporally, had the apartment to himself—and Elaine. Their love-making became less frantic and their closeness as two people in love began to grow. It was wonderful, except there was always that time of day or night when Elaine would have to leave and return to her real life—with Lewis.

Francis began to talk, ever so gently, about Elaine leaving Lewis, but Elaine would always cut him off with the comment, "I have commitments that I can't break, Francis, commitments you don't understand."

No matter how he pressed her, she would never say more.

9

FRANCIS WAITED IMPATIENTLY—and anxiously—in the Columbus Sea in, as always, the booth with the hanging beads. This would be his second meeting with Elaine since the Chinese restaurant episode. Francis, like a fool, had taken Elaine to an upscale Chinese restaurant as a Valentine present. The restaurant had been recommended by some embassy staff. No English was spoken at the restaurant, so he thought he might impress Elaine with his skills in Chinese. But rather than impressing Elaine, all that he had been able to accomplish was to almost have her seen by a close friend of Lewis Franklin's—a friend who also knew Elaine. When Judge Higgins had entered the restaurant along with several other people, Francis had to use his Chinese not to order dinner, but rather to ask the way to the kitchen door so he and Elaine could sneak out without being seen.

And when he and Elaine met last week, Francis could tell she was still very upset about almost being seen—and the implications of that. She said the whole event had made her feel like a two-bit floozy. Francis had tried his best to make her not to think that, but wasn't very successful. Their lovemaking had been strained and mechanical.

Francis saw her finally enter the door of the bar. She shook and then closed her umbrella as she came toward the booth. Francis got up and helped her off with her damp coat, kissing her lightly on the cheek as he did so. She smiled—weakly. Francis signaled the bartender for a drink for her. There was no need to tell him what she would want; the bartender knew them as regulars now.

"Hello, darling. You're late. I was getting worried," Francis said.

"I just had some things to do—actually some thinking to do. I stayed a while at the office after Lewis left. I told him I wanted to do some shopping before I came home. He'll expect me about eight," Elaine said.

"Sounds serious," Francis answered in a lighthearted way, but thinking he didn't like what he was beginning to hear. Elaine's tone was remote, distant. Francis sensed something was terribly wrong.

The bartender brought her drink. "Cheers," Francis said. Elaine barely sipped her drink.

"Francis, I have made a decision. This will be our last time together." Elaine set her drink firmly down on the table, and pushed it away.

Francis' jaw went slack. "Elaine, you can't be serious. Are you crazy? What's wrong? If I have done something wrong, tell me. What did I do?" Francis reached out to take Elaine's hand. She pulled it back.

"Francis, my darling, you have done nothing wrong. You have done everything right—too right. I'm hopelessly in love with you, and I cannot handle it anymore. This sneaking around, pretending around Lewis, making up stories about why I won't be home or will be late. I just cannot handle it anymore. And I have commitments to keep," Elaine concluded with a firm, rigid voice.

"Darling, you don't have to handle it. I love you. Get a divorce. I want to marry you. Darling, marry me," Francis asked fervently.

"Francis, you know I can't do that. I'm a Catholic; it goes against what I believe. I have already sinned enough. I can't compound it any more by divorcing Lewis," Elaine said.

"Believe! My God, Elaine. Living with a man you don't love? That's not what your faith is asking of you. I love you, Elaine. You love me. Please don't leave me again. I thought I would never get over losing you when you left me on that train. Then by some miracle—yes, Elaine, miracle—I found you again. Don't leave me again, don't," Francis pleaded.

"My mind is made up. I know I have made the right decision." Elaine stood and put on her coat. Francis stood also, trying to say something, but not knowing what to say. Elaine started walking toward the doorway. Francis struggled to get some money out of his pocket, threw a dollar bill on the table, and went after her. The bartender watched them go, a frown coming to his face as he shook his head.

Elaine opened her umbrella as she stepped outside. It was raining hard now. She stepped to the curb and waved for a taxi. "Elaine, I'm not going to let you go." Francis grabbed her arm and pulled her back from the curb as a taxi rolled up.

"Francis, let me go. I can't change my mind. I can't see you any longer. People are depending on me to be there. They need me, now more than ever."

A cop stood on the corner. He looked over at them, then walked toward them. "Need any help, lady?" he asked.

"No, officer, no," Elaine answered.

The policeman continued to watch them, staring hard at Francis.

"Elaine, what do you mean? Lewis doesn't need you. He can take care of himself," Francis said angrily.

"It's not him, Francis. He never needed me. I have a son—and he is dying of leukemia."

Francis' hands dropped to his sides in shock. Elaine got into the cab. Francis stood in the cold rain, watching the cab drive off. The tears on his face mixed with rain drops. The cop turned away and walked into the corner café.

10

WITH THE LOSS OF ELAINE, Francis knew nothing else to do except bury himself in his studies. He focused his total energies on learning Chinese—to read it, to speak it, to make it become a part of him. And his efforts, irrespective of why he was so immersed in them, reaped unexpected results.

"Chief Marian," Professor Chi said to Francis after class one day in March, "perhaps I can interest you in an event tomorrow night at the embassy. A special guest from China will be there to talk about conditions in China. The guest—"

Francis interrupted excitedly, "Madame Chiang Kai-shek! I saw in the newspaper that she arrived in Washington yesterday."

"Yes, Chief, that is correct. Would you be interested in hearing what she has to say?" Chi asked.

"You bet I would! You can get me in to hear her talk?" Francis asked.

"Of course. The ambassador and I are very good friends. I will arrange for you to be on the guest list," Chi said. "Be there at seven-thirty."

BY THE TIME Francis' taxi got through the traffic, it was already seven-thirty. The embassy was packed. Everyone was talking about Madame Chiang Kai-shek.

After waiting in line to get checked against the guest list, Francis wandered about the large but crowded ballroom trying to find the professor. Finally seeing him, Francis worked his way through the crowd toward him. Just as Francis reached the side of the professor, an elderly, slightly balding but elegantly dressed Chinese gentleman in a tuxedo walked smartly to the podium at the front of the ballroom. Francis recognized him as the Chinese ambassador—Francis had spoken briefly to him a few times in the last several months. The crowd jostled for position, forming a large semicircle in front of the ambassador, straining the chord stretched between golden stanchions that had been set up to maintain space between the crowd and the podium.

"So there you are, Mr. Marian. I was getting concerned that you were not going to make it," the professor said in Chinese as he made space for Francis.

Professor Chi turned to look at the podium as the ambassador began to speak. The crowd quieted.

"It is my considerable pleasure," the ambassador began, "to present to you tonight an honored emissary from our Chinese homeland. She is the most gracious woman I have ever had the pleasure of meeting. She is intimately aware of the struggles and attacks our people are enduring, both from external and internal enemies. She is here tonight to seek your support and encouragement for the difficult years ahead. Ladies and gentlemen, may I introduce Madame Chiang Kai-shek."

Madame Chiang emerged from the tight group of people standing behind the ambassador. There was loud applause as Madame Chiang walked to the podium. She was slim and attractive. Her jet black hair, pulled back tightly in a bun in traditional Chinese style, was in striking contrast to her delicate ruby red lips. She was wearing Western style clothes—American high heels and a long chemise style red satin dress with a plain front and side panels that looked to be made from Chinese embroidery. A single string of pearls encircled her neck. Her face was strong and angular, giving her an aura of majesty.

Madame Chiang smiled and nodded to the audience as she reached the podium. The loud applause continued. She finally raised her hands to quiet the audience. As the applause subsided, she began to speak as eloquently as Francis had ever heard anyone speak in Chinese, explaining she was traveling across the United States to gain support and raise funds for the humanitarian needs of the Chinese people. She spoke of the trying times China was having and the hardships being endured by the Chinese people after the 1931 seizure of Manchuria by the Japanese. She spoke of the oppression that existed in Manchuria under the Japanese, as well as the bravery of the Chinese people who opposed them every day. As she spoke her final words— that China would soon, with the help of all China's friends in the United States, throw off the yoke of Japanese oppression—the applause became deafening.

After her presentation, a long line of people formed to meet Madame Chiang. Chi told Francis to get in the receiving line with him. They conversed in Chinese as the line slowly moved forward. Finally they were at the head of the line, where the ambassador was making introductions and ensuring that no one person spent too long with Madame Chiang.

"And, Madame Chiang, this is Professor Chi," the ambassador said as both Chi and Francis bowed their heads. "The professor is doing post doctoral research at Georgetown University here in Washington in governmental administration. He also teaches Chinese to fledging diplomats and the like in a program run by the United States State Department."

"It is an enormous honor to meet you, Madame Chiang," Professor Chi said as he bowed his head. Raising his head and looking directly at her, Chi blurted out excitedly, "Do you know that I came from the same city as you?"

Francis was surprised. The emotion that Chi was displaying was uncharacteristic of him. He had always been the emotionless teacher around Francis.

"Indeed, Professor. Chi… Chi, oh, yes. Was your father a teacher in the school for young children there?" Madame Chiang asked as she looked intently at Professor Chi.

"Yes, yes, that was he," Professor Chi answered as he nodded his head repeatedly.

"Oh, that is wonderful. He was my teacher… and you look so much like him. I remember the many times he would scold me for talking to the other children during our lessons," Madame Chiang said with obvious delight, as she clapped her hands together. "And how is your honorable father?"

"I regret to say that he died several years ago," Chi responded.

"I am so sorry. He was a wonderful teacher," Madame Chiang said.

"Thank you. When I finish my postgraduate studies in governmental administration here at the university, I hope to return to China and obtain a position at one of the universities, perhaps at Fudan University in Shang-hai where I obtained my degrees—and perhaps, as well, serve our government," Chi said.

"Well, perhaps I can be of assistance. We need more people with your expertise. Please forward some information on your background to me—the ambassador knows how to reach me—and I will see if I can get it into the hands of the right people," Madame Chiang said.

"I would be honored if you would," the professor said with obvious appreciation.

Then, apparently remembering who was standing beside him, the professor said in Chinese, "Excuse me for not introducing Mr. Francis Marian. He is in the United States Navy. He is one of my students. In fact, he is absolutely the best American student I have had since I have been teaching here in America," Chi said as he turned to look at Francis, smiling slightly and raising his eyebrows, as if expecting Francis to speak.

Francis was totally taken aback—"the best American student." Francis had never realized that Chi had such a high opinion of him. He hoped he was up to the challenge. Francis responded in the best Mandarin Chinese he could muster. "It is with great honor that I am able to meet you. Your reputation is second only to your eloquence. I hope that your visit to this country will be fruitful."

"My goodness, Mr. Marian, I am impressed, and I am honored by your kind words. How long has this man been studying under you, Professor?" Madame Chiang asked.

"Almost eight months," Chi answered.

"Indeed," Madame Chiang said slowly as she studied Francis. "Well, I am honored by the welcome that the people of the United States have given to me. Perhaps I will have the privilege of welcoming you to my country someday, Mr. Marian," Madame Chiang said.

"I would be honored if the opportunity were ever to arise."

11

FRANCIS WAS DEAD TIRED. Madame Chiang's visit had been less than three weeks ago and his involvement in embassy events had grown more intense than ever. He was regularly at the embassy several nights a week now. He had stayed long into the night at the embassy this day, speaking with some newly arrived representatives of Chiang Kai-shek's Nationalist Party—the Kuomintang. As he reached the door of his apartment, Francis saw an envelope tacked to it. It had his name on it. Written on its corner in the unmistakable scrawl of the landlady were the words: "A messenger brought this early this evening."

Francis opened the envelope. The message was from McDonald; it minced no words: "Meet me at 1500 hours tomorrow at Admiral Pratt's office in the Navy Building on Constitution Avenue. McDonald"

Admiral Pratt, Chief of Naval Operations! And McDonald—in Washington. What in the world was going on? Francis was damn sure it couldn't be good. Was he in trouble? Maybe so, but maybe, too, he might just find out, finally, why he had been doing what he had been doing for the last nine months in Washington—besides losing Elaine on that rainy night almost two months ago.

IT WAS THREE-FIFTEEN in the afternoon of the next day. Francis had arrived at Admiral Pratt's offices at about half past two just to be on the safe side. After being told to take a seat and wait, Francis did just that, wondering what was going on—and where McDonald was.

Suddenly, McDonald stuck his head out of Pratt's private office. "Get in here, Francis," McDonald said without any explanation. *Jesus, I must be in real trouble*, Francis thought. *Maybe he found out about me and Elaine.*

Francis entered Pratt's office and stood at attention. Pratt—who Francis recognized from various photos he had seen—was seated at a large mahogany desk. McDonald was standing by the desk, a solemn look on his face.

Pratt said, "At ease." Francis spread his legs and put his hands behind his back, but his back remained stiff as a ramrod. Nervous sweat began to run down his back.

"Chief, Captain McDonald and I have been reviewing your records, particularly the results of those aptitude tests you took several months ago. We have also received the reports of Dr. Franklin, that psychologist who worked with you. Captain McDonald has had some lengthy discussions with him as well."

Oh shit, here it comes, Francis thought.

"And the results were very positive in terms of what we are looking for," the admiral said.

Francis let out a low sigh.

"Something wrong, Marian?" the admiral asked.

"Uh... no sir. Excuse me, sir. Just a little tickle in my throat, sir. Nothing at all, sir," Francis said as he saw McDonald scowl at him.

"Well then, let me explain," the admiral said, "The political situation in the Orient is very unstable—has been ever since Japan invaded Manchuria four years ago. The War Department is not optimistic about what might happen in the Orient in the next several years, particularly as it might impact the Philippines. Captain McDonald and his special projects group over at ONI have concluded we need special people out there for intelligence-gathering—to find out what the Japanese may be up to."

McDonald and his group at ONI! Francis said to himself in shock. *I'll be damned. McDonald is part of ONI—no wonder he has been so secretive about this whole business. But why the fuck couldn't he have told me. It sure would have made things easier.*

"Your mental skills seem to be ideally suited for such a role," the admiral continued. Then, looking at McDonald, the admiral said, "Captain, feel free to expand."

"Francis, we need a few, select people who can gather intelligence through our listening posts in Hawaii and the Philippines. That's why I started searching for people like you a couple of years ago—and fortunately the training school commandant at San Diego brought you to my attention. I couldn't tell you about what was going on until I was sure that you filled the bill—high memory recall and linguistic capabilities in Oriental languages. So do you get my drift, Marian—about what we want you to do?" McDonald asked.

Holy crap! Francis could see it now. "I... think so. Spying?"

"Well, not in the usual way that you might think of it," McDonald answered. "No Mata Hari stuff. Just somebody who can work across the usual channels with our human intelligence guys—those are the real spies—and our signal intelligence people—the listening posts, traffic analysis—to ferret out what is happening in the Orient, or more to the point, what might happen. Maybe sometimes working with embassy people to bring the military perspective to sensitive negotiations. I can't give you more details, because I don't know what they are."

"What we are talking about is long range, Marian," the admiral said, "At least that's what the War Department and the Navy think right now. We have to be ready for whatever might happen. Knowing more about Japanese intentions and plans will help us in that. The specifics of what we need to do, what we might do, will be dictated by need and opportunity."

"But I don't know Japanese, and only a little Chinese, sir," Francis protested.

"We know that," McDonald responded, "But everything we see in the reports about you says you have a high aptitude for learning them. And according to your Chinese teacher and the people at the Chinese Embassy, you have been making remarkable progress with Chinese. You know a hell of a lot of Chinese, whether you realize it or not. So we will take care of the rest. You will receive a bunch of training over the next three years."

Three years! Francis thought. *That's an awful lot of training—and a hell of a commitment.*

"There is one thing, Marian," the admiral said, "The nature of your potential activities might put you in some rather precarious—I can't think of a more appropriate word—situations. Consequently, this duty will be volunteer. I am therefore asking, for the record, will you volunteer for this?"

The cardinal rule of the enlisted man, Francis thought, *is never, never volunteer. But shit, what is there to stay around here for? Elaine is gone. And there sure isn't anything waiting back in Chicago. Nothing could be worse than driving trolley cars for the CTA. What do I have to lose? And hell, what they are asking me to do looks a lot more interesting than anything else I might do if I turn down their offer.*

"Yes sir. I volunteer," Francis answered.

"Fine, my boy, fine," McDonald said, breaking into a smile.

The admiral picked up a pen from his desk and signed what appeared, from Francis' position across the desk, to be three identical, typed sheets of paper with "Navy Department" printed across the top. Then the admiral looked at Francis and smiled for the first time. "Can't do anything in the Navy without it being in triplicate, you know." He handed one sheet to Francis.

"Captain McDonald has convinced me, not without considerable effort I must admit, that to effectively carry out your duties, you need to be an officer. He told me of some experiences of his own which were very informative. As of this moment, you are Lieutenant, j.g., Francis S. Marian. Congratulations," the admiral said.

"Thank you, sir," a stunned Francis answered.

"Well, Captain, you want to tell Marian what's next?"

"Like I said, Francis, no Mata Hari stuff," McDonald said casually. "But just as a matter of covering all the bases, there is one other thing."

Francis groaned to himself.

"After you finish you language course here in D.C. this spring, and before you get into more language training, you need to take a little officer's training—just a few weeks of instruction, no big deal. You can get that right here in D.C. After that, we think it would be useful if you had a little special training down at Quantico. Nothing much, really."

II

SHINAKO

12

THE AFTERNOON SHADOWS were beginning to lengthen in the carefully manicured garden surrounding the home of Shinako Fujimori in the outskirts of Tokyo. Shinako looked up at her handsome suitor, soon-to-be navy first lieutenant Seiroku Takamatsu, as he approached the bench where she was sitting. *He looks so*—she knew no better word how to describe him—*beautiful. Like a sleek young tiger moving quickly through the jungle. How I love him so.*

Seiroku reached out to Shinako. "Come," he said, "Walk with me." Shinako rose and came close to Seiroku as he pulled her to her feet. Shinako could feel the warmth emanating from him. It made her almost giddy—his closeness, after so long, was intoxicating. It was the first time he and she had been together—and alone—since the 1935 April holiday celebrating Emperor Hirohito's birthday nearly two months ago. Slipping away from Shinako's ever-watchful Aunt Chieko was always a challenge. But Shinako doubted that anything would really be said about it. Chieko seemed to understand the need for Shinako and Seiroku to be alone from time to time, for youthful love to grow.

Shinako was so happy for Seiroku. All afternoon he had talked to her so proudly about his coming graduation—only six weeks away—from naval flight school. He would be graduating near the top of his class and he was sure that he would receive an important posting in Japan's growing cadre of naval fliers—perhaps to one of the new aircraft carriers being commissioned. He was sure of it, he had boasted—his flying skills almost assured it. "Why," he had proclaimed, "I might even be assigned to Vice Admiral Yamamoto's First Air Division!" And then, soon after, so Shinako hoped with all her heart, marriage to Seiroku would follow.

"Shinako, will you be at my graduation ceremony—to see your mighty flier accept his new wings?" Seiroku asked, as he guided their steps toward the thick, bushy trees at the rear of the garden.

"Of course I will. How could you think otherwise?" Shinako answered. Then with a mischievous smile, she playfully scolded Seiroku. "But perhaps I should not come. You may think you are too important. A woman must keep her man in his proper place. Did your mother not teach you that?" she teased.

"My mother taught me many things, among them how to win a woman's heart." Then with a sly, happy grin, he added, "And how to seduce a beautiful woman."

"Your mother did no such thing. Seducing women is an art learned by experience only. And I imagine you get plenty of time to practice seduction at Ita Jima. I hear the girls of the town all have cadet boyfriends," she replied lightly. Then more seriously she asked, "Seiroku, you do not have a girlfriend at Ita Jima, do you? Tell me the truth."

"No, of course not. It is you I love, only you," Seiroku answered in a beguiling voice.

"Do you really, really love me?" Shinako asked, wanting reassurance.

"Yes, I do," Seiroku answered.

"Oh, Seiroku, I do love you so. I do not know what I would do without you." Shinako pressed close to him as Seiroku stopped walking, turned, and put his arms about her.

Shinako could feel Seiroku begin to stir. "Seiroku, maybe we should go now?"

"No, please, Shinako. I long for you so. Soon we will be together. We can be one now. Please, Shinako, no one will know," Seiroku said.

Shinako's body was stirring too. She looked at Seiroku, her body filling with desire. She took Seiroku's hand and placed it over her breast. "Come, behind the trees."

13

"MY BROTHER, I MUST SPEAK with you." Chieko said as she entered her brother's study.

"My sister Chieko, what is it that makes you so serious today?" Yukihiko Fujimori asked as he looked up from the letter he was so meticulously preparing, straining to see her through the morning sunlight streaming through the window.

"Yukihiko, I must speak to you about your daughter, Shinako. I must tell you something with sorrow in my heart, as would your beloved wife tell you were she alive. It is with shame I must tell you I have not done my duty in care of Shinako, whom I, like you her father, love so much. I have allowed her to be too often alone with Seiroku," Chieko said, her voice shallow.

"But, my sister, where is the harm in that?" Yukihiko asked. "Both you and I know that Shinako and Seiroku are in love and will marry soon, once they get the courage to ask my blessing. I fully expect Seiroku to seek my approval when he comes home next week."

"Youthful love, my Brother, is not without passion, passion which may become released at unforgiving times," Chieko asserted.

"What are you saying, Chieko? Speak directly," Yukihiko demanded.

"Shinako came to me last week, before you returned from your Philippines trip. She did not know what to do—her monthly menses had not come. She was afraid that she might be with child... Seiroku's child... and she is..."

Stunned and unbelieving, Yukihiko asked, "Are you sure?"

"Yes," Chieko answered. "I have asked all the necessary questions."

14

THE WATER GURGLED soothingly over the algae-covered rocks. A cooling evening mist was slowly settling over the well trimmed miniature pines, subduing the sharpness of the brightly colored flowers surrounding the gazebo and the two tall men—the proud father and the obedient son—standing in it.

"You have made me very proud, Seiroku. Your excellent performance at the Kasumigaura Flight School has been recognized by important people," Jiro Takamatsu beamed.

"I am very happy that I have been able to please you, my Father," Seiroku said earnestly. "I am excited about finally being able to serve the emperor and help fulfill our country's true destiny."

"Yes, that is something about which I wish to speak to you now, before we return to your graduation dinner and our guests arrive. As you know, I am a good friend of Vice Admiral Yamamoto. If he conducts himself well and can prevent making too many enemies in these turbulent times—many in the military do not trust him—he will continue to rise in power and importance," Jiro said.

"Yes, my father, I am aware of the considerable respect with which Admiral Yamamoto is held by many. References to his naval views were often made by my instructors at Kasumigaura; his days there are well remembered," Seiroku responded obediently.

Jiro continued. "I believe that to be successful in the coming years it would be well that you become a member of his staff. I wish to recommend to him that you be appointed to his staff—in a junior role, of course, but with time, such an appointment could lead to important advancement and opportunity."

Seiroku could hardly contain himself. To be on Vice Admiral's Yamamoto's staff would almost assure him of rapid advancement. He would be in a position of authority, in a position to make important decisions. What an opportunity!

"But," Jiro went on, "to be on his staff you must not only be highly qualified—which your record of achievement thus far clearly demonstrates—but your personal life must be above reproach. And I do not mean the geisha at Kasumigaura—that is nothing. I am talking about your political and social relations."

Seiroku was puzzled. He was devoted to the emperor and the service of his country. He was sure that there could be no question about that. What was his father suggesting? "About what are you speaking, my Father?"

"I speak of your relationship with Yukihiko Fujimori's daughter, Shinako Fujimori," Jiro answered. "I know you and she have deep feelings for each other. It has been so even before you entered the navy."

"Yes, Father, I hold Shinako warmly in my heart, as she holds me in her heart. We hope to soon be seeking her father's blessing as well as yours for our union in marriage. And with an appointment to Yamamoto's staff, our future could not look brighter," Seiroku said.

"It is a blessing I cannot give. I cannot recommend you for Yamamoto's staff if you continue to see her," Jiro warned sternly.

Seiroku was stunned. "But why, my Father, why?"

"You should know as well as I. Shinako's father is a pacifist, perhaps even a Communist," Jiro said angrily.

"But Father, I have heard of no such thing," Seiroku objected.

"I have my sources! Do you doubt what I say? And Fujimori's views are becoming more widely known in important circles. He raises his voice more and more in public and important private circles, questioning our people's right to our destiny in Asia. His voice attacks all that I, as well as our most revered military leadership, believe we must do to regain our rightful place of leadership in the Orient. Do you not believe as I that we—Japan—are the rightful leaders of all the lands of the Orient? Do you not believe we should rule China?" asked Jiro.

"Yes, I believe as you, my Father, but Shinako's father's political views are his views, not hers. They have nothing to do with my devotion to the emperor and my ability to perform dutifully for Admiral Yamamoto—"

Jiro broke in angrily. "It has everything to do with your ability to be trusted as a member of Yamamoto's staff and your ability to rise in rank—to someday, perhaps, stand beside Yamamoto himself. Terminate this relationship with Shinako. I will not allow anything to stand in our way to be among those who will decide Japan's destiny, those who will throw off the yoke of Western imperialism and return Japan to greatness," Jiro stated with finality. "Consider what you must do and then join me as we await our guests." Jiro turned and strode toward the house.

Seiroku watched his father march off, his heart pounding. To not have Shinako, how could he endure that? But what was the alternative? He must serve the emperor and serve him to the best of his ability. Was there no way to have Shinako and still receive his father's recommendation to Yamamoto's staff?

The limbs of the small pine trees near the gazebo seemed to bend low with the weight of the evening mist upon them—like Seiroku—as he turned to join his father

15

CHIEKO ANSWERED the light knocking on the door. Opening it, she saw Seiroku Takamatsu standing there, in full dress uniform. "What is it that you want?" Chieko asked.

"Most honorable *oba san*, may I come in? I wish to speak to Shinako," Seiroku said.

"You may come in, but whether you speak to Shinako will be for her father to decide. Wait here while I summon him." Seiroku was surprised by Chieko's hostility; she had always greeted him in a friendly way before.

In a few moments, Yukihiko Fujimori came to the hallway where Seiroku was waiting. "What is it that you want with Shinako?" Yukihiko asked in a tight, hostile voice.

"I wish to give her this note—to be able to explain," Seiroku answered as he raised a white-gloved hand holding a pale blue envelope.

Yukihiko snatched the note from Seiroku's hand. "That is for Shinako!" said a startled Seiroku.

"What my daughter receives from you from now on will be as much my business as it is hers." Yukihiko tore open the envelope and quickly read its contents.

"You despicable snipe. How dare you now break off your relationship with my daughter! Have you no honor?" Fujimori asked as his voice rose in anger. "You, your father, and the rest of that military trash—you destroy people. And you want to destroy this country."

Seiroku responded to the attack with youthful impetuousness. "Military trash! It is people like you who are ruining this country. I will save this country," Seiroku shouted back. He was confused and hurt. His anger was his protection.

"Get out," shouted Yukihiko.

"I love Shinako," shouted Seiroku, just as Shinako ran in.

"Father, what is going on?" Shinako asked, her eyes wide.

"Shinako, I must talk—"

"I said get out." Yukihiko raised his hand and slapped Seiroku across the face.

Seiroku staggered back from the forceful blow, his hand to his face. "I shall not forget this disgrace," Seiroku said as he turned and left, slamming the door.

Shinako started to run after him, but Yukihiko grabbed her arm. "No, my child. He is not worth it," he said.

"But Father, I love him. I ... I am with his ... his child," Shinako said softly.

"I know, my daughter, I know. I have known for some time now. Read this and you will understand." Yukihiko handed her Seiroku's note.

She read its few words. Seiroku bid her a loving farewell, saying that they could no longer see each other, that the time was not right for their union. But he gave no reason why his love for her was not strong enough for him to marry her as he always said he would.

"Oh, Father, how could he do this to me?" Shinako asked as tears came to her eyes. She looked at her father, then Chieko. Then she ran from the room.

FOR THE NEXT WEEK Shinako seldom left her room, avoiding her father—hoping against hope that Seiroku might come back, try to contact her somehow. But he did not. She cried the hours away, until she would slip into a sleep of exhaustion—then waking only to cry again.

Chieko would come to her each day, to try to comfort her, and to watch the innocent beauty of Shinako slowly give way to resignation.

Finally, the day came when Shinako could cry no more.

Chieko spoke slowly and lovingly to Shinako. "Shinako, I know you are beginning to face reality now. As your heart empties, your mind fills with new awareness. It is time for you to think of what you must do—before it is too late to do anything. Do you understand what I mean?"

Shinako looked at Chieko, understanding coming slowly to her eyes. "But, it is our child—Seiroku's and mine. I can't," Shinako protested.

"Think, child, think! Seiroku has shown where his devotion lies. He does not know what he did to you. And he need never know. You can go on with your life—have a truly loving husband and family someday—if the knowledge of what has happened remains within this house. You have such a bright future; your father has so many hopes for you. Do not throw them away. The problem of the baby can be resolved, quietly and safely, and your life can go on."

"But what will Father think? Would he ever forgive me?" Shinako asked in desperation, not wanting to lose the only remaining tie with her beloved Seiroku. She wondered if she had the courage to do what Chieko was asking her to do.

"Forgive you? It is your father who asked that I discuss this with you, dear Shinako. He loves you so very much. For him, there is nothing to forgive. You brought the sunshine back into his heart after your mother died. He wants only the same for you," Chieko said.

Shinako's father knew what was best for her. He had always known, and Shinako had never questioned his decisions. She could not question them now. Shinako slowly nodded her head. "Tell Father I will do as he wishes."

THREE WEEKS LATER, Shinako and her aunt stood on the afterdeck of the *Futenma Maru* and watched Tokyo Bay slip into the distance. Shinako leaned heavily on the railing for support.

"Your body will heal soon, dear Shinako. And though you do not think it possible, so will your heart. If you could only know the pain I felt when my young husband did not return from the fight with the Russians. The pain seemed unbearable, but it did pass. Time can heal many things," Chieko said calmly.

"I pray that you are right, dear Aunt Chieko. My shame is heavy upon my shoulders, but it grows lighter each day when I think of my father. I never realized he could love me so much as to bear this shame with me—to be with me through this time. I do not know if I could ever love anyone more than him," Shinako said.

Shinako turned her face into the warm summer breeze coming across the outer bay. "But for Father's wisdom and love, I might not have allowed myself to live," Shinako said as she squeezed the railing tightly, as if trying to drive the demons of death from within herself.

"You do not need to talk like that, Shinako. We will soon be with our cousins in Hawaii. And life, you will see, will look brighter. I wish my mind were young enough to learn the American language, as you will. What you will learn in Hawaii should open many doors for you. Knowledge of Western ways and the American language will be important to our country in the coming days, I am sure," Chieko said as she turned to look up at the sky. "Come, let us go to the stateroom. You need your rest. And besides, it looks like it may rain. Dark clouds are gathering."

III

HYPO

16

NOTHING MUCH, REALLY. DAMN! Francis bitched to himself. McDonald's "little special training" was an understatement if there ever was one. Ever since he had arrived at the U.S. Marine training base in Quantico, Virginia, Francis, along with the other seven men who were in the special unit with him, had been doing everything at double time. The Marine colonel in charge of the special unit, a wiry fellow by the name of Brackston, had been running them around like a bunch of raw recruits, despite the fact that all of them were officers.

Of course, Francis really didn't feel like an officer. It had been less than a month since he had finished his crash course on being an officer—"no big deal," McDonald had said in that meeting nearly three months ago with Pratt. Ha! Four weeks of intense twelve-hour days of instruction. And now this. Shit, he was finally beginning to figure McDonald out. Whenever McDonald said something wasn't a big deal, watch out.

Colonel Brackston was a no nonsense officer. He had made it clear on the day they had arrived at Quantico, that if anyone didn't like the way he was conducting their training, that was just too bad. "If you don't like it, you can just get your ass out of here and on a train back to wherever you came from," he had told the group upon their arrival at Quantico.

But no one did, of course. Each man had been handpicked because, as they soon all learned, each had some very special skills. Besides being able to read and speak at least one foreign language, each had at least one other special skill. For Francis, of course, it was his memory. For Pulaski, it was small arms and ballistics. There wasn't a pistol in the armies of the world he wasn't familiar with, and not know its range and accuracy. For Simone, it was radios. He could make a radio work with just wire and spit. For DeFlorio, it was engines. He had been a design engineer for Ford in Detroit before the Depression wiped out the need for his talents. He had turned to the Army for a job and wound up getting a commission in the engineering corps.

They all were sticking it out through the grueling physical conditioning and the training in all sorts of useful skills—useful, at least, for a spy: hand-to-hand combat, small arms use, radio communications, codes and ciphers, even clandestine entry. By the time the training had gotten to the point of learning how to crack a safe, Francis figured that he could probably quit the Navy and make a good living as a burglar.

The explosives training in the fifth week of instruction had scared Francis shitless. He didn't see how anyone could have the nerve to set or defuse explosive charges. But to Woodruff, the Army officer who was the most senior of the eight of them, it was no problem. He was as cool as a cucumber in unpacking the explosives, fixing the charge, lighting off the fuse, and then calmly ambling back to the bunker before the charge went off. When Francis asked, "Paul, how do you keep so cool in handling that stuff?" Frances was really surprised by Woodruff's answer, since Woodruff was a lawyer in the Army's Judge Advocate General's office specializing in the legalities—or ill-illegalities—of covert operations. Woodruff replied it was just practice. It was just about all he had done in Europe during the year before the U.S. officially sent its doughboys "Over There" to the "Great War."

And last week's training, in addition to being physically demanding, was emotionally draining for Francis. The hand-to-hand combat training had been expanded to include—Francis knew of no better way of saying it—murder by stealth.

For three days, their instructor had shown Francis and the seven others the many ways to silently kill a man—by breaking his neck while severing his vocal cords. Francis and each of the other men became a temporary victim and then attacker as different techniques were demonstrated. With and without the knee; with ropes, cords, piano wire, garrotes; with knives, scissors, and razors—even a way to lower the butt of a heavy pistol into the neck to smash the spinal cord. The instructor practiced with each man, carefully guiding his hands and knees through the proper motions. Francis couldn't believe there were so many ways to kill a man.

Then this morning, Brackston had herded all of them aboard a bus for a long ride to an Army base outside the small community of Highstown, New Jersey, about twenty miles east of Trenton. The sign at the entrance read, "U.S. Army Training Facility."

"Colonel, what are we going to do here?" Simone asked as the bus squeaked to a stop.

"Nothing much. Just learn how to jump out of airplanes."

"Y'ALL ARE AT THE U.S. ARMY TRAINING FACILITY for parachuting," the just-introduced Sergeant Jackson began in a thick Georgia cracker accent. To Francis, Jackson's words sounded like a bowl of mush. "Y'all" came out like a drawn-out "yawwwl" dripping with homemade syrup. Francis had to strain to understand what Jackson was saying. "Probably y'all didn't know that the Army has this type of training school. I'm proud to say that this school is the first of its kind in these United States. Y'all should feel honored for assisting your country, and the United States Army, in perfecting the techniques that y'all are going to learn here."

Perfecting techniques, Francis thought. *Jesus H Christ. Does he mean that we're guinea pigs for figuring out how to parachute out of a plane?*

"For the next two weeks, y'all are going to learn the fundamentals of jumping. Y'all learn what a parachute is, and how to properly wear it. Y'all learn how to make it open. Y'all learn how to drop from a plane with a parachute on. Y'all learn the proper stance for landing. Y'all learn how to cushion your fall. Y'all learn how to guide your chute so y'all don't land in a tree or a lake. Y'all learn how to get out of your chute while in water without drowning. Y'all learn how to get yourself down from a tree after you land in one."

Francis wondered whether Jackson's contradiction was intentional.

"If y'all don't learn these things, y'all will probably get killed on your first jump," Jackson said as his eyes bore into each of them for a long moment. "When the colonel here figures y'all learned these things—and only then," Jackson finally continued, "we will do actual jumps from a plane." Jackson then turned to Colonel Brackston. "That's all I have to say for now, sir."

"All right, men, follow me," Brackston shouted.

FOR THE NEXT TWO WEEKS, they did just what Jackson said they would. All went without a hitch, except Francis began to think more and more about what was awaiting him, and the others. Finally, on a Saturday afternoon, Brackston said they were ready and that the first jump would be on Monday. Francis—along with the others in the unit—went to the local chapel on Sunday.

IT WAS SIX-THIRTY Monday morning. Colonel Brackston stood in front of the eight men on the edge of the runway. "Gentlemen," Brackston begin, "I will be your jump master for the next three days of actual jumps. You will pay special and close attention to what I say. Your life will depend on it." Brackston paused, as if to let what he had just said sink in. But Francis didn't need any convincing; he was damned scared already.

Brackston continued. "You will do three jumps: one today, and if all goes well, one tomorrow and one the day after. You have only one objective for this first jump today: to be alive and well to do the jump tomorrow. The objective for the second jump is to try to remember, without being told, what we have been trying to teach you during these last two weeks. The third and final jump, if you are still with us at that time, will be to make a jump and reach a designated assembly point with your weapon, ready to fight, within five minutes after hitting the ground. If you do not make it within five minutes, I will personally arrange for the airplane to take you up again so you get another chance. So I suggest that you get there in time the first time." Another long pause by Brackston. "All right, let's get our equipment on."

Forty minutes later, Francis and the others, each loaded down with two parachutes, climbed into the plane, a converted Martin B-10. Five minutes later they were airborne. Francis looked at the others lining the inside of the fuselage, sitting on two parallel, low benches built into the metal skeleton of the aircraft. Each looked like death warmed over. There was no doubt about it. Each was scared shitless—and that included Francis.

As the plane started to go higher, heavy turbulence set in. The plane bounced, rolled, and shook. Brackston stood and began to walk down the narrow aisle between the two rows of men, yelling at the top of his voice so as to be heard above the roar of the wind and motors. "Now, remember when you go, relax. You count to ten, at a nice even pace—one, two, three, four, five, six, seven, eight, nine, ten—and then, and only then—pull your rip cord. If something goes wrong, we are at a high enough altitude that if your chute doesn't open, you will have plenty of time to pull the rip cord to your emergency chute. Remember, pull the emergency cord if something goes wrong—and you don't have to count to ten. Can you remember that?"

Everyone nodded, too frightened to answer.

Francis looked at Woodruff across the aisle. Woodruff literally looked green. As Francis leaned forward toward Woodruff to ask how he felt, the plane hit another air pocket and dropped suddenly. Woodruff started to gag. Francis yelled, "Look out," as Woodruff began to puke, splattering Brackston and Francis.

There were groans from everybody as they tried to distance themselves from the vomit rolling down the center of the plane towards the open drop hatch. "Aw, shit" seemed to be the most common reaction.

Brackston looked at Woodruff with disgust. "Woodruff, that will not get you out of anything." The overhead light turned red.

"All right, everybody up. Line up," Brackston hollered.

They all stood up. Francis slid his feet through the vomit as he moved towards the drop hole in the center of the fuselage over the modified bomb bay. The light turned green and a loud buzzer came on. "Go, go, go," Brackston yelled as he grabbed each man by the arm, got him to the edge of the hatch, checked to see that the man had his hand on his rip chord, and, when necessary, pushed him down and out.

Then it was Francis' turn. He stepped to the hole, hesitating as he looked down through the hole to the vast green and brown landscape, far—sickeningly far—away. Francis closed his eyes in fright, and then felt Brackston push him down—and out. Francis did a fast count to ten, then pulled. He felt a jerk. *Thank you, God!*

Francis opened his eyes. He saw clouds in the distant, then the horizon, and then—*oh, my God*—the ground below: a multi-colored landscape with green fields, tiny buildings, brown lines of roads, and little moving ants—no, not ants, people! Francis almost gagged. Then he felt the wind blowing in his face—moist and cool, refreshing. He felt the pull of the parachute straps across his chest and shoulders, and the helpless feeling of his feet dangling in the air. Then, as he began to become accustomed to the strangeness of his fall, he looked down again, and saw the earth rushing up at him—coming, accelerating, ever faster towards him, finally rushing up to meet him. Francis remembered his training—"be loose, roll when you hit the ground."

Francis hit the ground and rolled over. He couldn't believe it. He was alive. As he looked up, he saw the rest of the chutes, some on the ground, the rest floating down. Everybody seemed to be coming down okay. As each landed, each pulled off his chute, gathered it up, and then threw it over his shoulder, like a load of dirty clothes. Then they all started running towards each other, hugging each other, happy to be alive.

Jackson, who had been on the ground observing the jump, joined the jubilant crowd. "All right, quiet down. Y'all did as expected—lousy. Let me tell y'all what I saw y'all doing wrong on the way down, and in your—I don't know no better way to describe them—shit poor landings. It is a wonder any of y'all is still alive after what I saw. Pulaski, when you jumped, you let your legs spread out like a whore on Saturday night. That's a damn good way to turn upside down and get tangled up in your chute. And you, Simone—was there a reason you tried to land on your hands and feet? You looked like a cow taking a piss. And Marian, what's that goddamn smell on you? Did you puke?" Francis looked at Woodruff with a scowl.

Jackson continued to rattle through his observations on everyone, giving them hell. But Francis knew there had to be only one thought on everyone's mind: only two more jumps to go.

"ALL RIGHT, YOU PEOPLE, your second jump yesterday seemed to show that maybe you can be trusted to jump without somebody holding your hand!" Brackston yelled. "So, today, don't forget what you did yesterday. And remember what you have to do today. When you land, look for the flag. It will be on the edge of the field. You have to collapse your chute, get your rifle out and get to the flag within five minutes after landing. Sergeant Jackson will be on the ground timing you. And I will be jumping with you today. I'll buy a round of beer for each person who beats my time to the flag. Anybody I beat has to buy a round." The red signal light came on. "Everyone up and in line," Brackston shouted.

Francis was the seventh in line, after Simone and before Woodruff. Just jump like last time, Francis told himself, and everything would be okay—and over.

The red light turned to green. "All right, out you go," yelled Brackston as he stood by the drop hatch. No one hesitated. Francis moved to the drop hole. He stepped into nothingness, counted to ten, and pulled his rip chord.

Francis felt the reassuring jerk of the chute as it opened. He looked upward at the billowing chute. Only a few clouds decorated the sky. The sun was so bright that it seemed to make the white chute shine. In the distance, he saw what looked like Colonel Brackston floating downward. He thought he saw Brackston wave. Francis lifted his arm and returned the wave. Then Francis looked down at the landscape below. It looked peaceful, idyllic, like a painting done by one of the Dutch masters, as it seemed to reach gracefully upward to gather Francis into its fold. Francis could see the landing area. It looked small, but was growing rapidly larger. But then Francis felt the wind. It was starting to pull him away from the open landing area. Brackston hadn't been waving; he had been struggling to direct his chute! Francis was moving toward trees— far too near the trees. Francis yanked at his shroud lines, struggling to get away from the trees. The trees were coming up fast! Then, thankfully, a sudden gust of wind shoved Francis back toward the landing area. He missed the trees, but hit the ground hard—very hard. He felt a sharp pain in his left ankle as he hit.

Francis started to get up. The pain shot through his left ankle and leg, forcing him to the ground. "Jesus, what have I done?" But there was no time to contemplate what had happened. He pulled in his chute as he sat on the ground. Then he pulled his rifle off his pack, struggled to get up, made it, and looked for the flag. He saw the flag about two hundred yards away and tried to run. It hurt like hell, and he knew he could not run—at least like a normal person. Francis did the only thing he could think of. He started to hobble and hop, using the rifle as a crutch, towards the flag. The pain was almost unbearable, but he had to make it. He just had to do it. He couldn't fail. He just couldn't!

He hobbled and hopped, swinging his bum leg along with his rifle. Time was running out. He looked towards the flag; everybody else was already there. He could hear them all yelling for him, "Come on, Francis, come on. You can make it. Come on!" The yelling grew louder and louder, cheering him on. He didn't know how much time he had left, but he knew it wasn't much.

Francis collapsed on the ground as he grabbed the flagpole. Arms went around him, hugging him, pulling him up. Brackston looked at Francis. "Well, Jackson, did he make it?"

"Looks like he did, Colonel—by three seconds."

"Well, Marian," Brackston said with apparent delight, "I guess you're going to be buying quite a few rounds of beer."

17

FRANCIS STROLLED CASUALLY along the promenade deck of the cruise liner, looking out at the broad Pacific and just enjoying the opportunity to not have to be doing something. It probably was the first time in a year that he wasn't jamming Japanese or Chinese into his head. After he had been released from the hospital at Quantico, McDonald had assigned him to the Oakland Naval District headquarters across the bay from San Francisco so he could, in addition to continuing to study Chinese, study Japanese at the University of California, a small university located in the snug, little mainland community of Berkeley.

Francis had begun his instruction in Japanese nine months ago, at the beginning of the fall semester under the tutelage of a Japanese language instructor named Takeda. Learning Japanese was not easy for Francis, but at least Professor Takeda did an excellent job of distinguishing the different styles of Japanese—*intimate* for family and close friends, *polite* for strangers, and, for older people and superiors, *honorific*—and identifying similarities, which were surprisingly few, when they existed between Chinese and Japanese. Intonation, as in Chinese, was also crucial in understanding the language, making doubly difficult the interpretation of written characters, though Francis' knowledge of *kanji* from his Chinese instruction made the task easier. The context in which groups or strings of characters appeared was essential in effective interpretation of written materials—and here Francis' memory played a critical role. His memory enabled him to subconsciously and rapidly consider potential interpretations and then identify and connect the subtle train of thought that sequentially evolving *kanji* characters were intended to convey as they followed one another down a page.

Within a few weeks, Francis was able to speak and write elementary Tokyo Japanese, the more commonly used eastern Japanese dialect, sufficiently, so Takeda said, to at least get by—but only as an obvious tourist—

should he ever get to Japan. Encouraged, Francis redoubled his efforts trying to learn the language, but it was a mentally demanding and time-consuming task, particularly since Francis still had to attend several classes a week to keep up his Chinese.

And maybe, as Francis thought about it, it was just as well. Christmas had been emotionally difficult for Francis. It brought back memories of the previous Christmas—with Elaine. When allowing himself to think about her—when he could stand the still present pain of her loss—he knew how much he still loved her. Even the autumn fling with a girl from San Francisco that his roommate, in an effort to get Francis out of his melancholy, set him up with didn't really help. The several nights he had spent with her were pretty much a flop. Emotionless sex, as Francis found out, was not, after Elaine, a totally satisfying thing for him. He was just glad the girl was not interested in anything permanent.

Francis' sorrow over Elaine had gotten progressively worse after Christmas. His brief interlude with even another girl he met in Berkeley just made him miss Elaine more. But that fling, too—fortunately, Francis concluded in retrospect—also came to an end in April, when McDonald had arrived, unannounced, in Oakland, and casually told Francis of his new assignment.

"I'm on my way to Hawaii for several days, Francis—I leave in about an hour from the Alameda Air Station. One of the things I will be doing will be getting the groundwork ready for you to transfer to Hawaii," McDonald told a surprised Francis as they stood in a hallway of the District's main administration building.

"Hawaii?" Francis said in surprise.

"Yes. Here are your official orders," McDonald said as he handed Francis a large envelope. "Pratt and I told you we wanted to use you in the Orient, so don't act surprised. Hawaii is the stepping stone to the Orient. You are to continue your instruction in Japanese there while assigned to a signals intelligence unit. As any fool can see, our relations with Japan are deteriorating. The time is getting close when the Navy will want to really start using your special skills—to help monitor Japanese intentions in the Orient. Not only does the Navy want you to become fully proficient in Japanese, we want you to learn how a signals intelligence unit really works. We—I—fully expect that after you get the hang of things, we will move you to another unit—maybe putting you in charge—sometime in the next year or two. So get your personal matters in order; you leave in one week."

"A week!" Francis said in disbelief.

"You got any problems with that—some reason you can't leave here by then?" McDonald asked, looking searchingly at Francis.

Francis thought a moment. *Why can't I leave? I have lost Elaine. Everything at home seems okay—at least it's no worse than it has ever been. And I certainly don't want to stay around just for that girl in Berkeley I have been seeing. So there really is no reason why I can't leave.* "No sir, no problems."

"Good. You'll be going by ocean liner; I'm giving you a little time off. It's been about a year and a half since you started your training in D.C., so I figure you deserve it." Francis didn't know whether that was meant to be a compliment or not, since McDonald didn't pause in his words. "When you get to Pearl Harbor on Oahu, you will report to a Lieutenant Rochefort—it's all in your orders." With that, McDonald bid a hasty goodbye and left for the airfield.

And, so, here he was, on a spring day on an ocean liner to the Hawaiian Islands, looking out at the white clouds on the Pacific horizon, contemplating the events of the last two years, wondering if he would ever see Elaine again, or ever return to the States again. His training at Pearl Harbor, as McDonald had pretty well said, would be his last step before Francis would start really doing intelligence work for the Navy. The time was almost at hand when McDonald would be making full use of Francis' developing skills. Francis' life in the Navy had spanned the country, from West Coast to East Coast and then back to the West Coast, in those two years. Now it was on to the Hawaiian Islands. Francis felt as if he were being drawn inexorably toward the Orient. And what that would bring he had little idea.

AS HE CONTINUED TO WALK the deck, Francis realized that he was approaching the three Japanese businessmen he had seen on the first day of the cruise. They were again gathered at the railing, talking animatedly. Francis casually stopped his walking and leaned on the ship's rail near the three men. He could hear what they were saying.

The three men were taking in a combination of Japanese and English. As Francis listened, he heard a reference to "Admiral Yamamoto"—and that struck a bell with Francis. Yamamoto—Francis had heard about him. He was an up and coming admiral in the Japanese Navy, an admiral who apparently believed a great deal in naval air power. *Why are these businessmen talking about Yamamoto?* Francis wondered. *Is this the type of thing McDonald might have me doing a year from now—eavesdropping on suspicious*

Japanese? Not that Francis expected to really hear anything earth shattering, but he was just plain interested. *And besides,* Francis thought, *eavesdropping on them might be a good opportunity to see just how well I can understand Japanese outside the classroom.*

As Francis leaned casually on the railing and listened, he gathered that the men were returning to Japan from an extended period in the States. From the comments they made, they were apparently practicing their English as part of the discussion, dropping in and out of English as their discussion wore on. As he discreetly listened, Francis realized that the men were actually Japanese naval officers. Their discussion seemed to center around some military conferences in which they had been involved. The names of Yamamoto and Nagumo were mentioned several times, particularly by the tall, handsome, young man who seemed to be in charge. Francis finally heard enough to sort out their names. Kobi and Sueno were junior officers. The tall one who seemed to be in charge was called Seiroku—the one called Kobi addressed him as Lieutenant several times. Somehow—it was not clear from what Francis heard—Seiroku was connected to Yamamoto.

About the time Francis realized that the men had apparently been military attachés at the Japanese consulate in San Francisco, the men seemed to notice that perhaps Francis was listening. They stopped their discussion, looked suspiciously at Francis, and walked away. Francis tucked their faces and names away in his mind, and wondered what connection a naval lieutenant named Seiroku would have with one of Japan's most important admirals.

As the remaining days of the voyage passed, Francis encountered Seiroku and his friends from time to time, sometimes merely walking about the deck and sometimes engaged in whispered conservation. Each time Francis would draw near, even if only in innocence, Seiroku would stare at Francis with a look of hatred.

18

FRANCIS' ASSIGNMENT at Pearl Harbor was to a special signals intelligence unit engaged in listening operations on Oahu—at an operations complex informally referred to as the HYPO station. The primary job of the unit, under the direction of a young lieutenant named Rochefort, was to intercept, decode, and decipher Japanese military radio traffic in the Pacific. Supporting that primary activity was a variety of others, including ship-tracking. Francis' initial job was to work in the ship-tracking section.

The task of ship-tracking was to keep tabs on where foreign military vessels were in the Pacific—in particular, Japanese ships. Different messages, particularly weather reports, made by ships at sea were used to estimate where the Japanese ships were. Regular daily reports of weather and position made by commercial ships in standard international code, readable by anyone, were matched with coded weather reports from naval vessels. The coded weather reports from Japanese warships were deciphered by another of Rochefort's sections, a section behind locked doors that led to a basement that, as a newcomer, Francis was not allowed to enter. Matching of the commercial and decoded military weather reports provided a means to estimate military ship locations. The tracking process was one of logical deduction, although Francis and those with whom he worked would be the first to admit, when forced to do so, that oftentimes the estimates of Japanese naval vessel locations were little more than educated guesses.

His times at the HYPO station were squeezed between mornings and several afternoons a week with Takeda, who had come to Hawaii shortly after Francis arrived, to continue his instruction in Japanese to a number of young naval officers.

Francis' Japanese improved dramatically in the weeks of instruction after his arrival in the islands. And to speed Francis' learning process, Takeda also arranged for an individual tutor for Francis. She was a young Japanese national by the name of Shinako Fujimori visiting relatives in Hawaii. Takeda had learned of her through the family with whom she was staying—a well respected Japanese family in the Islands whom Takeda had known since he was a young man. She spent a few evenings a week with Francis.

Francis enjoyed his sessions with the young Shinako. She was intelligent and eager to help Francis learn Japanese. And as he soon learned, Shinako was in the process of also learning English, so he began, in return, to help her as well. Their times together rapidly became mutual teaching sessions. They would chatter back and forth in Japanese, then English, then Japanese, and then English again. They would often laugh at each other as they learned of each other's customs and, what to the other, often seemed strange ways of thinking.

Francis and Shinako became warm friends, but nothing more than friends. Francis could sense some sorrow in Shinako that she seemed to be hiding, or at least not willing to talk about. That sorrow would not allow her to move beyond friendship, and Francis did not seek to break the barrier that her sorrow created. He just enjoyed being with her, and appreciated not having to be concerned about anything beyond that. He did not want to be caught up in a personal relationship with a woman.

Even if he had wanted to, he was bothered by something else. Shinako was such a gentle person. Her personality, her views about the world—at least to the little extent she talked about them—just didn't seem to match with what the Japanese were doing in China. She seemed to be so different than what Francis had come to know of about the Japanese from the times he had spent at the Chinese embassy in Washington. She remained, in so far as her political views were concerned, an enigma to Francis. But trying to understand her more—to really sort through her inner mind and emotions was something Francis was just not ready to do. He was just too busy.

Not only was he learning Japanese from Takeda with the assistance of Shinako, he also had to remain fluent in Chinese. And to do that, Francis also attended Chinese classes two nights a week. All in all, the load under which Francis was working was enormous. But his efforts began to pay off.

In early August, only three months after arriving in Hawaii, Rochefort reassigned Francis to the secret decoding and decrypting section working in the basement, or, as those who worked there called it, the "dungeon." The name "dungeon" had not been randomly chosen. The basement was without windows and air circulation was limited. The body smells of those who worked there permeated the air—and did not go away. The few visitors that came there—and there were only a few, since a security clearance was necessary to enter—always left gasping for fresh air.

Over the following months, Rochefort and some of the others in the decoding group began to explain to Francis the intricacies of the deciphering and analysis process. Actually, it was quite complex, especially for a language like Japanese. Signals first had to be intercepted, decoded, decrypted, and—then—interpreted, a difficult, mentally demanding and always tedious process. Rochefort started Francis on apparently less difficult messages. But, by late fall, Francis had developed his deciphering capabilities to the point he was working on the same level of messages as Rochefort. And as he became more involved in the deciphering work, Francis, like Rochefort and the others working in the dungeon, became totally absorbed in what he was doing, spending longer and longer hours at HYPO.

But Francis' absorption in his decryption work was disrupted in late March of 1937 when McDonald, who now spent most of his time in D.C., arrived unexpectedly one day at the HYPO station, pulled Francis into an office, and told the young ensign there to go make himself busy somewhere else for an hour.

"Francis," McDonald said as he pulled back a chair and propped his feet up on the one lonely table in the office, "things appear to be heating up in the Orient again. The Japanese look like they are going to try to gather in more of China under their wing, just like they did in Manchuria back in thirty-one and two. It's probably only a matter of time before the Japs turn their attention to southeast Asia. So we think it's time we try to find out more about what they may be planning to do."

Francis knew McDonald well enough by now to know McDonald had something up his sleeve.

McDonald looked at Francis with a smile. "Francis, in three weeks, you will be officially terminating your duties here at Pearl, including your Japanese language instruction, and going to Manila."

Francis looked at McDonald in surprise.

"Yes, I know. I thought you would probably be working on intercepts and decoding for some time here too. But I checked with Takeda—as well as that young Japanese woman who tutors you. According to him—and her—you have become damn good at handling Japanese. You've had more than a year with Takeda. He thinks he's done about all he can for you. So we are going to make use of your talents where we need them—now. We have other people like Rochefort who can work on the intercepts here, but we don't have people like you—with all your other talents," McDonald explained.

"You will be assigned to Cavite in the Philippines for the primary purpose of setting up a listening post there. I say setting up a listening post—actually I want you to revamp the operations already in place there. It's called Post Y. The current operation, which I want you to take over, needs a whole bunch of upgrading. Model it on the setup that you have been working in here, with the prime objective of intercepting Japanese naval and diplomatic communications in the western Pacific and East Indies," McDonald said.

"Who will I have working with me?" Francis asked.

"There are five officers and sixteen enlisted men now. After you get your feet on the ground, you will probably want to increase the number of people—but you will have to give me solid justification. The brass back in D.C. will need a lot of convincing," McDonald said as he pulled a sheet of paper out of his chest pocket and unfolded it. He handed it to Francis. "Since you will have to be the senior officer for the operation, you are being promoted to full Lieutenant, effective the end of the month. Congratulations, Francis."

Francis was surprised. "Thank you, sir."

"And there is something else, Francis," McDonald said.

Damn, I should have known, Francis thought. *There is always something else.*

"I am sending you to take over the Post Y operation, but you are going to have to run that place so that it can get along without you for extended periods of time, if it has to. I may want you to be taking on some special assignments from time to time," McDonald said.

"Anything in particular you have in mind, sir?" Francis asked with a mixture of interest and apprehension, wondering what McDonald would want Francis to do.

"No, not specifically—at this time. But I'm not going to let all that training at Quantico go to waste."

IV

BREIDSTEIN

19

WERNER BREIDSTEIN could still hear the whistling of the bitterly cold wind outside the walls of the old castle as he followed Hauptmann Gehlen through the entrance hall and then into the office of Brigadegeneral von Schnell, commandant of the *Wehrmacht's* Special Training School at Stuttgart, Germany. While not acknowledged in its name, it was widely known in more senior German military circles that the Stuttgart castle was a training school for spies. And Werner Breidstein was one of its most recent graduates—except that Werner Breidstein had not graduated from the Stuttgart school. Willy Rosin had been the one to graduate. Werner Breidstein was the cover name given to Willy Rosin for his first assignment.

Willy was tall and muscular, with blue eyes and sensuous lips—the epitome, except for the tan hue of his skin, of Germany's Aryan race so prized by Adolph Hitler, the new Fürher of only five months, a position with which Hitler had anointed himself in August of 1936 after the death of President Hindenburg. Willy had been selected by the Fürher himself, so Willy had been told by his father, Count von Rosin—a confidant of Hitler—to play the role of Werner Breidstein for one of Hitler's most prized and secret projects.

Von Schnell turned from the glow of the fireplace to look at Breidstein. Breidstein drew to attention, clicking the heels of his leather boots. Von Schnell nodded and then sat down in a chair with intricate woodcarvings forming its high back and arms.

"Well, Breidstein—I assume you are becoming accustomed to that name by now," von Schnell said without waiting for an answer. Breidstein was not surprised by von Schnell's use of the name. He had been forewarned by Gehlen, von Schnell's aid, that von Schnell would address him only as Breidstein. Von Schnell believed, so Gehlen said, that a successful spy, particularly one in a role such as Willy would be playing—that of a highly successful and very visible international businessman—must always use his cover name, even when it didn't seem to matter, to prevent accidental exposure.

"This is to be your final briefing, to make sure that all is ready. Gehlen, has Breidstein been provided with all the necessary background on the operations of the Hamburg Import-Export and Economic Development Company and—what's the name of that local company there in Manila that we, Hamburg Import-Export that is, purchased?" von Schnell asked.

"The Philippine Transfer Company," Gehlen answered.

"Yes ... yes, the Philippine Transfer Company. Well, Gehlen, did Breidstein get all the necessary information on the operation of the two companies?" von Schnell asked.

"Yes, *Herr* General. We have spent the last three weeks in Brandenburg with Count von Rosin going over information on the two companies," Gehlen answered.

"Well, Breidstein, do you agree? Have you all the necessary information?" von Schnell asked.

"Yes, *Herr* General," Breidstein answered confidently.

"Good. Then tell me about these two companies, Breidstein," von Schnell ordered. "And tell me in English. I want to hear how good your training of the last year has been."

Breidstein was surprised that von Schnell would ask him to speak in English; he hadn't known von Schnell spoke English. Breidstein spent almost twenty minutes describing the complex operations of Hamburg Import-Export, a very real and very successful German company doing business in Europe and Asia—and the company upon which Count Rosin, until his very recent retirement, sat as chairman of the board. The operations of the Philippine Transfer Company, on the other hand, took only a few minutes to describe. It was a nearly bankrupt, struggling export company in Manila, which Hamburg Import-Export had purchased and which would become Breidstein's base of operations in the Orient and East Indies.

As Breidstein finished talking, Von Schnell nodded his head and pursed his lips. "All right, Breidstein. I have heard much better, but your English is adequate. Fortunately, there will be no reason for you to hide your fluency in English, or Spanish for that matter."

Von Schnell then casually asked, "Count Rosin was vice governor of Germany's Pacific island possessions before the World War, was he not?—In German please. My mind is too old to carry on anymore conversation in English."

"Yes, *Herr* General," Breidstein answered in surprise. *Why is von Schnell asking me that?* Breidstein thought. "He was vice governor for most of our island possessions in the Pacific region, primarily the Palau, Marianna, and Caroline island groups, until the beginning of the Great War. My father was interned in Manila in 1914 by the Japanese when they took control of most of the islands."

"No, Breidstein!" von Schnell exploded. "Not your father—Count von Rosin. You must remember that you are Werner Breidstein. Only we here at Stuttgart, Count Rosin, and the Fürher know who you really are. Even the German ambassador in Tokyo and the consul general in Manila will know of you only as Werner Breidstein."

Breidstein was shaken, realizing how easily von Schnell had tricked him. Breidstein hesitated a moment, and then said. "I shall not forget again, *Herr* General."

"Good, and let that be a lesson to you—how easily, unless you absorb your total being into the role of Breidstein, it would be for you to become exposed." Von Schnell paused a moment as he looked at Breidstein, and then continued, "But, tell me, I am interested. When did you return to Germany?"

Breidstein was again surprised. *Surely von Schnell does not think I would make the same mistake again.*

"The ... young Willy Rosin returned with Count Rosin at the end of 1918, shortly after the death of his mother." Breidstein's stomach tightened with the mention of his mother.

"Yes ... the sad death of young Willy's mother. So young, I understand," von Schnell asked in a fatherly tone, as he brought his two hands together at their fingertips to form a steeple.

Breidstein's stifled an anguished sigh. Von Schnell's remark brought back painful memories, dulled only by the haziness of time. *Why is von Schnell talking about this?* Breidstein wondered. *Why is he probing my past? Von Schnell has already made his point about always acting like Breidstein.*

"Yes ... ah ... Willy Rosin's mother's death was very unexpected. The stress under which she was placed by the Americans during our ... the Rosin's family internment was just too much for her heart."

"Yes, it is sad," von Schnell said. "But, Breidstein, that is past," von Schnell said as he dropped his hands to the arms of the ornate chair and crossed his legs. "Tell me what are the objectives of your mission?"

Breidstein answered von Schnell with ease. "There are four objectives. The first is to report upon American and Japanese military activities and fortifications in the Philippines and the islands of Micronesia. The second is to provide information on mineral and petroleum resources and their development in the region, with special attention to their impact on the capabilities of Japan to wage war. Third, to export raw materials from the Orient and the East Indies to Germany and other countries supportive of German views. Fourth, to purchase or gain controlling interest in individual mines, petroleum developments, and rubber plantations to secure economic leverage for activities that may be initiated by Berlin in the Orient or the East Indies in the future."

"And, Gehlen, what type of arrangements have been made for Breidstein to transmit this information to us?" von Schnell asked.

"Two, *Herr* General. One, by apparent business report sent by ordinary letter or cable when the message is innocuous, and two, by diplomatic courier out of the consulate in Manila or the embassy in Tokyo, if the information is sensitive," Gehlen answered.

"And your bank in Manila, Breidstein?" von Schnell asked.

"The Manila branch of *Bank-Hamburg Geschäftlich*," Breidstein answered. "Hauptmann Gehlen has informed me that the bank can provide any legal services I may need."

"Including the means for transmitting and accessing money in the company's account—for various needs, legal or illegal?" von Schnell asked.

"That has been explained to me, *Herr* General," Breidstein answered.

"And the various documents to get him through immigration in Panama and Hawaii, Gehlen?" von Schnell asked.

"Also taken care of, as we have previously discussed, *Herr* General. Our forgery unit has done outstanding work."

"Good, good. Things seem to be in order. Therefore, let me say a few final words to you, Breidstein," von Schnell said as he rose from his chair. "You are to be in the lead of Germany's return to power in the South Pacific, Breidstein, but I emphasize that it is not your responsibility to set the time or define the means by which we re-establish our control of that region of the world. Your mission is to provide Germany—the Fürher—with the means to facilitate our return to the Pacific by developing appropriate relationships and knowledge that we here in Germany can use. This mission will require the use of all your ingenuity and resources and may be long, possibly years in length." Von Schnell concluded with a somber, final statement: "In many ways, Breidstein, the future of Germany's leadership in the whole of the Pacific rests upon your shoulders."

Breidstein returned von Schnell's penetrating stare with what he hoped was an appropriate look of seriousness, trying to contain his building excitement—after all these years, to return to the land of his birth, and play a pivotal role in the future of Germany! Behind his emotionless exterior, he was ecstatic.

"All further instructions for your mission will be provided by Gehlen. For now, return to your quarters, Breidstein," von Schnell ordered. "Gehlen, you remain. I have some other matters to discuss with you. Breidstein, close the door as you leave."

Breidstein's mind began spinning as he left the room. What an important role in Germany's future he had been given! And to be able to accomplish that in the land of his—no, Breidstein rebuked himself with a silent laugh; he was Breidstein, only Breidstein—the land of Willy Rosin's childhood. Finally, an opportunity to avenge the death of... Willy Rosin's beloved mother caused by the arrogant and stupid Americans. A determined smile came to Breidstein's face as he strode confidently out of the old castle building into the still blowing wind.

VON SCHNELL WATCHED Breidstein exit the room, waiting for him to close the door. Then he turned to look at Gehlen. "Well, what do you think, Gehlen?" von Schnell asked.

"I am not sure he fully appreciates the importance of what he is expected to do," Gehlen responded. "He is rather young for this mission—only thirty."

"If he does not know now, I think he soon will," von Schnell countered in a pensive tone. "Besides, he looks older than he really is. My worry is that we don't lose control of him. He is going to be out on his own, in a highly visible position, if things develop as we desire. He will be cut off from people he has known here in Germany. He will have to become an entirely different man. That might do strange things to a man's psyche."

Von Schnell paused a long moment, and then continued in a matter-of-fact tone. "But the more immediate concern—is he fully prepared for his mission? Much of the training he has received here in the last several months is not going to be of particular benefit to him."

"I agree, *Herr* General. But we had no choice," Gehlen said.

"I know, Gehlen, I know. Our orders are clear. He is to be in Manila by the end of spring. I just hope Berlin knows what it is doing—sending this man halfway around the world to some god forsaken islands in the Pacific, all for the Fürher's grand new vision for Germany," von Schnell said in ill-disguised disgust.

Then von Schnell's expression became troubled. "Do you think he has any idea about his mother's death—what really happened?"

"From what he said, I would say no."

"I hope he does not find out," von Schnell said slowly. "I'm not sure what would happen if he did. But, for now, Gehlen, we have one other matter."

Gehlen looked expectantly at von Schnell. Von Schnell paused a long moment before he spoke. "Do you think Breidstein's preparation in Brandenburg is complete?"

"I am not sure what you mean, *Herr* General," Gehlen said.

"Let me put it more bluntly, Gehlen. Do we have any further need of Count Rosen's assistance in preparing Breidstein?"

Gehlen hesitated, then answered, "No... I think he has provided us all the assistance he can. Why do you ask, *Herr* General?"

"I am concerned that the count knows too much about this mission," von Schnell said.

"But, *Herr* General, it could not be helped. He had to know the reason, at least partially, for his son's new identify in order to gain his assistance," Gehlen responded.

"I know, I know. But I have had encounters with Count Rosen before. The count thrives in his own self-importance. He may just say too much about Breidstein trying to impress someone. We need—for the benefit of the mission—to deal with that," von Schnell said.

"But, how—" Gehlen started to ask.

"The count is getting old," von Schnell broke in. "His health is not all it should be. Few would be surprised if the count were to have a heart attack at his age."

Gehlen looked at von Schnell with growing understanding.

"Do you understand what must be done, Gehlen?" von Schnell asked.

"Yes, *Herr* General, I do. I will make arrangements for... it... immediately," Gehlen answered.

"Good," von Schnell said. "Now, when is Breidstein to leave the country?"

"He will board the *Ciudad de la Habana* in three days. We have made very elaborate arrangements for him to enter the Philippines as Werner Breidstein without any chance of connection to Oberleutnant Wilhelm Rosin, the *Oberkommando der Wehrmacht*, or the Chancellery," Gehlen said.

"Good... good," von Schnell said with a slight smile. "And by the way, Gehlen, the son of Count Rosin need not be informed of his father's sad death when it does occur... say..." von Schnell paused to look at Gehlen with raised eyebrows, "within the next month." Gehlen nodded his head. "*Herr* Breidstein," von Schnell continued, "will have more important matters about which to be concerned."

20

BREIDSTEIN COULD SEE the ships on the horizon beginning to form up for their transit through the Panama Canal. The captain had said that if he could coach this old tub along fast enough, he would be able to pass through the canal to the Pacific by Sunday morning. And old tub it was. It had taken seven weeks to sail from Hamburg to the Panama Canal. But Breidstein was not concerned about reaching the Pacific by Sunday morning. His plans called for him to leave the *Ciudad de la Habana* at the western end of the canal at Balboa and make his initial contact there.

Gehlen had said it was imperative to Breidstein's arrival in Manila that no connection be made between Willy Rosin's military life, the Stuttgart school, and the life of Werner Breidstein, the successful German businessman—and thus the necessity of breaking the direct connection between Germany and Manila. To do this, Breidstein had boarded the *Habana* in Hamburg under the name of Franz Lundstrom, the same name with which he would leave the *Habana* at Balboa tomorrow. After a few days stay in Balboa, he would board a Japanese ship under the name of Pedro Sanchez for travel to Hawaii where he would also depart the ship as Pedro Sanchez. With the forged papers and passport for Breidstein recovered from the German consulate in Honolulu, and the history of Breidstein in place, he would have no trouble passing as Breidstein when seeking passage on a luxury cruise ship leaving Hawaii for Manila.

The troubling aspect of the Balboa layover was what was to happen while there. Gehlen's plan called for Breidstein to leave the ship when it docked at Balboa, as if he were going on a short tour of the city. The ship's captain had been instructed not to be concerned when Breidstein did not return. A contact with appropriate passwords would pick him up at the dock and take him to a hiding place where he would remain until the time to leave. But, Gehlen had said, for the connection to really be broken, one thing would have to be done before Breidstein left Balboa. The local operative, whose only allegiance was to money, could not be left alive to tell tales.

As the ship worked its way up the relatively short transit through the locks to *Lago Gatun*, and then began the longer downward passage to Balboa, Breidstein mulled over what he would soon have to do: kill someone— something he had never done. It wouldn't be murder, of course. He would be doing only what his mission demanded. But it would not be quite like killing someone in battle, and he still had mixed feelings about it.

As Breidstein continued to ponder what he must do, lush shades of green and brown, punctuated by brilliant spots of color from flowers and birds, slid by the ship. They reminded him of the Philippines and the intensely happy days he had spent there with his mother at the Villa San Fernando north of Manila on the Luzon coast. His mother had grown up at the villa, continuing to return there whenever she was able, as a young woman and then as a mother. She had continued to use the villa even after the death of her father, vice-regent of the Philippines until the Spanish-American War, to get away from the rigid formality required of the family of Count Rosin, vice-governor of the German island colonies of Micronesia. When she and her son, Willy, were able to return to Villa San Fernando, even if only briefly, all the formality was dropped. Willy's mother became so different, so vibrant—her Spanish upbringing spilling out. Through his times at Villa San Fernando, Willy became proficient in Spanish under his mother's private tutelage, a tutelage that built a profound bond between them.

But the American internment during the World War had changed all that. The internment had thrust his mother into an alien life, one without the elegance, grace, and power she had known as a young woman. She had tried to retain a semblance of the old ways, but in the end she failed. One night she had held Willy tightly, telling him how much she loved him. Then, the next morning, Willy's saddened father had awakened him to tell him that his mother's heart had failed during the night, that she was gone forever. *I never saw her beautiful face again after that night. That internment, in the ultimate analysis, is responsible for her death—no, not death, but murder. But for the stress of the American internment, my mother would be alive now.* What Breidstein must soon do was only part of the grand scheme for Germany to reclaim its rightful place in the world—and only part of just retribution for past wrongs, like his mother's death.

AS THE *HABANA* EDGED UP to the Balboa docks, Breidstein casually returned to his cabin, where he gathered up only his money, pistol, and passport. He stuffed his pistol into the back of his pants, inside his waist band and under the money belt. The forged passport and visa he needed for his return to the docks in three days, were already sewn into the lining of his coat. Everything else he put in the suitcase to be left behind, to be dealt with by the captain. Breidstein then strolled back on deck and walked casually down the now extended gangway into the noisy crowd.

"*GRACIAS,*" BREIDSTEIN SAID as he smiled and took back the passport for Franz Lindstrom from the immigration officer standing behind the small inspection table. He turned and walked into the main lobby of the port building, his eyes searching for someone who might be his contact. His eyes locked onto a short man with dark Panamanian skin but bright blonde hair wearing a well-wrinkled and not-too-clean white suit. The man approached Breidstein.

"*Señor*, do you wish a guide? My name is Carlos. I speak many languages: English, French, and, of course, Spanish," said Carlos in Spanish.

Breidstein answered in Spanish. "I'm not sure. I am really looking for someone."

"But, *señor*," Carlos said, pausing as he looked directly into Breidstein's eyes before continuing to speak. "I am not only a man of many tongues, but also a man of many worlds." Breidstein's body tensed, hearing the code words for which he had been waiting.

Breidstein returned Carlos' stare, and then spoke the necessary response. "Do you believe in new worlds that are yet to be found?"

"Yes, for those with the courage and the might," Carlos answered immediately.

Breidstein relaxed, and quickly said, "Let's get out of here."

Carlos led the way out of the port building. As the two men exited the building, Carlos waved his arm, pointing toward a parked car. Breidstein recognized it as a Metz. It was a bright, but scarred red, with dented fenders, one broken headlamp, and well-worn tires.

"My car, *señor*," Carlos said with obvious pride. "You like the car, *señor*? It was willed to me by my cousin upon his death—such an unfortunate death he suffered."

Breidstein decided to humor Carlos. "It looks like a wonderful car," Breidstein said, trying to sound sincere. A big smile came to Carlos' face.

Nearing the car, Breidstein asked out of curiosity, "How did your cousin die?"

"I killed him. He tried to cheat me," Carlos responded in a matter-of-fact tone, the smile still on his face.

Breidstein looked at Carlos in surprise, wondered whether to believe him.

"Now, *señor*, if you would be so kind as to adjust the choke and spark while I crank the engine," Carlos said as he walked to the front of the car with the cranking bar in his hand.

Breidstein did as he was told. Carlos pushed down on the crank, giving it a full turn. The engine caught with a sputter and then roared to life. Breidstein adjusted the choke and spark so the engine hummed steadily. Carlos quickly ran to the car door and climbed into the driver's seat.

Carlos maneuvered the Metz into the mass of humanity along the street, beeping the horn belligerently from time to time to get people or animals out of the way. "I was concerned that you might not easily get through the passport check, but you seemed to handle it okay," Carlos said as he honked the horn again.

"What would you have done if it had not been so easy?" Breidstein asked.

"I was prepared to rush forward and grab you as a customer, slipping the guard ten balboas in the process."

"Oh," Breidstein answered, but thinking that a great deal of his mission depended upon this rogue, and his ability to potentially bribe a guard. This would probably not be the last time that his mission's success would hang from such tenuous threads. He had better get used to it—and he had better get used to what he would soon have to do to Carlos.

THEY RODE UP INTO THE HILLS TO A HOUSE—not a villa but a good-sized house, well separated from the other houses on the hillside. Once in the yard in front of the house, Carlos parked the car so that it pointed down the hillside, explaining, "I let it coast down the hill to start it." Inside, Carlos led Breidstein to his room.

"Your clothes are in the closet. I was instructed as to your height and build and given a list of things to obtain—pants, suit, shirt, tie, all those type of things, as well as appropriate luggage. The clothes are fine Panamanian clothes, as I was instructed to obtain. I presume they will be adequate for whatever purpose you may have," Carlos explained before he left Breidstein alone.

Breidstein took stock, pulling out his documents and checking to see if he still had everything, remembering that he would have to destroy the documents with his old identity before leaving. He kept his money belt on, knowing that the thousand American dollars in it would be a huge attraction to anyone, including Carlos.

There was a knock at the door, followed by, "*Señor*, may I come in?" But the voice was not that of Carlos. It was a woman's voice.

Startled, Breidstein answered, "*Si*." Gehlen had not said anything about another person being at the hideaway.

The woman, young but obviously more than a child, entered the room. "I am the housekeeper, Christina. Carlos asked me to see if you needed anything—anything at all."

"Not now," he responded, thinking that, except for her round-like face, she looked very attractive—raven black hair and dark green eyes. Just what he thought Spanish harlots probably looked like. *Is she more than a housekeeper?* he wondered.

"Fine, *señor*. We will be having our dinner in about an hour. Please join us," Christina said as she made a turn and paused before she walked out of the room, momentarily outlining her very full breasts against the sunlight spilling through the doorway.

BREIDSTEIN WENT DOWNSTAIRS to the small verandah where Christina was setting out dinner platters and bowls of fruit. The sun was falling beneath the tree line around the house. Carlos was already sitting at the dinner table.

"You have met Christina? She is my housekeeper—and my friend," Carlos said as he put his arm around Christina's waist, pulling her close to himself and then slipping his hand down to firmly grasp her buttocks. "She does many things for me. She even bought your clothes."

Chistina slipped from Carlos' grasp. Carlos gave a small laugh as she did so. Breidstein no longer had doubts about the relation between Carlos and Christina.

"Yes, we met. What does she know about my visit here?" Breidstein asked.

"*Señor*, she knows no more than I," Carlos said, as he reached for some fruit and began eating.

Not knowing what else to do, Breidstein sat down and began to eat also.

21

IT WAS THE NEXT DAY. The three of them were finishing their afternoon meal when Carlos turned to look intently at Christina and speak. "I must go into town—to the *mercado*. And I must attend to other matters."

"So soon?" Christina asked.

"Did you not say we needed more food. And I must see to things at the other house, as well. I will be back later tonight, just like I usually do, just as always—no different than any other time," Carlos said slowly to Christina, as he pushed his chair from the table.

Breidstein started to object. "What do you mean, other house? Where are you going? What is this about?" Breidstein didn't trust Carlos, and he didn't like the idea of Carlos going off by himself, and doing who knows what—*maybe,* Breidstein thought, *even letting it slip that I am hiding here.*

"*Señor*, to maintain such a fine house as I have here, with Christina, I must have many business ventures. My house in town has many fine ladies who provide enjoyment for the more successful men of the city. I must periodically assure the well-being of my ladies, is that not correct, Christina?"

"Yes," Christina said with downcast eyes.

"Do not worry, my friend, I am sure Christina will be able to take care of you while I am gone," Carlos said with a smirk at Christina.

With that, Carlos walked out the door. In a moment, Breidstein heard the car engine catch as Carlos started driving off.

Christina rose from the table, looking out of the window as she spoke to Breidstein. "Do not worry. He will be back." Then she turned to look at Breidstein. "He goes to collect the money from the girls—and spend the evening with one of them, like he used to do with me before I came here… to work here with him. He will probably get drunk and… maybe… not return until morning. It is just as well that he not return tonight… just as well."

"Why do you say that?" Breidstein asked.

"He asks too much… when he gets drunk," Christina answered.

Carlos must be very mean when he makes love to her—probably beats her when he's drunk, Breidstein thought.

Then Christina's voice became sullen. "But one day… one day he will demand too much of… one of them… or me."

THE REST OF THE AFTERNOON passed quietly. Breidstein carefully packed his clothes in anticipation of his departure the next day. After a light evening meal fixed by Christina—Carlos still had not returned—Breidstein went out to the patio as Christina began to heat water to wash the dishes.

As he sat on the patio, watching the moon come up, he thought about what he knew he was soon going to have to do to Carlos, and wondered what to do about Christina. There was no doubt that Carlos would have to be killed. Gehlen's instructions were quite clear on that. Carlos' death was critical to the success of Breidstein's mission—Carlos was scum anyway. Breidstein could do it when they left the house for the drive to the city tomorrow. Shoot him on the way down through the hills and dump his body into one of the streams that the road crossed; there were numerous places along the road that were deserted enough. All he had to do was have Carlos stop the car—Breidstein could pretend he had to piss—get Carlos out of the car momentarily, and then do it. It would not be difficult.

Christina was a different matter. Did she really pose a threat? He didn't like the idea of having to kill a woman, even if she was a whore. And if he did kill her, it would mean driving back to the house after he killed Carlos. He certainly could not kill her before he killed Carlos, unless he could fake some accident that resulted in her death. But that might not work. Carlos had to be totally surprised. Breidstein pondered what he should do, almost wishing he could ask Gehlen for advice. Coming back to the house was not without risk, so killing her was not necessarily the right thing to do. Breidstein juggled the pros and cons in his mind for a long while, struggling with ideas about what might be done.

Then Christina appeared in the doorway to the patio. "Do you wish to take a hot bath tonight? I can heat some water on the stove for you. There is a wooden tub in my room you can use."

Breidstein thought a moment. He was getting tired of the cold water sponge baths he had been taking ever since he had set foot on the *Ciudad de la Habana*. "Yes. Where do you want me to put the tub?" A good bath might be just what he needed to clear his thoughts.

"It is fine where it is. You can take your bath in my room. I will start heating the water," Christina answered.

Breidstein went to Christina's room. It was a simple room, but the mirrored dresser had numerous cosmetic items spread about on it. The chifforobe, which he opened out of curiosity, had simple dresses and skirts, and, not totally surprisingly, two fine, rather exotic-looking dresses. The bed in the corner was much wider than the one he slept on and it had a pale blue bedspread over it. The tub sat in a corner behind a dressing screen.

Christina entered with a large bucket of steaming water. Walking behind the dressing screen, she began to pour water into the wooden tub. She left the room for more water.

After the third trip, Christina said, "I think it is ready now. Go ahead," and then walked toward the bedroom door.

Breidstein stepped behind the dressing screen. The tub waters looked inviting. A large bar of soap rested on a stand by the tub and two small towels hung on a rack. He heard the bedroom door close. He began taking off his clothes, laying them across the top of the dressing screen. He hung his money belt on the soap stand. He got into the tub, slid down as far as he could into the hot water, and began to enjoy himself.

Christina came around the dressing screen with a washcloth in her hand, totally surprising Breidstein. He thought she had left the room. "Let me wash your back. I know how hard it is to do in this small tub."

Breidstein didn't say anything, neither encouraging nor discouraging her. She pulled off her shoes and knelt down, pulling her skirt above her knees to do so. Her coarse, black stockings went up her slightly fat but still shapely legs and disappeared under her skirt. She shifted the money belt and took the bar of soap in her hand. She began to soap Breidstein's back with smooth strokes. Breidstein said nothing, but he could feel himself begin to stiffen. He dare not look at himself. She moved closer, as if to wash him better, and her breast pushed against his arm. Breidstein could feel the closeness of her; her nipple pressed into his arm. He turned and looked at her. The air was humid from the hot water. Perspiration had begun to wet her blouse. She pulled her shoulders back from him. Breidstein could see her large nipples through the wet cloth of her blouse. She looked at him, coolly, and put the bar of soap on the floor.

She leaned towards him again and put her hand into the soapy waters, searching for him. When her hand found him, she squeezed gently and began to slide her hand up and down, along with a gentle twisting motion. This was not the first time for Breidstein, but this was far different from the whores of *Ku'damm* in Berlin. "Come," she said, as she stood and then helped him stand.

He rose, exposing himself fully. She stepped back from the tub. She picked up a towel from the stand and wiped the dripping water from him, but left him still wet and slippery.

She turned her back to him, saying, "Loosen the ties." He did and her skirt fell away, revealing the full length of her stockings and her short pantaloons. She reached about herself, pulled her blouse over her head, and turned, presenting her two full globes to him. He reached out to her, grasping one, and slowly began to caress it. She moved closer, pulling his head down. "Kiss my nipples, make them hurt." As his mouth began to work, she used her free hand to push her pantaloons down. She wiggled and they finally fell to the floor. She stepped from them and then took another step back.

Breidstein looked at the dark, black, soft patch she had uncovered above the top of her stockings. She came to him. He grasped her legs and lifted her, her legs wrapping about him as he did. She clasped her arms around his neck. He slid his hands to her buttocks and positioned her. He slid himself into her. As he began to push into her, she used her arms to pull him into herself even farther. They began to move in rhythm, both grunting. Low and satisfied moans began to come from her.

Then in the same moment as she gave a ragged cry, they both came. After a moment of stillness as they savored what had just occurred, she loosened her legs and Breidstein let her down, slowly slipping out of her. He was satisfied, but still hard, able to do more. She pulled him to her bed, and pushed him flat on the blue bedspread. Then she mounted him, her breasts heaving, seemingly alive. Loud, animal-like sounds of joy began to come from her lips. Breidstein began to urge her on.

Then, suddenly, a gunshot came from somewhere in the house, startling them both, breaking their rhythm. "What was that?" Breidstein asked in surprise, as he heard heavy thuds—what sounded like furniture being overturned. As he pushed Christina off himself and stood up, he heard a door slam and then more sounds of furniture being overturned, as if someone were knocking aside furniture as he came down the hallway toward Christina's bedroom.

A look of fright came to Christina's face as she got up from the bed. "¡*Dios mio*! I didn't think he would do it this time—I didn't believe he really wanted to do this again—with you."

"Again? What are you taking about?" Breidstein asked in a frightened voice.

"To have you ready, so you would give him no trouble. He is coming to kill you! Quick—behind the door," Christina said hurriedly, as she pushed Breidstein toward the door.

Breidstein stood with his back against the wall, naked and defenseless, the sweet inner juices of Christina still wet on his now sagging penis.

The door burst open and Carlos staggered in, drunk, a gun in his hand. "Where is he?" Carlos demanded. "I want his money. You should have been with him in his bed so I could kill him."

Christina looked towards the dressing stand, but Carlos was not fooled. He turned around and saw Breidstein standing there, naked. "Well, at least you will die a happy, satisfied man," Carlos said as he pointed the gun toward Breidstein. "She is good, isn't she? One of my best girls. Did she do the other as well as the fuck? She's really good at it. But that doesn't matter now. Where is your money belt? It's full of money, isn't it?"

Breidstein was immobile, petrified. He was looking into the face of death for the first time.

As Carlos spoke, Christina moved toward the dresser and picked up the long bladed scissors lying there. Christina's eyes had become black orbs.

Breidstein's eyes began to widen. Christina stepped toward Carlos' back and drove the full length of the scissors' blades into him, between his shoulder blades. As the blood spurted outward and dotted her face, she screamed at him, "You bastard—no more, no more. I will not let you kill anymore. You are done hurting me." She pulled the scissors outward and pushed them back, twisting them, deepening the crevice in Carlos' back.

Carlos howled, trying to grab his back with his free hand. His eyes rolled, seemingly on fire. He finally broke free from Chistina, as the blood covered scissors slipped from her hands. He turned and fired his pistol. Christina slumped to the ground, a black, powder-rimmed hole in the middle of her chest. Breidstein jumped forward, grabbing Carlos and reaching for the gun. Carlos offered no resistance; he could not. He was dead. And so was Christina.

22

BREIDSTEIN LET CARLOS SLIDE from his grasp. Carlos' blood made a gory red swath across Breidstein's naked chest and stomach. Christina's blood spilled from between her breasts and onto the floor.

"Carlos? Carlos, did you get him? Did you kill him? I found his gun. Where are you?" yelled a voice from somewhere outside the bedroom.

Breidstein jumped. There was someone else! For a moment, Breidstein did not know what to do. Then, with no further hesitation, he pulled the gun from Carlos' hand.

Breidstein carefully opened the door. At the end of the hall, coming out of Breidstein's bedroom was a man—a man with the light skin and angular face of a European. The man saw Breidstein and stopped. The man reached under his shirt, withdrawing a pistol. Breidstein fired twice, and the man crumpled to the floor. Breidstein ran towards him, waiting for him to move, but there was no life left in him. Breidstein bent down to look at the man, the first man he had ever killed.

God, Breidstein thought, *what is happening here? Everything is falling apart! I've got to get out of here.* Breidstein took the man's gun, realizing that it was his own, that it must have been found in his room by the man whom he had just killed. He ran to the open hall window. He saw the Metz at the far edge of the yard, farther downhill from where it had been parked earlier in the day. No wonder he hadn't heard Carlos drive up. Tied to the rear bumper of the car was a saddled horse, obviously the horse of the man that Breidstein had just shot.

Breidstein looked for signs of other people. But all was silent. No one was stirring in the other houses scattered along the hillside. Only a single dog barked, but it soon quieted. Either the people of the houses had heard nothing, or they didn't care. Or they were afraid. Breidstein's emotions began to calm and reason began to take hold again. He went back to the man lying on the floor. Breidstein emptied the man's pockets, finding only a hotel key, a large wad of money, and, in the man's shirt pocket, a blood-wetted passport. Looking at the passport, he saw it was American; then he realized that the man had spoken in English, not Spanish.

Clothes—he needed to get some clothes on and get moving—get out of this potential trap. But what about the bodies ... ? Let them be—Carlos and Christina, and the other man. Let it be a lover's quarrel, or more accurately, a fight between a pimp, his whore, and her customer. Breidstein put the roll of money back into the man's pocket; it should look as if there had been no one else there to steal the money. Breidstein carried the man's body into Christina's bedroom and dropped it at the foot of the bed. Then, finally, he dropped a gun by each man's hand.

BREIDSTEIN APPROACHED the gangway of the *Katsuragisan Maru* in the light of the rising sun piercing the morning mists that shrouded the dock. His thighs were still sore from the horse ride into the town. He reached the top of the gangway. He was blocked from going any farther by a surly-looking ship's officer.

The man said something in Japanese that Breidstein did not understand.

"I don't speak Japanese," Breidstein said in Spanish. "But I have a ticket." Breidstein pulled a set of papers from his coat pocket. "My name is Pedro Sanchez."

The ship's captain stepped out of the shadows. "We have been expecting you, *señor* Sanchez," he said in poor Spanish. He took Breidstein's passport, studied it for a moment, and handed it back to Breidstein. "Did you enjoy Panama and its treasures?" the captain asked.

Breidstein spoke his prepared answer to the code words. "It is a jewel second only to the islands of Japan."

Satisfied, the captain motioned to the officer at the gangway to let Breidstein board. "Follow me," the captain said as he turned and led Breidstein along the deck, toward a cabin door.

The *Katsuragisan Maru* reached the open Pacific before the sun rose the next day.

BREIDSTEIN'S TWO-WEEK PASSAGE to the Hawaiian Islands was uneventful. Upon arrival, he made contact with the German Consul in Honolulu and retrieved Werner Breidstein's business reports and personal documents, including a passport—stamped appropriately for Breidstein's travels as an international businessman. Leaving the consulate, he found a decent hotel, took a long bath to rid himself of the smell he had acquired on the *Katsuragisan Maru*, and then went on a shopping spree, buying a wardrobe suitable to his position. The metamorphosis of Willy Rosin into Werner Breidstein was complete.

Five days later, Werner Breidstein boarded the *Empress of Canada* for Manila.

V

SORGE

23

IT HAD BEEN FOUR DAYS since Breidstein had departed Hawaii for the Philippines. He had been doing his utmost to act the successful international businessman, strutting about on deck as if this type of trip were a common thing for him. He sometimes tried to strike up a conversation with passengers who looked to be rather important.

The only conversations of any substance, however, were those at the dinner table. He regularly shared his table with a naive young American university professor of apparently wealthy background enthralled with Communism, a Canadian government official whose primary responsibility seemed to be promotion of lumber sales, a Filipino doctor and his wife—only she of the two had passable English-speaking skills—and a suave Argentinean who could barely speak a word of English and was an obvious gigolo—without current attachment. Since Breidstein was the only one of the six who could speak Spanish and English fluently, he became the *de facto* interpreter for the Argentinean. However, the political connotations attached to every topic of the dinner conversations by the American—no matter how inane—made Breidstein nervous. Breidstein was a businessman, not a politician!

But tonight would be different—no stupid riffraff with their idiotic questions and adolescent views of world politics. The engraved dinner invitation for April 4, 1937 had been delivered to his stateroom yesterday. Werner Breidstein was on the list for the captain's table.

THE FIRST OFFICER made the introductions to the ship's captain as the guests gathered at the table. In addition to Breidstein, the captain, and the first officer, there was the elderly Mr. and Mrs. Dwyer from New York; another American but younger couple, Mr. and Mrs. Cairnes, recently of Rio de Janeiro; a young Japanese woman named Shinako Fujimori; and two U.S. Navy officers, a Commander Ellington and a young lieutenant by the name of Francis Marian. Breidstein surmised, from the way they greeted each other, that the young Marian and the Japanese woman already knew each other well. Of them all, Breidstein recognized only Dwyer, the millionaire oilman whose name often appeared in the business section of international newspapers—and whose company was one of Hamburg Import-Export's frequent sources of business.

Breidstein was seated between Miss Fujimori and Mrs. Cairnes. The two naval officers had Mrs. Dwyer between them. The rest of the men filled the remainder of the large circular table.

As the captain began his dutiful remarks about how pleased he was to be dining with those gathered at the table, Breidstein cast a sideways glance toward Miss Fujimori. Breidstein was mildly surprised, and intrigued, by her mixture of Oriental and European looks. While certainly Oriental, her cheeks were softer than those of an Oriental, and her sculptured chin and neck seemed faintly Roman in character. *Being the world traveler I am*, Breidstein thought as he smiled inwardly, *I am attracted to an array of women, not just Aryan women. There should be no reservations about my having an interest in Oriental women, particularly this very attractive one.*

As the captain finished his welcoming remarks, the waiters came forward with the first course. As they did, the captain turned to Mr. and Mrs. Cairnes, who, the captain quickly made known, were American diplomatic personnel.

"Yes," Albert Cairnes responded to the compliments of the captain, "I will be working directly with the high commissioner in Manila. Judith," Cairnes inclined his head toward his wife, "will also be on the high commissioner's staff, dealing with cultural affairs. Since the Philippine Commission's offices in Manila are run much like an embassy, the State Department thought it would be good experience for us—what with the Philippines being so close to Japan and all. We have been informally told that our next assignment will be Japan itself."

Albert Cairnes then embarked upon a monologue of the couple's experiences in Brazil, the country of their last assignment. Judith Cairnes frequently interrupted her husband to emphasize the importance of some of their responsibilities during their time in Rio de Janeiro. When she did, Breidstein nodded his head, sometimes asking a question, as if intrigued by the comments of the two Americans, which in a way he was. Here were some people, particularly the woman, he might cultivate to learn more about what went on inside the high commissioner's offices in Manila.

Breidstein's interest in Judith Cairnes was also perked by the substantial cleavage she displayed—but he did not let his eyes often focus there. He was too much a man of the world—so he reasoned—to be distracted by such as that. None the less, despite his attempt at nonchalance, he could not completely stop his eyes from slipping downward momentarily from time to time to Judith Cairnes' ample endowments. It was during one of those careless moments that Judith Cairnes smiled discreetly at him. Then as her husband continued his monologue, Judith Cairnes leaned toward Breidstein, exposing her bosom even more, and whispered to Breidstein, "Wonderful views on this trip, are there not, *Herr* Breidstein?" Breidstein smiled, pretending innocence, in return.

The American, Dwyer, eventually cut into the Cairnes' remarks, starting a discourse about the poor state of world affairs—and the importance of oil development to the United States and the world. Dwyer eventually offered his definitive comment about international oil development, saying, "By God, it's what's keeping America and the world economy from going totally down the drain."

Seeing his chance to impress Dwyer, Breidstein chimed in. "Yes, that's very true. And I'm glad I represent a company that is helping people like Mr. Dwyer."

Dwyer turned his head to look at Breidstein. "Why do you say that?" he asked.

"I am the new Orient representative of the Hamburg Import-Export and Economic Development Company. I believe we provide services to your company on a regular basis."

Dwyer hesitated a moment. "Ah... yes, yes. That's correct. Yes, a fine company... Hamburg Import-Export and... ?"

"Economic Development," Breidstein said to assist the fumbling Dwyer. To ease the obvious, but denied lack of recognition of Hamburg Import-Export, Breidstein turned toward Mrs. Dwyer.

"What brings you on this particular trip, Mrs. Dwyer?" Breidstein asked.

"We're taking a trip around the world, ostensibly a vacation, although, I'm afraid, it appears it is turning into one of my husband's business trips."

"Well, you have to seize the opportunities when they occur, don't you agree, Breidstein," Dwyer said as he interrupted his wife. Breidstein nodded in agreement, thankful that he seemed to be still in the good graces of Dwyer, after almost embarrassing him.

"It's like the Philippines," Dwyer went on. "Those islands will be exploding some day. If we can get ourselves well situated before the Philippines become independent in forty-six—at least if that damn Tydings-McDuffy Act isn't changed—then I, my company that is, have the opportunity to make some real money, not this penny-ante stuff we make from China. If we don't take advantage of the opportunities down there, the Japs will. American know-how is what's needed there these days," Dwyer said with blustery conviction.

Breidstein saw Miss Fujimori's jaw tighten. And across the table, he saw the young Lieutenant Marian raise an eyebrow as he tilted his head to look at Miss Fujimori. Breidstein wondered if anyone else had seen her reaction to the "Jap" reference.

"Speaking of the Orient," Mrs. Dwyer interjected in a condescending tone, "how is it that a young girl like you is off traveling by herself, Miss Fujimori."

"I am going to meet my father in Manila. He has a business there. He periodically meets with the local managers of the company." Dwyer gave a knowing glance to Breidstein, as if to say I told you so. "After he finishes his business, we will return home to Japan together. As to my traveling alone," Miss Fujimori said with acidity, "my father has always allowed me more freedom, perhaps, than most. He finds many of the Western ways attractive. I have been living in Hawaii for the last two years with my cousin's family, attending English language school. Perhaps you can tell me if my studies have been successful?"

"Amazingly so, my dear. But, my dear, how is it that you know the lieutenant? I gather you are *very well* acquainted—perhaps you are tiring of traveling alone?" Mrs. Dwyer asked with a hint of titillation.

"We are not traveling together—I didn't even know Lieutenant Marian was on board until this evening. We met in Hawaii about a year ago," Shinako responded defensively.

Francis nodded his head. "Yes, I am as surprised as Miss Fujimori," Francis said as he smiled toward Shinako.

Shinako smiled in return.

"But why would you be meeting a Jap—Japanese in Hawaii, Lieutenant?" Mr. Dwyer asked accusingly.

Breidstein could see the young lieutenant's jaw tighten.

"I took some language instruction from her," Francis said in an obviously irritated tone.

Language instruction—it could be nothing else but Japanese, Breidstein thought. *So what is this Lieutenant Marian into—is he involved in intelligence matters?*

"Oh, but of course, now I understand, Lieutenant," Mrs. Dwyer said with an icy smile. "And why is it that your father became so enthralled of Western ways?" Mrs. Dwyer asked as she pointedly turned her face back toward Shinako. The arrogance in Mrs. Dwyer's voice was obvious to Breidstein.

"He was Japan's ambassador to Germany for nearly six years," Miss Fujimori said proudly.

Breidstein now understood why Miss Fujimori had been invited to the Captain's table. Breidstein smiled inwardly to himself. *I hadn't expected to be so lucky tonight—getting introduced to a United States Navy lieutenant involved in intelligence and a young woman whose father is part of the Japanese diplomatic community. She, through her father, might open many doors for me. And who knows what I might get out of this Lieutenant Marian.*

Dwyer spoke. "Still having all those assassinations in Japan? Every time I read anything about Japan in the *Journal*, it seems that some Jap politician is getting shot. Wasn't your prime minister—Tsuyoshi, or whatever his name was—murdered not too long ago… and the prime minister before him—wasn't he assassinated too?"

The discomfort of Miss Fujimori was apparent to Breidstein. "Yes, we have had difficult times, but those events occurred more than five years ago—"

Dwyer interrupted. "Yes, but the way I understand it, you people have a bunch of secret societies over there and—"

Breidstein was about to come to the aid of Miss Fujimori when the captain broke in. "But Mr. Dwyer, what is past is past. Perhaps, Mrs. Dwyer, you might tell us more about some of your travels? Is this your first trip around the world, or is this just a regular thing for you?"

Mrs. Dwyer immediately began to inform everyone at the table of just how much of a world traveler she really was.

As Breidstein listened with feigned interest to the words of Mrs. Dwyer, he realized that a hand, a female hand, was on his leg. And it certainly wasn't Miss Fujimori's.

Breidstein didn't quite know what to do. He couldn't remove Mrs. Cairnes' hand without the likelihood of someone noticing. And for that matter, Mrs. Cairnes was not an unattractive woman. But she certainly was a married one, and this was not the place to explore her interests.

The hand continued to move tantalizingly over and up his thigh beneath the white linen tablecloth draped over the table. Breidstein stole a glance at Mrs. Cairnes. She smiled discreetly. But then the main course arrived and she removed her hand. Breidstein tried to maintain a reserved demeanor the remainder of the meal as Mrs. Dwyer, unimpeded by her husband's frequent interruptions, talked on until the serving of dessert broke her stride, at which point the captain turned the group's attention to the two naval officers. "Well, Commander Ellington, why are you two officers traveling to Manila?"

"We are reporting to Cavite," Ellington replied. "We have a big base there, you know—several miles south of Manila. I'm joining the fleet staff there to work on some new war plans. Lieutenant Marian here is into communications. He's going to head up a special communications unit there. Isn't that right, Marian?"

Breidstein could see the young Lieutenant almost shrink in his chair as attention was drawn to him.

"Yes sir," Francis answered, responding to Ellington's question.

Navy war plans, special communications, Japanese language training—interesting, Breidstein thought. "War plans? The United States isn't at war," Breidstein said, trying to get Ellington to talk.

"It's an ongoing process. Always have to be prepared, you know—that type of thing. Of course, the Navy's focus is on the Pacific, what with the Japanese Navy ... ." Ellington hesitated, looking toward Miss Fujimori.

"Well, I would hope to God you would be concerned about the Jap navy," Dwyer interjected.

Breidstein winced to himself. This was not the way he wanted the conversation to go.

"Lieutenant, what are these special communications you are into," Breidstein asked, trying to steer Dwyer away from Ellington.

"Oh... just radio communications—listening and talking," Francis answered.

"But what do you listen to?" Breidstein asked pointedly.

"Yes, what does a radio person listen to, especially out in the middle of the Pacific?" Mrs. Dwyer asked. "Why would we want to use taxpayer money to listen to the radio in the Philippines?"

"Be quiet, dear," Mr. Dwyer said to his wife. "The Navy has to spend money some way, to justify all that money Roosevelt keeps asking for—even if it is on boondoggles." Breidstein winced again.

"Actually, sir, there is quite a bit of radio traffic in the Pacific," Francis said. "Most of the world's leading navies are active in the Pacific."

"You mean you listen to people other than Americans?" Mrs. Dwyer asked in surprise.

Breidstein saw a look of exasperation come to the young lieutenant's face.

"Yes ma'am," Francis said, "it's pretty necessary—if you want to understand what other people are doing."

"Isn't that what most people would call 'signals intelligence', Lieutenant," Breidstein asked innocently, but immediately realizing that perhaps he had said too much. Such a term was seldom used except by those in the military.

"Yes, it is usually called that, Herr Breidstein," Francis answered, without, as best Breidstein could discern, any hint of suspicion.

Breidstein didn't ask anymore questions of the young Lieutenant Marian. He was satisfied with what he had already learned about Marian, information to report to Berlin—and information that might become very useful in the future.

24

ACCOUNTING AND WAREHOUSING reports from the Philippines Transfer Company were strewn across the floor. Breidstein turned out the light. He had tried, after returning to his cabin from the captain's dinner and a short, innocent walk about the deck with Miss Fujimori trying to get to know her more, to study more reports on the Philippines Transfer Company. But the dinner and the intensity of the evening playing the role of Breidstein had been too much. He had given up trying to study the reports any more that night.

He was almost asleep when he heard the knock, followed by, "Werner, let me in—hurry."

Breidstein opened the cabin door slightly, looking out. Judith Cairnes pushed the door open widely and stepped into the cabin. "I thought I'd never get Albert off to sleep," she said as she closed the door and moved close to Breidstein.

"Mrs. Cairnes, what are you doing? Why are you here at this time of night?" Breidstein asked as he pulled his untied robe together.

"Why do you think, Werner. I knew what you were thinking when you looked at me. I haven't seen a man as attractive as you in a long time." She put her arms inside Breidstein's still untied robe, sliding them up and down his back. Breidstein began to respond.

Judith Cairnes pushed against him, feeling his hardness. "Go ahead, Werner. We don't have much time. I will have to get back to the cabin soon."

Breidstein contemplated a moment. Obviously she was reading a great deal more into the evening and his straying eyes than he had intended, at least for the present—even if he had not removed her hand from his leg during dinner. But was this good or bad? If he turned Judith Cairnes away, it might create problems, particularly with the position she would be soon assuming on the Philippine High Commission staff. If he did what she obviously wanted him to, not only would he prevent the ire of a scorned woman, but she might well become a valuable source of information. Besides, she was quite attractive.

Breidstein reached up to Judith's shoulder and slid down the straps of her gown. "Oh, Werner," Judith said in a throaty voice. She pulled his hand to her breast and moved her body with Breidstein's toward the narrow bed as he let his robe fall from this body. The papers on the floor crinkled noisily as they backed over them. Judith let her dress fall amid them.

25

THE DAYS OF THE VOYAGE to Manila were down to their last after nearly three weeks. Breidstein had been trying to expand the relationships that had been started at the Captain's dinner, but the only truly deepening ones were those with Judith, which had resulted in several nights similar to the first with her, and the young Japanese woman, Shinako Fujimori, with whom Breidstein was becoming quite friendly, if only in a Platonic way. It was clear to Breidstein that Shinako was lonely, but not for the affections of a man. And Breidstein did not want to try to disrupt the character of the developing relationship; he only wanted to capitalize on it and meet Shinako's father.

Dwyer was friendly, having a drink with Breidstein from time to time, but not apparently wanting to develop a stronger friendship—he seemed to spend most of his time in the ship's telegraph office sending or receiving wireless cables. As to the two naval officers—Breidstein seldom saw them, which was fine with Breidstein. He wanted, at least for the time being, to distance himself from the young, possibly suspicious Lieutenant Marian.

Contemplating how he might strengthen his ties with Dwyer, Breidstein almost bumped into Shinako coming around the corner from the second deck cabins. "Excuse me. Oh, hello. How are you today, Shinako?"

She answered excitedly, "Wonderful! We dock today and I am so looking forward to seeing my father again. It has been almost two years."

"Yes, I imagine you would be. I hope you will remember to introduce me when we arrive. He seems to be a very interesting man, from all you say," Breidstein said.

"No, Werner, I won't forget. I am sure you and he will like each other," Shinako said.

"Well," Breidstein said with a smile, "shall we go on deck and watch our passage into the harbor?"

"If you wish," Shinako responded.

"I do so wish," Breidstein repeated after her, mocking her in fun. "After you, Shinako-*san,*" Breidstein said as he gave a silly little bow, laughed, and swung his arm with exaggerated graciousness toward the stairway. Shinako gave a wide grin, and then turned toward the stairway.

Breidstein followed Shinako up the narrow stairway to the deck. Despite what he knew had to be hands off, he could not take his eyes from her smooth hips as each of her small legs beneath her long dress went up, step by step.

They walked over to the railing. The sun was up by now, but still low enough that they had to squint to see the lush landscape off the side of the ship several kilometers away. They had apparently entered Manila Bay earlier in the morning. As far as they could see was land, both off the sides and toward the bow of the ship in the direction they were headed. Farther ahead, in the distance, they could see the beginnings of a city, shrouded in a morning mist.

The purser walked by. Shinako stopped him, asking when they would dock.

"Nine o'clock, Miss, about an hour from now."

"Is that Manila coming into view?" Shinako asked.

"Yes, it is," the purser answered.

"And what is that large island behind us, there?" Shinako asked as she pointed with upraised hand toward a mountainous looking mass in the far distance.

"Why, Miss, that is the island of Corregidor."

BOTH BREIDSTEIN AND SHINAKO stood behind the crowd of Americans as the gangway was being lowered. Breidstein watched Shinako straining to look into the waiting crowd on the dock, looking for her father, but thought it would be difficult to pick out anyone because there was so much milling about.

"What does he look like? Perhaps I can help you find him," Breidstein offered.

"He's about fifteen centimeters taller than me. He has big, bushy eyebrows and dark brown hair. And he looks, well, Oriental," Shinako said.

"Is that him, with the dark suit, there by the gate?" Breidstein volunteered as he raised an arm to point toward the dock below.

"No, no," Shinako said.

"Well, that's the only person I see that seems to fit the bill," Breidstein said.

As the moments passed, Breidstein could see that Shinako was becoming agitated, saying something in a whisper over and over in Japanese. It was apparent that Shinako was worried.

"Well, it's no use standing up here. Perhaps when we walk down the gangway, he will see you and come out of the crowd," Breidstein suggested, trying to ease Shinako's anxiety.

"Perhaps you're correct," Shinako said, as her eyes continued to search the dock.

By the time they had gotten past the immigration agent at the bottom of the gangway and reached the wide dock beyond, Breidstein could see that no father was stepping forward. But the Oriental man in the dark suit Breidstein had seen before was approaching Shinako.

As the man neared Shinako, he said something in what Breidstein thought must be Japanese. All Breidstein could catch was the name "Fujimori" being said. Perhaps Shinako's father had been delayed and had sent someone in his place. But as the conversation between Shinako and the man continued, it became heated. Shinako, for some reason, didn't seem to like what the man was saying, and was apparently arguing with him.

Then the man raised his left arm and made a signaling motion. A large car with diplomatic plates and prominently displayed Japanese flag on the fender pulled towards them as the man clasped Shinako's arm with his hand. Shinako yanked free of the man's grasp.

Breidstein didn't know what was being said, but he didn't like what seemed to be an attempt to take Shinako away—forcibly. Breidstein stepped in. "Now listen here, what's going on?" he demanded, hoping the man understood English.

"Who are you?" the man asked accusingly in strongly accented English.

"I am Werner Breidstein. I represent Hamburg Import-Exports. Miss Fujimori and I are friends. Who are you?" Breidstein demanded.

"You are not Japanese, are you?" the man asked.

"Well, no, but—"

"Then this does not concern you," the man said as the car drew closer.

Shinako then broke in with a demanding voice, as if asking a question of the man.

The man stepped back, let out a long sigh, and then began to speak softly to Shinako.

Shinako looked at the man one brief moment before turning to look at Breidstein. Then she fainted. Before she hit the dock pavement, Breidstein grabbed her, wondering what the man had said.

26

BREIDSTEIN BEGAN SHAKING Shinako's shoulders as he held her in his arms, trying to revive her. Slowly she began to open her eyes. They were glassy as she stared at Breidstein. Breidstein turned to look at the man, who now had a look of fright on his face. "What did you say to her," Breidstein demanded.

"I am the second deputy to the consul general at the Japanese consulate here in Manila. I was sent by the consul general to bring Miss Fujimori to the consulate," the man replied in his stilted English.

"Why did she faint?" Breidstein demanded, almost yelling at the man.

"Regretfully, I had to tell her—she would not come without me telling her—that her father is dead."

With that, a loud cry came from Shinako's lips, and she began to cry uncontrollably.

"May I suggest," the second deputy said, "that I get Miss Fujimori to the consulate where our doctor can attend to her—and she can speak to the consul general."

Breidstein hesitated a moment, and then said, "Yes, that sounds like a good idea."

Breidstein lifted the still crying Shinako and helped her into the consulate car. He didn't give any opportunity for the second deputy to keep him from also getting into the car.

Inside the car, Shinako buried her face on Breidstein's shoulder. She wept the entire drive to the consulate.

Arriving at the consulate in about twenty minutes, Breidstein half-carried Shinako into the consulate foyer. The consul general quickly led them into the library, where Shinako collapsed on a couch.

After a few moments Breidstein introduced himself, using English as the common language between himself and the Japanese consul general. "I am

Werner Breidstein. I am the newly appointed agent for the Hamburg Import-Export and Economic Development Company. Miss Fujimori and I met on the trip from Hawaii. I was very concerned about her distressed state and felt she needed a friend."

"I am Consul General Agawa. I appreciate your concern." He turned to the second deputy, asking, Breidstein surmised, what had happened. The man looked very uncomfortable as he apparently tried to explain.

"I don't think you should blame your man. I think he tried not to tell Miss Fujimori the news at the dock, but she insisted," Breidstein offered.

"Well, it does not matter now. Miss Fujimori, do you feel any better now? Can you talk?" Agawa asked with a gentle voice.

Shinako responded weakly, "A little. Tell me what happened," Shinako asked in English, apparently for the benefit of Breidstein.

The consul general cleared his throat. He spoke in English, as had Shinako. "Two days ago we received a wireless message from the Foreign Ministry in Tokyo. It seems they had been contacted by your father's sister, who was trying to contact you on the ship through the liner offices. She was unsuccessful and so she turned to the ministry. We learned only yesterday of your arrival date. By that time, we thought it better we inform you here rather than on the ship."

"Yes, but what about my father? What happened?" Shinako asked.

"We know little. He was apparently going to give some speech or public announcement at the Foreign Ministry on the day before he was to sail here. As he was walking up the steps to the ministry building, he was shot by a small group of unknown men who ran away and escaped. That is all I know," Agawa said.

"Shot! My father assassinated! Oh no, oh no." Shinako began to weep again. At that moment a doctor entered the room. After examining Shinako for several moments and talking to the consul general, he took some pills out of his bag and had Shinako take them.

"The doctor has given her some sedatives. She needs to get to her hotel and rest," Agawa said to Breidstein.

Shinako said faintly, "I have no hotel room. My father was going to arrange all that."

Breidstein spoke. "She can have my room at the Manila Palace Hotel. I'll call the German consulate—they are expecting me—and arrange for a car to pick us up immediately. Could you connect me with Consul General Bogner?"

Agawa hesitated, but only a moment. "Certainly, *Herr* Breidstein," Consul General Agawa answered. Breidstein saw the slight hesitation, and then realized that Agawa was impressed—by the man named Breidstein who could demand that a German consulate car be sent to pick him up.

Fifteen minutes later, the German consul general's personal limousine came up the driveway to the Japanese consulate.

As Breidstein and the doctor helped Shinako into the car, Consul General Agawa said to Breidstein, "*Herr* Breidstein, please call me when you have an opportunity. I believe we would have much of mutual interest to discuss."

27

IT HAD RAINED all morning in Tokyo—a light drizzling rain from a pale gray sky. The ground was still wet as the mourners gathered by the graveside for the burial service of Shinako's father, Yukihiko. It had taken more than a week for Shinako to get back to Tokyo from Manila—Shinako had arrived in Tokyo only two days ago—so Chieko, Yukihiko's sister, had taken care of the actual arrangements. Though difficult, Chieko had arranged for a Christian burial service for Yukihiko, as he often had said to Shinako and Chieko that he would want when he died. A Christian burial was not well received by many of the people that once claimed Yukihiko to be their friend, so the funeral was only sparsely attended.

As Shinako sat and listened to the words being said over the grave, she thought of what would happen now. Her grief had reached the limit; it had permeated her every fiber. Her beloved father was gone. Now she had to think about the future. She and Chieko were the only ones left in the Fujimori family. Her father's estate would last only so long; creditors were already gathering at the doorstep. His business was likely to go under soon unless she sold it to someone who could actually run it. It was unrealistic to think that she could run it; Japanese women just did not do that. Any attempt at it would be useless, considering the resistance she would encounter.

True, a distant cousin of Chieko said he would take them in, but it was clear that he was making the offer only out of reverence to Chieko's dead husband—and his own needs. The cousin was a widower, and he was looking for companionship as his later years approached. Chieko had said, "He will probably ask me to marry him. And I suppose it would not be too bad. He wants a mother more than a wife." Left unsaid was what would happen to Shinako.

AS THE MINISTER said his closing words, Shinako's eyes wandered. She saw a strange face in the back of the small crowd—a dark, foreboding face with heavy eyebrows, a thick mustache and the heavy jowls of a Westerner. Shinako wondered who it might be; she knew everyone else.

The minister finished and Shinako and Chieko each stood and placed a rose on the grave. They gave one last look and then turned away. The light rain started again.

As Shinako and Chieko walked to their limousine, the unknown man walked up to them. "Excuse me for interrupting in your hour of grief, but my name is Richard Sorge. I represent the *Frankfurter Zeitung*, an international business newspaper. I was with your father at the time of... of his passing. I wonder if I might talk to you ... at another time, a more convenient time?"

Shinako looked at him in surprise. *At the time of my father's passing; what is he talking about?*

Chieko spoke quickly, in an irritated tone, "Yes, you are correct; this is not the time. Please call for an appointment." Chieko quickly turned and ushered Shinako to the waiting limousine, leaving Sorge standing in the rain.

The chauffeur was about to drive away when a taxi came quickly up the small cemetery roadway and stopped in front of the limousine. Lieutenant Seiroku Takamatsu got out, opening an umbrella as he came around to the window of the limousine.

Seiroku looked through the limousine's side window, motioning for it to be lowered. Chieko rolled the window halfway down and peered out at Seiroku. "What do you want? Why do you come here and blaspheme my brother's memory?" Chieko asked.

"I only wish to speak to Shinako, to express my sorrow. I would have been here earlier, but I did not know until an hour ago that the ceremony was being held today—that she is here in Tokyo," Seiroku said.

Shinako stared at Seiroku, then said, "It is just as well." Then she turned her head to look toward the front of the car.

"Drive on," Chieko ordered the driver. The limousine pulled out around the taxi, across the edge of the wet grass, leaving muddy tire marks. Water splashed on Seiroku as the car made its hurried exit. Seiroku slowly walked back to his taxi and got in. The taxi tore up the wet ground as it turned around and pulled away.

A short distance away, Richard Sorge was still standing in the rain, watching what had happened. As the taxi sped away, he reached inside his coat and retrieved a small pad of paper. He wrote something down on the paper and returned the pad to his coat pocket.

TWO HOURS PASSED BEFORE SORGE RETURNED to his small office in midtown Tokyo. The first thing he did was to check the teletype to see if any important news stories were in the process of breaking. None were. Then he called his contact at the taxi company. As he explained what he wanted, he read a number from his pad—the number of the cab that had brought the Japanese naval officer to the funeral—repeating it twice so that there was no mistake.

Sorge received a return phone call the next morning. A brief conversation then followed as Sorge negotiated a price for the information the contact had obtained, with Sorge assuring him that the money would be delivered by the end of the day. That done, the contact told Sorge what he had found.

"Admiral Yamamoto's headquarters," Sorge said in disbelief. "Are you sure that was where he was picked up and dropped off—at Yamamoto's headquarters at the War Ministry building." Assured that there was no error in the information, Sorge hung up the phone and leaned back in his squeaky chair. "A member of Yamamoto's staff—how very interesting." It didn't seem to make sense to him at all, but there seemed to be no doubt.

Sorge then unlocked his top desk drawer and pulled out a file labeled "Organizations." He spent several minutes adding some notes on the several pages contained in the file before he returned it to the drawer.

28

"I DO WANT TO THANK YOU for seeing me today, Miss Fujimori," Sorge said as he knelt down with Shinako in her Tokyo home a little more than two weeks after the funeral.

"Yes, it has been a very difficult time, but I will manage, somehow." *I wonder if this man has any idea how difficult it really has been for me—my money almost gone, my father's so-called friends doing their best to avoid me, and even my father's life-long servants leaving*, Shinako thought as Sorge nodded in understanding.

"Now, as to the reason why you are here, *Herr* Sorge. You said you were with my father at the time of ... of his death," Shinako said as she looked inquisitively at Sorge.

"Yes, I was. You see, as I said before, I represent the German paper *Frankfurter Zeitung* here in Tokyo. I am a foreign correspondent for a variety of international news services as well," Sorge explained. "I maintain a small office here in Tokyo. I had heard that your father was going to the Foreign Ministry to make some important statement about the growing power of the military in civil matters. I had gone there to interview him." Sorge paused, then continued. "I understand he was an outspoken critic of the military, that he was concerned about the increasing lack of civilian control in the government," Sorge said.

"That is correct, though I did not follow his political activities closely," Shinako responded. "You may know that I have been, until recently, in the Hawaiian Islands." Shinako slipped into English without realizing it. "I spent two years there learning English and trying to understand the Western mind, at least as it was evidenced in Hawaii. My father had a great concern about the Japanese being able to understand Western culture."

"I did not know that you had spent time in Hawaii," Sorge answered as he straightened his body in surprise. "Your English is remarkable, at least as much as I can tell."

"Thank you. I apologize if I presumed too much," Shinako said, realizing that she had not asked Sorge if he spoke English.

"No, not at all. I speak English, but not nearly as well as you apparently do," Sorge replied.

"Perhaps," Shinako continued, "you do know, since you are from Germany, that my father was Japanese ambassador to Germany in the nineteen-twenties," Shinako said.

"Yes, that I did know," Sorge said.

"Well, my mother and I were with him at that time. The little German I know came from the time I was there. My father insisted that I take courses in the German language while we were there. I did so until we had to return to Japan, when my mother became so ill. She died shortly after our return," Shinako said.

Shinako then slipped from English into German, as if to emphasize her point. "He said I would never have a better chance to learn the German language. He did not think opportunities like that should be wasted. He was a very wise man, a very loving man. He gave me much love and support when I needed it during some very difficult times. I do not know if my pain over his loss will ever go away." Shinako paused to take a deep breath, almost feeling real physical pain, and then gathered her thoughts.

"Well, what do you think? How bad do I sound to a real German?" Shinako asked.

Sorge smiled. "Actually rather good, for an Oriental tongue. Certainly not perfect, but certainly understandable."

"But back to what you were saying, *Herr* Sorge," said Shinako, as she slipped back into Japanese. "Please tell me what happened. I really don't know any details. Perhaps knowing them would help me deal with his death more easily."

"Well, I had followed him up the steps, to try to ask him a few questions before he went into the Ministry. He didn't seem to mind when I asked if I could ask him some questions. There was quite a crowd around him. Just as I started to ask him my first question, there was a shot—actually two. One apparently missed him and wounded a young woman in the crowd behind him. The second, unfortunately, struck him in the heart. I must say to you that I believe that he died instantly, that he did not suffer," Sorge said.

"Did you see who did it? The police have done nothing. They say they have no idea, no clues. I know that is a lie, but I can do nothing about it," Shinako said angrily.

"No," Sorge answered. "Actually my back was to the direction from which the shots came. By the time I turned around, I saw only several people running away. I could not really see much of them, except that they ran fast enough to indicate that they were young men."

Tears were coming down Shinako's face. "I am sorry. It is just that it is... it is so senseless. Why did this have to happen to him?" Shinako said.

"I'm afraid it's part of these times, Miss Fujimori—just a part of these difficult times."

Shinako finally recovered her composure, wiping her eyes with a crumpled handkerchief. "I want to thank you for coming, *Herr* Sorge. And I appreciate your coming to the burial service. So few people actually came, as you could see. The newspaper censors did their best to bury the announcement of the service."

"Well, I felt it important that I be there, given the circumstances... although it looked as if not everyone got there that wanted to be there. That young naval officer that came up at the last minute, for instance—a friend of the family?" Sorge asked.

"Oh, Seiroku Takamatsu. A friend... no, just a memory from long ago," Shinako answered.

"Takamatsu! Not the same Takamatsu that sits on the war ministry council?" Sorge asked.

"No—his son," Shinako answered, startled at Sorge's surprise and apparent interest in Seiroku. She became uncomfortable as Sorge looked intently at her for a long moment. She broke his stare by speaking to him. "Thank you, again, *Herr* Sorge. Your words have provided me some comfort. Perhaps we shall meet again."

"Perhaps." Sorge started to rise, but then stopped. "Miss Fujimori, may I speak to you a moment more?"

"If you wish, but about what?" Shinako asked, wondering what this strange man wanted now.

"Well, I somehow feel partially responsible for your father's death. If I had not stopped him to ask my questions, well ... who knows?" Sorge said.

"*Herr* Sorge, his death was not caused by you. I do not think you are in any way responsible," Shinako said.

"Thank you, but still, I want to help. I know that this must be a difficult time for you. And, perhaps your financial condition is not, shall I say, very secure. But you have some particularly unusual talents. You speak German and English, a rare combination for a Japanese. I could use the assistance of someone with your skills," Sorge said.

"What are you suggesting, *Herr* Sorge?" Shinako asked.

"Quite simply, I would like you to come to work for the *Frankfurter Zeitung* as my assistant. Your skills would be invaluable in improving my reporting capabilities. I have an appropriate budget for hiring qualified people to assist me. I could offer you a salary of ... six hundred yen a month," Sorge said.

Shinako thought for a moment. Sorge's offer might be a godsend. With the salary he was offering and by stretching out her father's estate money, she just might be able to carry on in a reasonable fashion, at least for the foreseeable future, without the help of Chieko's cousin. And if she could get any reasonable amount of money for her father's business in the Philippines, she could provide for an appropriate dowry for Chieko's marriage to her cousin, in keeping with the stature of the Fujimori name. Shinako could then be reasonably independent and secure.

"Yes, *Herr* Sorge, I think I might like that." Shinako repeated her acceptance again, this time in German, and then another time in English for good measure.

29

THE DAYS AFTER BREIDSTEIN'S ARRIVAL in Manila and his first face-to-face meeting with Consul General Bogner passed rapidly. The consulate's legal officer worked with Breidstein to get the old Philippine Transfer Company out of its doldrums and into a fully functional business again as part of Hamburg Import-Export. With the help of the consulate offices, the way was smoothed for Breidstein to become the registered agent of the company in the Philippines. Breidstein was now in a position, as the legal officer assured him, to not only carry on import and export activities throughout the region but also consummate the purchase of other companies on behalf of Hamburg Import-Export.

The previously made arrangements for the Manila branch of *Bank-Hamburg Geschäftlich* to provide appropriate cash and credit to Breidstein and the Philippine operations of Hamburg Import-Export were confirmed. Once the bank president, Karl Jahnel, realized that the credit line authorized for Breidstein by the home bank in Germany was one of the largest ever handled by the Manila branch, Jahnel quickly assigned himself as manager of the Breidstein account.

Breidstein worked initially out of a temporary office at the consulate, spending long hours to get the company back into shape. He replaced the dock manager with a local man named Macarat recommended by Jahnel as not only a good manager for the rough crowd that worked the Manila docks, but also someone who knew his way around the docks—should Breidstein need some extra assistance. Macarat spoke not only Tagalog, but also Spanish and a smattering of English. Under Macarat's watchful eyes, Breidstein also had the warehouse offices remodeled and a sturdy wall safe installed in his private upstairs office, to better accommodate the range of business needs he contemplated.

Shortly after the remodeling began, Breidstein received a call from Consul General Agawa's secretary asking whether he might be free to meet with the consul general the following day. "Yes," Breidstein had responded. "Tell him *Herr* Breidstein would be very pleased to meet with him."

"I AM SO GLAD that you were able to join me, *Herr* Breidstein," Consul General Agawa said in their common language of English the next day as Agawa gave a slight bow and then shook Breidstein's hand in the Western style of introduction.

"The pleasure is all mine," Breidstein said in response. "I have been saying to myself that I needed to come by and visit you, but getting the business back in running order has been very time-consuming." Actually, Breidstein was very pleased with the way things were working out. Agawa had come to him, rather than Breidstein going to Agawa. "You may know that my company, the Hamburg Import-Export and Economic Development Company, purchased the Philippine Transfer Company. My intent is to get the operation back on its feet and generate a healthy profit from its operations before year's end. Your invitation is a welcome respite from my efforts."

"I did feel that I ought to express my personal gratitude to you for your assistance to Miss Fujimori in her time of sorrow here in Manila. Your assistance in making the necessary arrangements for her return to Japan were very appreciated, I am sure, by her," Agawa said. Then after a pause, he added, "It was a very difficult situation, not only for her, but for the consulate—and me."

"You, personally? I am not sure I understand," Breidstein said, puzzled.

"Yes. You see," Agawa began to explain, "Mr. Fujimori was well known in political and diplomatic circles. His political views had not been, how shall we say, well received in the last few years. He had created quite a bit of animosity among many in political circles because of his public remarks about the influence of the military on national policy and the character of Japan's leadership in the Orient. Too much overt assistance to Miss Fujimori by the consulate, and by me in particular, would not have gone unnoticed," Agawa said.

"Well, I am glad I was able to help. She should not have to bear the consequence of her father's views," Breidstein said.

"I know that, but things do have a habit of spilling over from one thing to another in the diplomatic and political world," Agawa said with a smile and a tilt of his head.

"I suppose you're right," Breidstein mused.

"Tell me, Herr Breidstein, what type of things have you been doing to get your operation moving again?"

"Well, there have been many. Renewing our contacts with our various clients and making sure that the terms of the contracts with them are appropriate has occupied much of my attention," Breidstein answered.

"But apparently your company does more than just ship goods. Economic development ... now just what does your company do in that regard?" Agawa asked politely.

"Well, we are always open to actually acquiring businesses, or working with an ongoing business in an appropriate type of joint venture, if we feel the business operation is particularly profitable, or has the potential for becoming so," Breidstein answered.

"Why would a business owner want to sell part of his operation if it were profitable?" Agawa asked.

"There might be a variety of reasons—personal, such as health or age, or perhaps temporarily distressed financial conditions. You know the world is not yet recovered from the economic disaster of nineteen-twenty-nine. Such conditions are not often readily resolved without an infusion of a significant amount of cash," Breidstein answered authoritatively.

"Do you ever work with silent partners?" Agawa asked.

Breidstein paused. *How do I know whether Hamburg Import-Export works with silent partners? I wasn't briefed on such a possibility. Besides, why is Agawa asking that question?* "Sometimes. It depends upon the situation." Breidstein answered, guessing that any business arrangement could be worked out if there were a need. "Why do you ask?"

"Well, since Miss Fujimori's return to Japan, her father's business here has been floundering. I made some inquiries and it seems that the business is about to go under. Miss Fujimori is not in a position to give proper guidance to the Philippine manager for its operation. It is, as you say, one of those businesses which is financially distressed," Agawa answered.

"What kind of business is it?" Breidstein asked.

"Chromite mining. Mr. Fujimori owned one of the few independent chromite mining operations here in the Philippine archipelago. There are only a very few sources of chrome in the Eastern Hemisphere, and the Philippines is one of them. Over the years, in his visits here, I spoke with him many times about the operation. The profits were very sizable," Agawa said with a tight-lipped smile.

"What are you suggesting, Mr. Consul General?" Breidstein asked.

"That Hamburg Import-Export and I form a partnership to purchase Fujimori's company," Agawa answered.

"Why would I want to recommend to my company that we do such a thing? If the Fujimori company is ripe for takeover, why should my company not just buy it outright?" Breidstein asked thoughtfully.

"It would be difficult, if not impossible, because," Agawa explained, "while the company is located here in the Philippines, it is legally organized—incorporated is the term I believe you use in Europe—in Japan. It is a Japanese company merely doing business here in the Philippines. The Japanese government would not allow someone who is not Japanese to assume ownership of the company. Conversely, new ownership—at least open ownership—of the company by a Japanese entity would not be well received here in the Philippines in the current political environment."

"But what could the Philippine government do about it?" Breidstein asked, slightly confused.

"New Japanese ownership would potentially open the company to punitive actions by the American government. Roosevelt's re-election last year does not portend good relations between Japan and the United States and, therefore, the Philippine Commonwealth. Roosevelt's anti-Japanese views are well recognized by my government. So we must move cautiously in our dealings where American power is strong, at least for the time being," Agawa answered.

"Thus, in this situation of which we speak," Agawa continued, "if the buyer, in so far as what appeared to be the case here in the Philippines, was, say, a well-respected international company such as yours, with undisclosed partners—of various nationalities such as Japanese, Korean, or Chinese from Manchukuo—owning at least fifty percent of the company, then we could overcome both Philippine and Japanese concerns," Agawa concluded.

"But would these investors, such as yourself, Mr. Consul General, have enough capital to acquire the necessary fifty percent?" Breidstein asked.

"I am sure they would, *Herr* Breidstein. The necessary resources would be more than sufficient," Agawa said with apparent confidence.

Breidstein realized then that Agawa was merely fronting for the Japanese government. But so what? That might be even better. The closer Breidstein was able to work with the Japanese government, whether openly or not, the more likely it would be that he could obtain useful information from them. And that was part of his mission.

"But would Miss Fujimori be willing, as the heir to her father's estate, to sell the business?" Breidstein asked.

"I believe so. I received a letter from her last week asking for my assistance in locating a potential buyer here in the Philippines." Agawa paused, and smiled again. "I would anticipate that the business would sell at a very attractive price considering how speculative such a purchase would be and how difficult it is to find willing buyers in such economically depressed times."

"I will have my bank's legal department begin drawing up the necessary papers," Breidstein responded.

30

IT WAS A WEEK LATER that Breidstein moved from the apartment where the consulate had located him to a larger, more luxurious apartment in Manila's consulate district, a location that better befitted Breidstein's status as the agent for the Hamburg Import-Export and Economic Development Company.

Breidstein had been living in the new apartment only a few days when he received an invitation, hand-delivered by messenger, to the July Fourth celebration at the mansion of the Philippine High Commissioner. The printed invitation had a personal note written at the bottom of it: "Hope very much to see you there. Judith."

AS HE ENTERED the main ballroom of the high commissioner's mansion, Breidstein saw it was filled with people, military and civilian, and obviously not all American. Many were clustered in small, tight groups, while numerous others wandered about among them. Breidstein wandered about as well, making small talk with various people, as he looked for Judith. Then standing in a small group of army and navy officers he saw the young Lieutenant Marian. *Perhaps now is the time to initiate some discussion with him,* Breidstein thought. *All I have to do is be careful.* Breidstein walked over to the group of men.

"Hello, Lieutenant Marian. How are you," Breidstein said warmly. Francis turned and saw Breidstein. Francis stepped away from the other officers and their conversation. "Well, *Herr* Breidstein, we meet again. I'm surprised to see you here—at a July Fourth celebration."

"Why should you be surprised, Lieutenant? I enjoy parties—and your Fourth of July parties are supposed to be grand, are they not?" Breidstein said, trying to be friendly.

"Yes, they usually are, although I really don't have the time for a party— I probably wouldn't be here except for the orders of the base commander—

104-ceiving line is?" Breidstein asked.

Francis answered, "I believe it's over that way," as he pointed to the far end of the ballroom.

"Thank you," Breidstein said as he started walking to the back of the room.

In a few moments, Breidstein saw the receiving line; Judith was at the high commissioner's side, assisting in the introductions. Breidstein went to the end of the slowly moving line. As Breidstein got closer to the head of the line, he saw that Judith had seen him. She had given a short, quick smile to him. Finally Breidstein reached the head of the line.

Judith looked directly at Breidstein, her eyes aglow, as she introduced Breidstein. "Commissioner Lambert, may I introduce to you *Herr* Werner Breidstein. He is the Orient representative for the Hamburg Import-Export and Economic Development Company."

"It is a pleasure to meet you, Commissioner Lambert," Breidstein said.

"*Herr* Breidstein has recently arrived here in Manila, Commissioner. He has only begun to appreciate the beauties of the Philippines," Judith chimed in with a smile. Breidstein wondered whether she intentionally implied a double *entendre*.

"And what will you be doing here in the Philippines, *Herr* Breidstein?" the commissioner asked.

"My company has recently assumed ownership of the former Philippine Transfer Company. I hope to expand my company's business here in the Philippines and the Dutch East Indies," Breidstein answered.

"Interesting," Lambert said. "That should go hand-in-hand with your Chancellor Hitler's stated desires to return economic health to Germany, should it not? How will your activities relate to what *Herr* Hitler says he will be doing, economically or ... otherwise?"

"They relate only to the economic health of my company and the natural benefits that follow," Breidstein parried back, not wanting to get into a political discussion.

"And, I suppose, the political influence such economic benefits can achieve?" Lambert asked.

Breidstein responded coolly, "Perhaps, but, as a simple businessman, I know little of that."

Lambert looked at Breidstein, smiled, and said, "I suppose not, *Herr* Breidstein. Well, please enjoy our party. Have you ever gotten to watch an American Fourth of July fireworks celebration? It is quite an event."

"Yes, they usually are, although I really don't have the time for a party. I probably wouldn't be here except for the orders of the base commander—all new officers have to attend the commissioner's official parties when Navy officers are invited," Francis said as he gave a small laugh. "So how is the exporting and importing business, *Herr* Breidstein?"

"Going very well—hard work, but going well. Are you settled in with your communications unit? You must be busy, from what you say. If I remember correctly, you were going to be in charge. It must be really a challenge commanding a communications unit, what with so many people and your relatively...low rank, Lieutenant."

Breidstein could see Marian pause before answering. "I don't have any problem—besides I only command a small group, only five other officers," Francis answered.

"Only five? Then you must all be very specialized. Sounds intriguing. Just what type of special communications are you into, Lieutenant?" Breidstein asked, trying to pry something from Marian.

"Things I am ordered to be into," Francis answered. "And just what type of special things are you *into, Herr* Breidstein."

"Lieutenant, you must have some misconception of what I do. I just buy and sell goods—trying to make money," Breidstein countered, beginning to feel that he had made a mistake in talking to Marian. But, it was not all wasted effort. It was clear now that Marian was heavily involved in directing some small group at the Cavite base that must be doing some very specialized signals intelligence work on Japanese activities. That would be additional useful information for Berlin. But Marian didn't sound like he was going to be saying much more of value.

"Well, Lieutenant, if you get here to Manila again, come by my office—it's down on the main dock road near pier eleven—and we can have lunch, perhaps," Breidstein suggested.

"Thanks for the invitation, but I don't get up to Manila often—about the only time is for a monthly report to Commander Ellington—and those are pretty busy days. I sure you remember Ellington—from the cruise," Francis answered.

"Oh, yes, I do," Breidstein answered, thinking, *so Marian provides a monthly report, apparently to a war planning group. That can only mean one thing. Marian and his group must be intercepting and deciphering Japanese Imperial Fleet transmissions, and, maybe, making some sense of them. Marian doesn't even realize what he has let me know.* "Well, should you ever get the chance, please come by. Now, I think I had better introduce myself to my host. Have you seen where the commissioner's receiving line is?" Breidstein asked.

"No, but I am looking forward to seeing it," Breidstein said.

"I'm sure he will enjoy it," Judith added.

DARKNESS HAD FALLEN when the announcement was made that the fireworks display was to soon start, and that all guests were invited to the patio and large garden at the back of the ballroom to watch. Breidstein began to move with the crowd towards the patio area. As he did, he suddenly felt a hand on his arm. It was Judith Cairnes.

"*Herr* Breidstein, how good to see you again. I might suggest that we watch the display from the garden area below. It provides a much better view of the bay where the fireworks will go off. Let me take you there," Judith offered in a ceremonial voice.

"Well, thank you, Mrs. Cairnes. That is certainly kind of you," Breidstein said as his part of the charade. He could sense that Judith was speaking for the benefit of those around them who might be listening. They walked together, an appropriately proper distance between them.

They stopped at the edge of the crowd, near the lower end of the garden. As they did so, the first fireworks explosion went off over the bay. The faces of the crowd turned toward the exploding light. Breidstein, too, turned to look. Another explosion followed. Then he felt Judith begin to pull him away from the edge of the crowd. The fantasia of exploding light continued. All eyes were turned toward the fireworks as Breidstein and Judith slipped away. In a few moments, they were behind tall bushes, out of the sight of the crowd.

"Oh, Werner, why have you taken so long to see me?" Judith said as she put her arms around him and pressed against him.

"Judith, it has been so hectic these first weeks. Besides, I wasn't quite sure what excuse I could use to contact you. I was concerned that someone might draw some inferences that would put you in a compromising position," Breidstein said.

"Werner, don't worry about that. I can handle that type of thing. Everyone is discreet here. I already know of a couple of women who have ... friends ... here in Manila," Judith said.

"Really? Well, I still think we should be careful." Breidstein wondered how discreet they really were if Judith already knew about them.

"Of course we should, but that should not prevent us from seeing each other. We can meet for lunch next week. But we can talk about that later," Judith said.

A very large fireworks explosion went off, a precursor to the building finale of the display.

"Let's don't waste time," Judith said with urgency. "The fireworks will be finished in a few minutes." Judith pressed her mouth against Breidstein's, her tongue probing. Then she began to quickly undo the buttons of his pants. In a moment, he sprang free and she grasped him. Breidstein slid his hand down Judith's leg and lifted her dress. He slid his hand between her thighs—she had nothing on to impede his probing fingers.

"Oh, Werner, do it now. I want you." Breidstein slid his finger into her, probing her, rubbing her. "Oh, God, Werner, God, don't stop, don't stop," Judith moaned in his ear. Breidstein, sensing her approaching climax, allowed his excitement to build. She came rapidly, with a huge shudder that racked her whole body. Breidstein did not hold himself back anymore as she moaned deeply in his ear. The milky liquid spew from him.

31

AS THE DAYS of Breidstein's first summer in the Philippines passed, Breidstein became, with the discreet assistance of Judith, more and more involved in the social activities of Manila's elite foreign community of diplomats, dignitaries, government leaders—and those who served them.

He also began regularly attending social functions at the German consulate and arranging for influential people in the Manila area to be invited as well. Among the first to be invited, before they departed Manila for the continuation of their world travels, was Dwyer and his wife. Dwyer's views and those of Consul General Bogner on international commerce and the necessary abilities to manage it were in considerable accord. After that evening, Breidstein began to receive inquiries from petroleum importers seeking the assistance of Hamburg Import-Export in expanding their sources of supply.

Jahnel and his wife were also soon on the list of invitees to consulate functions. Not only were they ecstatic about the invitations, but also began, in turn, introducing Breidstein to many of the more wealthy people in the islands, many of them long time clients of *Bank-Hamburg Geschäftlich*. The name "Werner Breidstein" began to appear more and more on the list of invitees to important social and business functions in Manila. People seemed to sense his power almost immediately.

But amid the afternoon receptions and cocktail parties and evening dinners, Breidstein attended closely to the development of more financially profitable activities. He made effective use of the letters of introduction that Count Rosin had provided to introduce Breidstein "as a long time and trustworthy friend." Doors began to open wide for Werner Breidstein. People with knowledge of important pending, and lucrative, business deals began to let Breidstein know about them—well before they became generally known in the business community. Breidstein capitalized on such often little known information—including that about under-the-table deals, and those who participated in them—by sending it on to Berlin. But he also made sure to use the information to reap revenues for Hamburg Import-Export, irrespective of whether those revenues were quite legal or not.

Breidstein's financial success seemed unstoppable. Each deal he made generated more opportunities for Hamburg Import-Export. Breidstein began visiting the islands of the Philippine archipelago and the nearer islands to the west in the Dutch East Indies, visiting and meeting owners of various mining and rubber operations—making deals, outbidding competitors and crowding them out. His competitors could not understand how it was Breidstein and Hamburg Import-Export could make such bids, never knowing that the coffers of the German government were making up any losses Hamburg Import-Export incurred.

Even the speculative Fujimori mining business, whose purchase was consummated in midsummer under the partnership name of Manila Enterprises, began to generate significant rewards for Hamburg Import-Export—and its silent partners. And as the success of Manila Enterprises grew, Agawa and Breidstein became friends, distant and reserved, but friends. World politics became the continuing theme of discussion when they met. Breidstein became a trusted confidant of Agawa.

And somewhere amid Breidstein's successes, the tools of Breidstein the spy—money, prestige, and power—mutated into the insatiable appetites of the man who only a year ago had been selected by Hitler to spearhead Germany's return to power in the Pacific.

32

FRANCIS RAN from his General Purpose vehicle—most people were calling it by the nickname of "jeep" now—through the driving rain to the Post Y operations building, darting inside as he yanked open the door. He pulled off his raincoat and hung it and his hat on a wall hook to dry. He sat down at his desk, opened its top drawer and removed the letter from Marge. He read it again, not because he didn't remember its words, but because the words troubled him so—and still made him angry. Both Ma's and Pa's health seemed to be going downhill, despite the efforts of Marge and Marty, her finance—Marty had finally made it official by giving Marge an engagement ring on July Fourth. Even more troubling was the news about Hal—or more precisely, the lack of news. Hal had gone, with Pa's blessing and encouragement, to Central America again in February, almost seven months ago, saying he wanted to follow up on some business opportunities he had come across in his third trip to Mexico back in 1936. But two months after he left Chicago, the few letters from him stopped. The last letter, written from, of all places, Panama, said, so Marge wrote, Hal had gone into partnership with a man who ran a tourist business—and that Hal was making good money selling tours and cruises to rich Americans and Europeans visiting Panama and other nearby countries of Central America.

Francis didn't know with whom he was more angry, Marge or Hal—Hal for not writing or Marge, for taking so long to let Francis know that Hal had stopped writing, that she had lost contact with him. Francis knew that Ma and Pa—or at least Ma—had to be worried, and that couldn't be good for her health. Hal, the damn squirt, was probably making money hand over fist and shacked up with some gal—and couldn't care less about letting anybody know what was going on. Or so at least Francis hoped—and that nothing worse had happened. Francis threw the letter back in the drawer in disgust. He would write Marge tomorrow and tell her in no uncertain terms to contact the American Embassy in Panama and have them locate Hal—and stop everybody's worrying!

With a sigh, Francis picked up the yet incomplete draft of his August report to McDonald on the Post Y intercept operations. The report was to be used as part of McDonald's continuing effort to demonstrate to the Navy Department the importance of the Post Y operation and the need to increase its size and support.

And support was one thing that Francis really needed. Getting and setting up the new communications equipment for the revamped listening post operations had taken almost two months after Francis' arrival in the Philippines. Because the Post Y operation was not part of the regular communications setup at Cavite, Francis and his gang, as he liked to call them, were treated pretty much like outcasts. Obtaining necessary supplies and just day-to-day support for Post Y's operations was an ongoing struggle.

But Francis had made considerable headway in getting the five officers and sixteen enlisted men working as a well-oiled group, although the workload on all of them was becoming immense. They all regularly put in ten to twelve-hour shifts six days a week, irrespective of rank. It was only because of their dedication that Post Y was able to function as well as it did. However, one advantage, Francis had to admit, of the intense effort they all gave was the camaraderie that it produced. After only four months together, they were working with each other on a first-name basis.

IT WAS LATE EVENING. McDonald had arrived at Cavite earlier in the day. He and Francis sat hunched over a table in a small office in the Post Y operations building. Steaming coffee rose from two cups. They were going over the Navy's Department yea's and nay's on McDonald's budget request for Post Y operations that McDonald had submitted in late August. Many of McDonald's requests—the recommendations made to McDonald by Francis—had been turned down.

"The worst thing, I think Francis, is that only four more enlisted men are authorized. You are still going to be understaffed, and I knew that you were going to be really disappointed about that. That's why I'm here—to give you some news that should perk you up. Because of its sensitive nature, I needed to tell you in person," McDonald said in a quiet voice as he picked up his cup and then took a long swallow of coffee.

Francis' sour expression lightened. "What is it, sir?"

"This is top secret. Only a handful of people back at HYPO know about it, so it goes no further than this room—got that?' McDonald asked.

"Yes sir," Francis answered.

"Rochefort is telling me we are getting close to breaking the Japanese operational naval code—"

"Holy shit!" Francis said excitedly. "If we could do that—boy, would that make a difference. We would still have a lot of tough translating and decrypting to do, but holy cow, it's hard for me to even realize how that might impact what we do. To have the up-front decoding worked out—damn, that could really change things."

"Yes, so I want us to figure out what it might do for your needs—and think about how we might integrate what you do here at Post Y and what we would do at HYPO— "

There was a loud knock. "Excuse me, Lieutenant," a voice said through the door, "but you have an urgent telegram."

McDonald looked at the door with irritation. "Go ahead, Francis. See what it is."

Francis got up and unlocked the door. An enlisted man handed Francis a red-bordered envelope. "It was just delivered from Admiral Hart's message center."

Francis took it. "Thanks. Return to you duties," Francis said as he closed the door.

Francis looked at McDonald. "Go ahead and read it, Francis. The red border—it might actually be important."

Francis tore open the envelope. It was a teletype message from Marge:

RECEIVED WORD FROM AMERICAN EMBASSY PANAMA HAL FOUND DEAD. PA HAD HEART ATTACK RIGHT AFTER EMBASSY MESSAGE AND DIED 3 HOURS LATER. WILL TRY TO DELAY FUNERAL AS LONG AS POSSIBLE SO YOU CAN GET HERE. PLEASE COME. MA REALLY BROKEN UP. LOVE, MARGE.

"Damn," Francis said.

"What's wrong?" McDonald asked.

"My father, and half brother—both dead. My brother's been missing—and he's been found—dead in Panama. My step-father apparently had a heart attack when he found out."

"I presume there's going to be a funeral," McDonald said in a tentative voice.

"My sister says she wants me to come. My mother is really all broken up," Francis said as his jaw tightened in an effort to hold back tears.

McDonald picked up the phone on the desk and spoke. "Get me Admiral Hart's office."

As he waited for the connection to be made, McDonald asked Francis, "How quickly can you get some things together and get out to Clark Field—how many hours?"

Francis hesitated a moment and then held up four fingers.

Six hours later, Francis was on a B-17 bound for Hawaii as the sun was beginning to rise over the Philippine Sea.

33

PA'S FUNERAL and Hal's memorial service had been thankfully short, but it made Francis do a lot of thinking during the chain of military flights back to Manila after his two week-stay in Chicago. Francis learned in Chicago that Hal had been apparently dead since April—almost six months—but had not been identified until a few weeks ago when Hal's passport photo was compared to autopsy photos. Information was still not clear, but his apparent murder involved some woman—something that didn't surprise Francis—who was also killed.

The American embassy was still trying to sort out the details. Because of the confused circumstances and the lack of a passport for the man, the local police didn't expend too much effort, so the American embassy said, trying to find out who the dead man was—until the American embassy, at Marge's request, started some inquiries. One thing led to another and eventually the American Embassy was notified that perhaps a death to an American citizen had occurred some time ago. The embassy got copies of Hal's passport photo and confirmed with the police that Hal was the dead man. Pa's grief over Hal's death, once the embassy contacted Pa as Hal's next of kin listed on his passport application, was just more than Pa's heart could stand.

Pa's and Hal's deaths, despite the ugly and tragic circumstances, didn't remove the old wounds Francis carried from his years growing up with Hal, but it did make them less painful.

As Francis thought it over, he knew that a lot of the hatred—that was the only honest way he could describe it—he had for Pa was because of Pa's obvious favoritism of Hal. And Pa had never stopped making Francis feel worthless because of what Francis could do with his memory. That was something Francis would probably never understand—why Pa thought so little of Francis' special skill. Maybe that was something Dr. Lewis Franklin—he was a psychologist—could explain.

Thinking of Franklin, however, just made Francis think about Elaine—and just caused Francis to become even more melancholy. The running around in Hawaii—something he didn't do in Manila; he had neither the time or desire—hadn't made anything better. He hadn't been actually unfaithful to Elaine. How could he, given the situation? But he still felt some pangs of guilt. He was, he knew, still deeply in love with Elaine.

By the time Francis returned to Cavite, he was not only physically exhausted but also emotionally drained. His work, as it had many times before, became his solace—for the love from Pa that he never had, and the love from Elaine he was determined, somehow, to recapture.

VI

CHINA

34

BY OCTOBER, only six months after Breidstein's arrival in the Philippines, Judith and Breidstein were meeting so often at Breidstein's apartment that Breidstein kept a closet full of lounge wear and lingerie there for her. And more and more, Judith began to share with Breidstein what went on inside the high commissioner's offices.

Today, Breidstein could tell Judith was very tense. She had come to his apartment and shed her dress almost immediately. She put on a silk robe and sat on the couch, next to Breidstein, smoking—something she seldom did—taking long drags on a cigarette. As Breidstein began massaging her stocking-covered legs exposed by her partly open robe, she began to unwind by talking, almost complaining, to him. Breidstein had realized for sometime he was becoming not only her lover, but also her release from what she saw, as she said repeatedly, as her boring life inside the commission offices—with her husband Albert.

"Werner, it has been so hectic of late. And you seem to be so busy. We don't get to see each other often enough," Judith complained.

"I know, my dear," Breidstein said as he continued the movement of his hand up and down her legs. "The business is just so demanding. I am finding I must be out in the islands more and more. The goods we handle seem to come from every little island in the Philippines and the East Indies. The travel here takes so much time." He slide his hand higher, to the top of her stocking. Judith leaned her head back, stretching her body.

"Have things been busy at the commission offices?" he asked casually.

"Oh God, yes," Judith answered as she slowly exhaled cigarette smoke from her lungs. "The Japanese fighting with the Chinese, the bombing by the Japanese, the capture of Peking—it has put everything in shambles at the commission offices, so to speak. And, then, the attack on Shang-hai a few weeks ago—you would think that what happens in China wouldn't be our concern here, but, God, we seem to have all sorts of activity going on because of what's happening up there."

"My goodness. Like you, I don't understand that either," Breidstein answered soothingly.

"Oh, I don't know, but I keep hearing rumors that the State Department is so concerned about what might happen if the Japanese are successful in their attacks that we might go to war over it. I think that's absolutely stupid. I think Commissioner Lambert is even trying to see if he can exert some influence on the Japanese consulate here to get the Japanese to negotiate with the Chinese rather than fight."

"Negotiate?" Breidstein asked.

"I don't know, something like that. Maybe some type of negotiated settlement. Albert says Commissioner Lambert believes he could score a real coup if he could get negotiations between Japan and China going. I suppose it would mean a real feather in his cap. But I don't really know; I just hear tidbits and rumors. I think Albert said Lambert is even scheduled to meet with the Japanese consul general next week about some possibilities."

Then Judith paused, taking a long drag on her cigarette. "But why are we talking about that when we could be doing other things, Werner?" Judith said as she pulled her robe apart, revealing the darkness of her thick, black pubic hair, now damp and glistening with reflected light from the afternoon sun streaming through the window.

35

BREIDSTEIN WAS GLAD the embassy's evening festivities were soon to start. The grilling by Ambassador von Dirksen had been intense. But now it didn't look as if it would resume, at least today. The request by von Dirksen for Breidstein to come to Tokyo had come in the second week of November under the guise of an invitation to the German embassy's celebration of the ninth anniversary of Hirohito's inauguration as emperor. The real reason for the visit, however, was for von Dirksen to receive a firsthand report on what Breidstein was accomplishing. Von Dirksen wanted to know what made what Breidstein was doing so important to Berlin. Von Dirksen and Breidstein had been in almost continuous discussion ever since Breidstein had arrived in Tokyo yesterday.

The discussion had resumed this morning, only, however, to be terminated when von Dirksen was given a note by his appointments' secretary, Krug. Von Dirksen had looked at the note and then quickly dismissed Breidstein, with a brief comment that he would see him at the party that evening.

THE PARTY WAS WELL UNDERWAY. The ballroom was packed with diplomats, military officers, government officials, and socialites from the Tokyo European community. Breidstein had been talking about half an hour with various people to whom he had been introduced by Krug when he saw her, talking to a dark-complexioned man. Breidstein looked again to be sure. Yes, it was Shinako Fujimori.

Breidstein began to move through the crowd toward her. As he did, Shinako saw him. Her eyes widened and a smile came to her face. She immediately began walking toward him.

"Werner, how wonderful to see you. What are you doing here?" Shinako asked.

"Just on one of my business trips. The ambassador invited me to the gala once he learned I was coming to Tokyo. The consulate in Manila helps me a great deal in my financial dealings in the islands, so I suppose my reputation preceded me," Breidstein said with a laugh.

Then, turning serious, he asked, "But how have you been, my dear Shinako? The last time we saw each other was not a happy time for you."

"Yes, it was most difficult. I will always be thankful to you for the comfort and assistance you gave me. But I have put that time behind me. My father is at rest now," Shinako said.

"Well, what have you been doing? Have you been managing well?" Breidstein asked.

"Oh, yes. Things were looking rather grim for awhile, but then I came upon a wonderful opportunity—"

At that moment, the dark-complexioned companion of Shinako walked up. "And here it is. Werner, I want you to meet my employer, *Herr* Richard Sorge. He is the local correspondent for the *Frankfurter Zeitung*. Perhaps you have heard of it?" Shinako asked.

"In fact, I have. I read it whenever I have the opportunity. I think I have seen your by-line quite often. You do excellent work, *Herr* Sorge," Breidstein said as he extended his hand toward Sorge.

"*Herr* Sorge, this is Werner Breidstein. He heads the Hamburg Import-Export Company in Manila," Shinako said.

"It is a pleasure to meet you, *Herr* Breidstein," Sorge said as he took Breidstein's extended hand. "And thank you for the compliment. And, I must say I have heard quite a bit about you, even here in Japan. You seem to be doing wonders with your import-export business, particularly for a man as young, I must say, as you," Sorge said.

"Well, thank you, but you overstate my accomplishments." Breidstein was surprised by Sorge's remarks, wondering who else was taking note of his activities. Was he creating too high a profile?

"Perhaps... but that aside, how did you come to know Shinako?" Sorge asked.

"Werner and I met when I was returning from Hawaii. He was very helpful and kind to me at the time of my father's death," Shinako said before Breidstein could respond.

"Oh, really. What brings you to Tokyo, *Herr* Breidstein?" Sorge asked.

"Oh, just working on some business arrangements—actually just possibilities—here in Tokyo, trying to line up some buyers. The ambassador heard I was coming to Tokyo and invited me to the affair this evening." Wanting to avoid discussing why he was in Tokyo, Breidstein changed the subject. "So Shinako works for you. What does she do?" Breidstein asked.

"I happened to learn about her considerable linguistic skills—both German and English," Sorge said.

"I know. She is a very talented woman," Breidstein answered in agreement.

"Well, I hired her as an assistant to help in my reporting activities—gather background information for my news stories. She has been working for me for almost six months now. I am very pleased with her," Sorge said as he looked toward Shinako.

Shinako begin to blush.

"That's wonderful," Breidstein said. Seeing Shinako blushing, he wondered if Sorge and Shinako had more than just a business relationship.

"*Herr* Breidstein," Sorge continued, "perhaps we might get together for lunch sometime soon, while you are still here in Tokyo. Perhaps we could talk about business conditions in the Philippines—and your successes there."

"Perhaps, *Herr* Sorge, perhaps." Breidstein didn't like the idea of an interview. Too much publicity could result. He probably would have to fend off Sorge's request for the rest of the evening.

Suddenly, Breidstein saw Shinako's face drain of color. "What's wrong, Shinako?" Breidstein asked. "You look like you have seen a ghost."

"You are almost correct. I see someone I once knew. Over there, in that group of Japanese naval officers," Shinako said as she pointed across the room.

"In the group gathered around Admiral Yamamoto?" Sorge asked as he turned to look where Shinako was pointing.

Breidstein's interest was immediately perked. *So that is Yamamoto.*

"Yes, there next to him, on his left, the taller of the two men is Seiroku Takamatsu. You remember him don't you, *Herr* Sorge? He arrived late at my father's burial service," Shinako said as she continued to look toward Seiroku.

"Oh, yes, that's right," Sorge said. "Is he on Yamamoto's staff?" Sorge asked in a voice that sounded a bit too casual to Breidstein. "You never did tell me how is it that you know him, Shinako?" Sorge asked.

Shinako ignored Sorge's questions. "Werner, could you escort me over to the group. I would like to say hello to Seiroku."

"Certainly, my dear," Breidstein answered.

Shinako slipped her hand into Breidstein's extended arm and started towards Seiroku. Sorge followed behind.

Halfway across the room, Breidstein could see that Seiroku had seen Shinako. Breidstein watched Seiroku rapidly excuse himself from the group gathered about Yamamoto and walk quickly toward Shinako. As he got closer, Breidstein could see he had an angry expression on his face.

As he neared Shinako, Seiroku spoke angrily, at least so it seemed to Breidstein, to Shinako in Japanese. Then he grabbed Shinako's arm and forcefully guided her to the edge of the room, away from Yamamoto, leaving Breidstein and Sorge to follow.

Breidstein watched Shinako speak to Seiroku, a questioning look on her face.

Seiroku spoke again to Shinako, now in a softer tone. As he did, Breidstein saw Shinako's face grow somber, then grim, as tears came to her eyes. She spoke again, the hurt in her voice evident.

Then, finally, as the tears began to roll down her cheeks, Shinako turned to Breidstein, speaking in German. "Werner, please get me out of here. It seems that Lieutenant Takamatsu wishes that I were not here. He is afraid I may upset Admiral Yamamoto."

Not sure of what had been said, but sure that it had not been pleasant for Shinako, Breidstein escorted her out of the room and toward the front door. Once outside, a taxi quickly moved to the portico, and Breidstein helped a tightlipped Shinako into the vehicle. She would only say she wanted to be alone—and adamantly refused to let Breidstein escort her home.

Breidstein returned to the ballroom, still wondering what the young naval officer had actually said to Shinako. Seeing Sorge, Breidstein went over to him and asked, "Do you know what that—"

"*Herr* Breidstein," Krug interrupted as he walked hurried up to Breidstein, "the ambassador wishes to see you—immediately, please." Krug looked arrogantly at Breidstein, as if daring him to object.

Breidstein thought it strange that von Dirksen would want to resume their discussions in the middle of the celebration. Breidstein turned to Sorge. "Please excuse the interruption, *Herr* Sorge. Perhaps we can speak again later," Breidstein said.

"Yes, perhaps," Sorge responded gracefully.

Krug looked at Breidstein. "This way, please, *Herr* Breidstein," Krug said impatiently as he led Breidstein out of the ballroom and down the hall to the ambassador's study.

"Breidstein, come in here," von Dirksen said as Krug opened the door to the study and then walked away. "We need to talk."

Breidstein entered the study and saw that von Dirksen was not alone. In the corner of the room stood a man that Breidstein did not know.

"Breidstein, this is Ambassador Trautmann, our ambassador to the Nanking government. He arrived this morning from China," von Dirksen said.

Breidstein straightened and clicked his heals, as if he were in uniform. "A pleasure."

Trautmann nodded. "*Herr* Breidstein."

"This morning I received a message from Berlin ordering me to contact the Japanese about their recent actions near Shang-hai. You know what's happening, don't you?" von Dirksen asked.

"Certainly," Breidstein answered. "The Japanese landed troops near Shang-hai several weeks ago. They appear to be overcoming the Nationalist Chinese forces, driving them out of Shang-hai and inland toward Nanking."

"Yes, that's correct. But," von Dirksen paused, and lowered his voice, "now this is totally confidential, top secret—Berlin is not happy about that. *Herr* Trautmann, perhaps you had best explain."

"The Japanese actions may precipitate an unwanted response from the Americans. The United States government may feel it necessary to rush to the aid of the Chinese or the international community in Shang-hai, increasing the likelihood of American military intervention in Asia. Such actions would be detrimental to Germany's plans at this time. Berlin wants me to negotiate a truce and then some sort of peace accommodation between the Japanese and Chiang Kai-shek," Trautmann said.

Von Dirksen interrupted. "This morning, after I left you, Ambassador Trautmann and I went directly to the Japanese Foreign Ministry and sounded them out about possibly making some type of accommodation. They seem interested."

Trautmann continued. "I am to be the negotiator for an arrangement which will allow the Japanese to peacefully occupy Shang-hai and Nanking. But they also said they want you involved in the negotiations. It seems that you come highly recommended by the Japanese consul general in Manila," Trautmann said to a surprised Breidstein.

"Your reputation has apparently preceded you, Breidstein," von Dirksen said with a smirk.

"Well… I don't know… are you sure that I should get involved?" Breidstein asked. He was taken aback by his requested involvement, and concerned it might it raise too many suspicions about him.

"Yes. Berlin made it clear that we are to do whatever is necessary. And the Japanese made it clear that they want you to be involved. They themselves cannot meet with Chiang—it is a matter of face to them. It might appear they were attempting to appease him. They want you to represent them. They made it very clear. You are to look after their interests."

"Well, I suppose… I can… if it will facilitate Berlin's desires. When do you plan to leave?" Breidstein asked.

"You and I will leave immediately after the celebration is over tonight. Ambassador von Dirksen will arrange for your things to be brought over from the hotel. He can cancel any appointments you may have had. Now, return to the party as if nothing has happened. Return here by midnight. We leave by Japanese military transport at two a.m."

36

FRANCIS SIGHED, took a swallow of burned, lukewarm coffee, and turned his eyes to stare again at the jumble of Japanese symbols and partial words on the paper in front of him. Even with the assistance of the broken Japanese naval code, decoding and decryption of Japanese Navy messages was still a terribly difficult process, with perhaps only a small percentage of the messages being decrypted to an extent that would provide understandable information. Because of the volume of intercepted messages, many messages were not fully decrypted before, after perhaps one or two weeks of effort, they would have to be sent, as per McDonald's explicit instructions, on to Hawaii for further evaluation and decryption effort. In Francis' view, this strategy was not working well, but McDonald insisted that Post Y's job was immediate intelligence—longer-term intelligence efforts were the job of the HYPO station in Hawaii. Thus it was often that by the time Francis or one of the others at Post Y would begin to really understand a message, the message would have to be forwarded to Hawaii with, at best, only a partial understanding of what the message said. As Ensign Lewis Frankhill, the youngest of the Post Y officers, complained, "Christ, Francis, it's like sex with a hooker. Just when things are beginning to get good, your hour is up." Francis was in full agreement.

The phone rang. Francis answered it.

What followed was a curt order from the officer of the day at Cavite that an emergency message had been received from the Office of Naval Intelligence ordering Francis to be at Clark Field, with sidearm, by 1800 hours to meet an army captain coming in from Hawaii. Francis was to be temporarily assigned to a Captain Paul Woodruff. When Francis asked if there were any more details, he was given a gruff "no" and a sharp, irritated comment that it wasn't the OD's job to know what some goddamn Army captain from Washington wanted "from one of you people from over there at that fucking Post

Y outfit." Francis didn't try to find out more. He gave his best, "Aye aye," and hung up the phone.

Francis wondered what was going on? *But*, he thought, *if Woodruff is involved—more than two years since Quantico—something must be up.*

Francis looked at his watch. Wasn't much time. He walked to the radio room and told Louis that he had been ordered up to Clark Field.

When Louis asked why, Francis answered, "Damn if I know," and went outside to the jeep.

THE PILOT LEANED through the open cockpit doorway and yelled to the two men in the back of the plane, "We just crossed the Chinese coast."

"All right, Francis, I can tell you what this is all about now. If we get shot down from here on in, we won't likely land in the Jap's lap," Woodruff said, as the airplane's motors hummed loudly in the background.

"Here," Woodruff continued as he pulled out some Chinese peasant clothes from a bag at his feet, "put these on—just put your uniform back in the bag. You can't be wearing a Navy uniform for what you are going to be doing."

Francis looked strangely at Woodruff, but complied. He took off his parachute and began unbuttoning his shirt.

"Since we don't have much time, let me give it to you fast and sweet," Woodruff said as Francis continued changing clothes. "Ever since the Japanese landed reinforcements near Shang-hai a month ago, the Japs have been pushing Chiang Kai-shek's Nationalist forces steadily back towards Nanking. We—the War Department—think this is the beginning of a major push by the Japanese to take central China. We are concerned that Chiang and his Kuomintang party may not put up much of a fight. The Nanking capital may fall to the Japanese soon. But, more important, we are worried about Mao Tse-tung and his Communist Party." The plane took a nasty bounce. Woodruff's eyes rolled.

Woodruff continued. "Ever since Mao gained control of the north, Chiang has been deathly afraid of losing control of central and southern China to Mao. Letting the Japanese gain temporary, at least in Chiang's mind, control of central China may appear to Chiang to be a way to lock out the Communists. And now the Germans appear to be getting involved. There is the possibility that the Germans may have enough influence with Chiang—they have been schmoozing him for a long time—to induce him to reach an accommodation with the Japanese," Woodward said as he put imaginary quotation marks with his fingers around the word "accommodation."

"Accommodation?" Francis asked.

"Yup. Chiang hands over cities for money. Simple as that. The Germans may offer him some deal so good he will accept an arrangement with the Japanese. State was pushing something like that for awhile, but the President nixed that when he found out." Woodruff drew an imaginary knife across his throat with his index finger.

"From the German perspective, such an accommodation would be a win-win situation. The Japs take over practical control of central China and keep the Commies out while the Germans make points with the Japs by helping them move farther into China. And that's something the War Department does not want to happen," Woodruff said as he shook his finger in the air.

"Any reason why—beyond stopping Japanese expansion?" Francis asked.

"Yes. If Chiang accepts some accommodation, Chiang would probably be thinking he could let the Japs and the Commies fight it out. Then after the Japs and Mao's crowd have worn each other down, he would come back to fill the vacuum, at least so Chiang would reason. But what happens if the Communists are able to beat the Japs, or maybe later, when Chiang tries to return, Chiang cannot beat Mao? Then Mao Tse-tung and his Communist party have won all of China, not just northern China. And then we have a Communist China. And that is the worst of all possible worlds, as far as the War Department is concerned," Woodruff said emphatically.

"Besides that general line of reasoning, what makes you think the Germans are going to offer Chiang some deal?" Francis asked as he folded his uniform into a tight bundle and stuffed it into the bag at Woodruff's feet.

"We have it from very reliable British sources—and don't ask me how they know—that Trautmann—that's the German Ambassador to Chiang's government in Nanking—has already met with the Japanese and gotten their agreement to offer Chiang a deal. We know that Trautmann and some of his people in Tokyo have already gotten to Shang-hai. We suspect that they are already trying to see Chiang to make a deal," Woodruff said.

"But why should Chiang accept?" Francis asked. "All he has to do is withdraw further inland, into central China, far enough to where the Japs can't easily get to him. Why should he make a deal just because this Trautmann brings an offer from the Japanese?"

The plane took a jolt as it hit another air pocket. Woodruff's face turned sour. Then he answered. "Because Chiang needs money—lots of it—to keep his power base intact and purchase war supplies. The Germans will probably offer enough money that Chiang just cannot refuse to make a deal," Woodruff answered.

"All right. So you don't want Chiang to make a deal with Trautmann. But, hell, why not just send some people from the State Department to China and have them talk directly to Chiang?" Francis asked as he finished strapping his parachute back on.

"No way, Francis. The political heat would be unacceptable—just create all sorts of problems for the President in trying get future support for China if it became generally known—and it would if people from State went to see Chiang—that the War Department wanted to prevent a cease-fire agreement between Japan and China. The isolationists in Congress would have a field day," Woodruff said with a smirk.

"Okay, so I'm supposed to prevent Chiang from making a deal with the Germans. How do you expect me to do that?" Francis asked.

"You make him a better one," Woodruff answered.

"Make him a better deal? I don't even know the guy. Why should he even listen to me?"

"Well, Francis *Soong* Marian, according to a certain Captain McDonald, you're not quite right about knowing Chiang," Woodruff said with a grin.

McDonald—I should have known. "What the hell do you mean?" Francis asked.

"Isn't your grandmother an adopted sister of Charlie Soong, the elder head of the Soong family in China?" Woodruff asked.

"I'm not too sure. I never really knew my father's side of the family. He died when I was only four years old. And my mother said my uncle—actually half uncle—died back in the early twenties in China," Francis said.

"Well, let me tell you that your grandmother was adopted by Soong. Apparently Soong took her under his wing quite a few years ago, at turn of the century, after her first husband died in some fighting. She and your uncle became part of the Soong household—until she remarried her second husband, a cousin of Soong—your grandfather. He died during the Boxer Rebellion shortly after your father was born. After he died, your grandmother returned to the household of the elder Soong. And your uncle did die in the early twenties, another one of those casualties that seem to always occur when there is internal strife. But your grandmother is, as far as we know, still alive and kicking in Canton.

Francis wagged his head, a skeptical look on his face. "Are you sure about all this?"

Woodruff answered. "It's been all checked out, before you and I ever met. And, even important, the elder Soong also had a natural daughter named Soong Mei-ling who got married quite a few years ago. That name strike any bell?" Woodruff asked.

"Should it?" Francis asked.

"Damn right," Woodruff answered. "That's the maiden name of the wife of Chiang Kai-shek. So in a round about way, Chiang is your uncle-in-law."

"Holy shit!" Francis said in surprise.

"Once that piece of information gets to Chiang, we think he will at least listen to you," Woodruff said. "A professor Chi—you knew him in D.C. I am told—" Francis nodded his head in agreement, "will meet you at the drop site and arrange for you to get in front of Chiang."

"So what deal do I offer Chiang when I do?" Francis asked.

"Five things," said Woodruff as he held up five fingers, "in return for not making a deal with the Japanese, with or without German encouragement." The plane bounced heavily again. "One, a promise that the U.S. will stand behind him until the Japanese are kicked out of China. Two, we, that is the United States government, will not back the Mao crowd. Three, we will set up, in China, an air force group composed of American flyers—Navy and Army—to fight the Japs, and this air force unit will be under his nominal command, with an American officer providing tactical command. Four, we will guarantee him enough U.S. treasury credits to rebuild his army and to effectively fight the Japs. We fully expect, though we will not admit it to Chiang—nor do you tell him—that he will use the credits to rebuild his army to fight the Communists once the Japs are out."

"This first letter I am giving you," Woodruff said as he pulled an envelope from inside his shirt, "is a letter from the president making the first three of these commitments. If there is any possibility of this letter falling into anyone's hands other than Chiang's, destroy it. It's written on rice paper so you can eat it if necessary. Open it and read it."

Francis opened the envelope and began to read the letter. It was written in both English and Chinese. After several minutes, he looked up.

"Now here is a second letter, signed by both the president and the secretary of the treasury, dealing with the fourth commitment—the credits. Read it," Woodruff said as he handed the letter to Francis.

Francis studied it for a minute. "The amount of U.S. Treasury credits we will guarantee to Chiang is left blank. Did someone forget something?" Francis asked.

"No. You will fill that out when you make the deal with Chiang. You are authorized to offer more than the Germans if it's necessary. But Francis, make damn sure Chiang doesn't just keep upping the price. Make him an offer that is obviously better than that of the Germans, and then hang tough—don't get into a bidding contest. Try to make it clear to Chiang that you won't get into a bidding fight with the Germans. He accepts the deal or you walk away. And, this I am supposed to tell you directly, nothing on paper: We can't break Fort Knox, so don't go over ten million dollars," Woodruff said emphatically.

"Ten million? Did you say ten million?" Francis asked incredulously.

"Yes, I did," Woodruff said.

Now that's some serious money, Francis thought. "You said five things."

"Oh, yeah. You are going to give Chiang some money for his own, shall we say, treasury—on the spot, to really close the deal—right then and there if he accepts our deal." With that, Woodruff unhooked his parachute, looking a little uneasy about doing so, and undid his shirt. He wrestled off a bulky money belt. The pockets on the belt had wire seals. "Here. This is the money you are going to give him if he accepts the deal," Woodruff said as he handed Francis the money belt.

"And put your John Hancock on this piece of paper," Woodruff said as he unbuttoned his shirt pocket and extracted a short pencil and a piece of paper. "It says that I gave you this money belt with nothing taken out—that the seals are still unbroken. It's the only proof I will have to stop me from being thrown in the hoosegow when I get back."

Francis signed the receipt and handed it back to Woodruff. Woodruff carefully put the receipt back in his shirt pocket and buttoned it. Then he began struggling to get his parachute back on. The engines of the plane began to accelerate, getting louder. The plane began to rise, gaining altitude for the drop

"Five minutes to drop!" the pilot yelled from the cockpit.

"And by the way, Francis, don't lose that money belt. It might be pretty hard for you to replace," Woodruff shouted.

"Why?" Francis yelled as he twisted his body to get the money belt on.

"That belt has one thousand 1000-dollar bills in it. In case your math isn't so good, Francis, that's one million U.S. dollars, direct from Uncle Sam."

FRANCIS FLOATED DOWN to an open field. As he landed he saw a man run out of the surrounding woods towards him. The man called to him. "Mr. Marian, Mr. Marian. It is I, Professor Chi."

It took a moment to recognize Chi's voice; it had been a long time since hearing it in D.C. As Francis pulled off his chute, Chi reached Francis' side. "It's good to see you, Professor," Francis said in Chinese.

"It is good to see you again, Mr. Marian, and good to see my lessons with you were not forgotten. Gather up your parachute. The others are waiting at the edge of the clearing. We will have time to talk later," Chi said.

As they got to the edge of the clearing, Chi introduced the three others with him. Each held machine guns. "Come now," Chi directed, "we go to my home on the edge of Nanking where we wait to meet with Chiang."

Three hours later they reached Chi's house. Francis began to quiz Chi. "How did you get involved in this, Professor—and how did you get here—from D.C.?"

"As to the first question, we, that is, our foreign affairs office, received a request three days ago from your War Department via the Chinese embassy in Washington that your government wished you to meet with General Chiang. Since apparently your War Department knew I knew you, I was requested to assist you," Chi answered. "As to your second question, you will remember that I expressed a hope to Madame Chiang Kai-shek that I could serve the Nationalist government. Well, a year ago, General Chiang extended a request to me to join his foreign affairs office as an advisor—I accepted his request. I have been here in China since last February, advising the government on relations with the United States."

"Can you get me in to see Chiang?" Francis asked. "I must present some important information from my government to him—directly to him."

"I am trying to arrange that, but it is very difficult. General Chiang is not only an extremely important man but also a very busy one at the present time. We are having a very difficult time fending off the Japanese attack. None of us is very confident that we will be successful in our effort," Chi said glumly.

"But that is why I am here. I need to talk to the general about the Japanese," Francis said.

"As I say, I am doing what I can. I have contacted a friend, Gong Jing-li. He is now an aid to General Chiang and controls people who meet with the general, at least outside of the general's closest circle of friends and advisors. Because we became good friends during our university days, Colonel Gong has agreed to see me sometime tomorrow. I will go to his offices and wait to meet with him. I will tell him that you wish to meet with the general, but I am not optimistic that he will allow you to meet the General at the present time," Chi said.

"Well, I have something that might make him more receptive to allowing me to see the general. Tell your Colonel Gong that I not only bring important information directly from the president of the United States, but that I am also General Chiang's nephew from the United States," Francis said with a slow, deliberate voice.

"What? What are you saying, Mr. Marian?" Chi asked.

"Just what I said. General Chiang is my uncle-in-law."

37

COLONEL GONG led Francis into the sitting room of General Chiang's home—and headquarters of the Nationalist Chinese Army in Nanking. Two days had passed, and Francis had almost given up hope of seeing Chiang—until an hour ago when Gong had picked Francis up in old American Buick and brought Francis to Chiang's palatial home.

General Chiang was sitting on a large, brocade-covered couch with a pot of steaming tea on an ornate table. Francis bowed as the colonel spoke in Chinese. "Generalissimo, this man says he brings a message from the president of the United States, and greetings to you, his uncle-in-law."

"Lieutenant—is that not correct—Marian? What brings a lieutenant in the United States Navy—and as you claim, my nephew—to me here in Nanking?" Chiang asked.

"Yes, Generalissimo Chiang, it is remarkable but true. I am a lieutenant in the United States Navy, and I am your nephew. My name is Francis Soong Marian. My father was from China and his mother is the adopted sister of the honorable elder Charlie Soong, whom I believe you know well as the father of your most honorable wife," Francis said.

"Well, how remarkable. And how, may I ask, is your honorable father and mother, whom I have never had the opportunity to meet?" Chiang asked politely.

"I regret to say that my father died many years ago. My mother is well and lives in the American city of Chicago. She has a son and daughter by another marriage to an American," Francis explained.

"This is very interesting," Chiang said, "but I must with due respect question what you say, since you bring me no proof that you are who you say you are, and—"

At that moment, the door to the room opened and Madame Chiang Kai-shek entered the room. "I must apologize for interrupting you, honorable husband, but the gentlemen from the German embassy have arrived and are waiting."

Francis' heart skipped a beat. *German embassy! Woodruff was right. The Germans are here trying to negotiate a deal.* Francis rose from his chair and bowed in the direction of Madame Chiang. "It is a pleasure to meet you again, Madame Chiang."

General Chiang looked at Francis in surprise. Madame Chiang turned her eyes and studied Francis for a moment. Then, after what seemed like hours to Francis, Madame Chiang responded, "Yes, Mr. Marian, it is a pleasure to see you again. I am honored to have the opportunity to welcome you to my country as you did me to yours ... how long ago was it ... two years?" Madame Chiang asked.

"Yes, in April of nineteen-thirty-five. You were most eloquent in your remarks that evening. I shall always remember what you said," Francis said.

"Thank you, Mr. Marian, I appreciate your kind thoughts, now—and then. But you do not wear a uniform. Are you still in the United States Navy?" Madame Chiang asked.

"Yes, I am still in the Navy. I wear these clothes so I do not draw undue attention to my visit to your most honorable husband," Francis answered.

"You know the lieutenant, my dear?" Chiang asked with interest.

"Yes, in a way," Madame Chiang answered. "On my nineteen-thirty-five visit to the United States, I met Mr. Marian at our embassy in Washington. He was taking instruction in the Chinese language under Professor Chi, that professor who advises us in Western affairs and politics. Professor Chi spoke very highly of him."

"Professor Chi's instruction was apparently very successful. He speaks like the true Chinese that his father was," the general said.

Chiang's words "true Chinese" were not lost on Francis.

"Now, my nephew, what is this message you bring from your president?" Chiang asked as he inclined his head toward Francis.

MADAME CHIANG LEFT the room with instructions from Chiang to tell the German representatives that he would be delayed in meeting with them and for them to return that evening. Colonel Gong sat silently in the back of the room as the discussion between Chiang and Francis began. Francis spoke with caution and dexterity.

"My president wishes to extend to you his fullest support in your struggles against the Japanese and those others in your land who do not recognize your government's rightful and legal representation of all"—Francis stressed "all," knowing that Chiang would understand Francis meant Nationalists *and* Communists—"the people of China. The president believes it in the fullest interest of China that it can not accept an accommodation with the Japanese in its struggle with them. The president is prepared to have the United States provide major commitments to the Nationalist Chinese government in support of that belief."

"And what commitments might they be, my nephew?" Chiang asked politely.

"President Roosevelt has authorized me to offer the following to assure your continued and ultimate success in your struggle against the Japanese." Francis then formally presented the first three elements of the president's proposals—the same things that Woodruff had explained to Francis, but with a considerably greater degree of political commentary.

"How can I be assured that your president will maintain his commitments that you make for him now?" Chiang asked with raised eyebrows.

Francis reached inside the front of his shirt and withdrew the first of the president's letters. He handed the letter to Chiang. Chiang read it slowly, and then handed it to Colonel Gong, who also read it.

"Yes, I see that the president is firm in his commitments. But, as you and he must realize, the most significant impediment to our continued struggle with the Japanese is our limited capability to purchase needed war supplies. Unless that problem is addressed," Chiang said as he tilted his head, "my guarantee to continue my struggle with the Japanese in an uninterrupted fashion cannot be provided."

"My president fully understands that need. He is therefore prepared to provide to the Nationalist Chinese government United States Treasury credits to assure a continuing capability to purchase needed military supplies."

"And how much might those credits be?" Chiang asked with polite firmness.

Francis knew they were now down to the nitty-gritty. The bargaining had begun.

"That is a difficult question to answer without more evaluation of your needs. And perhaps it would be wise, before determining that amount, to consider what other resources might be available from other friends of the Chinese government," Francis responded with what he hoped would lead to the final step of negotiations—a face-to-face meeting with the German representatives.

Chiang looked at Francis. He smiled. "Yes, that is perhaps what should be done. Will you be able to join me for some additional discussion this evening?"

"I would be most pleased to do so, most honorable uncle-in-law."

FRANCIS WAS BROUGHT BACK into the sitting room by Colonel Gong after several hours. He had hoped—and expected—that Chiang would not be alone, that the German representatives would be there, but he was surprised as to who one of the representatives was.

"Ah, Mister Marian," Chiang said as Francis entered the room. Francis thought Chiang's use of "Mister" rather than "Lieutenant" was at least a good sign. Francis surmised that Chiang probably thought the Germans might not be too impressed by a lowly lieutenant negotiating for the government of the United States. Of course, Chiang did not know that Francis and one of the Germans in the room had met before. In addition to Ambassador Trautmann, there was Werner Breidstein.

Trautmann looked stiffly at Francis as Chiang made introductions. As he did, a smirk came to Breidstein's face. Breidstein leaned over to Trautmann and whispered to him. Trautmann raised his eyebrows as he listened to Breidstein. Finishing his introductions, Chiang said, "And *Herr* Breidstein is... an advisor to Ambassador Trautmann."

"Ambassador Trautmann," Francis said as he dipped his head toward Trautmann in acknowledgment. "As to *Herr* Breidstein, we have previously had the... pleasure... of meeting." *What the hell is he doing here?* Francis thought.

Breidstein nodded slightly in acknowledgment.

Chiang's brow wrinkled as he tightened his eyes and he stared questioningly at Francis. A moment of silence passed. Then Chiang began to speak. "Ambassador Trautmann is here to offer the assistance of his government in reaching an accommodation with the Japanese government. His government feels that continued fighting between China and Japan in the province of Kiangsu serves only to make conditions worse, for everyone. In return, the German government is proposing to extend credits for purchase of needed resources by my government. Is that not correct, Ambassador?"

"Indeed it is, Generalissimo. Chancellor Hitler has authorized me to offer five million marks in credits to your government to use in whatever way that you and your government consider most needed."

Francis did some quick figuring in his mind. *Five million marks—about one and a half million dollars.*

Francis spoke. "That is a very generous offer. But my government feels that accommodation with the Japanese serves no effective long-term purpose. My government is willing," Francis took a mental leap over a wide chasm, "to offer two million American dollars in credits, if the Generalissimo is willing to agree now with the American position not to accept such an accommodation."

Trautmann looked stunned. He turned towards Breidstein and began whispering to him, apparently translating what Francis had said. Breidstein's expression became strained as he listened. Then Breidstein whispered back to Trautmann. Then Trautmann turned back to Chiang. "My government feels it is in the very best interests of China that it enter into an appropriate peace accommodation with the Japanese in regard to the fighting that is going on and approaching closer to Nanking each day. My government's belief in this is so strong that," Francis watched Trautmann turn toward Breidstein and take a deep breath, "it will provide fifteen million marks of credits to your government."

Fifteen million marks—about five million dollars, Francis thought. *This bidding has to come to a stop soon.* Francis had already overstepped his instructions not to get into a bidding war. Francis decided to go for broke. "The United States, in support of what it believes to be in the best interest of China, is prepared to offer ten million dollars, but must reiterate to the generalissimo that it is imperative that his agreement with the American position be provided—*now.*"

Trautmann's face became ashen. He turned to Breidstein and whispered for several moments. Francis saw Breidstein's eyes widened. As the Germans continued to speak in hushed tones, Chiang turned to look at Colonel Gong. Francis saw Gong ever so slightly nod his head.

Chiang spoke. "The American government has offered ten million dollars, Ambassador. This, I believe, is approximately twenty-five million marks."

Trautmann looked triumphantly at Francis. "The German government is prepared to offer thirty million marks."

Francis spoke quickly. "Is the German government prepared to guarantee that amount in writing, here and now?"

"Well ... well, we would have to confirm this with the Chancellery in Germany. But that is a mere formality."

Francis saw the skepticism in Chiang's eyes. Francis withdrew the second of the president's letters from beneath his shirt. He placed it on the table. He wrote ten million dollars in the blank space on the letter. "This is a written guarantee from the United States government, signed by the president of the United States, that ten million dollars in credits will be made available to the Nationalist Chinese government within ten banking days upon delivery of this letter to any United States embassy in the world." Francis slid the paper across the table to Chiang.

Chiang picked it up and read it. He handed it to Gong. After a moment, Gong nodded his head. Chiang turned to Trautmann. "Ambassador?"

"Well, I am sure that the Chancellery would approve our offer here. They might even increase it a considerable amount … a considerable amount, I am sure."

Francis played his trump card. "Most honorable Uncle," Francis began. He saw the look of astonishment and disbelief on the face of Trautmann, and then on the face of Breidstein as Trautmann translated to Breidstein what Francis had just said. "There is a saying in the United States. It goes, 'A bird in the hand is worth two in the bush.' " Francis again reached under his shirt. He drew out the money belt and placed it on the table. He undid the pockets and pulled the bills from them, placing the bills in ten stacks on the table. "As further evidence of our good faith and desire to help the Chinese government, the United States gives now to you, Generalissimo, for your immediate use to help the Chinese people, one million American dollars, in addition to the ten million dollars of guaranteed credits, if you will now—immediately—agree not to accept an accommodation with the Japanese."

Chiang looked at Trautmann with questioning eyes.

Trautmann said nothing.

"I believe our discussion is over, gentleman. I regret I must leave you now. I must attend to the defense of our capital and our continued resistance to the Japanese, with whom an accommodation would not be in the best interests of China."

38

FRANCIS STAYED THE NIGHT at Chiang's home, spending some of the evening talking with Madame Chiang about the future of China. In the morning, one of Chiang's officers brought Francis back to Chi's home, to await completion of arrangements for a plane to fly up from Honk Kong to get Francis.

But shortly before the noon hour, Colonel Gong arrived at the house. He was excited. "Lieutenant Marian, we must leave. Conditions are deteriorating. You are in great danger. You cannot stay here any longer. We can no longer wait for the American Army airplane as you planned. General Chiang insisted that I get you out of the city. It is important that you report to your government the results of our negotiations," Gong said as he anxiously waved his hand, urging Francis toward the car.

Colonel Gong drove Francis to the Nanking docks, stopping the car near a ship flying the American flag from its bow. It reminded Francis of the ship he had seen in the picture in Captain Bates' office so long ago. The ship's name on the bow was barely visible through the crowd of people on the dock. The name read USS *Panay*.

"It's a U.S. Navy gunboat," the Colonel said to Francis as they worked their way through the jostling, dense crowd towards the gangway. "Its usual duty is to guard Standard Oil barges from attacks by bandits along the river, but it is departing within the hour to take some of the British and American nationals still here in Nanking upriver to Hankow where they can be safe from Japanese attack."

Refugees were crowded on the afterdeck of the *Panay* under the watchful eyes of several armed marines. More refugees were still climbing aboard using makeshift gangways to cross from the dock to the stern of the *Panay*. "Once in Hankow, you can contact your military people to get you back to the Philippines somehow. I will radio one of General Chiang's officers in Hankow, a Captain Cheng Kai-nam, to meet you when you arrive."

Francis shook the colonel's hand and walked up the *Panay's* main gangway. As he reached the top, he drew to attention and saluted the colors.

The officer on the deck put his hand on Francis chest, preventing Francis from going any further. "Where do you think you're going, bud?" the officer asked, as he lowered his other hand to the pistol at his side.

Francis stiffened in surprise, then smiled at himself—he was still dressed in Chinese clothes. Francis saluted the officer. "Lieutenant Francis S. Marian, U.S. Navy, requesting permission to come aboard, sir!"

The officer looked at Francis. "What the fuck is going on? Who the hell are you?"

"Lieutenant Francis S. Marian, on special assignment with the Office of Naval Intelligence."

The officer looked at Francis again. "We better see the Captain. And I'll take that forty-five you have there under your shirt," the officer said as he drew his own pistol.

Francis gingerly removed his pistol from his belt and handled it to the officer.

The officer turned to a burly marine with a rifle slung over his shoulder. "Take over the deck watch, Murphy. Nobody else gets up that gangway until this gets straightened out—nobody."

Francis was quickly taken to the captain of the *Panay*. Francis explained to him what he was doing in Nanking—at least as much as he felt he could, which was not much. When the captain asked for more details, Francis said, "Sorry, sir. I'm really not at liberty to discuss them, sir."

The captain looked at Francis, scrunched his nose up tight, and finally said, "Well, I guess I have to believe you. You didn't have to tell the OD that you were Navy; you could have just come on board in that mass of those people out there and I would have never known the difference. Anyway, I don't have time now to worry about you. We'll do some more talking later. In the meantime, just to be on the safe side, you're going to the brig."

IT WAS NOW MIDAFTERNOON. The ship had left Nanking almost three hours ago but now had temporarily stopped near Hohsien, about twenty-five miles upstream from Nanking, to let more refugees on board.

Francis looked out across the wide expanse of the Yangtze River from the one small porthole in the smelly room that served as the brig. Things looked so peaceful now. And, as best Francis could tell from the lack of noise, even the mass of refugees crowded on board the *Panay* appeared to have quieted down.

But then Francis heard a noise in the distance. As it grew louder he realized what it was—airplanes. Francis twisted his neck back and forth, trying to see the airplanes through the small porthole. There, over the treetops—there they were. They rapidly came into focus—Japanese light bombers. He heard someone on the afterdeck scream. Then others began to scream. Then he heard the captain's voice, amplified by a megaphone. "There is no need to panic. We are an American ship. They will see our flag. They will not attack us. Don't panic."

Then as Francis continued to watch the planes, he saw the planes begin to turn towards the ship. *My God*, Francis though, *it looks as if they're going to make a bombing run.*

As a bomb dropped from the first plane, the screams started again. Francis watched the bomb's fall, until he could not see it anymore. It had looked as if it were going to fall ahead of the ship into the water. It did, making a muffled explosion in the water. But second and third bombs were already on their way as the first bomb exploded. Francis could hear people on the barge screaming, "We're American, we're American!"

Francis heard the whistle of the second bomb. It struck the ship somewhere above him, causing a huge, deafening roar. In a frightening instant of time, everything began to shudder and vibrate as the metal bulkhead twisted. The door of the brig banged open and a large hole tore through the metal in the ceiling about him. Pieces of raw, jagged iron and wooden planking flew through the air. Francis momentarily saw something moving toward him. He felt what seemed like a baseball bat hit his shoulder. Then things went blank.

39

FRANCIS OPENED HIS EYES, slowly and painfully. He could feel his face was swollen. And then he realized his shoulder was bandaged so it immobilized his upper chest and shoulder. He slowly moved his eyes and looked about. He could see he was in some sort of hospital—the room was packed with injured people—but where he didn't know. A Chinese doctor and nurse stood at the foot of the bed, talking.

Francis attempted to talk. His swollen face made it almost impossible. "Where... am... I?"

The doctor turned to look at Francis. He moved to the side of Francis' bed. "You are at a hospital in Nanchang." Francis remembered a map—from somewhere—showing Nanchang several hundred miles south of Nanking.

"How—"

"Later—rest now. Nurse, get that Captain Cheng in here."

In a moment a Nationalist Chinese Army officer rushed into the room. "Is he awake, Doctor?"

"Yes, but don't talk to him too long—he needs plenty of rest."

"Lieutenant Marian—are you Lieutenant Marian?" the officer asked.

"Yes." Francis could see the look of relief come to the captain's face.

"Thank the gods. We found your identification, but were not sure it was you since you did not wear a uniform. The generalissimo wishes me to express to you his kind thoughts and wishes for your fast recovery. He was afraid that you were one of those killed in the bombing. I am to be personally responsible for your safety until you can return home."

"How did I get to Nanchang?"

"You were taken to a small hospital near Wuhu after the bombing, but that hospital had to be evacuated when the Japanese got near. You and the other wounded were brought here by train last night, well beyond the reach of the Japanese."

The doctor broke in. "That is enough. You can talk later."

"Yes, Lieutenant, we can talk later. For now, rest. I will get a message to the generalissimo that I have found his nephew and that he is recovering."

OVER THE NEXT SEVERAL DAYS, as his bruises and two cracked ribs slowly healed, arrangements were made for a British plane to fly up from Honk-Kong, about six-hundred miles to the south, to get Francis. In the days as he rested, trying to heal, and waited for the airplane, Francis listened to what were first rumors and then confirmed reports of horrendous atrocities being committed by the Japanese as they overran Nanking: rape, torture, murder—all the vile evils that a conquering army might do. Francis wondered what good had come from convincing Chiang not to accept a peace accommodation with the Japanese. Chiang's army would probably still be intact, and perhaps, if he had made the accommodation, the appalling events occurring in Nanking might not be taking place.

By the time the British plane picked Francis up and returned him to Luzon fifteen days after the *Panay* bombing, Francis was convinced that what he had done in China, what he had convinced Chiang to do, had been wrong—that a terrible mistake had been made.

The first person to get on the plane after it landed at Clark Field was McDonald. "God, Francis, you have had one hell of a time. How do you feel?"

"Great, just great," Francis answered sarcastically.

"Well, you look like you are all in one piece, at least, although you sure look like hell," McDonald said as he surveyed Francis' battered and bandaged body.

"That Jap attack on the *Panay* was no damn accident like they are claiming, you know," Francis said, neither able nor wanting to hide his anger.

"I know it, you know it, a lot of people know it wasn't an accident, but as far as the official line is concerned, it was all an accident. Nobody wants to start a war over the thing," McDonald said with resignation.

"Well, maybe we shouldn't have gotten involved. Maybe if we hadn't stuck our nose in, then maybe none of that... maybe the Japs might not have done what they did," Francis said with an angry voice.

McDonald stared at Francis. "What do you mean, Francis... that the Japs might not have done what they did?"

"Nanking... don't you know? They're dying there by the thousands!" Francis said with anguish.

McDonald was quiet for a few moments, looking Francis straight in the eyes. Then he spoke. "Yes, I know, Francis, probably more than you. But, let me make one thing very clear to you, *Lieutenant.* What you did in Nanking—even with all the loss of life that has occurred—is damn important to the long term stability of the Asian continent and the defense of the United States. In the long run of things, that stability will probably save more lives than you or I will ever know. I hope to hell you realize that—and how damn important what you did with Chiang is."

Francis said nothing as a nurse assisted him off the plane.

VII

MANILA

40

"RICHARD, WHAT IS THIS?" Sorge heard Shinako ask from across the room as he closed the window, trying to shut out the noise of the busy Tokyo street below. It had been almost a year now that Shinako had been working for the *Frankfurter Zeitung*, and her relationship with Sorge, while strictly business-like, had grown quite informal. She no longer called him "*Herr Sorge.*"

"What are you talking about, Shinako?" Sorge answered from the other side of one of the two rooms that represented the "Tokyo Office-*Frankfurter Zeitung.*"

"This list—this list in this folder labeled 'organizations.' I was rearranging some of this mess that is on the file table here—I can never seem to find anything—and I came across it."

"Oh, that," Sorge said, trying to sound casual. *How did that get over there! How could I have been so careless?* Sorge thought. He rose quickly from his chair and walked toward Shinako "Well, I try to keep tabs on who belongs to what—as a way to sort out the players. You know, everybody who is anybody seems to belong to some organization here in Tokyo. Just give it to me, and I will take care of it," Sorge said as he extended his hand, watching with apprehension as Shinako began looking at the contents of the file.

Shinako continued to casually scan through the several pages of organizations and lists of names below some of them. "Why are some of these organizations circled, like... the Blood Pledge Corps... Cherry Blossom Society... the Imperial Way... East Asia Supremacy Association?" she asked.

Sorge put his hand on the folder. "I don't know that you really need to look at that, Shinako. Please give me the file," Sorge said as he began to gently pull the folder from Shinako's grasp. *Please give it to me, Shinako, please*, Sorge implored in his mind. *Don't open a Pandora's box!*

"But Richard, I am just trying to help," Shinako said as Sorge watched her continue to run her eyes through the pages of the file.

"No. No. That's not necessary," Sorge said, finally pulling the file from Shinako's hands, knowing that she had already seen too much.

"As you wish, Richard," Shinako said with a haughty voice. She returned to her desk and sat down, her back to Sorge. She picked up some loose papers and began reading.

Oh, God, Sorge thought, *now what I'm I going to do. I can't let her stay around here knowing about that list.* Sorge put the file in his desk drawer and locked the drawer.

BREIDSTEIN PICKED UP the telephone on the table by the couch. "Werner Breidstein speaking."

"*Herr* Breidstein, this is Richard Sorge. So good to have you back in Tokyo again."

"Thank you. How did you know I was back?" Breidstein asked.

"I was at an embassy gathering last week—spoke to Ambassador von Dirksen while I was there and asked about you. He told me you were expected back in Japan this week," Sorge answered.

"Oh, I see." *That von Dirksen talks too much,* Breidstein thought. *Not that there is anything wrong with Sorge knowing I am here, but still, I think von Dirksen is a little too friendly with Sorge.*

"I was wondering if we might get together soon—perhaps dinner? Some things I would like to talk to you about," Sorge said.

Well, Breidstein thought, *I'm finally going to have to relent and give Sorge an interview. Actually, given that Hamburg Import-Export operations has been doing so well of late, there is plenty to talk about that poses no risk.* "Yes, dinner would be fine. Perhaps… tomorrow evening. Would that be acceptable?" Breidstein asked.

"Excellent. Suppose I come by your hotel at, say, seven and take us to a place I know. It has excellent French cuisine—the best you will find in the Orient outside of Indo-china," Sorge said.

"Fine. I'll see you at seven," Breidstein said.

THE DINNER HAD GONE like Breidstein thought it would—Sorge asked questions about the character and financial health of Breidstein's export operations and his business acquisitions, making notes on a small pad from time to time. As the evening progressed, Breidstein realized that Sorge was subtly steering the discussion toward the people Breidstein met in his business dealings and their views, particularly their political views. "Well, Richard, I'm really an apolitical businessman. My purpose is to make money for the company. The politics of my customers and suppliers are of no particular concern."

"I find that difficult to believe, Werner. The restrictions on sale of goods, tariffs, embargoes—the whole lot of them—make it important for you to have good insight into what international politics are going to do to your business opportunities, and to the people here in the Orient with whom you must deal to nurture those opportunities. The Oriental mind, you know, is nothing like anything you will ever see anywhere else. You have an assistant familiar with the political scene and the culture it meshes with here in the Orient working for you, of course?" Sorge asked.

"Actually, no. I rely quite a bit on the advice of the consul general in Manila, as well as von Dirksen here in Tokyo." Breidstein was surprised by Sorge's question, thinking that Sorge must already know that he had no such assistant.

"You mean Consul General Bogner? He's a fool," Sorge blurted out. But then, in a mollifying tone, Sorge said, "Excuse me, that is perhaps an exaggeration. I did not mean to say he is not a capable man. It is just that he is not, let us say, particularly well versed in the culture of the Orient."

Breidstein tended to agree with Sorge's first assessment but did not say so. "Well, perhaps I could use some greater insight. I try to do the best I can, learning as much as I can from different people, such as yourself, for example."

"You know, Werner, your business might really take off if you had an assistant—someone who understands the Japanese mind particularly well, someone who could really help you communicate with the different people you meet," Sorge said.

"Perhaps," Breidstein said, wondering what Sorge was up to—where Sorge was trying to go with the conversation. *He can't be asking me for employment,* Breidstein said to himself. Breidstein let Sorge continue to play out his line.

"You know Shinako Fujimori. You remember she works for me?" Sorge asked.

Ah, is that what this is about? "Of course. Shinako and I are good friends. Why do you ask?"

"Well, perhaps we could make an arrangement," Sorge answered. "I would like to have a correspondent working for me in Manila, someone right in the

Philippines, where so much is happening these days. But I can't really afford to support one, at least full-time. My budget just won't handle it. The only reason I am able to employ Shinako now is because of the relatively modest salary I give her. Shinako might be willing to go to Manila, working for me on a part-time basis, if she could be assured of an appropriate income from other sources. Perhaps you might like to hire her as your assistant and have her work in your Manila office."

Breidstein hesitated. "Well... it's a possibility." Breidstein wasn't quite sure what he might be getting into. *And why,* Breidstein wondered, *is Sorge even offering this deal? What is his reason—it can't be really what he says it is. It sounds like he wants to get Shinako out of Japan. If so, why? But having Shinako in Manila—that is very appealing. It presents some interesting possibilities.*

Sorge continued. "Werner, she is an attractive woman. I'm sure you have noticed that. She might be particularly useful in cementing deals with some businessmen whose eyes are attracted to the Oriental woman. And her ability to speak not only Japanese but German and English would be of no small benefit."

"Well, what type of arrangement were you thinking about... financially, that is?" Breidstein asked.

"Perhaps increase her salary, say by about thirty percent, to about fifteen hundred yen a month. That would seem an appropriate incentive for her to go. You could pick up a thousand and I would pick up the rest, roughly the split of time I suggest she would be making between us," Sorge said as he smiled at Breidstein. "I would, of course, pay all her expenses that she might incur as part of her reporting activities... travel and whatever," Sorge said.

"Well, Richard, even with the salary split, that's quite a bit," Breidstein responded, wondering what Shinako really made in salary from Sorge. *But,* Breidstein thought, *all things considered, it is not unreasonable, and money is not really a concern anyway. The real concern is what would be the value of having Shinako in Manila. And why should I help Sorge?* "And I'm not sure how effectively I could use her. She might well end up working most of the time for you." Breidstein could sense that Sorge was willing to give more, that he was pushing very hard for the deal. Breidstein continued to act reluctant to accepting the deal. "But, still, Richard, I just don't know...."

Sorge leaned close to Breidstein. Breidstein could see beads of sweat on Sorge's brow. "Werner, there is perhaps something else I have that might be useful to you—enable you to know a little more, actually a great deal more, about the people with whom you deal. Something that could increase your leverage in difficult situations. I would be willing to share it with you, if we could consummate this arrangement for Shinako."

Breidstein's interest rose. "What is it?" he asked.

"I think you will be more impressed if you see it. I have it at my office," Sorge answered, as he signaled the waiter for the check.

41

OVER THE LAST FEW DAYS Shinako's interest in the file that Sorge had so abruptly taken from her had grown. She had been surprised to see both her father's and Seiroku Takamatsu's names on one of the pages just before Sorge had so forcefully pulled the file from her hand. And both names had been circled in red. What was that list and why were their names singled out? She had recognized some of the names of the organizations—what some, particularly her beloved father, would call radical. Was it a list of radical organizations here in Japan? But that didn't seem right if Seiroku's and her father's names were on the list.

The more she thought about it, the more she knew she had to see the list again. Was Seiroku in trouble? Was there something about her father she should know? She was determined to find out. And tonight seemed to be the time to do it. Sorge had left the office about six, saying he had a dinner appointment. Sorge should not be coming back to the office until tomorrow morning.

AS SHINAKO WALKED up the street toward the small building that housed the *Frankfurter Zeitung* offices, she looked to see that Sorge's car was not parked in front of the office. Nor did she see any lights as she looked up at the office windows. But to be sure, she went to the back of the building. Sorge's car was not there either. She entered the side doorway and went up the stairs to the office.

She opened the office with her key and locked the door behind her. She turned on the small lamp on Sorge's desk. It gave off a tiny glow. Shinako had to get into Sorge's desk drawer somehow to see that list. She didn't intend to harm Sorge in any way, so she didn't see that what she was doing was really wrong. But she also knew that Sorge would be very angry if he found out.

She tried to pull open the drawer, just on the chance that Sorge had forgotten to lock it sometime in the last several days. The drawer wouldn't budge.

Maybe she could open it from beneath. She got down on her hands and knees and began working at the metal catch that held the locking bar under the drawer. She pulled and tugged. Nothing would move. But she just had to get into the drawer!

But wait, the keys—the extra set of keys that Sorge kept in the file room! She remembered now. When she started working for Sorge, he had gotten an office key for her from the loose keys in that back cabinet drawer. Maybe, just maybe, there might be a spare key to his desk there.

She got up and walked to the file room door. She opened it. The windowless room was pitch black. She felt along the wall for the light switch. She turned on the switch and two dim bulbs in the archaic lighting fixture hanging from the ceiling came on.

But then she heard a car stop and, a moment later, a car door slam. Then another. Was that Sorge? Shinako ran to the office window and pulled the shade back slightly from the window. Yes, it was his car! He must be coming back to the office for something. She ran to Sorge's desk and turned off the lamp. She scurried back to the file room, closed the door, and turned off the light. Blackness enveloped her.

In a few minutes, she heard the office door open. She put her ear to the thin file room door. She saw light slip under the bottom of the door by her feet as the office ceiling light was turned on. She could hear two people walk across the room. The scrape of the legs of the straight-back chair at the work table as it was pulled across the wooden floor followed. Sorge's swivel chair squeaked loudly like it always did when he sat down. Then a voice in German she didn't recognize, at least at first. "Remember, Richard, I'm not going to go through with this—it could be quite expensive—unless it is as good as you say." *It's Werner! What is he doing here? What is he talking about?* she wondered.

"I think you will be quite pleased... " The squeaking, scraping noise of a moving chair blocked out what Sorge was saying. "...show you."

A moment's silence followed. Then Shinako heard Sorge say, "Here, take a look at this, Werner."

A longer silence.

"What are these organizations? The Young Officers, Young Men's Patriotic Storm Troops, *Ketsumeidau*, these others—and the names below them?" Shinako could hear Breidstein ask.

Shinako then knew. *Richard is showing Werner the list!*

"The organizations—many are factions or groups in one of the military arms or bureaus—are ones I have identified, from various sources, that have tried or are still trying in some cases to take over the government or ministries in the government—by force or subversion—to generally move Japan into a more militant stance, possibly trying to expand the war beyond its current bounds in northern China. The Japanese have essentially consolidated their power there, so many are looking to more fertile areas in Asia—and beyond. A few of the organizations are fairly well known in political circles, but many are not."

"And the names under the organization names? I presume those people are members of the organization," Shinako heard Breidstein ask.

"That's correct, or are at least connected with the group in some important way. Very few people know that those people belong to those groups. In fact...." The scraping chair again drowned out more words. "...others in the group. These organizations are very secretive," Shinako heard Sorge said.

"Then how did you find out about them?" Shinako heard Breidstein ask.

"I maintain many contacts that most people don't know about. In fact, some of the people in some groups are actually ... uh ... friends of mine who share their knowledge with me, for various reasons—including a common vision of the world order, or a need to obtain information from me. They scratch my back and I scratch theirs, so to speak. And you would be surprised how well bribes continue to work, even in these days," Sorge said.

"And the circled information?" Breidstein asked.

Yes, Shinako wondered, *what is so special about the circled names? Why are Seiroku's and my father's names circled—why?*

"Ah, yes, the most interesting part of the list. That I will tell you now, if you ... ." This time a squeaking chair blocked Sorge's words. Shinako could see him in her mind's eye, rocking back and forth.

There was a long silence. Then Breidstein spoke again. "Yes, it's...." The chair again blocked out Breidstein's response.

Werner, stop fidgeting, Shinako shouted in her mind.

"...me, but how do you know you can trust me not to expose you, to let the authorities know about this?"

"Very simple, Werner. I know that using this information can be much more beneficial to you than merely causing difficulties for me. You and I both recognize the potential for use of this information. Letting the authorities know about this serves no useful end, for you or me. Shall I go on—do we have agreement?" Shinako heard Sorge ask. She wondered what agreement he was taking about.

"Yes," Breidstein said.

"Good, we have agreement," Sorge answered.

There was a long moment of silence, then Shinako heard Sorge speak again. "The circled organizations are those I know or have very good reason to suspect have been directly involved in actual or attempted assassinations, both here in Japan, Manchukuo, and...." More noises, more lost words. "... circled people were those directly responsible for the assassination, or the targets of the assassination attempt."

A long silence followed. Then Breidstein spoke, the amazement in his voice clear, "Are you sure? Is this really all accurate?"

"Yes, it is. For example, look on the second page. You see a name that is particularly familiar in the first column?"

A moment's silence. "Yes, Yukihiko Fujimori."

"Yes, Shinako's father. He was assassinated was he not? And you see the circled name opposite him—that is the man who assassinated him. You know of him, do you not?"

Shinako almost screamed. She knew the name; she had seen it!

"Yes, but it cannot be. He is on Yamamoto's staff. He and Shinako were probably lovers at one time, maybe still are," Breidstein said.

"It is true," Sorge said. "I was there when Fujimori was assassinated on the steps of the Foreign Ministry building, interviewing him. I was looking directly into the face of the man who fired the shot that killed Fujimori. You are the first person to whom I have ever told this. It was Seiroku Takamatsu."

FIVE WEEKS LATER, Shinako arrived in Manila. After that night she realized she could no longer stay in Tokyo. The memories hurt too much. She also knew that to bring Seiroku to trial would be impossible. The police would not listen to her. The politics of the times did not care about justice; justice sought only what was politically correct—and her father had never been politically correct. And anything she would do might bring retribution not only on herself but also her Aunt Chieko. Who could know what might happen if Shinako tried to bring Seiroku to the attention of the police. And none of it, none of it, would bring back her father.

She had considered confronting Sorge directly about what he knew but then realized it was not Sorge's fault. He had merely been an observer. The fact that he did not tell the police was nothing at which to be surprised; he knew the political situation as well as she.

So when Sorge asked her to think about moving to Manila and becoming a local correspondent there for him, Shinako jumped at the chance. And, as to working for Breidstein—so what if Breidstein knew about her father's murderer? It was even better that way. Breidstein might help her get some action from the authorities some day if she could somehow tell him that she knew, without letting Sorge know. *Maybe,* Shinako thought, *Werner can do what I cannot—get justice for me and my father. No, more than justice—revenge. Someday, somehow, Seiroku will pay.*

BY THE END OF THREE WEEKS in Manila, Shinako had found an affordable apartment on the outskirts of Manila's downtown area and was into the routine of her new responsibilities. By the end of another two weeks, she had forwarded her first write-up to Sorge in Tokyo, and he seemed pleased. She felt renewed, able to face the world again. The pain and outrage of Seiroku's treachery moved to her subconsciousness, where it continued to smolder.

42

BREIDSTEIN STOPPED his writing and turned his swivel chair to look down to the docks below. Dock hands were swarming over the topside of the Spanish freighter still unloading under the dim lights of the dock. The freighter was scheduled to leave Manila tomorrow for its destination to the west, Camranh Bay, where its holes would be filled with zinc ore from the mines of southern Indo-china. That was one of Breidstein's most profitable shipping operations, another convenient arrangement for which Agawa's influence had been so useful.

Earlier in the day, Breidstein had carefully watched the unloading of his new black Mercedes—finally a car suitable for his position, one that could be driven by a chauffeur. It had taken almost six months to get it ordered and shipped from Germany. Now, thank goodness, he could stop driving that atrocious convertible Bogner had arranged for him to use. He would speak tomorrow to Macarat about finding a suitable chauffeur, one who could be trusted to perform other duties of a more discreet nature beyond those of just a chauffeur, should such need arise. Macarat's background was just shady enough that he might know how to find the type of person Breidstein wanted.

Breidstein turned back to his desk to review his just finished monthly report. It described the various recent business deals he had concluded, including the lucrative contracts he had secured with five sugar plantation owners on the Vogelkop Peninsula of Dutch New Guinea. But his successfully concluded business ventures were only a sidelight to what he had found on the islands of Palau. In his visit to the silver mining operations on Ceram and Halmahera in the Moluccas east of the Celebes, Breidstein head rumors about a Japanese military buildup on the Palau islands. He immediately altered his plans and, as Breidstein noted in his report, hired a boat in Sansapor and made the five-day cruise to the Palau's for the ostensible purpose of finding possible products for export.

His unexpected arrival at Peleliu and its little harbor town was not warmly welcomed by the local Japanese constabulary. And the situation was made doubly difficult by Breidstein's inability to speak anything beyond the most elementary Japanese. The magistrate seemed very adamant, as best as Breidstein could determine, about getting Breidstein to leave—and getting more demonstrative by the minute. Breidstein was afraid the situation was about to get out of hand when a local plantation owner named Lothar Kohl arrived. Kohl had come to the magistrate's office out of curiosity when the news was quickly spread by the natives that a European had arrived on the island. Kohl, fortunately, knew enough Japanese, and of course German, to act as a translator. He was able to calm the magistrate, assuring him that Breidstein was only an exporter trying to drum up new business—and promising to keep Breidstein from wandering too far from the town.

Breidstein soon learned that Kohl had migrated to the East Indies and then Micronesia from Africa's Ivory Coast shortly after the World War started, hoping to avoid the conflict's tentacles. He might have succeeded, if Germany had won the War. But that was another story, Kohl said as they left the magistrate's office.

"But I am a survivor. I can manage to make the best of a difficult situation," Kohl said as he and Breidstein started walking down the sand-covered lane that formed the main street in the town. "And, it looks like things are going sour again," Kohl went on as they neared a small bar—the only bar in the island's one town, or as Kohl said, "At least the only town with white people living in it."

"Sour again? What's happening?" Breidstein asked as the two entered the bar and sat down at a wobbly table.

"Well, it's pretty straightforward," Kohl said as he held up two fingers and said, "Whisky," to the bartender. "When I first started my plantation here on Pelielu—well, not actually started it, but bought it from the widow of the original owner; she wanted out so bad she sold the place for a song and a dance—I was pretty much on my own. When the first Jap magistrate arrived here in nineteen-twenty, after they were given control over all the islands out here, nobody paid too much attention to him, particularly me—until he distributed a notice that an export fee had to be paid on goods shipped from the islands by all non-Japanese, unless they were being shipped directly to Japan. Well now, that wasn't where I was shipping my stuff, so things got a little rough, financially—other ways too—until I could break my delivery contracts and ship directly to Japan. Then, of course, things started to improve. Like I said, I'm a survivor."

"But you said that things were getting bad again?"

Kohl took a swallow from his glass. "Yeah, they are. Everything was going along pretty good until about two years ago. Then the Japs," Kohl said as he paused and looked around the bar to see if anyone was close enough to hear, "brought in some army troops. Not a lot, maybe one company, but still they were military, not civilians. A short while later they brought in Korean laborers, and by God if they didn't start building an airfield and pier on the other side of the island. Actually, there is a better harbor there, but it was never really developed because of some crazy native superstitions—couldn't get the natives to work the boats over there. But that didn't stop the Japs."

"You mean they are building a docking facility and an airfield on the other side of the island?"

"They aren't building anything; it's already built. Planes come and go all the time. And here's the bad thing," Kohl said as he paused to take another swallow of his drink, finishing it. He held up his hand and motioned for the bartender to bring another. Then he continued. "The Japs have closed down that side of the island, and I can't get to all my planting areas over there. I complained to the magistrate—that ass that gave you such a hard time—but crap, he wouldn't do anything. Said I shouldn't complain or talk about the situation if I knew what was good for me."

"Is there any way I could get a look at what's going on?" Breidstein asked in a low voice.

Kohl looked at Breidstein for a few moments. "I don't know, it might be difficult. I might get fined, or something worse."

"Well," Breidstein volunteered, seeing what Kohl apparently was hinting at. "I would certainly be willing to pay you for your time, say…" Breidstein paused as he watched Kohl's eyes, "two hundred yen."

"Well now, that puts a different light on it. Come on, my truck is across the street. And you will need to pay the tab before we go. Leave the barkeep a nice tip. He's a good guy—sets me up with a native gal when I get the urge."

It took about two hours for Kohl to reach a high hill overlooking the bay on the other side of the island. From their vantage point, Breidstein had an excellent view of the new pier. Several small boats—launches and patrol boats—were tied up at the pier, but the pier was big enough to dock a moderately sized naval vessel. And beyond the inland shore of the harbor was a landing strip. Other buildings lay beyond the end of the runway. On the runway itself sat what appeared to be two scout planes and six fighters, each with a large rising sun painted on its fuselage. On the hillsides opposite from where

Breidstein and Kohl stood were several buildings. Breidstein could see soldiers walking about, entering and leaving the buildings.

"We better not stay here too long," Kohl warned. "Might get noticed."

"Yes, you're right," Breidstein agreed. "I don't need to see anymore."

"And so," Breidstein had concluded in his report, "the Japanese appear to be making a concerted effort to develop military bases in outlying islands. These islands could become important stepping stones to expansion of Japanese control beyond the islands of the Japanese mandate."

The final portion of Breidstein's report summarized the recent American activities in the Philippines on the Bataan Peninsula, including Subic Bay on the western, ocean side of the peninsula. He had already made several trips to the area, as if on a weekend outing, driving on the peninsula's back roads in the Subic Bay area, trying to see what was going on. He had seen quite a few small military fortifications and supply dumps. But that ruse could not be used again. The last time he had been stopped by a U.S. Army military police truck and told to keep to the main road. Considering what little he did see, however, it appeared that major military construction was underway throughout much of the peninsula around the Subic Bay area.

"The Americans," he wrote in summary, "like the Japanese, are also making considerable strides in building up their military capabilities in the areas under their control."

Yes, Breidstein thought, *the report seems to be quite good—has the right tone about it.* With that, he picked up the report and his notes and put them in the safe. He left the office thinking he would drive his new car to the consulate tomorrow morning to give the report to Bogner for delivery by diplomatic pouch—perhaps even take Bogner for a spin.

As he walked down the stairs to the back of the building where his shiny new car was parked, he thought about the problem of having a more convincing reason to be on the Bataan Peninsula on a more regular basis. He needed to keep track of what was going on there, but what could he do, besides act like a tourist? And that, as the experience with the military police patrol had shown, was not going to work anymore without raising too much suspicion. He had to think of something else.

43

IT WAS ONLY A WEEK later that Jahnel, Breidstein's banker, invited Breidstein to lunch. Meeting Jahnel at a restaurant in Manila's banking district, Jahnel quickly broached the reason why he had invited Breidstein to lunch.

"Werner, you mentioned the other day that you wished you could find a getaway for the weekends. Well, I may have found something for you. One of the bank's best customers, a family by the name of Hoffmann, owns a villa near Mauban on the west side of the Bataan Peninsula—right on the ocean. About two years ago, Herman Hoffmann died unexpectedly, leaving the villa, along with some other very sizable holdings, to his wife, Marlene, and his son, Eric. Marlene doesn't have much interest in using the villa anymore. Eric spends most of his time on Palawan managing their plantation, while Marlene likes to stay here in the city when she's not at the plantation. I think she misses her life in Berlin—she grew up there."

"So she wants to sell this villa?" Breidstein asked, thinking a villa on the Bataan Peninsula might be just the excuse he needed to regularly be on the peninsula so he could monitor the military activity there.

"Well, not sell, but lease, on a long-term basis. Given her situation and interests, she might be willing to make you quite a good deal," Jahnel said encouragingly.

"What is she asking and what is this place like?" Breidstein asked.

"Her asking price is seven hundred pesos a month. As to what the place is like, maybe the thing to do would be to go and see it," Jahnel said.

"Probably would. When could I do that?" Breidstein asked.

"Marlene will be in the city this weekend, I understand. Perhaps she could show the villa to you. Why don't I arrange for you two to meet?" Jahnel asked.

JAHNEL INTRODUCED THEM over brunch the following Saturday. As brunch progressed, Breidstein realized that Marlene, from the things she said, did in fact have significant financial holdings, although it was not quite clear why she implied that they were difficult to access. And Breidstein could sense, as he often could with women from the tones of their voices, the nuances of their words, even the slight movements of their head and hands, that Marlene was taking an interest in him—sexually. And Marlene, despite her age—which was only partly hidden by the layers of makeup she wore— had a certain voluptuousness that somehow appealed to Breidstein.

By the time the meal was nearing its end, Marlene and Breidstein had agreed to drive to the villa, with Breidstein purposely demonstrating an unwillingness to immediately accept what seemed to be a rather steep lease cost, despite Marlene's assurance that Breidstein would love the villa. Of course, Breidstein was already certain that the villa would not only meet his needs to have a reason to be on the peninsula, but also might lead to other benefits. Marlene, or at least her deceased husband, was well known on some of the islands of the Dutch East Indies and had many important friends— friends to whom Marlene could introduce Breidstein.

"MARLENE, I THINK the villa might be about what I am looking for, but what I said about the price remains. The rent is quite a bit more than I had hoped to pay, so I am just not sure. I may need to lower my expectations," Breidstein said as he turned the Mercedes onto Highway Seven.

"You just wait and see, Werner, you just wait. And I want you to remember, Werner, that this drive is the long way around to get to the villa. We can go this way—it's a lovely drive—but it will be late afternoon before we get there," Marlene told Breidstein. "It's much quicker to take the car ferry from the Manila docks—when it operates—over to Limay and drive up the bay road to Highway Seven. We just keep on Seven now, until we get to Olangapo on Subic Bay, and then we'll go south along the coast to Mauban."

"Subic Bay?" Breidstein asked.

"Oh, yes, we will be driving right along it much of the way to Mauban. There's a big U.S. Navy repair yard there, you know. But don't worry, we are far enough away from it that we're not bothered by all that goes on up there. The villa," Marlene explained, "is several kilometers south of Mauban. Of course, if you are really in a hurry to reach the villa and bypass the Subic Bay area, you can cut across the peninsula at Orion to Bagac; but the road is not nearly as good across the pass in the Mariveles Mountains as it is going by Olangapo. But who's in a hurry when going to the villa?" Marlene said with a laugh.

"Well, I might just use both, depending upon how adventurous I feel," Breidstein said. *And,* he mused, *depending on what military activities I might want to see.* The villa seemed ideally situated for monitoring military activities on the peninsula.

A few moments of silence followed as Breidstein and Marlene watched the flowers and foliage slide by. Then Breidstein spoke, wanting to find our more about Marlene's son and how he might figure into any relationship he might have with Marlene. "Jahnel said that your son, Eric, runs your Palawan plantation. That's quite a way from Manila, isn't it?"

"Yes, he does—and it is. When my husband, Hermann, died, he left the plantation to Eric and me, with the provision—damn him—excuse me, Werner, that just slipped out—that I would have part ownership only so long as I lived at the plantation! That requires that I live there, so my lawyer tells me, at least fifty percent of the time. I suppose that was Hermann's way of assuring that the plantation would be properly taken care of," Marlene said with resignation. "And he had to do something. It is such a God-forsaken place down there, particularly with no one of my age or interests there. Of course, I love Eric, but it can be very lonely there," Marlene said as she smiled at Breidstein.

Breidstein returned the smile, gently placing his hand on her knee. Marlene did not remove it.

THE SUN WAS LOW when they reached the villa. After unlocking the gate through the perimeter wall, they drove up to the house, a large rambling structure with wings on both sides jutting out from the central portion of the house.

"I had no idea it was so big, Marlene," Breidstein said.

"Oh, yes. My husband was a great one for entertaining. When we bought it from the original Spanish owners, he thought we could use this place not only as a getaway but as sort of a mini-palace to bring people from throughout the Philippines. He had ambitions of becoming some type of a political power-broker in the Orient. We used to spend three or four months here during the course of a year," Marlene said.

"This looks grand," Breidstein said as they walked into the large living room fronting on a verandah open to the ocean view.

"Yes, it is, isn't it," Marlene agreed. "And up the coast about a kilometer is a dock as well—on a spit of land poking out into the ocean. You can bring a large yacht right up to it. And, just out back, there is a small stable, tack shack, and bungalow—just in case you want to keep some horses. When we were staying here, we had several. Of course the servants would take care of them. The servants—actually some locals from Mauban—only come out now to periodically check up on things for me, or when I have a special need for them to be here."

"How do you notify these local people in Mauban to be here when you want them?" Breidstein asked.

"Oh, that's easy. I can phone the constable in Mauban—we had a telephone line run out quite a few years ago—and he will get a message to them. I send him a nice Christmas present each year to keep him on my good side—and do little favors like that for me," Marlene said with a laugh.

"Will they—the people from Mauban—be here tonight?" Breidstein asked.

"No, Werner, they won't. I called the constable from Manila yesterday and got a message to them to bring some food up to the house this afternoon and then be here in the morning to fix us breakfast. I was rather certain I could get you up here to see the villa. I can fix dinner for us. I thought you would like some privacy tonight. Did I misjudge you?" Marlene asked.

"Not at all, Marlene, not at all," Breidstein answered.

"Good. Why don't you take a walk around—get the feel of the place—while I start on dinner."

MARLENE HAD CHANGED CLOTHES and was setting out dinner by the time Breidstein returned to the kitchen. His hour-long walk had convinced him the villa would be ideal for his needs.

"Well, Werner, how do you like it?" Marlene asked.

"I like it, Marlene, but I am going to be frank with you. The price you are asking is rather steep." Breidstein felt that he still needed to show some modicum of resistance.

"Well, Werner, that's the price Jahnel suggested, in view of the fact that I would no longer have use of the villa," Marlene said.

Breidstein paused for a long moment. "Well, Marlene, I was thinking about that. I would hope that we might be able to share some considerable time together, not only in Manila, but perhaps here as well, so it would not be as if you did not have use of the villa." He stepped close to Marlene. She did not move away. "In fact, I would see no difficulty in having you use the villa whenever you like as long as I continued to have access to it whenever I wanted," Breidstein said.

"I think that would be a fine idea." Marlene moved closer to him. "I think having access at any time would be very nice." Breidstein felt himself getting hard. "We probably could have some very enjoyable times together, don't you think?" Marlene dropped her hand and put it on Breidstein's crotch, and began to rub him.

"Yes, Marlene, I think we could."

"Speaking of access, Werner, why not let me have a little access right now?" With that, she began to undo the buttons on Breidstein's pants. Breidstein began to kiss her as she did so. He could taste her thick lipstick and feel her hands. Her perfume was overpowering.

"Here, Werner, now, here," Marlene said with a deep, husky voice.

She pushed him down on a kitchen chair and pulled his pants, and then his underpants, off. His penis rose like a lightning rod. Marlene gave a low growl. Then she pulled up her dress. It was apparent now to Breidstein why she had changed clothes. Marlene wore nothing beneath her dress. "Like what you see, Werner?" Marlene asked.

"Oh, yes, my dear, very much," Breidstein answered.

"Well, you can have your... access... whenever you want." With that, she straddled him.

THE FOLLOWING WEEK, Marlene had Jahnel's legal department draw up a lease agreement. Marlene and Breidstein signed the lease one night at Marlene's Manila apartment after dinner. Breidstein didn't return to his apartment that night.

44

BREIDSTEIN STOPPED a few moments as he entered the waterfront bar to let his eyes adjust to the darkness after the brightness of the Manila sun. There were only a few men—they looked like fishermen or out-of-work dock hands—at the bar. Breidstein walked up to the bar.

"Is Enrique here?" Breidstein said in Spanish to the bartender.

"Who wants to know?"

"Me," Breidstein said as he pushed two pesos across the bar.

The bartender took the coins and pointed to a table.

Breidstein walked to the table and looked at the small but very muscular man sitting there.

"I'm Breidstein. Are you Enrique?"

"*Si*," the man said as he looked up. "Sit down. Want a drink? Pedro, another round over here, for both of us," Enrique called to the bartender without waiting for Breidstein's answer.

"Now what is this about some job? Macarat said you were looking for a chauffeur?" Enrique asked.

"Yes, that's right." Breidstein said.

"Well, I'm your man," Enrique said.

The bartender brought the two drinks. He waited while Breidstein dug out some bills and threw them on his tray. He didn't offer any change. Breidstein waited until the bartender left before he continued.

"There is one other thing," Breidstein said.

"I was waiting for that," Enrique answered with a slight bobbing of his head.

"I may have need of assistance, from time to time, in carrying out some activities that might... uh... shall we say... provoke some question from the authorities... if they were to find out about them," Breidstein said.

Enrique looked at Breidstein a long time, from beneath partly closed eyes.

"I know how to keep my mouth shut. And I have a quick hand when needed." Then, within a bat of an eye, Enrique had his knife out, the long blade up against Breidstein's throat. "Does that answer your concerns?"

"Yes it does," Breidstein answered. Enrique took the knife away.

"How much do I get paid?" Enrique asked.

"Three hundred pesos a month, and you can live at the bungalow at my villa on the peninsula when I don't need you here in town, if you want. When I'm here in the city and not traveling, I'll expect you to be available five days a week—and maybe more if I need you," Breidstein said.

"Five hundred," Enrique shoot back.

"Four," Breidstein countered.

"Done," Enrique said.

"When can you start?" Breidstein asked.

"How quick can you give me the money to get a chauffeur's outfit?" Enrique asked.

45

"THERE YOU ARE, Werner. What took you so long?" Judith asked Breidstein as he entered his apartment, whipping the perspiration from his brow with his linen handkerchief. The heat was merciless in Manila during the summer.

"I had to finish some business. It just took longer than I thought it would," Breidstein lied, remembering the way Marlene had come to his office shortly after lunch, presumably on business, and decided to spend, as she often did, some extra time with him on the couch in his private upstairs office.

"Well, I have some important news—actually bad news, I'm afraid," Judith said.

"Oh, is something wrong at the commission offices?" Breidstein asked. Getting tidbits of information from Judith was a regular occurrence now. It was the real reason he continued to see her; her lovemaking was becoming rather uninspiring of late.

"Albert and I have been transferred to Tokyo. We leave at the end of the month," Judith said as she looked at Breidstein with what he thought she probably believed were sorrowful eyes.

"My goodness. Well, you have been expecting it, have you not? Besides, that is what you want, isn't it?" Breidstein asked, thinking of the possibilities that might develop with Judith in the American embassy in Tokyo, assuming he would be able to maintain contact with her.

"But Werner, what about us? Aren't you concerned about us?" Judith asked.

"Judith, my dear, you know as well as I that our relationship could not go on forever. It has been exhilarating, but there is nothing we can do about the transfer, is there? You really don't want to turn down that opportunity, do you?" Breidstein asked pointedly, knowing that Judith's ambition would not let her do any such thing.

"Well, no, but—"

"No 'buts' about it, my dear. You must go, for your own good—your professional growth," Breidstein said with feigned sadness at her loss.

"Well, yes, I should. Actually, it's a very good opportunity. I will be put in charge of all cultural affairs. And Albert is going to be an assistant deputy ambassador—and that's a very important position." Breidstein began to savor the possibilities that Judith's and Albert's new positions would create.

"Of course, Judith, you know how much I am going to miss you. But," Breidstein paused, "remember that I go to Tokyo every three or four months now—so...." Breidstein hesitated, wanting Judith to make the commitment.

"Oh, yes, Werner. We can see each other when you come to Tokyo. Your schedule wouldn't be so crowded that we couldn't manage to spend some time together?" Judith asked.

"No, it will not, at least not for you, Judith. We may see each other less often, but we will just treasure the moments more," Breidstein said romantically.

"That sounds wonderful, Werner," Judith said, the tenseness in her voice disappearing. "Now, Werner," Judith answered with a wicked smile, as she moved closer to him, "I have the rest of the afternoon free. Have you any suggestions as to what we might do?"

VIII

TAKAMATSU

46

ONCE AT CLARK FIELD north of Manila, Francis went directly to the flight dispatcher. "Name's Marian. I'm supposed to meet a plane from Hawaii coming in via Guam about fifteen-hundred."

The dispatcher picked up his clip board. "Yes sir. It's scheduled for touchdown about a half an hour from now. You can wait in here if you like, sir."

As he waited, Francis picked up yesterday's English edition of the *Manila Times* from a table. The front page had an article with the headline, "Germany Says Peace Goal In Sudetenland." He read it and other background articles on the situation. He already knew, of course, about the Munich accord and Hitler's October occupation of the Sudetenland a week and half ago, but the paper had an interesting analysis from the perspective of those in the Orient. Among the contributors to the article Francis was surprised to see the name of Shinako Fujimori, "Manila correspondent for the *Frankfurter Zeitung*." He wondered if it were the same Shinako Fujimori he knew—*probably is*, he thought, *although I am surprised that she is working in Manila. How did she become a correspondent for the* Frankfurter Zeitung?

Francis looked at this watch. Forty-five minutes had passed. He went back to the dispatcher's desk. "What's the status on that flight coming in?" Francis asked.

"I'm not sure. Should have landed by now. I'll see if I can find out what's going on, Lieutenant," responded the dispatcher.

Francis continued to wait. Another half hour passed.

Finally, the phone rang. Francis looked up. An orderly answered, and then turned to the dispatcher. There was a moment of conversation. Then the dispatcher looked toward Francis. "Your plane is finally coming in, apparently without a radio."

FRANCIS STOOD OUTSIDE the dispatch building as the C-47 landed. He ran toward the plane as it taxied to a stop at the edge of the tarmac. The two engines continued to turn over. The fuselage door opened, a ladder was dropped down, and Paul Woodruff emerged. Ten minutes later, Woodruff and Francis entered an empty room in the dispatcher's office. Woodruff made sure the door was closed behind them.

"All right, Paul, what's all the hush-hush about," Francis asked as he and Woodruff settled into two old leather chairs.

"Well, first of all, you will be dropping into China again—tonight," Woodruff said calmly.

"The hell you say!" Francis said in surprise.

"Yes. Now let me explain why. First of all, I'm here to brief you. I was sent specifically because you know me and, shall we say, because of our mutual interest in China," Woodruff said with a grin.

But Woodruff's face quickly lost its smile as he continued. "The Japs are still on the offensive in China. As you know, they took Amoy in May and Swatow this June. ONI analyzed the radio traffic from around that time, including what you picked up at your listening post, and concluded that there was a big increase in traffic out of Formosa shortly prior to the invasion of Amoy in May. That's not very surprising since we know now the attack was launched from Formosa. But, here's the interesting part. A large increase in traffic has again developed from the same general area, so we think another attack may be planned. The War Department thinks it may go either toward the north, toward Foochow, or, and this is the one everyone is betting on, to the south toward Canton, using Swatow as a staging point."

"Two things, Paul," Francis broke in. "Is Chiang being warned? And why is Swatow a staging point? Why not Formosa again?"

"As to the first question, yes, but I don't know the details. Chiang has been told enough to get his help in this mission. A Colonel Gong is going to be your contact. I've been told you know him." Francis nodded in agreement. "He's going to meet you at your drop site. Beyond that, I don't know. As to your second question, it gets to the guts of why I'm here. And, for that matter, why we were late getting here today," Woodruff said.

"What do you mean?" Francis asked.

"We think, from pieces of information we have been getting, that Japan is in the process of developing a new fighter, a highly improved fighter being built by Mitsubishi, the big industrial and weapons manufacturer. We don't think it's really perfected—that it's still being tested. In the attack on Amoy, we received reports from some of our Chinese contacts that a new plane appeared to be in use. We think it may be a major modification to their high-speed Type 97 recon plane that set some international speed records a year or so ago. We believe what was reported in the attack on Amoy was some type of test model. Testing of the new plane may be going on in several places. Coming out of Guam after refueling, we had a little brush with some Jap planes, probably out of one of the Marianas. They didn't shoot, but they got damn close. If we hadn't scooted into some heavy clouds and done some fancy back tracking, they might have forced us down—literally. We took a round-about direction to get here, just to be on the safe side—that's why we were late. One of those planes that buzzed us might have been one of these test models."

"Why do you think that?" Francis asked.

"Our pilot—he didn't recognize one of the three planes at all—and they sure got close enough to be recognized," Woodruff said.

"What did it look like?" Francis asked.

"Sleek and fast—that's about all this old army man can tell you," Woodruff said.

Francis gave a little laugh.

"But back to China, Francis. If an attack is made by the Japanese on Canton, we think the plane will see more testing there. But because of the distances involved, we think any attack on Canton using the plane will have to be made flying out of Swatow. It's too far for a fighter to come all the way from Formosa and still have enough time over the target for full testing under combat conditions."

"That's an awfully lot of hypothesizing, Paul, an awful lot."

"Well, Francis, as of the end of last week, it's not all hypothetical. We received a report from some of our Chinese contacts in Swatow that two of these apparently new planes landed in Swatow. As far as we know, nothing has yet occurred with them, but we are betting that they will be used in an attack on Canton, an attack that could happen anytime now," Woodruff said.

"So I suppose you want me to see if I can get a look at those planes. Maybe I can, but security around them must be tight. Getting close enough to really see much is going to be difficult," Francis said.

"Well, Francis, that's not quite what we have in mind. Our Chinese sources say that the two test pilots, as well as some engineers, likely from Mitsubishi, are staying in the main hotel in town. Apparently that's where many of the Japanese officers stay. There is a good possibility that discussions about the plane's performance will go on there. So, rather than looking at the plane, we want you to find out what's being said about it. There may even be some documents about the plane there. You will have to just play it by ear once you get into the hotel. But if you do find some documents, don't bring them out. We can't have the Japs knowing that we know anything about this plane. It might just speed up their development schedule. And that's the last thing we want to do. Just look at any documents you can find, and use that memory of yours to bring back the information," Woodruff said.

"Great. All I have to do is say, 'Hey, guys, can I sit in on the conversation. And maybe you could let me look a little at those plans, as well.' Good God, Paul, who in the hell dreams up these schemes?" Francis asked in exasperation.

"Well, it's my understanding that—"

"Stop. You don't have to tell me, Paul, I know—McDonald."

FRANCIS DROPPED from the plane seven hours later. He was already in Chinese clothes and his face was shaded with cream to darken it—to make him look, if not closely inspected, Chinese. The only other thing he had, besides the parachute, was the .45 that Woodruff had given him. "Don't be afraid to use it if you need to, Francis," had been Woodruff's parting words as Francis had gotten on the plane at Clark Field.

As Francis hit the ground, he rolled easily to break his fall. As he got up and began gathering up his chute, he saw three people coming from the edge of the clearing. Francis squatted and pulled the .45 from under his shirt.

"Mr. Francis Soong. Mr. Francis Soong. It is I, Gong." Francis relaxed and stood up.

"It is good to see you again, Mr. Francis Soong. The generalissimo sends his greetings. Come, we must go quickly. There may be Japanese patrols in the area." Francis followed obediently.

ABOUT FOUR HOURS LATER, as the false dawn before the sunrise was appearing, they reached a house on the edge of Swatow. "It is the house of a friend. A useful friend, as you will see," Gong informed Francis.

As they entered, the master of the house greeted them. "Welcome. I am Fong Chu-liu. This is my wife, and there, yet asleep, are my son and daughter. And the old one, there, is my most honorable mother." Francis bowed to the old woman and Fong's wife. "Come. I have a room you can use to rest." Francis was worn out. He figured it had been close to twenty-four hours since he had slept.

"I will return at my usual hour, Colonel, and bring the latest news from the hotel. Good bye for now." With that, Fong Chu-liu left.

Fong's wife came into the room with two bowls of rice porridge. "You eat, then sleep. I will wake you later."

As Gong and Francis ate, Francis started asking Gong questions.

"Why are you here, Colonel?"

"When the generalissimo received your request, that is, the request of your government, for assistance, he suggested that I be the contact for this venture, once he was told who would be coming from the United States," Gong answered.

"And just who is this Fong Chu-liu?" Francis asked.

"He is one of the generalissimo's loyal soldiers, as we all are. Fong is also one of the managers of the Swatow Harbor Light Hotel, the hotel where the Japanese officers and pilots are staying. We will use his assistance to carry out your plan," Gong said.

"What plan, Colonel?" Francis asked.

"Why, the plan you have to sneak into the hotel and listen to the talks about the airplane. You can describe your plan to me after we get some sleep, when Fong Chu-liu comes home."

"Oh, yes, that plan." *Shit*, Francis thought, *nobody has any damn idea how I am supposed to do this.*

47

FRANCIS WOKE about midday. He could hear the voices of children playing. The colonel's bed was empty. Francis cautiously opened the bedroom door. He saw Gong sitting at a table, drinking tea.

"Come, Mr. Francis Soong. Sit with me and have some tea to warm your belly. Fong should be back soon," Gong said as he looked up at Francis.

Francis sat down at the table. Fong's mother poured a cup of tea for him. The two men talked as they sipped their tea. Then Francis asked Cong the question that was burning in him. "Nanking, Colonel Cong—what really happened? Was it as bad as some news reports said? It is hard for me to believe some of the reports—thousands murdered?"

"It was worse, much worse than most news reports said. Tens of thousands died in the most horrifying ways. The Japanese were able to control much of the news that got out. It was only from those few that were able to hide and then escape that we learned the extent of the atrocities. No one was spared—men, women, even the children. It was ghastly. The men were dismembered and then disemboweled—or beheaded. Women, no matter their age, were raped in front of their husbands and children; then they too were killed." Then Cong's voice began to crack. "And my own ... father ... and mother ... ." Tears came to Gong's eyes. Gong took a deep breath, to hold back a sob.

"I am sorry ... I am sorry, Colonel. I shouldn't have asked you." Francis said with anguish. *And*, Francis thought, *maybe, despite what McDonald had said, I shouldn't have arranged that deal with Chiang. Maybe it would have been better if Chiang had made a deal with the Japanese—maybe none of this horror would have occurred.*

Francis said no more, not wanting to intrude upon Cong's emotions anymore. Cong became silent, turning away from Francis to look out the window. Only the noise of the children at play outside broke the silence. Francis made no attempt to disturb Cong in his sorrow.

Finally, Cong turned toward Francis, and spoke. "I shall remember only the good days of my life with my mother and father. When the Japanese are conquered, I shall then remember their final days. I will then obtain my retribution and put their souls to rest."

Francis fervently hoped that what he would do would hasten the day when Cong would obtain his revenge.

Another hour passed as Gong spoke more, but now about Japanese military activities since Nanking, describing how Chiang and his army were trying to fight the Japanese. Then, as Fong's wife began to set out rice bowls for dinner, an excited Fong returned.

"They attacked Canton today. News came by radio to the hotel. Our people at the airport said the new planes went out this morning, with the regular planes. But only one of the new planes came back. What are we going to do?" Fong asked.

"Are the pilots still staying at the hotel? And who else is with them?" Francis asked.

"The pilots are there, including, I think, the ones who fly the new planes. And there are engineers there too. Yes, they are there, at least tonight. They came in very upset, looking very tired," Fong said.

"Well, that is understandable, if they lost one of their test planes," said Gong.

"Tell me their schedule, Fong Chu-liu. What do they do at the hotel?" Francis asked.

"They leave early in the morning to go to the airfield. I think they train most of the time, at least until today. The engineers go with the pilots to the airfield. They take rolls of drawings with them. When they all return in the afternoon, they usually take a bath and then have dinner. After dinner, my waiters say they discuss things, in one of the engineer's rooms. My waiters say they sometimes gamble, rather than talk. We sometimes serve them drinks and desserts while they do this," Fong said.

"Where are these rooms? How do you get into them?" Francis asked.

"The engineers have rooms on the top floor. The pilots are scattered on the top two floors. Each room has entry from the main hallway. There are balconies outside each window, but they are too small to go directly from one room to another using them; they are not that close. The only way to get to the balcony is from inside the room. There are no outside stairs or ladders. There are inside stairs, of course, but they usually have many people, often Japanese officers, on them—the elevator often jams. But of course we can always see when it does; the people in it always start waving their arms and yelling," Fong said.

"How are the food and drinks brought to them?" Francis asked.

"The cooks prepare what is needed in the kitchen on the first floor. It is put on the dumbwaiter and sent to the proper floor. A waiter gets it off the dumbwaiter and takes it to the room," Fong said.

"And does this dumbwaiter go to the top floor?" asked Francis, beginning to see a plan.

"Yes, it does."

"And how is the dumbwaiter repaired? How are the ropes and pulleys inspected?" Francis asked.

"Why, the maintenance man goes up to the roof and opens the access door to the pulley shed—" Fong stopped in mid-sentence.

"Colonel, can we get some good, strong rope by tomorrow morning?" Francis asked.

IN THE EARLY MORNING, Fong took Francis into the city, finally leading him down a dirty alley to the hotel delivery door leading to the kitchen. "Wait while I distract the guard at the door," Fong said.

Fong entered the kitchen while Francis stood in the wetness of the early morning with two bags of purposely rotten, smelly fish, as if waiting for the kitchen door to open. They and the nearby piles of loose garbage made it difficult to breathe. After several minutes, Fong opened the door. "Quickly, the guard is having some tea and cakes set out by my cook."

Francis followed Fong through a room stacked high with empty crates and boxes. Garbage pails, as well as more loose garbage, were pushed back against one wall. Then they entered the main kitchen. Francis could see the back of the guard hunched over a table, eating. The cook stood nearby, with a steaming pot of tea. Francis saw the cook motion with his eyes. Fong and Francis walked quickly to the end of the kitchen and the dumbwaiter, beyond the sight of the guard.

Fong took the fish out of the tops of the bags. Then from one bag Francis pulled out a coil of rope and swung it over his head and shoulders. From the other bag, he pulled out the .45, a candle, some matches, and a handful of rice cakes. The .45 went under his belt, the candle and matches into one pocket, the rice cakes into the other.

Fong pulled the dumbwaiter doors open, and cranked the dumbwaiter down until the top of it was at the level of the bottom of the door.

Francis climbed onto the top of the dumbwaiter, keeping most of his weight off it by bracing his back and feet against the walls of the shaft.

Fong closed the dumbwaiter doors and pulled out a folded piece of paper from his pocket. Unfolding the large sheet of paper, he stuck it to the doors with tacks. It announced that the dumbwaiter was out of service and not to be used without the permission of the manager.

FRANCIS PUSHED HIS LEGS and back against the walls of the dumbwaiter tower, the pulley ropes between his legs. He put some of his weight on the top of the dumbwaiter itself. He took the candle and matches out of his pocket and lit the candle. He looked upward, as much as the candlelight would allow. He could see only rough concrete walls, with pulley ropes coming down from the darkness of the tower. He put the burning candle in his mouth, and began to push himself slowly up the tower. Every few feet, he would pull the dumbwaiter up and transfer some of his weight to it, so he could rest his legs.

Francis continued working his way up the tower, his back and legs becoming more and more tired, despite the temporary rests using the dumbwaiter. His calves began to cramp. He began to wonder if he were ever going to reach the top of the tower, when, finally, the top began to appear in the light of the candle. His legs and back gained renewed strength as he saw sunlight coming in around the edges of the access door at the top of the tower.

He finally reached the top. Francis took his foot and pushed on the access door, forcing it open. The midmorning light streamed into the tower. Francis pulled himself onto the roof, looking quickly about to see if anyone was on the roof. There was no one.

Francis closed the access door and crawled around to the back side of the small roof door tower so that he would be out of the immediate sight of anyone coming to the roof. He began to massage his aching legs.

Francis remained undisturbed throughout the rest of the day, listening to the miscellaneous sounds of the city below. During the midafternoon, he ate two of his rice cakes.

As the hours passed, Francis allowed himself to think about... Elaine. He would seldom allow himself to do so... it hurt too much. But as the time slowly passed, he couldn't help himself. Their moments together had been too wonderful for him to ever forget. His times with Elaine, and the love that had grown out of them, had been like the rush of a wild river engulfing him as he swam in it, never quite sure where it was taking him but always growing bigger and more gentle as it flowed toward the sea. Her devotion to her son had brought a damming end to their moments together, but as time passed, the river, Francis could only hope, would someday flow again… and the pain of her loss would be gone.

Francis' thoughts were broken by the drone of planes in the distance. He looked to the southwest and saw Japanese fighter planes approaching the city, slicing through wispy clouds sparking in the late afternoon sun. They were too far away, however, for him to see any of their details. They soon began to circle downward for landing.

As night settled, he crawled to the edge of roof and watched the lights of the hotel rooms spring sporadically into the darkening night. As he listened, he began to pick up conversations from partially opened windows. He finally decided which room, from the several that Fong had said the pilots would usually gather in to talk, was probably the one where the pilots were this night. Francis tied the rope onto a sturdy roof vent and carefully dropped it over the edge of the low brick wall ringing the roof. He grabbed the rope and climbed over the brick wall. He lowered himself down the building wall and toward the balcony of the room where he hoped the pilots and engineers were meeting. He climbed over the balcony railing and onto the balcony itself. He pressed his back against the wall as he moved close to the partially open window.

Francis could hear a heated discussion going on in the room. It took several moments for his mind to adjust to the Japanese words coming from the room. Then it became clear that the new plane was the subject of the discussion.

"…and I told you that something must be done about how that plane recovers from dives. I nearly crashed during a steep strafing dive. That's what happened in yesterday's loss, only Shimada wasn't able to pull up in time. The explosion when he hit the ground was horrendous. The plane does not handle well in a steep dive. We must find out what is wrong," a voice said demandingly.

"Well, just what happens?" someone else asked. "You can't expect me or anyone else to redesign for a problem when all you can say is that it does not handle well in a dive. What happens, Lieutenant? Here, look at the plans. With the information we get from this test model, we will be able to build the finest fighter in the world. What we have is better than anything already. You tell me what you want to change. Point to it, Lieutenant Takamatsu!"

"Well, you and the rest of your friends are the engineers. I thought Mitsubishi was supposed to have the best aircraft designers in the world," the first voice responded angrily.

"Please, please. We are all tired and overwrought. Yesterday's loss was most regrettable, but let us see if we can learn from it," another voice interjected.

"Seiroku, please describe what happened, very carefully," said another voice.

Silence. Then, "I was flying level at about a thousand meters. I saw a train moving along some tracks. I pealed off and started a shallow dive that I gradually steepened as I approached the target. Vapor eddies were swirling off the wings behind the cannon pods as I looked behind me to see if my wing partner was following. Then a slight buffeting started. It got worse. I began to pull up, but the plane would not respond. It took all my strength to pull back the stick to make the plane level off. I swear I must have been only ten meters from the ground when I leveled off. My body sweats even now when I think of how close I came to death—and what Shimada must have been thinking as he tried to pull out." A pause. "I need some air. The smoke in here is overpowering."

The man came to the window and pushed on the window panes to swing the window open more. Frances hugged the wall, trying to submerge himself into the brick wall. *If he looks to the side he's going to see me*, Francis thought as he carefully pulled the .45 from his belt.

"Ah ... that is much better." The man leaned his head out the window, his eyes closed, taking a deep breath. *My God*, Francis said to himself. *That's the man who was one of the three Japanese officers on the ship to Hawaii. Seiroku, that's right, that's his name. So that's who he is, Lieutenant Seiroku Takamatsu.*

"What do you mean you saw vapor eddies?"

Takamatsu pulled his head back from the window and turned toward the questioning voice.

"Little wisps of swirling vapor coming off the trailing edge of the central portion of the wing behind the cannon pod," Takamatsu answered.

"Vapor eddies. That shouldn't be happening. That plane does not fly fast enough to cause low-pressure vaporization; its design speed is only two-hundred-sixty knots, significantly less than the two-seventy that we want in the final design. That should not be happening ... unless there is a low-pressure pocket... separation of the flow... an isolated pocket that forms on the wing behind the cannon pods. Just maybe... that could explain the loss of lift, why you could not pull up like you should be able to. Maybe... if we reduced the size of the cannon, eliminated the wing protuberances. Twenty-millimeter cannon require a great deal of structural support... or maybe we could even eliminate the cannon altogether so—"

"Fire! Fire!" came the call in Chinese from outside the room. *Right on time*, Francis thought.

Francis heard the door open and someone ask, "What is going on? What are you yelling about?"

"Fire! Big fire. There is big, big fire in the kitchen. Get out, get out. We may not be able to stop it. Down the stairs quickly before it spreads."

"What's he saying?" someone asked in Japanese.

"I think he's yelling about a fire, something about a big fire in the kitchen. Maybe we had better get out of here until we find out what's going on."

There was clumping of hurrying feet as everyone rushed out of the room.

Francis leaned toward the window and carefully looked in. There was no one. It was time. He had maybe twenty minutes—if Fong had been able to jam the elevator. He opened the window wider and climbed into the room.

On the table was what he hoped he might find—a roll of engineering drawings. Two drawings were already pulled from the roll. One was a top and side view of the new plane, with dimensions. On the corner of the drawing was the title "Mitsubishi - 12Si Program Design Number 1." The other drawing was a detail of the wing shape, with sections cut at intervals showing the wing configuration. Francis began to look intently at the first drawing, trying to put every detail into his mind. Then he turned to the other drawing. More difficult to visualize, more difficult to remember. He finally put it aside, realizing he could not absorb any more.

Francis turned to the roll of drawings, flipping through the corner of the stack of drawings to look at their titles, trying to select one to study. There— "Landing Gear"—detailed drawings of a retractable landing gear. He unrolled the drawing and studied it for several minutes, then reinserted it in the roll of drawings. Then a search for another. He pulled out one labeled "Fuel System" and studied it, and then slid it back into the roll of drawings. Only a few minutes left—maybe time for one more. He quickly scanned the drawing titles again—this time selecting the one titled "Armament." He opened up the roll so the drawing was fully exposed. The drawing showed where protective armament was placed under the plane's skin. *Damn*, he thought, *almost none. Why?*

Francis heard voices coming from the hallway. "Stupid Chinese, don't know how to put out a simple grease fire." Francis quickly rolled up the drawings and set them back on the corner of the table. "And that elevator—my legs are not used to climbing six flights of stairs—we should hang the manager of this place up by his balls." Francis was putting the window back to its original position when the door opened.

"Well, let us get back to where we were."

Then came a voice with a name he now knew. "I think that until Mitsubishi looks at the possibility of—what did you call it, Horikoshi, a low-pressure pocket on the wing—we will not endanger more pilot's lives. I will recommend to Admiral Yamamoto that test flights of this model be limited until this problem appears to be corrected and that consideration be given to re-evaluation of the cannon size. We will not fly any more combat test missions with this model until this issue is resolved," Takamatsu said.

"Are you sure you want to do that, Seiroku?"

"That is why I was assigned to this mission by Admiral Yamamoto himself: to make the necessary evaluation and decisions. And that is what I am going to recommend to him," Seiroku answered.

"Well, is that it, then?" another voice asked.

"I think so. Give those drawings to me so I can lock them up with the others."

Francis stepped over the railing and began to pull himself back up to the roof.

FRANCIS SPENT THE REMAINDER of the night and part of the next day on the roof. He went over and over in his mind what he had heard and seen, trying to maximize his retention of what he had learned, including Seiroku Takamatsu's apparent connection with Yamamoto. As the sun passed its zenith, he finished his last rice cake and then climbed back into the dumbwaiter tower. Going down the tower was easier than coming up, but it was still a long, difficult effort to reach the bottom of the tower.

Francis had been waiting about half an hour when he heard a knock on the dumbwaiter door. "Mr. Marian. Mr. Marian." Francis pointed his .45 at the door as it began to open.

Fong's face appeared in the door opening, then disappeared as he jumped back from the .45. Francis lowered the .45. Fong reappeared, leaned toward Francis, and whispered, "It is all right. No one is here. Quickly, get out."

Francis uncoiled his tired body and climbed out of the dumbwaiter tower.

Fong put his finger to his lips to warn Francis to be quiet. Fong gave Francis a bag and had him put his rope and gun in it. Then Fong dumped a smelly load of food scraps into the bag. Then he gave Francis another two full bags of garbage. The smell was sickening. Fong tied a dirty white apron around Francis' waist. "Are you ready, Mr. Marian?" Fong asked in a whisper.

Francis nodded.

Fong and Francis stepped out from behind the wall that had shielded them from the view of the rest of the kitchen. Fong began to yell at Francis.

"You son of a bitch dog, don't you know better than to leave garbage in this kitchen. Take it outside, get it out! You will ruin everything we have here. Do you want to make our guests sick?" Fong yelled.

Francis ran toward the back of the kitchen, where the guard stood at the door, with the bags held high in front of his chest, blocking the view of his face. "Get out of here with that, you stupid pig. I knew I never should have hired you. Take that outside and never come back, you stupid pig. Get out. Get out!" Fong continued to yell.

Just as he neared the guard, Francis dropped the two bags of smelly garbage. Their rotten contents spew out across the floor. The guard jumped back, trying to distance himself from the smelly mess, backing away from Francis and the yelling Fong running after him. Fong's yelling followed Francis outside as he ran with the remaining garbage bag, his .45 in it, down the alley. Fong stood at the end of the alley shaking his fist as Francis got to the street and started the long walk back to Fong's home.

A DAY LATER, Colonel Gong said goodbye as Francis stepped from a small fishing boat to the ladder hanging from the side of a large junk gently swaying in the ocean swells.

The next afternoon, some sixty miles off the South China coast, a U.S. Navy PBY landed by the junk.

48

FRANCIS WAS MET by McDonald as the PBY edged up to the seaplane ramp at Cavite. Francis was dead tired, but McDonald hustled him into a staff car that took off into the night to a lonely, old barracks building on the edge of the Cavite base. As McDonald got out of the car, he turned to Francis and said, "The people you meet here tonight—forget them after tonight, if you can."

Francis followed McDonald into the barracks building, still carrying the notes and drawings he had made on the PBY after his pickup only six hours ago. Two Marine guards remained stationed outside as McDonald closed the door behind Francis. The six men in the room looked expectantly at Francis.

"TWO-HUNDRED SEVENTY KNOTS! You have to be kidding. Are you sure that you heard that right?" The small group of aircraft design engineers listened with disbelief to what Francis was telling them.

"That's what they said. The test model itself has a design speed of two-sixty," Francis said.

"Well, if that is right, we really need to make some radical improvements," said Malcolm, the engineer from Northrop. "You said that you looked at wing sections. What did they look like?"

"I have tried to reconstruct what I saw about that here on these sheets," Francis said as he pulled a drawing from under the pile of papers on the table.

Malcolm studied them for a minute. "Umm," he would say every few moments. "Look at this, Jim, will you," Malcolm said to another engineer. "If Lieutenant Marian's drawings are reasonably accurate, it looks like the Mitsubishi engineers have altered the aspect ratio quite a bit, and maybe stretched the wing width quite a bit near the fuselage. But is that for aerodynamics or additional strength at the wing-fuselage transition?"

"You may be right, Gerry. Lieutenant, were any names of the Mitsubishi people mentioned?" the engineer asked.

"There were three names mentioned. One was a Lieutenant Seiroku Takamatsu. He was one of the test pilots. I think he's on Admiral Yamamoto's staff. The test pilot who was killed was called Shimada. The other was Horikoshi. I don't know what he was."

"Horikoshi—isn't that one of Mitsubishi's lead designers, the one who was really behind the design of their type 97 recon plane, that plane that set that speed record back in April of thirty-seven?" another engineer asked.

"Damn, I think you're right," said Roger Mangarella from North American. "If that's so, I can guarantee you that the wider width is for aerodynamic purposes. One thing that Hirokoshi is really good at is insuring the best aerodynamics. He force-fits the structure to give him the aerodynamics he needs. And that makes sense with the design specifications the lieutenant found—lots of speed, high maneuverability."

"But where is he going to get the strength he needs? You put in the strength and the weight goes up; then the speed goes down," Malcolm asked.

"May I make an observation?" Francis asked.

"Please do, Lieutenant," said Malcolm.

"Well, take a look at this sheet, here, that I drew up, the one that's labeled 'Armament.' Now, I'm not an airplane designer like you people are, but doesn't it look like they don't have much armament?"

Pauli, another engineer from Northrop, studied the drawing that Francis had brought to their attention. "Damn. Almost nothing, at least compared to our designs. Knocking out armament would certainly cut the weight down. But this plane may be a flying coffin."

AS THE DISCUSSION DREW to a close, Mangarella, with a dry, tired voice, turned to Francis and said,. "I will have to hand it to you, Lieutenant. I don't know how you got to see and hear all this—"

"And don't ask, gentlemen," McDonald cut in from where he had been sitting quietly during the entire discussion.

"…but I am damn sure this information is going to put us a year or more ahead in design of a new generation of fighter that will be able to knock the crap out of this Jap plane."

Francis saw a big grin come to McDonald's face.

IX

MARIA

49

"WELL, WERNER, how have you been? World conditions have certainly taken on a new twist since we last talked, have they not?" Agawa said as he stood and welcomed Breidstein into his consulate office.

"They certainly have. The German liberation of Poland, I have to admit, did catch me a bit by surprise," Breidstein responded, thinking, *it caught me completely by surprise, totally disrupting my plans for getting back to business after that miserable trip for the Chancellery. Three months sailing through south seas on a miserable sail boat to gather information for the Chancellery about Japanese military activities in the Marshall and Gilbert Islands—dropping everything to meet their asinine schedule. And now I know why they wanted the information before the end of August—to somehow feed it into their plans before the invasion of Poland. But why the hell couldn't the Chancellery have warned me about what was going to happen before I left, so I could have been better prepared. Now all my East Indies operations are in chaos.*

"What has been the impact upon your business operations? Is it affecting you a great deal?" Agawa asked politely.

"Only somewhat," Breidstein lied. "I am in the process of re-evaluating my operations in the East Indies to see what impacts the British and French war declarations may have. Some of the rubber plantation operations in the East Indies in which Hamburg Import-Export is a partner will suffer. But my other operations will survive without undue damage," Breidstein said, pretending confidence.

"It is interesting you should use the word 'survive,' Werner. We, by which I mean the Japanese government, have that same thought in our mind when we look at United States activities here in the Orient, a place where Americans really do not belong. We are concerned that they may take aggressive and unexpected, as well as unnecessary, actions that might damage our rightful position in the Orient. Japan and Germany are in agreement, as you well know, with the need for political power to be exercised by those with appropriate historical and cultural ties—as it is for Germany in the case of Poland, and, for example, as it is for Japan in the case of Korea and Manchukuo," Agawa said.

"You say aggressive and unexpected acts, Heihachiro. What do you mean?" Breidstein felt that Agawa was leading the conversation somewhere, but as to where he could not see.

"Well, it is obvious that the United States government, despite the law it passed about the Philippine commonwealth becoming independent in nineteen-forty-six, appears more interested in exerting its power than recognizing the inherent right of those living here in the Orient to determine their own destiny. Japan is particularly concerned that the United States might take some inappropriate action—some military action—to further cement its power in the Pacific," Agawa finished in a ominous voice.

Breidstein was truly surprised by what Agawa said. "Do you really think the United States would undertake some overt military action here in the Orient that would pose a threat to Japan?" Breidstein asked.

"Until several months ago, I would not have thought that to be the case. However, we have begun to hear rumors and learn various things that suggest conditions may be changing. We are becoming very concerned, a concern that is considerably heightened by our lack of detailed knowledge about U.S. military intentions in the Pacific," Agawa said.

"But what can you do about it?" Breidstein asked.

"Well, Werner, I… we… were hoping that you might help in that regard," Agawa answered.

"I am not sure I understand, Consul General," Breidstein answered, not liking what he was hearing.

"Allow me to explain, Werner. The United States has for some time had plans dealing with potential war with each of the major powers. These war plans are coded by colors according to the country against whom the United States would act should one of these scenarios evolve. The scenario against Japan is called Plan Orange. Periodically, we believe, these plans undergo major revision. The last major revision, until very recently we believe, took place in mid to late nineteen-thirty-seven," Agawa said.

"Interesting…" Breidstein said, remembering the remarks of the navy commander Ellington on the *Empress of Canada* two years ago, "but what is your concern?"

"Another major revision has apparently been recently made, and we are suspicious that Plan Orange has become offensive rather than defensive, as we believe it was in the past. For our own protection we need to know if this is the case," Agawa answered.

"How do you expect to determine if such a change in this 'Plan Orange' has occurred?" Breidstein asked.

"Very simply, we would like to look at the plan," Agawa answered.

Breidstein looked at Agawa, finally realizing what Agawa had been leading up to and what he might be asking of Breidstein. "But I do not think I can help you in this regard, Mr. Consul General," Breidstein answered, hoping to distance himself from Agawa's request.

"Certainly you can, Werner. We have been able to work together so effectively to our mutual benefit in the past. And I would hope that such cooperation can continue—and besides, we need from you only some minor assistance," Agawa said.

Breidstein looked at Agawa, recognizing the implied threat. "What is it that you would have me do?" Breidstein said in defeat, knowing that what Agawa was asking him to do was very dangerous. One slip and Breidstein would be labeled a spy.

"We know that a Filipino woman, Carmen Sanchez, works as a senior clerk in the main military files offices of the Philippine Army here in Manila," Agawa explained. "We would expect that certain components of this Plan Orange as it might affect us would be in those files because the Philippine Army would likely be involved in any actions of the type we fear. Now, Miss Sanchez, a very lovely woman, at least for a Filipino, has struck up, shall we say, an intimate relation with an American naval officer whom we believe is on the command staff involved with revising the plan. It would have obviously serious repercussions if the U.S. Navy, as well as this officer's wife, were to find out about this relationship."

As Breidstein listened to what Agawa had to say, beginning to see Agawa's developing plan, he began to realize, while surely dangerous, that here was a possible gold mine for himself. If he were going to do this, he might as well get some benefit from it. *I'll let Agawa think I don't want to do this,* Breidstein thought, *but I'll find a way to see whatever he sees, without him knowing.*

"I see that Miss Sanchez has a hold over the officer, but what hold do I or you have over her?" Breidstein asked.

"We are fortunate that Miss Sanchez lives with her mother. The mother is now a housemaid in some of the American military officers' homes here in the Manila area; she started working as a maid after her husband died. If you were to hire the mother, Juana, as your full-time maid at a lucrative salary—at least in terms of what she is used to seeing—both Juana and Miss Sanchez might soon become dependent upon your largess. Once that occurred, you could readily induce Miss Sanchez to help us if her mother were threatened with the loss of the job to which she and, indirectly, Miss Sanchez had become accustomed."

"That is asking a great deal, Mr. Ambassador," Breidstein said, pretending to be still reluctant to avoid what Agawa was asking.

"Not really. All you have to do is make sure the Sanchez woman cooperates with us. You yourself would not have to be involved in asking her to do anything. All you have to do is get the mother to convince her daughter, Carmen, to assist us."

And, Breidstein thought, *convince her daughter to help me as well.*

A WEEK LATER, Breidstein met Juana Sanchez in the lobby of his apartment building.

"*Senõra* Sanchez, thank you for coming this afternoon," Breidstein said in Spanish to the short, mid-aged Filipino woman standing in front of him in a pink and white maid's uniform. Breidstein could see in her haggard face the look of desperation that comes with living on the edge of poverty, without a hope of change—just the thing he needed in this woman for what he intended to do.

"Your chauffeur said you wanted to hire me, *Herr* Breidstein," Juana Sanchez said as she looked about at the elegant lobby.

"Yes, that's why I had him pick you up at the military base. I am in need of a very good maid, a full time maid, here at my apartment."

"I work for many officers now—at the army base. I am poor ... working for just ... one person," Juana said hesitatingly.

"You come highly recommended, Juana. What if I were to offer you a hundred pesos a week? Could you work for me then—work for me only?" Breidstein said, knowing the amount had to be several times larger than what the woman was making now.

"Do you mean that, *Herr* Breidstein," Juana asked with wide eyes.

"Well, I know it's not as much as you deserve, but perhaps you can see your way clear to take the position. Perhaps, if I gave you some extra money now, a bonus—a gift from me—that you could use to find some place to live nearer to my apartment—my apartment is on the sixth floor here. Would a thousand pesos be enough to make you change your mind and work for me?" Breidstein asked with a smooth, innocent voice.

Juana looked at Breidstein. "Can I start tomorrow?"

"Of course, of course. You come tomorrow and I'll have my little gift for you too," Breidstein said.

50

"GOOD AFTERNOON, *Herr* Breidstein. You are home early today. Will you be going out for dinner or do you wish me to fix dinner?" Juana asked as Breidstein entered his Manila apartment early one March afternoon. It was nearly four months since Breidstein had offered Juana the job as maid in his Manila apartment. It was time to spring the trap.

"Neither, for the moment, Juana. I must talk to you." Breidstein sat down on the couch, as if very tired. "I want you to know how satisfied I have been with you since I hired you."

"Thank you, *Herr* Breidstein. My life and that of my daughter have become so much better since you hired me," Juana said.

"Unfortunately, Juana, that may be coming to an end. The war in Europe is causing serious difficulties for my business. I may have to let some employees go—I may have to let you go." He saw the look of surprise and then fright on Juana's face.

"Do you mean that I cannot work for you... anymore?" Juana said with a crack in her voice.

"Well, it might come to that, Juana. I'm so sorry," Breidstein said with fake remorse.

"Oh, no! Please, *Herr* Breidstein. If I lose my job, it would be terrible. I cannot even think of going back to the way I lived before I met you. Please, *Herr* Breidstein, isn't there something I can do?" Juana pleaded.

"Well, Juana, let me think." Breidstein purposely cupped his chin in his hand and stared out the window a few moments, as if in deep thought. Then he said with grave seriousness, "Perhaps there is something that can be done, Juana. Perhaps your daughter—Carmen is her name, isn't it—could help me with some problems I am having. Do you think that she might help me if she could?"

"Oh, yes, *Herr* Breidstein. Oh, yes," Juana answered.

"Well, that sounds promising, Juana. Why don't I meet with Carmen after she finishes work tomorrow. Have her meet me, say, in the park down by the docks near my office. Do you know where that is?"

"Oh, yes, *Herr* Breidstein. I know it."

"Good. Why don't you have her come about, say, six-thirty. Would that work out?" Breidstein asked.

"Oh, yes, *Herr* Breidstein. I will bring her myself," Juana answered.

THE NEXT DAY Breidstein sat on a park bench, casually reading the afternoon paper. Shortly before six-thirty, Breidstein saw Juana hurrying into the park with a strikingly pretty, well-dressed woman. Her hair was black but with a noticeable tinge of red. Her wide mouth was sensual, and seemed to fit perfectly with the air of wanton mystery that her smoothly swaying hips evoked as she came toward Breidstein. Breidstein could understand why someone might be attracted to her. Breidstein rose and smiled.

"*Herr* Breidstein, this is my daughter, Carmen. I have brought her as you wanted," Juana announced.

"*Señorita* Sanchez, it is a pleasure to meet you. Your mother has told me that you may be able to help me. With your assistance, I will do my utmost to assure that I can continue to provide employment for her. Am I correct in my understanding that you will be able to help me?" Breidstein asked with dripping politeness.

Carmen spoke for the first time. "Yes, if I can," she answered.

"I'm sure you can," Breidstein said in a soft, beguiling voice, keeping up his charade of friendliness. "Juana, why don't you sit on the park bench, over there, and rest," Breidstein said as he pointed to a bench a considerable distance away. Juana nodded and shuffled away.

"Why don't you sit down here so we can talk," Breidstein said as he sat down and extended his hand in invitation to Carmen to do the same. Carmen sat down at the opposite end of the bench from Breidstein.

"This is what I would like you to do," Breidstein began. "Tomorrow—here at the same time as today—I will introduce you to an associate from the Japanese consulate. He will ask you to help him to gather, from time to time, some materials from your place of work."

Carmen's eyes widened, and she opened her mouth to speak. Breidstein raised his hand to stop her protest. "If it is something you cannot do, my dear Carmen, please tell me now... and I will prepare a letter of recommendation for your mother to find a new place of employment." Carmen closed her mouth. "Good, you are in agreement. Let me continue," Breidstein said without the false politeness of his earlier words.

"When he asks these things of you, you shall do them. But you shall also tell your mother what you tell him, so she can tell me—and you tell her to tell me. If you get any papers, you give them first to your mother for delivery to me—I will return them to you the next day for delivery to the man from the Japanese consulate. And you will do these things, for me, without telling the man from the Japanese consulate. Do you understand—without telling the other man?" Breidstein asked.

"Yes, but my mother ... does she have to be involved?" Carmen asked.

"Yes," Breidstein answered with a harsh voice.

"I... I... just don't know... if I can go through with it. Isn't there something else, anything else," Carmen said with pleading eyes.

"No, and you will go through with it, unless... perhaps, you would like your relationship with your young naval officer to become known to his superiors. Would you like that to happen?" Breidstein asked menacingly.

Carmen's eyes widened as she looked at Breidstein, and then slowly shook her head.

51

"SO FRANCIS, WASHINGTON CONCURS with the British. Something is going to happen soon in Malaya or French Indo-china, or perhaps even Siam. Ever since the Germans took on the Brits this last year after they invaded Poland, the Japanese have been anxious to spread their wings more. The whole of Southeast Asia is high on Japan's agenda for takeover, either politically or militarily. But as usual, our information is hazy as to precisely where or when," Scott, Francis' old roommate from D.C., said in summary to Francis as they sat in an office at Post Y.

Scott had flown the previous day to Cavite from Singapore, where he was stationed as liaison to British naval forces there, with orders signed by the commander of the Asiatic Fleet, Admiral Hart, telling Francis to give the British some unspecified assistance. When Scott told Francis that McDonald was behind the offer of assistance, Francis was not surprised.

"Well, I would have to agree with that," Francis said. "Considering where the Japanese are now, and the intercepts we have been getting at Cavite since July, I would put my bet on Indo-china. But you're right, they might jump almost anywhere."

"Quite so, Lieutenant. That's why we want you, at the suggestion of your Navy Department, to help us narrow things down a bit," chimed in Major Mason. Mason had come from Singapore with Scott. "We think it would be useful if you could spend some time, so to speak, in Bangkok, and gather some information about Japanese intentions while you are there. It would, we think, help us considerably in keeping our options open in Burma and Indo-china."

"Why Bangkok, and why me?" asked Francis, thinking it perversely funny the way the major referred to the mission they were handing him as if it were just a holiday jaunt.

"Quite simple, old man," answered the major, despite the fact that he was at least twenty years Francis' senior. "Bangkok is a hotbed of activity. The

Japanese embassy is a major base of diplomatic—and other more devious—activity in Southeast Asia. But with the Burma Road closure earlier this summer, the Japanese demands and all, you know, we Brits are having a rather difficult time moving about reasonably unnoticed in that part of the world. You Americans still can get about without undue notice, though I'm not sure how long that is going to last either. So you should be able to get past the scrutiny of the local government to get closer to where we need to be. As to why you ... I've been told that you have considerable powers of recall, a considerably useful talent should you just happen to get a chance to look at some Japanese documents. You can spend some time taking a look and they will never be the wiser," Mason said.

"What do you mean 'get closer to where we need to be'?" Francis asked.

"Old boy, I thought you understood," Mason said, looking at Scott with a frown. "We want you to be invited to the Japanese embassy in Bangkok so you can break into their radio communication files."

Francis looked at Scott. "What the hell does he mean 'be invited,' Scottie? Just how am I supposed to manage that?"

"Francis, it's not as bad as it sounds, really," said Scott, obviously trying to smooth Mason's rather abrupt introduction of what he expected Francis to do.

"We see no problem there, Lieutenant," Mason said with an assuring smile. "We have, shall we say, a well-connected contact in Bangkok who can arrange for your invitation to a big bash planned for the Japanese embassy about three weeks from now. Once inside the embassy, it's down a hall, into a room somewhere, and back out again. Easy as that."

Good God, thought Francis, *is this guy serious?*

"And," Francis said with resignation, "just who is this guy who is supposed to be so well connected?"

"Actually, Lieutenant, it is not a 'guy.' It is, as you Americans say, a 'gal.' She is the mistress of the Thailand deputy minister of foreign affairs."

52

"WE'RE PRETTY SURE that the communications operations are on the second floor on this side of the building. The antennas and wires that you can see from the outside all point to that," Scott said as he and Francis slowly drifted down the klong, the wide waters of the canal murky and dark from the sediments and human wastes it carried past the back wall of the Japanese embassy compound in the heart of Bangkok's commercial district. "See the antenna wires—almost hidden in the vines—leading down from the roof and into that alcove."

"Where is the communications file room?" Francis asked as the water taxi floated around a bend and the Japanese embassy passed out of sight.

"Well, we're guessing that it might be close to the radio room, but we're not sure," Scott answered. "You can confirm it with your contact. She is supposed to be familiar with the Japanese embassy." Then Scott looked at his watch. "It's almost time. You'll meet her at a tea shop not too far from here." Scott stepped to the back of the boat, spoke briefly to the oarsman, and then motioned him to a dock a short distance down the klong.

In a few minutes they were climbing out of the boat onto a small dock. Scott told the oarsman to wait. Scott slowly turned his head back and forth, looking up and down the klong. As he did so, Scott asked casually, "Whatever happen to that gal in Washington—what was her name ... Elaine?"

"Yes, that's right, Elaine. Things... just didn't work out," Francis answered, his emotions stirred by the memory of Elaine.

"That's too bad. She seemed like a nice gal," Scott said.

"She was," Francis said.

Scott stopped his perusal of the klong. "Looks like nobody is taking undue notice in us, so here's where I leave you, Francis. Go up this street here to the first corner, where it intersects Phra Sumen Road. The tea shop is on the corner. There's a sign hanging from the corner of the shop with a large red rice stalk painted on it. Enter from the side door on this street, here," Scott said with a nod of his head, "at exactly three-twenty. Time your entry using the clock on the bank across the street. That's what your contact will use. She will come in from the entrance on the main street at three-nineteen and be watching for you, or rather, that miniature Chinese bell flower in your lapel. Check her out with the pass words. From there on, you're on your own, buddy. See you back at the embassy," Scott said as he climbed back into the boat.

A few moments later, Francis was ambling slowly up the crowded side street. He reached the busy intersection and looked across the street. The hands on the clock moved to seventeen minutes after three. He looked at the curios in the shop next door to the tea shop for three minutes, checked the clock across the street again, and then opened the side door of the tea shop.

The room he entered was a large, simple dining area, filled with small tables and chairs—and packed with people, drinking tea and eating snacks. Francis looked across the room, trying to see who might be standing near the other door. He saw her when she waved to him, as if he were an old friend. She came across to him, kissing him on the cheek. "It is so good to see you again; you have a lovely El Capitolio in your lapel," she said in Chinese, as she pulled the small pink bell flower out of Francis' lapel, sniffing it.

Francis responded, "It has been paled by the moon of Saigon."

"Yes, but it has been brightened by the sun of Bangkok," she responded properly.

Relieved, Francis asked, "Where shall we sit?"

"Over there, where those two people are getting up," she continued in Chinese.

As they sat down, a boy with a dirty apron came to the table. The pretty young woman ordered two cups of tea and a plate of rice cakes for them. "You may call me Suu. What shall I call you?" she asked. "Do not tell me your real name. I do not want to know."

Francis hesitated. "Call me Cam. It's the name of a friend, a friend far away from here."

"All right, Cam. Here, take this." She pushed some bills across the table; a small envelope was under them. "You can pay the waiter when he comes back; a woman should not be seen buying a man's food. Give him two of the bills; that will be enough." Francis put the extra bills, along with the envelope, in his coat pocket.

"The envelope has your invitation to the Grand Celebration at the Japanese embassy, a week from now. It is the first anniversary of the new Thailand—out foolish leaders think changing our country's name will secure peace for us," Suu said with a low—and sarcastic—voice. "The crowd should be enormous for this event. You will be the guest of my friend, the deputy minister, if you are asked. His name is Jusef Habibie; the minister's name is Bacharuddin Saleh Raidy. Avoid meeting either of them. I told Jusef the invitation was for a relative of mine, not a European. I would have a difficult time explaining how you got an invitation if someone were to find out I gave it to you."

The boy with the apron returned with two cups of steaming tea and several rice cakes. Francis pushed the two bills across the table to him. The boy scooped them up as he turned and left.

"I expect quite a few Germans, along with their Vichy French sympathizers, to be there. Some other Europeans too. Bangkok's social set has quite a collection of Europeans. They are always at these type of things. An American should not raise any particular notice, although I wouldn't try to purposely make it known that I was an American."

They sat quietly for a moment, savoring the tea and rice cakes. Then Suu started to rise. "I hope you get done whatever you may be trying to do." Suu said.

"Wait! Wait. Don't go yet. You mean you don't know what I am trying to do?" Francis asked.

"No. All I was told was that you needed to get into the embassy celebration," Suu answered.

"Well," Francis took the plunge, hoping his estimation of her was not wrong. He needed her help. "I need to get into the embassy communications file room. I need your help."

"What? I was not told about that. I cannot help you any more than I already have. I cannot break into any files—" Suu objected.

"I am not asking you to. I just need your help to figure out where the communication files are kept in the embassy. I was told you know the layout of the embassy building. I think the records room would be on the second floor, on the back side of the building where it faces out towards the klong, next to what I think is the embassy's radio room. But I don't know for sure. What can you tell me—how can I get to the file room without being seen?" Francis asked.

Suu studied Francis for a moment. After a long sigh, she said, "All right, I will tell you what I know, but I can't do it in here." Suu surveyed the crowed room. "Come. Let us walk across the street to the park. Take my arm, as if we were lovers."

They both rose from their chair and Francis took Suu's arm. He led her out the front door, keeping her close to himself and smiling at her.

They worked their way across the busy street to the park. "There, go to the bench on the dirt, not the one on the stone walk," Suu directed. Francis wondered what she was up to.

"Well?" Francis asked anxiously as they sat down.

"I have visited the Japanese Embassy several times. Once, while I waited for Jusef to finish some private discussions, I asked to use the ladies' room. When I was in the ladies' room—it is on the second floor—I looked out the window in the toilet cubicle. The windows of the toilet and the radio room both open onto the same alcove. At least I think it was the radio room. I could see what looked like radio equipment through the window."

Suu took the toe of her small foot and scratched out a simple layout of the alcove area in the dirt. "Here," she said as she pointed with her toe, "is where the ladies' room is. Just beyond it—the next door—is the men's toilet," Suu said as she scratched more lines in the dirt. "The hallway off the stairway coming up from the ballroom on the first floor is along here. Here is where the radio room is. Between that window and the one I was looking from was another window. It could have been a file room. It looked like the room was filled with file cabinets."

"Did it look like there were people in the room?" Francis asked.

"As best I could see, no. It looked as if only storage cabinets were in there. But, the most important thing, I think, was the hallway off to one side between the ladies' room and the men's toilet," she said, pointing with her toe again. "I got a good look down the length of it. It is fairly narrow, but it looked like a hallway that might go to the radio room. It had several doors along it. You might be able to go down that hallway to the file room," Suu suggested.

Maybe, Francis thought, *but which door? And if it is locked, which it probably is, I will have to stand in a hallway trying to pick the lock. That is almost sure to lead to disaster.*

"What about a ledge, did you see a ledge—maybe a ledge on the outside of the building between the first and second floors?" Francis asked anxiously.

Suu thought for a moment. "Yes, I saw a ledge. It extends around the length of the alcove, beneath the second-story windows. Vines cover much of it, but it does extend from the window I was at all the way around to the radio room," Suu said.

"That's it then," Francis said with relief. "I go in through the ladies' room."

53

IT WAS NOW OR NEVER. The room was crowded with people, the conversation was animated, and the drinks were flowing. Francis no longer had time to ponder why Seiroku Takamatsu—the test pilot from Swatow—was among the Japanese naval officers in the small group of people, including Suu, gathered about several Thais, one of whom Francis was certain was Jusef. Francis turned from the table of hors d'oeuvres, one of the several he had been circulating among to avoid being drawn into conversation, and set his wine glass down. He took his handkerchief from inside his coat pocket, lightly wiped his fingers, and put the handkerchief back into his outside breast pocket. He looked intently toward Suu. She finally turned to glance at him; Francis saw her eyes widen in recognition.

Francis saw Suu lean close to Jusef and whisper to him. Francis could almost see her body tensing as she excused herself to go to the ladies' room. Francis saw Jusef nod absentmindedly to her and then turn back to his conversation with the naval officers.

Francis watched Suu walk briskly toward the stairway leading to the second floor, twice slowing, but never stopping, to give a bright smile to the several gentlemen who turned towards her. Suu started up the wide stairway. Francis followed.

As Francis reached the top of the stairs, he saw the door marked *Hwajang sil - Yoja* close. He proceeded down the hallway, as if toward the men's toilet beyond the ladies' room. As he reached the first door, it opened. A woman with bright blond hair and obviously fresh lipstick stepped into the hallway, glanced at Francis, and continued on toward the ballroom. Francis nodded slightly and continued walking towards the men's toilet, but slowing, trying to delay having to enter the men's room, knowing that to enter would only complicate what had to follow. Then he heard the ladies' room door open. He paused. "Come quickly," he heard.

He turned, looking past Suu's motioning hand towards the hallway to be sure that it was clear. He stepped into the ladies' room as Suu closed the door tightly behind him.

Suu pointed towards the window above the toilet in one of the two toilet cubicles. "Hurry. Hurry!"

Francis stepped onto the toilet seat. As he did so, Suu stepped into the cubicle and locked the lowered cubicle door. She pointed excitedly toward the window above the toilet.

Francis grabbed the window latch, pushed the window open, and began to hoist himself up. Suu put her hands under Francis' bottom and gave him a push.

THE EARLY EVENING AIR WAS HUMID, but the sweat dripping from Francis' face was not from the humidity. The ground was about twenty feet below and the ledge was narrow. He looked about himself as he held onto the window sill. All was just as it was supposed to be from Suu's drawing in the dirt—there were windows to three rooms: the ladies' room, the radio room, and, he hoped, the file room.

He began edging his way along the ledge, grasping some of the vines to help keep his balance. When he got close to the middle window, he grabbed the window frame. At first the partially opened window didn't want to move, but then he pulled harder—and it opened wide.

Francis listened for voices. He heard voices in the radio room, but not in what should be the file room. Francis looked in. The room was filled with file cabinets. He started to hoist himself into the room. He saw that two doors opened into the room. Both were closed. One apparently led to the radio room. The other door—probably leading to the hallway—was blocked by a file cabinet. Just as he was about to pull himself through the window, the door lock to the radio room rattled as a key was twisted in it. Francis quickly lowered himself back to the ledge. Then the door opened and a light was switched on.

"I hate this filing. Keeping these duplicates in here is a waste of time," said a voice in Japanese from inside the file room. Francis heard a file drawer being pulled open.

Then a voice came from the radio room. "Well, that is part of your job. And if you would do it right the first time, you would not have to come back here on your own time to do it again. Getting secret and non-secret files mixed up—how could you manage to do that?"

Then the voice from the file room said, "You can have this stinking job. When they told me that I would be working in an embassy, I did not think half my time would be spent in a file room."

"Complain, complain. Working here in Bangkok is much better than at home. I can get all the women I want, at good prices," the radio room voice said.

"You had better be careful about that. If the personnel officer finds out about your fucking around all the time, you will be shipped back home," the file room voice said.

"You do not need to worry about that; I am very discreet. Say, why don't you stop that for a minute and go downstairs and get us a plate of that fancy food they are serving down there. I bet you could get some from the kitchen and nobody would know the difference."

"That is a good idea. Anything is better than this filing." Francis heard the file room door close and the rattle of the lock as the door was locked. The light was still on. Francis edged up to the window and looked in. No one was there. Francis didn't wait any longer. He climbed through the window, wondering how long he had before the file clerk would return. As he lowered himself to the floor, he heard the radio operator twisting the radio dial, apparently listening for a particular station. In a moment, music started coming from the radio.

Francis saw a table by the end of the row of file cabinets. On the table amid a disorganized stack of paper were several file folders; one was marked "SECRET." Francis studied the mess on the table for a moment, memorizing the location of each item. Then he picked up the folder marked "SECRET" and began scanning the messages and letters in it. It was obvious why the file clerk was redoing the files; many of the items clearly dealt with only mundane embassy activities.

But then, near the end of the file, he found something—an extended memorandum to the ambassador, a summary report of some type, from the Foreign Ministry. Francis began concentrating on it, trying to store the words in his memory, only barely focusing on the meaning of them. "Burma Road... must close... one of three steps to isolate China... also control Indo-china and Thailand... providing complete blockage of southern border... conclude China War by attrition ... need political support ... French must close China-Indochina border... strategic importance... oil in southeast Asia."

Then another message, apparently a report on proposed military strategy considered in June by the War Ministry and the Imperial Staff. "Military strategy... proposed by Lieutenant-Colonel Nishiura Susumu... need to establish bases in southern Indo-china... support potential actions against... Dutch East Indies... Singapore... no attack on Philippines... in the event British actions draw United States ... maintain readiness... prepare for military actions."

Francis closed the folder and picked up the stack of loose papers. Two sheets down into the stack, he hit pay dirt—a message, stamped top secret, from the War Ministry, dated July 5, 1940, to the Japanese ambassador to Thailand. Francis' carefully read the message—not a policy review, not a proposed strategy, but actual information on forthcoming actions: "In anticipation of successful diplomatic efforts to secure closing of 'Burma Road,' accelerate efforts in Thailand to facilitate Imperial troop entry from China into Indo-china and potential landings in Haiphong within two months this date. Maintain contact with Third Army Commander liaison Captain Jiro Toshiba regarding schedule for possible troop entry and naval liaison Lieutenant Commander Seiroku Takamatsu regarding landing support group status. Seek: (1) continued political support in Thailand for stationing of our troops in northern Indo-china in interest of political stability of region; (2) Thai government requests to French government in Indo-china to agree to our use of Haiphong port facilities and airfields near China border in conjunction with (1) above; (3) Thai agreement to move its troops into Indo-china as show of support of our troops if French resistance encountered by our forces. Offer incentives of self-governance within new Great Asian Program and assurance that Laung Pibun Songgram will remain prime minister. Items (1), (2), and (3) must be achieved by September 30. Troop entry cannot be postponed beyond that date. Provide weekly report upon success towards these items."

Francis stopped as he heard a door open. "Well, here it is," a voice said.

"You really got a plateful. This looks good," the other voice said.

"You're welcome," the first voice said.

"Oh... thanks. Why don't you put the plate on the table here?"

Francis repositioned the papers on the desk and went to the window.

"No, I'm taking the plate into the file room with me—I have to have some diversion from that crap in there. Take a handful—and you can have this stuff here too—I'll take the rest with me."

Francis pulled himself up to the window sill and then hoisted himself though the window opening. As he eased himself down to the ledge, Francis could hear the key rattle in the door lock, with the door knob squeaking as it was turned. Then door to the file room opened. A disgusted voice said, "I hope this doesn't ruin the whole night."

Francis let out a low sigh as he started edging back to the other window. Then he stopped as the words he had just read sank into his consciousness. The message was dated July 5. *My God, two months from that date was last week ... and it is only three weeks until the end of September.*

54

SUU PULLED HER HEAD back into the ladies' room. "It looks clear. Go ahead," she said.

Francis stepped back into the hallway. Suu quickly pushed the door shut behind him. Then, at that moment, a Japanese naval officer—Seiroku Takamatsu—entered the hallway, walking toward Francis. It was too late for Francis to step back into the ladies' room, so Francis decided to just brazen it out, hoping that perhaps Seiroku had not seen him step from the ladies' room—and that he would not remember Francis from the voyage to Hawaii back in 1937. Seiroku looked at Francis, then at the door marked *Hwajang sil - Yoja* from which Francis had just exited. Francis put on a satisfied grin as Seiroku neared Francis. Then Seiroku tightened his brow, as if trying to remember something. Then, in an all-too-brief moment, Seiroku's eyes widened and Francis knew that Seiroku had recognized him. Francis knew he had to do something fast. Francis took one step closer to Seiroku and swung his fist with all his might—and connected with Seiroku's jaw. Seiroku slammed against the wall, his head banking loudly against it. Seiroku crumbled to the floor.

Francis turned and ran down the hall and then bounded down the stairs, taking three steps at a time. He reached the bottom, quickly slowing so as not to attract attention. He walked as rapidly as he could across the ballroom towards the doorway. Then it was out the door towards the embassy gate. Just as he reached it he heard a shout. Francis shoved the gate guard aside and started running.

Francis looked back as he ran. He saw Seiroku and two other men running after him. Francis ran harder, but the people in the street kept slowing him down. He pushed them aside as best he could. Behind him, he heard screams and yells as the three Japanese knocked more people out of the way. This could not go on for long, Francis thought, as he continued to run, crashing into people on the street.

Then he realized he was heading up Phra Sumen Road, the street that paralleled the Bang Lam Klong—the wide and deep canal separating the commercial district from the narrow streets of the Chinese ghetto, where he could easily lose the men—if he could just get there. But wait, at the next corner, the tea shop where he had first met Suu—the shop with two entry doors. Francis ducked into the shop. He ran across the room of surprised early evening diners, and then out the door on the side street leading to the klong.

The three Japanese ran into the cafe after Francis, stopped, and began looking at the diners. Then Seiroku shouted as he pointed to the side door.

As he heard the tea shop door bang open, Francis dived into the water of the klong, getting a mouthful of dirty water as he did. He spit it out as he came to the surface, took a deep breath, and dived deep. He opened his eyes, but all he could see was a brown murkiness. His eyes began to burn, finally forcing him to close them.

He continued swimming as long as he could, feeling a muddy current pulling him downstream as he did. He finally had to come to the surface, coughing, spitting, swallowing, and spitting again. He looked back. On the small dock from which he had dived, nearly a hundred yards away, were the three Japanese, surveying the water. Francis took another gulp of air, let himself go under again, and began swimming towards the opposite shore.

Francis came up again near a small dock with numerous small boats tied to it. As he pulled himself out of the water, a few people looked at him. Then they turned back to what they had been doing, saying nothing. Francis took his wet handkerchief out of his pocket, wiped his face, and then rubbed off the small globs of brown and black feces that had stuck to the front of his jacket. He threw the handkerchief into the water and began walking down the narrow streets of the ghetto, toward the American embassy.

55

FRANCIS WAS STILL TIRED. The sweat was pouring off him even now as he sat at his desk and began to look over last night's intercepts. He still hadn't gotten back into the swing of things; it was difficult to focus his thoughts.

He had arrived in Manila four days ago after a long, grueling flight from Singapore. He had repeated to Scott, in Japanese, the contents of the messages he had read in the Japanese embassy almost immediately after he had gotten back to the American embassy in the early morning hours, still wet from his swim in the klong. Then he had spent a long hour putting the same information down on paper; then another hour writing the English translation. Scott was ecstatic with what Francis had brought back. Then after only two hours of sleep, he was on a plane to Singapore with Scott where he gave the same information to Mason at the British Embassy. Mason was equally ecstatic. "Superb, old man, superb," was all that Mason could say, over and over. Then, the flight back to Clark Field on a U.S. Army Air Force plane. Back in his quarters at Cavite, Francis slept for nearly sixteen hours straight.

Yesterday had been his first full day back at Post Y. It had been sort of a confusing day, trying to get up to speed on what had been going on since he had left. It was hard to believe he had been gone almost a month.

Now this morning—he just couldn't seem to concentrate. Well, some coffee might help.

Ensign Louis Frankhill was standing by the coffee urn as Francis entered the small room which also served as Post Y's kitchen. "Morning, Francis. How are you doing?" Louis asked as he finished pouring his cup of coffee.

Francis smiled. "Okay, I guess. Little tired. I can't… seem to… get started." Francis suddenly felt weak. He stumbled, fell to knees, and then slumped to the floor. "Jesus Christ, I feel like I'm going to puke." That was the last thing he said before he lost consciousness. Louis began yelling for help.

FRANCIS SLOWLY OPENED his eyes. He could see he was in a hospital room. There was an intravenous needle in his arm with a tube to a glucose bag hanging on a stand by the bed. He felt like he had been run over by a truck. God, his mouth was so dry. He tried to say something. For a moment, no words would come out. Then a tiny noise—his voice: "Water, please, some water."

A nurse hurried into the room. "Lieutenant, did you say something? Are you awake?"

"Yes," came the weak response, "Yes, water."

The nurse poured some water into a paper cup from the pitcher on the bedside table and helped Francis lift his head to sip it. "Not too much, not too fast. You have been out for almost two days. Let me get the doctor."

A few moments later, a Navy doctor came in. "Well, I see you may be among the living again. How do you feel?" the doctor asked.

"Like crap," Francis answered.

"Well, that's to be expected. You have had a bout of typhoid; still aren't out of the woods yet. But at least you're conscious, and that's encouraging. But how in the hell did you catch typhoid?" Francis had a damn good idea, but said nothing. "Well, we have you pumped full of medicine. You're going to feel pretty rotten for the next several days. Just hang in there and let the medicine work. Go back to sleep for now."

FRANCIS WAS IN AND OUT of sleep for the next several days, not really sure—not really caring—what was going on. But finally he woke with his head clear, but not knowing what day it was. He still felt lousy, but at least he didn't feel like he was going to die. He lay there for a few moments, adjusting to the morning light and the sounds from the hallway. Then his discomfort began to grow as he realized he needed to pee—bad. He tried to lift himself up so he could go to the bathroom, but not realizing he had a catheter inserted in his penis. He was so weak he could barely move, but he tried to push himself up with his arms. The room began to spin. The intravenous needle in his arm pulled on the tube to the glucose bag; the bag and stand fell to the floor with a loud crash. The catheter pulled from his penis. Francis let out a feeble howl.

"Lieutenant, Lieutenant, please be careful," said a pretty, young Filipino nurse as she scurried into the room. "Why are you trying to get up? You must stay in bed."

"But I need to pee!" Francis said in pain.

"Well, here, let me help you," the young nurse said as she helped Francis to a sitting position. She reached down and picked up the catheter. "What do you think this is for?"

"I didn't know the damn thing was in me. And I still have to pee," Francis said weakly.

"Well, we always have this," the nurse said as she pulled a bed pan from under the bed. Then, to Francis' humiliation, she pulled back his gown, put the pan between his legs and said, "Okay, go ahead."

IN THE FOLLOWING DAYS Francis' condition continued to improve. And the visits of the young nurse who had helped him in his "time of need," as Francis delicately referred to it in his own mind, came to be one of the events to which Francis looked forward. Maria, as he learned her name to be, was effervescent in her care of him; she was just what he needed to get his spirits up.

And that was something he really needed. McDonald had flown in from Hawaii to brief him on the consequences of his exploits in Bangkok. Maria had helped Francis into a wheelchair and McDonald had wheeled him out to the hospital yard where they could talk without being overheard.

"You really had us worried there for awhile, you know, Francis."

"Well, thanks for the concern, but what pisses me off is that, from what I have seen in the papers, the Japs just walked right into Indo-china," Francis said.

"That's about right, Francis. Very little resistance. Practically welcomed with open arms by the Vichy French crowd there," McDonald said.

"Then what the hell did I go through all that crap in Bangkok for?" Francis asked.

"Francis, the information you brought back was invaluable. It has given us a much better insight into Japanese intentions in Southeast Asia, as well as some good information to add to our knowledge of the Jap Navy command structure—people like that Lieutenant Commander Takamatsu, who we figure is on Yamamoto's staff—a real right hand man. But in so far as it directly affected Indo-china—I know, I know, that's why you went in—it didn't make any difference. The British, so Mason tells us, concluded that the situation was deteriorating so badly in England that they couldn't offer assistance to the French. Without a guarantee of support and assistance from the British, any potential French resistance just collapsed."

Francis' last comment summed up the whole situation: "Crap."

56

"MARIA, WHY IS IT that I only see you every few days, and never on weekends? Are you out with your boyfriend?" Francis teased as Maria came in to check on him the day after McDonald's visit.

"You tease me, Lieutenant. But I do not have a boy friend. I am too busy for one now. The reason I do not see you every day, Lieutenant Marian, is because I am in training. I am here at the American hospital as part of my training. I spend much of my time at some of the Filipino clinics outside Manila. There are clinics at some churches on Battan and the west coast of Luzon that I spend several days at a time during the month. They are in dire need. Medical care, particularly for the children, is so limited here in the Philippines. Did you know that building hospitals, and filling them with good doctors, is one of the priority programs for the commonwealth. We even have a Department of National Health. It is projected to be one of the top programs in five years," Maria said.

"You seem to be quite an expert," Francis said in surprise.

"Oh yes, my uncle says it is very important that I know these things. But I talk too much. Here, take your medicine, and then you can get out of bed and get walking. You need your exercise," Maria said.

"Okay, okay. You're such a slave driver," Francis kidded as he started to get up and put on his robe.

"Oh, I almost forgot," Maria said, as she reached into her pocket. "This letter came for you today—from the United States."

Francis took the letter from Maria. It was from his sister, Marge. He opened it and began reading.

"Is it good news, Lieutenant Marian?" Maria asked in a moment.

"Well, it doesn't look like bad news," Francis said as he sat down on the edge of the bed and continued to read. Marge's letter, beyond the usual "how was everything and everybody" questions and answers, said she and her boy friend Marty had finally decided to get married—something Francis thought was about time. She went on about how she and Marty would continue to live in the house with Ma, so they could take care of her, which was a relief to Francis. But then, at the last of the letter, was a startling paragraph:

A strange thing happened last week, Francis. Ma told me about a telephone call she got one day from a woman named Elaine. Ma wasn't sure exactly when it was—you know she doesn't remember dates too well anymore—but it was probably in the last week or so. The woman said she knew you from Washington and that she was traveling through Chicago on her way to Colorado. She called to see if you were in town. Of course you weren't, so Ma told her that you were overseas. Ma was afraid to tell her where, because she was sort of suspicious of the woman, not knowing who she was and all. If I had been home when the call came, I probably could have gotten more information, but only Ma was home. Ma did ask if she wanted to leave a message, but according to Ma, the woman didn't. And here is the funny thing, Francis. Ma said the woman started to cry as she was hanging up. So who is this Elaine?

Francis' throat got dry, and tears began to well up in his eyes. Memories of the times he and Elaine had together in Washington came rushing back—as did that last rainy night in Washington. *Elaine. Jesus, after all this time. I can remember every detail of her. God, how I love that woman. And it still hurts losing her. But if Elaine tried to call me, maybe things are better now. Maybe, just maybe, things aren't over yet for us—at least Elaine's call gives me some hope.* If only there were some way he could find out what the situation with Elaine was. He didn't want to accidentally let Elaine's husband, Lewis, find out about Elaine and him, but he needed to find out what was going on. He needed to try to wiggle some information about Elaine out of Lewis Franklin without Franklin getting suspicious. *But before I can do anything,* Francis thought to himself, *I have to get out of this damn hospital.*

Maria looked at Francis. "Are you all right, Lieutenant Marian. Is there bad news?"

"I hope not, Maria—maybe, just maybe, it might be good news—very good news," Francis answered.

"Well, I have some news, and I am sure it is good news, Lieutenant Marian," Maria said.

"What is it, Maria?" Francis asked.

"The doctor says it will not be long before you can leave and return to duty. Since you will be leaving soon, I would be honored if you could meet my uncle. You have been my special training project; and I have mentioned you to him several times. He has expressed an interest in meeting you. There is a party this weekend. He and some others will be there. Would you care to go as my escort?" Maria asked.

"I think that would be great, Maria. Will they let me out of here?" Francis asked.

"I have already asked the doctor. He said it would be okay as long as I get you back before too late. I will have your uniform pressed and bring it with me when I pick you up Saturday afternoon."

MARIA PICKED FRANCIS up in a sporty, late model Oldsmobile convertible, not quite what Francis had expected. After about an hour drive, they turned into a long driveway leading up to a large, palatial-like building, with cars parked everywhere along the driveway. This was not just a simple little party. As Maria braked the car in front of the building, valets ran out and opened the car doors.

Francis took Maria's arm to steady himself and walked with her into the building. Quite a few people turned to say hello to her as they walked in. Once inside, she suggested some refreshment. Francis thought that was a good idea. He was still weak, and felt hot.

As Francis took the cup of punch offered to him, Maria looked about the large ballroom. "My uncle—I don't see him, Lieutenant Marian. Perhaps he is on the patio. Why don't you wait here and relax. I'll find him and come back and get you. He really wants to meet you," Maria said.

"That's sounds good to me. I wait here and cool off a bit," Francis answered.

Maria turned and started toward the tall French doors at the back of the room.

As Francis sipped his punch, he looked around the room. It was filled with a mixture of civilians and military personnel, clustered in small groups, talking. A small violin orchestral group played in the background. Some of the military types were U.S. Army, others were Commonwealth of Philippines Army. *Damn*, he thought, *there is a lot of brass here, and I may be lowest rank Navy guy here. Damn, what did I get into?*

Suddenly a voice came from behind him. Francis turned.

"Well, Lieutenant Marian, we meet again," Breidstein said.

Francis looked at Breidstein in surprise, then collected his thoughts. "Yes, so we do."

"What brings you here, Lieutenant," Breidstein asked.

"I might ask the same of you, *Herr* Breidstein," Francis answered.

"So you might, Lieutenant. I am only here with friends for an enjoyable afternoon party. But how long has it been, almost three years—since our, shall I say, encounter, in Nanking?" Breidstein asked.

"I believe you are correct. That *was* an interesting meeting, wasn't it," Francis answered mockingly.

"Yes, but the tables are turned now, aren't they? How does it feel?' Breidstein asked.

"What do you mean?" Francis asked, recognizing that Breidstein was trying to bait him.

"It is obvious, Lieutenant, isn't it? The Japanese entered Indo-china virtually without resistance. And the British have given into the Japanese demands not to use the Burma Road, have they not? General Chiang and his China will soon be completely isolated. And then all those millions your president gave to the generalissimo—to let the Chinese fight the Japanese and keep America's own feet clean—will have gone to naught. You Americans seem to be rather good at letting others do your dirty work—first China, *and now the Philippines.*"

Francis wasn't quite sure what to say. Breidstein had pretty well hit the nail on the head. *But by damn*, Francis fumed, *I am not going to admit it to this goddamn German, Breidstein.* Francis could feel his temperature rising, and it wasn't because he was still sick. *And just what does Breidstein mean by "and now the Philippines?" His comment doesn't seem to make any sense. Is Breidstein hinting at something?*

"Cat got your tongue, Lieutenant? You look a little peaked—a bit too close to the truth, perhaps?"

Francis was about to tell Breidstein to shove it when Maria walked up.

"I've found him, Lieutenant. Come on. I can't wait for him to meet you. He's on the patio," Maria said as she grabbed Francis arm.

Francis nodded towards Breidstein, "Another time, *Herr* Breidstein."

"Yes, another time," Breidstein answered, as he stared at Maria, a frown coming to his face.

"Did I interrupt something?" Maria asked as she led Francis across the ballroom.

"No, Maria, you didn't. Just a little friendly conversation with someone I run into from time to time," Francis answered.

Finally, after weaving through the crowd of people in the ballroom, Francis and Maria got to the tall French doors leading to the patio. What Francis saw on the patio made him gulp. "Maria, those people out there, in the middle of them—isn't that ... isn't that General MacArthur?" Francis asked.

"Oh yes, it is. Do you know Field Marshall MacArthur?" Maria asked.

"Only by reputation. What is going on here? Maria, just who is your uncle?" Francis asked.

"Come, let me introduce you to him. He is right over there." With that, she took Francis' arm and led him directly toward the group standing about MacArthur.

"Uncle," Maria said as she approached the group. A short, handsome Filipino man standing next to MacArthur turned.

"Oh, you finally got here, Maria. I thought you might have changed your plans. Is this your patient that you have been talking so much about?" the short man asked.

"Yes, Uncle. May I introduce Lieutenant Francis Marian," Maria said.

All Francis could see was MacArthur staring at him.

"Francis, this is my uncle, President Manual Quezon," Maria said.

"Uh... uh... a pleasure, sir." *I hope*, Francis thought, as he continued to feel MacArthur's stare.

"Maria, you remember General MacArthur?" President Quezon asked.

"A pleasure to see you again, General MacArthur. How is your wife?" Maria asked.

"It's my pleasure. And my wife is fine. In fact, she is here, somewhere. I am sure she would enjoy seeing you again. How long has it been, almost two months?" MacArthur asked.

"Closer to three months, General," Maria answered.

"May I introduce your guest, Maria?" Quezon asked.

"That's why I brought him along, Uncle," Maria answered.

"Uh, well, sir... uh... I don't want to intrude. Really... it's not necessary ... really," Francis stammered.

"Nonsense. My niece has said so much about you," Quezon said.

"Field Marshall MacArthur, may I introduce a friend of my niece—actually, a patient she has been working with at the Cavite naval hospital. She is in nurse's training over there, you know. Seems the Lieutenant has been going through quite a bout of typhoid fever. General, Lieutenant Marian," Quezon said, finishing his introduction of Francis.

"Good afternoon, *Lieutenant*," MacArthur said "What brings you here today? A little far from Cavite, isn't it?"

"Yes sir. You are certainly right about that, sir… General… sir."

X

TOKYO

57

FRANCIS WATCHED THE LAUNCH come across the windy bay, spray being kicked up by the bow as it bounced on the wave tops. The December day looked—and felt—cold. Francis pulled his coat tighter about himself. As the boat neared the side of the PBY, Francis picked up the two diplomatic bags handcuffed to his wrist and, bending low, stepped wearily to the rear door. He had gone from Manila to Guam, to Wake Island, to Hawaii, to Midway, to here—in less than five days, with a day of briefing in Hawaii by McDonald.

Several minutes later, Francis stepped from the boat to the dock, his legs more stable now. As he did, he saw someone get out of a large car with American flags on the fenders and hurry down the dock, pushing his way through the crowd of people. Francis recognized him as Albert Cairnes, the man from the cruise to Manila on the *Empress of Canada*, from what seemed like ages ago. *Apparently,* Francis thought, the *man got his transfer like he said he would on the cruise to Manila. I wonder if his wife was transferred with him?*

Behind Cairnes trailed another man, also forcing his way through the crowd, but with less success than Cairnes.

"I'm sorry I'm late, Marian, but as usual, the traffic in this country is unpredictable; damn bicycles everywhere—totally bog down the traffic," Cairnes said in obvious disgust as he got within speaking distance of Francis. "I see you have the bags. Let's go, Ambassador Grew is waiting."

Cairnes turned, obviously expecting Francis to follow. Francis knew Cairnes recognized him, but Cairnes acted as if their last meeting had been only yesterday, not three and a half years ago.

Seeing Francis look at the pile of packages and boxes in the launch, Cairnes said, "Smythe there will bring those items along later," as he pointed to the other man who had finally worked his way through the crowd. "Come on, Marian. The car is at the end of the dock."

Smythe, obviously a man who enjoyed food, smiled and, unlike Cairnes, extended his hand. "Welcome, I think, to Japan."

"Thanks." Francis started off after Cairnes.

AS THE BIG BUICK with the diplomatic plates moved through the city streets of Yokohama, Cairnes began a rambling commentary on Japanese life. The condescension in his voice was unmistakable. "It takes about an hour and a half to get to the embassy in Tokyo. Until they started restricting our landings to Yokohama, it would take only about thirty minutes. The restrictions have gotten pretty severe. I guess it all started in the spring of thirty-eight when the Japanese Parliament suspended civil rights for the country—it just sort of spilled over onto the embassy staffs here as well. When I got here after our transfer from Manila, there were already restrictions on movement of embassy people outside the Tokyo-Yokohama area. The arrest of some British subjects by the *Kempei*—military police, that is—here in July sort of put all of us on notice to be very careful about where we go."

Francis nodded. He had been well briefed on the *Kempei*, as well as the *Tokko*, the Japanese secret police, before leaving Pearl Harbor.

"I suppose the plane couldn't bring you along the route that lets you get a good look at Mount Fuji," Cairnes declared as much as asked.

Francis finally got a word in. "That's right. I didn't get to see it. The pilot said that if the day had been clearer we might have been able to see it in the distance. Actually, we were picked up by two Japanese escort planes about fifty miles out. They flew in with us all the way until we landed on the bay."

"See, what did I tell you? No freedom over here. Everything and everybody is watched."

THEY WERE NOW WELL INTO TOKYO. Cairnes was still doing most of the talking. "We are getting close to the Imperial Palace area. We will be swinging around the eastern side of the Imperial Palace grounds. We had better not stop to look—might be interpreted the wrong way, particularly by our escort."

"Escort?" Francis asked with surprise.

"Oh, you haven't noticed," Cairnes said with superiority. "Ever since the signing of the Tripartite Pact in September, things have gotten progressively worse around here. See the dark blue car behind us?" Francis turned and looked out the rear window, easily spotting the blue car. "*Tokko*—secret police," Cairnes announced. "A car always follows the embassy car. You can't go anywhere without being followed. God, I will be glad when Judith and I can return to the States. Judith—you remember her from the *Empress of Canada*, I'm sure—and some of the other nonessential personnel, mostly the wives, will be leaving within a couple of months. I might be leaving a few months after that."

With the comment about his wife, Cairnes became silent. Francis watched the city go by.

The car finally pulled into the embassy compound. A distinguished but tired-looking man, obviously Ambassador Grew, came down the front steps. Cairnes quickly jumped out of the car. Francis followed more slowly, struggling with the diplomatic pouches. Ambassador Grew shook Francis' free hand. "Well, Lieutenant Marian, I see Deputy Cairnes has successfully retrieved you from the docks. Did he give you his travelogue description of the city on the drive up from the harbor?"

"Yes sir." Francis answered with a stretch of the truth—and a loud voice. He had already been told that Grew was hard of hearing. "A very interesting city." And, as best Francis could determine thus far, consistent with his Hawaiian briefing.

"Well, let's get down to business. I want to know why State was so concerned about your arrival. Let's go up to my office where we can talk."

Grew led the way to his second-floor office. Cairnes followed behind Francis.

"All right, Lieutenant, let's get through the formalities. Here is your receipt for the two bags," Grew said as he signed a custody form and handed it to Francis. Francis reached into his pocket for the key to the handcuffs.

"Ambassador Grew, I was instructed to request that you read the letter in the red envelope as soon as possible, in my presence," Francis said.

Grew looked at Francis with raised eyebrows, but complied. Grew took the keys and opened the two pouches. After a minute of searching, he found the red envelope. It had "TOP SECRET" stamped on the front and back. He turned to his chair and sat down, carefully slitting open the envelope with the pearl-handled letter opener he took from his desk drawer. He began to read. Francis and Cairnes continued to stand.

After a minute, Grew said to Cairnes, "Mr. Cairnes, please leave Lieutenant Marian and me alone. I will call you when I need you." Cairnes left, with a quizzical look at Marian.

Grew returned to his reading as Cairnes left. After a few minutes, he pulled a large ashtray to the center of his desk, moving papers out of the way.

He put the envelope and its contents in the ash tray. He struck a match and set them afire. When the small blaze had extinguished itself, he looked at Francis. "All right, Lieutenant, you had better tell me the details."

58

"AND SO, MR. AMBASSADOR," Francis said to Grew some twenty minutes later as Francis honed in on his reason for coming to Tokyo, "Japan is under considerable pressure from Hitler to attack Russia along the northern frontier of Manchuria. The War Department believes the cease-fire treaty the Soviets and Japanese signed last year is good only so long as Japan thinks it serves their purposes. But how long will it be before the Japanese decide to expand their power base in Manchuria right across the Amur into Russia?" Francis asked rhetorically.

"I don't know, but I wouldn't be surprised if it were a damn short time," Grew answered as he pursed his lips, making his mustache bunch into a hairy mass under his nose.

"You hit the nail on the head, Mr. Ambassador. We don't know," Francis said emphatically. "But we can be sure the Japanese don't trust the Germans to keep the Soviets occupied or under control," Francis said.

Grew nodded in agreement. "Fighting along the northern Manchurian border could explode anytime. And the Japanese government's control of its army up there is almost nonexistent."

"And what happens, Mr. Ambassador, if either side, the Japanese or the Soviets, makes a move and attacks the other up there?" Francis answered his own question. "The Soviets will feel compelled to reinforce, significantly, its military strength along the Manchurian and Mongolian borders. And that's exactly what we cannot allow to happen," Francis said with finality.

Grew broke in. "Now I certainly do not want more fighting to start, but what if it did? Would not that relieve some of the pressure on China and Chiang Kai-shek?"

"Probably, but the War Department has a much greater concern. And here is the real crux of why I am here, Mr. Ambassador. For reasons I don't know, the War Department is convinced that Hitler plans to attack Russia this spring," Francis said.

"Jesus! That could change the whole complexion of things—the balance of world power! If Germany were to take over Russia like they did Poland, God help us," Grew said.

"Yes. And if Germany does attack, the Soviets can't have their forces spread out all across Siberia fighting the Japanese. Hitler would have a cakewalk all the way to Moscow. And it's not just an issue of Japan initiating an attack on the Russians. The Soviets cannot get the idea that Japan is so weak that they can attack the Japanese, grab a hunk of Manchuria, and get away with it. Either possibility puts us in a losing position if it diverts Russian forces from the German threat. That's where the real danger lies," Francis said.

"But can't we just let the Soviets know about the German plans?" Grew asked.

"Not directly, for several reasons. First, the War Department is worried this whole thing may be just some sort of ruse on the Germans' part. Second, it could compromise our intelligence sources by alerting the Soviets to what we know about German plans, an unacceptable compromise in the War Department's view. And if we tell the Russians directly, the Russians might decide to attack the Germans first, and then we would have a real mess. And finally, if we tell the Russians, they probably wouldn't believe us anyway," Francis explained.

"So what can we do, Lieutenant? We are damned if do and damned if we don't," Grew said.

Francis answered Grew's conundrum. "We are not going to tell the Russians. But what we are going to do is let them think they found out on their own that the Japanese are shifting their attention to the south, to the East Indies and Malaya, in preparation for an attack there. Then Russia, so we hope, will not feel compelled to mass its forces on the Siberian border. But we are going to let the Soviets know only after it's too late for them to try to move their forces from west of the Urals to mount a preemptive attack on the Japanese to grab Manchuria. And in the process, we are going to let the Japanese know that the Russians are not going to build up their forces on the Manchurian border, so the Japanese will not feel compelled to transfer more troops to the area," Francis said.

"You mean, Lieutenant, all we are going to do, in essence, is merely ensure that each side believes the other is going to honor the agreement they have already made?" Grew said in astonishment.

"Yes, Ambassador, that's all—if you want to call it that," Francis said with a grin.

59

"SEE LIEUTENANT," Judith Cairnes said, "didn't I tell you there would be a great crowd here? I told you it was about time you got out of the embassy and enjoyed some social life. Grew is just an old worry-wart. Now who would do anything on New Year's eve?"

Then Judith smiled and waved her fingers at a large-bosomed lady, saying under her breath to Francis, "God, there's the Spanish deputy ambassador's wife … ah … Violeta Gutierrez, or something like that. She is such a flirt. I don't care if the Spanish are hosting this party, I don't want to talk to her. Quick, over this way, Lieutenant."

Francis followed Judith as she led him in the opposite direction from the Spanish deputy ambassador's wife.

"Come along, Lieutenant Marian," Judith said, in a normal voice again. "There are so many people for you to meet. Aren't you glad I brought you along?"

Judith began working her way through the crowd before Francis had a chance to really say anything. She stopped every now and then, chatting briefly with acquaintances and introducing Francis as the new attaché, grabbing drinks from the trays of passing waiters as she did. By the time they were almost across the room, Judith had downed two drinks. But Francis held firmly onto his first. He was determined to keep a clear head. He had a specific purpose for being at the Spanish embassy party, and it was not to get drunk with Judith Cairnes.

Judith had just grabbed another drink off a swaying tray when Francis finally saw Breidstein in a small crowd of quietly talking men. Francis began moving toward them.

"There's someone I know—Werner Breidstein," Francis said. "You remember him, don't you, Judith—from the cruise to Manila. Why don't we say hello?" Francis asked.

Francis saw an embarrassed expression come to Judith's face. "If we must," Judith said.

In a moment, Judith and Francis reached Breidstein. He smiled as they approached.

"*Herr* Breidstein, it is so good to see you again," Judith said as she extended her hand to Breidstein. "And you must remember Lieutenant Marian. He's our newest attaché."

"Hello, Judith," Breidstein said as he took Judith's hand, brought it to his lips, and kissed it. "It's a pleasure to see you. I didn't realize you were here."

"I didn't know you were her either, until the Lieutenant saw you," Judith said as she pulled her hand from Breidstein's grip.

Breidstein turned his head to look at Francis. "Well, we meet again, Lieutenant. I *am* surprise to see you here—an attaché at the embassy. I am impressed. Your navy must have re-evaluated your talents. You were into radios at one time, weren't you," Breidstein said smoothly.

"I still am. I am only temporary—attaché, that is. I am providing some communication training to some embassy staff—trying to teach embassy people how to operate embassy radios a little more effectively. They need to use a little common sense when sending messages and not scatter embassy business all over Japan," Francis answered innocuously.

"How long has it been—only about ... five months—at President Quezon's residence, was it not?" Breidstein asked.

"That right," Francis answered, remembered how Breidstein had baited him and made him so mad. Francis wanted to say something—now—in return but, instead, held his tongue. Francis then continued smoothly, "Politics always makes for interesting discussion, irrespective of who has the upper hand. Of course, our emotion tends to be the one that always gets the upper hand—and only make us feel foolish later about the things we sometimes say."

Breidstein looked at Francis with a quizzical look.

Francis continued, "Fortunately I don't have to worry about politics anymore, except perhaps only in an academic way. Perhaps we can continue our discussion—later this evening, or over lunch sometime soon," Francis said with all the politeness he could muster.

Breidstein raised one eyebrow. "Perhaps."

"You two have met ... since the cruise?" Judith broke in.

"Yes, from time to time our paths have crossed. How long have you been in Tokyo, Lieutenant?" Breidstein asked.

"Several weeks. And you?" asked Francis.

"Several days," Breidstein answered. Francis saw Judith's jaw tightened.

"Some of my business operations are here in the home islands; they regularly bring me to Tokyo," Breidstein said.

I bet they do, Francis thought. *And,* he wondered, *why is Judith Cairnes so obviously upset by you?* Maybe there was more between Judith Cairnes and Breidstein than met the eye. He was going to have to check into that. It might be just what he needed to complete his plan.

WHY DIDN'T WERNER CALL ME WHEN HE GOT TO TOKYO, fumed Judith as she waited for her taxi to arrive. She had begged off from any more gallivanting with Francis, saying she wanted to get back to the embassy to get some rest before tonight's party, but really wanting to confront Werner. *He couldn't be so busy that he couldn't have called me when he arrived. And it's the holidays, no less. He couldn't be doing much business during the New Year's holidays. Well, I am going to get this straightened out—tonight. I am going to march right up to his hotel room and find out what is going on.*

She reached the Europa-Tokyo about six. If she knew Werner, he would be back before seven to change into dinner clothes; he seldom went out in the evening in Tokyo in ordinary business attire. She didn't even need to ask what room he would be in. It was always the same: top floor facing the bay.

She went directly to the top floor and knocked on the door, but there was no answer. She knocked again, only harder this time. No answer. One more time she pounded, so hard her knuckles hurt. No answer. Well, she would be damned if she were going to stand out here in the hallway waiting!

She went to the house phone on the table at the end of the hall. "*Herr* Breidstein and I accidentally locked ourselves out of his suite. Could you send someone up to let us in?"

"And what room would that be, madam?" the clerk asked.

"Why the bay view penthouse, of course, where he always stays when he comes to your hotel," Judith answered arrogantly, to assure the clerk she had an obvious right to be in Breidstein's apartment.

"Certainly. I will send up a bellboy immediately," the clerk answered.

Several minutes later, a bellboy, with a large key ring in his hand, got off the elevator.

"Oh, you finally got here. Thank goodness. Please open the door."

"But I thought *Herr* Breidstein needed the key," the bellboy said.

"Well, I am with *Herr* Breidstein. Please hurry, I have to go to the bathroom." She reached into her purse, extracting a large bill. *Thank God they take tips in this hotel.* For once she appreciated the Western custom of giving tips.

"Certainly, madam," he answered as he opened the door and pocketed the tip.

Once inside, she sat down and began to wait.

JUDITH HAD BEEN WAITING about half an hour when she heard the elevator stop. *That must be him, finally,* she thought. She got up to greet him, thinking of what might develop tonight if she could get things straightened out. But then she heard a woman's voice. Werner had brought a woman with him! *God, I can't be found here now,* she thought. She looked around, saw the closet and stepped into it, pulling the door closed. But thinking about it more, she opened the door slightly, so she would be better able to hear.

As the apartment door opened, the woman said, "Werner," but the rest was lost to Judith. They were talking in Spanish. But Judith didn't need a translation; she knew who it was. She had a perfect reflective view of the couch in the mirror opposite the closet door. Violeta Gutierrez was standing in front of the couch by Werner, reaching up to kiss him. Werner was responding, putting his hand on her back, then sliding it down to her buttocks. *Just the way he kisses me, damn it!*

As Judith watched, she became more and more angry. After several moments of increasingly arduous caresses, the lovely, buxom Mrs. Gutierrez sat down, pulling Werner down with her. He seemed to know what to do. He kneeled between her spread legs. Violeta smiled and slowly, tantalizingly pulled up her dress. Werner reached up and pulled down her panties. He lowered his shoulders, then his head. *God, he's going to do that to her?* Judith thought. *He said he had never done that with anyone but me. That bastard. How long has he been running around like this? Probably damn long. That bastard!*

Finally it was over, the moaning had stopped. Werner and Violeta had gotten up and gone into the bathroom to get themselves in order. Werner returned with a dinner jacket on. Violeta came out, her lipstick and dress straight. She reached over and put her hand to Werner's crotch. Judith didn't have any difficulty understanding Violeta's "Oo, la, la." Werner picked up her jacket from the couch and put it on her. He opened the door and they left.

Judith waited a few minutes more, fuming, before she got out of the closet. As she left, she said to herself, *I'm going to fix that bastard's balls somehow.*

60

"WELL, GOOD AFTERNOON, *Herr* Sorge, it is pleasure to finally meet you," Ambassador Grew said in a polite voice as Richard Sorge was ushered into Grew's outer office three weeks into the new year.

"I thought I should bring *Herr* Sorge here to your office, Mr. Ambassador," Smyth said. "Guests are already starting to arrive for the inauguration party and the library doesn't look like it will be undisturbed for very long."

Grew shook Sorge's hand with rigid formality. "That is quite all right, Smyth," Grew said. "You can return to your other duties."

"The pleasure is all mine, Mr. Ambassador. I am very pleased that you have agreed to an interview. You have always been on the top of my list of potential interviewees," Sorge said with his usual opening line to butter up an interviewee.

"You flatter me, *Herr* Sorge," Grew responded.

"Oh no, Mr. Ambassador, my readers will be extremely interested in what you may have to say, what views you have on the world situation," Sorge said, continuing his attempt to relax Grew before the interview really got under way.

"Not my views, *Herr* Sorge, America's views. Shall we go into my office?" Grew asked, as he extended his hand in invitation.

"A pleasure, Mr. Ambassador," Sorge replied.

Grew lead Sorge past his personal secretary, busy at work typing. "No interruptions, Miss Adams," he said in a perfunctory tone without a look at her.

"Yes, Mr. Ambassador," the stogy Miss Adams answered.

As Sorge passed Miss Adams' desk, he saw she was apparently typing up some handwritten notes—*probably Grew's*, he thought. But then he almost stopped, having to force himself not to stare. Sticking out from under the corner of the handwritten sheets he saw the top portion of an official-looking document. But it was not an American document; it was one with the official Japanese War Ministry seal at its top. As he hesitated ever so slightly, Miss Adams reached over and straightened the pile of papers into a well-aligned stack, covering the document. Sorge continued into Grew's inner office, seating himself in front of Grew's large desk.

"Well, how would you like to begin, *Herr* Sorge?" Grew asked.

"Perhaps I could start by asking why you consented to having this interview, such a long time after my request?" Sorge asked, thinking to throw an easy question to Grew to start the interview.

"I think it would be obvious, *Herr* Sorge. World conditions are deteriorating, in large measure, I might add, because of the actions of your government. The American government feels that by letting the German people know our views directly, through interviews like this, a better understanding between our countries, in the interest of peace and harmony, can be achieved," Grew said with a smile.

"Mr. Ambassador, I am apolitical. I attempt only to report the actions and views of others. But are you suggesting that the views of the German people are not in harmony with the German government?" Sorge asked accusingly.

"Well, let us consider the facts, *Herr* Sorge. It is generally recognized that *Herr* Hitler was elected by dubious means—"

Sorge cut in. "Mr. Ambassador, those are, as I understand them, only accusations of disgruntled losers. I have yet to see anything reported in any responsible fashion, by which I mean backed with substantiated information, that Hitler's election as Chancellor was anything except what it should have been—open and honest."

"But *Herr* Sorge, *Herr* Hitler's actions speak for themselves. He has led the German people into a bitter battle with England. In this last year alone, Germany has taken over control of the Low Counties and Norway. This is not something the German people want. Were it not for the forced conscription of the German people, I believe—President Roosevelt believes—that Germany would be unable to continue its, shall we say, aggressive acts," Grew said.

"But has not the United States instituted forced conscription—a draft, I believe you call it?" Sorge broke in, countering Grew's remarks.

"Yes, but... that... is of a different nature," Grew responded. "And be that as it may, America fully realizes the difficult economic times the German people have had to endure because of the worldwide depression. President Roosevelt wishes me to express to the German people the willingness of the

American government to assist, in a meaningful financial way, German economic development. America would not be adverse—"

There was a knock at the door. "Mr. Ambassador, please excuse me," said Miss Adams as she opened the door slightly.

"I said no interruptions, Miss Adams," Grew said.

"But Mr. Ambassador, the man with the weekly pouches has arrived. Your standing instructions are to have him brought to you immediately," Miss Adams said.

Grew looked at her. "Oh... yes, I forgot. Could you please excuse me for a few minutes, *Herr* Sorge? If you would please be so kind as to step into the outer office while I take care of this. It will be just a moment," Grew said politely.

"Certainly, Mr. Ambassador," Sorge said.

"Send the man in, Miss Adams," Grew said gruffly as Miss Adams let the man with the diplomatic pouches handcuffed to his wrist enter Grew's inner office.

Sorge followed Miss Adams out of the office and stood beside her desk as she sat down. Her typing was still stacked in a neat pile. She looked menacingly at him. "How long does this usually take?" he asked, wondering if the disruption was going to ruin the interview.

"Five or ten minutes," Miss Adams answered coldly.

"Miss Adams, get in here," Grew said as his office door opened and he stuck his head out. "We are out of custody transfer forms. Where are they?"

"Mr. Ambassador, they are where they always are, inside the stationary cabinet," Miss Adams answered.

"I'll be damned if they are. Get in here and find them," Grew demanded.

"But Mr. Ambassador," she said as she glanced at the stack of typing on her desk.

"I said get in here and find those forms, now!" Grew said loudly.

"As you wish, Mr. Ambassador." Miss Adams looked as if she were going to cry as she hurried into Grew's office.

Sorge hesitated only a moment. He stepped to Miss Adams' desk and started to leaf through the stack of papers beside the typewriter. Then Sorge found what he was looking for. Grew's handwritten notes, almost impossible to read—maybe some type of summary commentary, followed by the War Ministry document, in turn followed by what appeared to be a translation of some sort—handwritten asterisks, underlining, and explanation marks were scattered across the sheet, apparently written by Grew. *How in the world did Grew get this?* Sorge wondered. He began to read hurriedly. The Ministry document was apparently the minutes of a policy meeting held the first of the month by Prime Minister Konoe, after the return of Commerce Minister Ichizo from Batavia, where he had had discussions with the Dutch about the purchase of oil. Sorge continued to read; then his eyes riveted on the last paragraph:

The Council must therefore conclude that further attempts at expansion of the Manchukuo border along the Amur River are neither desirable nor feasible at this time. It is imperative that military actions that might precipitate an incident along the Trans-Siberian Railroad not be allowed to occur. In anticipation of priority preemptive actions against the Dutch, military planning and resources must be directed, without distraction, to development of capabilities to expand the Empire's boundaries to the East Indies, the Kra Isthmus, and the adjacent archipelagos.

Sorge was astounded by what he had discovered: Japan's strategy for expansion—in one unequivocal paragraph. But he didn't have time to contemplate it. He heard voices behind Grew's door; the door handle of Grew's office began to turn. Sorge quickly aligned the edges of the papers in the stack and stepped back from the desk just as the door opened.

The messenger came out, followed by a fuming Grew. "And you tell those people back at State to stop sending pouches over here with damn locks that don't work. I have enough goddamn problems over here without having to waste my time trying to open damn pouch locks. I don't have time to waste on crap like that!"

Miss Adams exited, with her eyes rolling and a look of exasperation on her face. She sat down at her desk.

"Oh yes, *Herr* Sorge. Shall we return to our discussion?" Grew asked with complete aplomb.

"Certainly, Mr. Ambassador," Sorge said, thinking, *Grew, the ultimate diplomat.*

THE DISCUSSION WENT ON for about an hour, but Sorge had a difficult time focusing his questions. His mind was spinning from what he had seen. Grew's remarks turned out to be the same old diatribe he could hear at any embassy party or read in any international edition of any American newspaper. As to Roosevelt's proposition of economic aid to the German government, it was obviously a feeler being put out by the American government to see if Hitler might consider stopping further military expansion into southeastern Europe if the United States were to guarantee some significant financial assistance to Germany. In simple terms, a bribe—a typical capitalist solution. Sorge was more than happy to end the interview. He had learned more than he thought he ever would—from the papers on Miss Adams' desk.

FRANCIS LOOKED DOWN from the second story window and watched Sorge walk out the gates of the embassy compound against the incoming flow of party guests.

Grew, standing beside Francis along with Miss Adams, asked, "Well, do you think he had time to read it?"

"I think so. I hope so. Only time will tell," Francis answered.

"Let's hope he gets the information to the right people," Grew said.

"If our intelligence about Sorge is correct, Mr. Ambassador, Sorge will certainly do that. What he saw in those papers should be in Moscow and on Stalin's desk before the end of the month. But," Francis continued, "that's all we can do about that. Let's hope our next piece of skullduggery goes as well as this."

"Yes," Grew said with a determined smile as he turned to Miss Adams. "Mary, get Judith Cairnes up here, alone and on the double," Grew ordered.

"Yes sir!" she said as she flashed a wide grin at the ambassador.

61

FOUR DAYS LATER, Judith stood under the shadows of a dock terminal roof along Tokyo's inner harbor, submerging herself in the throng of people—porters carrying luggage, dockhands standing by ships' ropes, friends seeing friends off, immigration officers checking passports and visas, and the ever-present *Kempei*. She watched Francis walk along with Breidstein toward the passport checkpoint, chatting amicably with him. Behind them was a porter pushing a wobbly cart with a mound of luggage.

Francis was quickly waved through once he showed his diplomatic passport. The check of Breidstein took a little longer, but he too was passed through after the guards took only a cursory look at his luggage. Francis followed Breidstein up the walkway to the passenger deck.

Looking carefully around the corner of the terminal building, Judith could see Francis standing at the ship's railing talking to Breidstein. She continued to watch them, waiting for Francis to take Breidstein into the salon for a drink, as Francis had laid out in the plan he had explained to her two days ago. As she waited in the shadows, she thought about the task she would soon have to do, hoping she would be up to it. But when she thought about Breidstein, she had no doubt. *I am going to fix that bastard.*

Finally, Francis and Breidstein turned from the ship's railing. Then the gangway was raised and the ship began to loose its lines. The space between the ship and dock began to widen. Judith knew it was time for her to act.

"Wait! Wait!" she yelled as she stepped out of the shadows on a run, her breasts heaving under the loose bodice of her low-cut dress. "Werner, where are you?" she yelled as she dashed toward the checkpoint, where the Japanese police guards were about to close down the guard booths. "God, you can't leave yet. Your bag!" she screamed as she waved a small briefcase in her hand.

The police grabbed her as she started to run through the checkpoint. Some people on the passenger deck of the departing ship looked down at her, but Breidstein was not among them.

"What are you trying to do?" the guards yelled in Japanese as they grabbed her. "You can't go past here." Judith didn't have to pretend she didn't understand them, but she knew what their intent was as they held her tightly to stop her from going any farther. That was what was supposed to happen. And it was apparent that the part of her body the guards were watching was not her hands; her ample breasts were dangerously close to being fully exposed. Then Judith, as she had practiced a hundred times the night before, unobtrusively turned the briefcase so its flap dropped open. Papers fell out everywhere.

Judith immediately bent down to pick them up, showing a large expanse of cleavage in the process. The guards looked down, first at her, and then at the papers scattered about. A "MOST SECRET" stamped in German was clearly evident on some of the papers.

As she continued to try to pick up the papers, other guards began to gather around her. Finally a man, obviously *Kempei*, stepped forward and reached down to take the briefcase from her. "Come with me please, madam." When it was obvious Judith didn't understand, he repeated in broken English, "Come, now!" as he grabbed her arm. She put up some pretended resistance but stopped when a second man took her other arm.

"I DEMAND TO SPEAK to the American Embassy. My husband is an embassy official—I'm an embassy official! I demand to speak to Ambassador Grew," Judith said for what seemed to her to be the thousandth time.

"Madam Cairnes, we must know what you were doing with this briefcase. Do you not know that it has secret military papers in it? To have such papers in your possession is very wrong, very illegal," said her interrogator in reasonably good English.

"I told you. *Herr* Breidstein accidentally left his briefcase at my... my... uh... uh... his office. I was merely trying to return it to him before he left. I know nothing about what was in the briefcase; absolutely nothing," Judith answered.

"Madam Cairnes, we know quite a bit about your relation with *Herr* Breidstein. Until you tell us the truth, we cannot call the embassy," the interrogator threatened again.

"You have no right to stop me from contacting the embassy... no right." Judith was getting a little worried—no, more than a little worried. She was getting damn scared. The plan was for her to contact the embassy when the police took the briefcase and started questioning her. But the *Tokko* had taken charge and they would not let her make the call. She wasn't even sure where she was. They had pushed her into a car and driven down streets she didn't know, to this place, a place that looked like a cell as much anything else.

"You have no rights," the interrogator said. "I consider you a spy. And spies have no rights. You Americans are so foolish, believing you can do anything you want. I am in charge here, and you are going to answer my questions. You are going to tell me the truth."

Then, outside the door, she heard voices—voices that got louder, voices that were American!

Ambassador Grew and Assistant Deputy Albert Cairnes burst through the door. "I am Ambassador Grew. What's going on here? Mrs. Cairnes is Deputy Ambassador Cairnes' wife. I demand an explanation," said Grew as Cairnes rushed to Judith, putting his arms around her.

Tears began flooding down her cheeks, creating long black streaks of mascara. "I thought you would never get here. God, Albert, you haven't looked so good to me since we left the U.S."

"Everything is under control, Judith. Don't talk now. We'll talk later," Albert Cairnes said.

"Ambassador Grew, I must tell you that this woman is under arrest for being a spy," said the interrogator. "She was caught trying to sneak military papers out of the country for Werner Breidstein."

"Spy? That's nonsense. Mrs. Cairnes is a respected member of the American diplomatic community here. And if she is not released immediately, I will take this all the way up to the Prime Minister. And as to your charges," Grew said with fire in his voice, "I understand that there was no sneaking about. I have eye witnesses that say she was quite open in her attempt to reach *Herr* Breidstein. If anyone should be questioned, it should be *Herr* Breidstein," Grew said authoritatively.

"Perhaps, but, unfortunately, he is already at sea and we cannot reach him for the moment," the interrogator said.

"Well, that's your problem," said Grew. "Undo those handcuffs, or you will have an international incident on your hands. Some very disagreeable discussions may develop between our two countries unless you release Mrs. Cairnes immediately."

The interrogator was silent for a long moment. Then he reached into his vest pocket for a key and undid the handcuffs. "I release her to your personal custody only. She is not free to go anywhere but with you back to your embassy."

"I understand. Come Mrs. Cairnes, Albert. The car is waiting," Grew said.

Judith leaned heavily on Albert's arm as they walked out. As they did, Grew turned to the interrogator and asked, "And where is Mrs. Cairnes' briefcase?"

The interrogator smiled. "Why, Mr. Ambassador, we do not have Mrs. Cairnes' briefcase. We have only a briefcase belonging to *Herr* Breidstein. We will take the matter of returning it to him."

"How dare you," Grew said portentously. "You are going to hear more about this matter."

"Yes, Ambassador, we may both hear more about this matter," the interrogator responded with a smirk.

Grew turned, ushering Judith and Albert out the door and down the hallway to freedom. "Quickly, before he has second thoughts," Grew said.

The chauffeur sat behind the steering wheel of the embassy car, with motor running and side door open. Grew practically shoved Judith and Albert into the back seat and then jumped in behind them. As Grew pulled the door closed, the chauffeur stepped on the gas pedal, and with a screech of tires, they took off.

"How did you know where I was? They didn't take me to the police office at the dock," Judith asked.

"We had some people watching what was going on," Grew answered. "We didn't think it would be a good idea to let you know about them ahead of time—might have given you stage fright. From what they said, you were superb. When the police put you in a car rather than taking you to the dock office, one of my men took off after you in one of our unmarked embassy cars. When they delivered you to the *Tokko* headquarters, he hot-footed it back to the embassy to let us know where you were."

"Thank God. I don't know whether I can handle this spy stuff or not," Judith said, as she straightened the top of her dress to finally provide a little more decorum.

THE NEXT DAY, Ambassador Grew received a formal letter from the Japanese Foreign Ministry:

Due to circumstances that need not be discussed, Assistant Deputy Ambassador Albert Cairnes and Cultural Affairs Officer Judith Cairnes are requested to leave Japan on the next available American airplane or steamship. Until then, the Japanese Foreign Ministry requests that Mr. and Mrs. Cairnes not leave the American embassy grounds and that, further, upon their departure, Ambassador Grew personally escort them to their point of departure for their return to the United States and assure that they get on board without incident.

Grew smiled to himself. *It just might have worked.*

XI

BETRAYALS

62

FRANCIS LOOKED in frustration at the letter from the clerk for Douglas county—the Colorado county in which Denver was located. It really didn't have much more information than what he had gotten in return from the carefully worded letter he had sent to Dr. Lewis Franklin in Washington in September, hoping to discreetly get some news about Elaine. He had written the letter to Franklin shortly after getting out of the hospital in August. But the only thing that had come of the letter to Franklin was a curt note—which was waiting for him when he returned from Tokyo—from Franklin's receptionist saying that Mrs. Franklin was no longer living in Washington. That had only raised more questions in Francis' mind. Was Elaine separated from Franklin, or maybe just living temporally in Colorado caring for her mother?

The Douglas County Clerk's letter had come only this morning, nearly two months after his February inquiry. Francis had asked if there were a ranch near Denver owned by a widow with the last name of Cotrall—Elaine's maiden name—who might have a grown daughter living with her with the name of Elaine Cotrall or Elaine Franklin. Francis knew it was a long shot, but that was the only thing he knew to ask. The clerk's letter said they had no ranch listed in their records owned by a Cotrall, but did provide the addresses of the county clerks for adjacent counties that Francis might contact for information. Francis knew what his next task would be: contacting the clerks of the other counties. Francis pulled some blank paper from his desk drawer.

Just as Francis twisted a sheet of paper into the typewriter and typed in the date, April 8, 1941, Ensign Louis Frankhill shouted out, "Attention on deck." There was a flurry of moving chairs as men rose to attention. Francis stood and saw McDonald entering the Post Y operations room.

"At ease. Continue with your duties," McDonald said to everyone as he walked by them to Francis' desk.

"Captain McDonald. How are you, sir? I thought you wouldn't be arriving until the end of the month, sir." Francis said.

"I decided to come a few days earlier. I've got some things I need to discuss with you—good and bad. Come on, we can talk as we walk over to the officers' mess. I'm hungry," McDonald said as he removed his hat and wiped the sweat from his forehead.

"Yes sir," Francis said as he pulled the county clerk's letter from the typewriter and shoved it into a desk drawer.

They started the long walk toward Cavite's base cafeteria. "First—about Russia," McDonald started. "It looks like your little charade in Tokyo might have worked. We've gotten information—don't ask how—that the Russians have called off some major planned troop movements to Siberia. They may even be talking about moving some troops from along the Amur and sending them to locations west of the Urals. I wanted you to know that, Francis—considering what happened in Bangkok," McDonald said with a nod.

"I appreciate that, sir, but don't remind me about Bangkok—please," Francis said with a wince—and a smile.

"Okay," McDonald laughed.

"Second thing. About some of that Jap diplomatic stuff you and your gang have been intercepting of late, including the word 'orange' that keeps popping up. You were guessing that it referred to the Navy's plan 'Orange.' You were right," McDonald said with a grimace.

"Damn. You mean the Japanese know about those plans?" Francis asked.

"Yes, we confirmed it," McDonald said. "The Japanese probably now know a lot of our thinking about how we would counter any attack they might make, including our defensive strategy for the Philippines and the rest of the South Pacific. But the one thing we don't know is how much they really know. And the bad thing is, if they know about Orange, what else do the Japs know? We just don't know how much has been compromised," McDonald said.

"How are the Japanese getting their information?" Francis asked.

"Based on some of your intercepts, as well as things we have pieced together in Hawaii and Washington, we believe there is a leak right here in the Philippines feeding the Japs information. And as far as we know, it is still going on. And it's pretty likely, just because of the way the Japs operate, that the Japanese consulate here in Manila is in the middle of it—they are probably coordinating the whole operation somehow. And we have to stop it."

"Are we going to confront the Japanese consul general about it?" Francis asked.

"No," McDonald said. "He would just deny it. All that we would do is just tip our hand. We have been investigating where the leak might be for the last couple of months. If we can find who, or what, the leak is, we can probably figure out how much the Japs really know and maybe give them some false information to boot—as long as we don't expose the leak. But first we have to find the leak."

"Do you have any leads?" Francis asked.

"Some. Based on our investigation thus far, we think we nailed it down to one of three staff planning groups here in Manila—two actually in Manila, one of which you regularly report to—and one right here in Cavite. Now we have to narrow it down further," McDonald said.

"How are you going to do that?" Francis asked.

"That's where I will be needing the help of you and your Post Y gang. We intend to plant some new, apparently important information in the planning sections and hope the leak picks up on it. I want Post Y to concentrate on intercepting that information and decrypting it," McDonald said.

"But how will that help figure out which staff group the leak is in?" Francis asked.

"The information we will plant in each of the planning sections will be different," McDonald answered. "What you and I need to do over the next couple of weeks is devise some apparently very important information—three different types of information—about Plan Orange that will be very obvious to decipher when you intercept it. So we have our work cut out for us," McDonald said.

"When do we start?" Francis asked.

"Right after lunch," McDonald said as Francis opened the mess hall door.

63

BREIDSTEIN'S MERCEDES pulled off the edge of the narrow road exactly one and a half kilometers beyond the entrance to the park on the edge of Manila's consulate district. Breidstein got out of the car and looked for Agawa. In a moment he saw him, sitting on a bench about fifty meters up a hillside. Breidstein began walking up the hill toward him.

As Breidstein neared Agawa, Breidstein spoke. "I got here as soon as I could, Heihachiro. Why all the secrecy?"

Agawa looked at Breidstein as he motioned for Breidstein to sit down beside him. "Werner, I had to speak to you alone, away from the eyes of the consulate. I'm afraid I've learned some disturbing news—news that will bring our relationship to an end."

Breidstein looked at Agawa in surprise.

"I shouldn't even be here talking to you, Werner. It is only because of our former friendship that I am here. If anyone in the Foreign Ministry were to find out that I am speaking to you, I would probably be dismissed immediately and ordered home to... what I am not sure," Agawa said.

Breidstein's eyes widen in alarm. "What are you talking about, Heihachiro?"

"Yesterday, I received a report, via indirect channels, that on your visit to Tokyo three months ago some secret military papers were found in your belongings by the *Kempei* as you were getting on the ship to return to Manila. The ministry was very upset about what those papers said," Agawa said.

"What are you talking about, Heihachiro?" Breidstein answered in shock. "No papers were found in my belongings. I didn't even have such papers."

"Werner, the report says that an American Embassy official, Judith Cairnes, was stopped at the dock trying to deliver your briefcase to you before the ship set sail. She apparently missed you only by moments. Search of the contents of the briefcase revealed the papers," Agawa said.

"What... apparently missed me? What do you mean?" a confused Breidstein asked.

"She arrived at the dock as the ship was departing—apparently screaming that she was bringing the briefcase to you. But the ship was already getting underway when she got to the dock. Her attempt to reach you was what apparently alerted the police at the dock."

Breidstein looked at Agawa, wondering what was going on. Then slowly, but certainly, Breidstein began to understand. Judith had been very cool after their meeting at the embassy party. And that Lieutenant Marian—he had been so friendly as they boarded the ship. And what a coincidence that Marian arrived at the dock at the same moment as he. Then, Marian's insistence that he buy them both a drink as the ship started to depart—inside the ship in the lounge, and away from a view of the dock. How convenient for Judith to arrive at the last moment with "his" briefcase.

"Heihachiro, that was not my briefcase. I think you and I have both been duped. Let me explain," Breidstein said confidently.

Agawa listened silently as Breidstein described his suspicions.

"So, Werner, you are hypothesizing that the incident was really contrived by this Lieutenant Marian," Agawa said.

"Yes," Breidstein answered. "Marian runs a communications unit at Cavite, and I suppose, in view of this, does a great deal more for the U.S. Navy than I fully appreciated." *And*, Breidstein thought, *I should have seen that when he said he was in Tokyo to "help with embassy communications."*

"Perhaps you should have been more circumspect in dealing with this Marian, Werner," Agawa said. Agawa's criticism was obvious to Breidstein.

"Perhaps... perhaps," Breidstein said as he silently cursed Marian.

"And the papers in the briefcase, Werner—what about them?" Agawa asked.

"Fakes, obviously fakes," Breidstein answered firmly.

"Perhaps, Werner ... and perhaps not," Agawa said slowly.

"But Heihachiro, they must be fakes—the whole thing was a ruse. What did the papers say?" Breidstein asked, seeking some way to exonerate himself.

Agawa looked intently at Breidstein. "I am sorry, Werner, I am not at liberty to say. In any case, my government must assess the implications of them, irrespective of whether they are real... or false. And, unfortunately, my government believes you are no longer to be... shall we say... entrusted with delicate information."

"But Agawa, they can't blame me. I didn't do anything," Breidstein said in defense.

"But, Werner, don't you see? If the whole episode was true, then you are a spy—for someone who poses a threat to Japan," Agawa said as he raised his hand to prevent Breidstein from objecting. "If the episode was a ruse, it means that the Americans are using you—to the detriment of my country. Either way, I cannot afford to be associated with you any longer," Agawa said.

Breidstein looked hopelessly at Agawa.

"And, one more thing, Werner—my last advice to you as a friend. Don't return to Tokyo. The consequences might be dire if you did." With that, Agawa rose, bowed formally to Breidstein, and then walked away, leaving Breidstein alone to contemplate his situation.

As Breidstein sat alone on the bench, he began to tremble. For the first time in years, Breidstein began to have doubts about his prowess.

64

AS FRANCIS SAW the PBY begin to descend to the waters of the Cavite harbor, he folded the letter he had received in the morning mail from the clerk of Clear Creek County southwest of Denver and put it in his shirt pocket. In response to his inquiry about a Cotrall family ranch, the county clerk said that a ranch in the county had been bought by a man and wife named Cotrall in 1928. The property title was transferred to a woman named Elaine Cotrall in September of 1940 and then sold by the same woman in February, 1941, only four months ago. The bad news was that the county clerk had no information about what became of the woman after the sale. *But the good news*, Francis thought excitedly, *is Elaine is using the name Cotrall, and that could mean only one thing—she isn't married to Lewis Franklin anymore! And if she isn't married to Franklin anymore and she isn't in Colorado, maybe she is in Fort Wayne, where she grew up. I might just be able to find her there, even by such a simple thing as a telephone call to directory assistance in Fort Wayne!* Francis' heart began to pound like the launch moving across the choppy waters of the harbor towards the dock.

As the launch carrying McDonald from the PBY bumped against the dock, the light drizzle that had been falling turned to a heavy downpour. Francis opened his umbrella and extended it over McDonald as he stepped from the launch to the dock.

"Thanks for the umbrella. How are you, Francis?" McDonald asked in almost a yell, trying to be heard over the beating rain.

"I'm fine, sir. But as usual, you have my curiosity peaked. What brings you to the Philippines this time?" Francis yelled in return.

"I need to make some reports to Hart and his staff about our general understanding of Japanese intentions in the Orient. And we need to have a long talk. But let's get out of this damn rain first," McDonald yelled.

"Yes sir," Francis said as the two began walking quickly down the dock toward Francis' waiting jeep. A short while later they were in a room by themselves at the Post Y operations building trying to get dry.

McDonald began to talk as he sipped coffee. "The first thing is that leak in the planning staff here in Manila that we have been trying to tie down for months now."

"Have you figured out who the leak is? Did our consulate intercepts help?" Francis asked.

"Yes, they sure did. If the leak is anybody in a U.S. uniform, it has to be one of three officers. And, I am very glad to say, Francis, you're not one of them," McDonald said.

Francis put his coffee cup down on the table with a bang. Coffee slopped over the side of the cup. He looked at McDonald.

"Yes, we had to check you out as well," McDonald said. "I'm sorry we had to do that, Francis, but we just had to be sure. That's why this investigation has taken so long, just to be sure about you. Sorry."

"Well, I guess you had to do what you had to do," Francis said with only slightly hidden anger.

"In defense of what we had to do, let me tell you, Francis, that you know a heck of a lot. You have to, for what you do and what we ask you to do. And sometimes you have had to do things that made you feel a little uncomfortable. That deal with Chiang—I know it was hard to understand, particularly in view of what happened to all those people … in Nanking." McDonald paused as he looked Francis directly in the eyes. "When things like that happen—at least in this business—it can cause people to do strange things. So because of what you know, we just had to be sure. Damn, if the Japs or anybody else ever got hold of you and somehow got you—or you decided—to tell them the things you know, we would be in deep shit, to say the least. You are a very valuable person, Francis. So just think about it from ONI's perspective."

Francis let out a long, heavy breath. "Okay, no hard feelings."

"Good. Now, about the three suspects: With the way we set up that planted information, along with other things we have been learning, it almost has to be one of the three," McDonald said.

"What's next then?" Francis asked.

"We have already put all three under surveillance—to see if we can catch them doing something they shouldn't. And in the case of one of them, it looks like he already has—a navy officer, I regret to say, who is a liaison to

MacArthur's planning staff. A man by the name of Ellington. I think you may know him," McDonald said.

Francis eyes widen in surprise. "Ellington, damn. Yes, I know him. I met him when I first came to the Philippines. I knew he had a loose mouth, but I didn't think he would do this type of thing," Francis said.

"If he is the right guy, we intend to use him for awhile before we quietly transfer him back to the States as if it is SOP. We will deal with him once he gets there. We will try to keep the Japs from realizing that we are on to them," McDonald said.

"How did they get Ellington involved?" Francis asked.

"Well, that's the second thing I need to tell you," McDonald said as he lifted two fingers in the air. "The main reason I came here was to give you some warning and some very special orders."

Francis wondered what McDonald had up his sleeve this time.

"We think that the Japs got to Ellington through some deal that was set up or initiated somehow by our friend, Werner Breidstein," McDonald said.

"Breidstein again. So our suspicions about him when I went to Tokyo are true. He is into the spying business—not just behind-the-door diplomacy?" Francis asked.

"Well, it looks more and more like that. The deal with Chiang and our use of Breidstein in Tokyo really didn't mean he was a spy. We fooled him, set him up—but that doesn't make him a spy. He could be, as he appears to be, merely very influential, very well connected—in tight with the Japanese politicos. But we have done some more checking on him. He has been apparently very friendly with Agawa, the Japanese consul general, ever since his arrival in the Philippines—that probably was the reason he was at the Chiang meeting. Agawa likely got him involved for some reason," McDonald said. "If Agawa and Breidstein are buddy-buddy, there're probably in a lot of things together, including this."

"Why do you think there's a connection between Breidstein and Ellington?" Francis asked.

"Pretty straightforward, once we had Army G-2 start bird-dogging Ellington a month ago. We found out Ellington has this thing going on the side with a Filipino woman. Not only is she a senior records clerk in the Philippine military files offices in Manila, but she also has a mother who is a maid for Breidstein. There is just too much coincidence there to believe that Breidstein is not somehow connected to Ellington, although we have never seen them together," McDonald said.

"Well, the connection makes sense to me. It explains something Breidstein said to me last August at a party," Francis said.

"What?" McDonald asked.

"He said 'Americans seem to be rather good at letting others do your dirty work—first China, and now the Philippines.' Maybe he had seen something in Plan Orange documents about Philippine Army plans for defense of the Philippines," Francis surmised.

"Sounds pretty much like he did if he made that comment. All the more reason to believe that Breidstein is mixed up with the Japs and Ellington somehow," McDonald said.

"So what do you want me to do?" Francis asked.

"Well, first of all, be damn careful in any dealings you may have with Breidstein. Be on your toes around him. Secondly, and very importantly, if any opportunity arises for you to find out more about this guy or what he is doing, take it. As of now, you have standing orders from me to follow up on any lead dealing with Breidstein that you come across that seems promising. I don't want you to spend your days bird-dogging him; we've got people in Army G-2 here already doing that. A Lieutenant Jack Burkhart will be your contact—"

"I know him," Francis interrupted. He and Burkhart had met during the summer of Francis's arrival in the Philippines. They got along really well, despite he being Army and Francis being Navy, once they realized they were both in the same type of business. They regularly traded bits of information without telling the brass.

"Good. G-2 will keep Breidstein under surveillance as long as they think he won't get suspicious, although with the crowd he runs around with, that will be hard. They will try to keep us informed about what he's up to. But like in China, he may just pop up somewhere unexpectedly. If he does, then follow up if it seems to make sense to you. Just keep me informed as much as you can," McDonald ordered.

"Yes sir," Francis answered.

LATE THAT NIGHT, after McDonald had left for the bachelor officer quarters, Francis made his call to find Elaine, in Fort Wayne, Indiana, across the International Date Line, where it was late morning—of the prior calendar day. After a long effort, he was finally able to get the overseas operator and make the connection to Fort Wayne. As he asked for directory assistance, his hands began to shake.

"Do you have a listing for Cotrall?" Francis asked over the heavy static.

"Would you repeat that name again," the operator asked.

"Cotrall—C-o-t-r-a-l-l," Francis almost yelled into the receiver.

In a few moments, the operator spoke. "We have no listing under that name, sir."

"Are you sure, absolutely sure—no listing under the name of Cotrall—C-o-t-r-a-l-l?" Francis asked again.

"Yes sir, I am," the operator answered through the heavy static. "Anything else, sir?"

Francis sighed in disgust—and dismay. "No. Thank you, operator." Francis heard a loud click as the operator disconnected the line

Just what Francis had been afraid might happen. Either Elaine didn't go back to Fort Wayne, or, maybe, she had moved in with her married sister—and he had no idea what her sister's married name might be. There seemed to be nothing else he could do so long as he was here in the Philippines. Despite the late hour, he walked back to the Post Y operations room, knowing the only way to stop thinking that he might have come to the end of his search for Elaine was to immerse himself in his work.

65

BREIDSTEIN PUT DOWN the morning newspaper, almost laughing aloud about the editorial outrage over the September fourth attack on the USS *Greer* by a German U-boat in the Atlantic. Then, looking at his watch, he wondered why Juana had not yet arrived to make his breakfast.

The phone rang. Breidstein answered it, thinking it might be Juana calling to tell him why she was late. But all he could hear was a crying woman. Finally, he was able to make sense of the woman. She was the landlady of the house where Juana and her daughter Carmen lived, and she was calling because Juana told her to call. Carmen had committed suicide during the night, and Juana didn't know what to do. "*Herr* Breidstein, Juana has no one to turn to—she is alone. She wants you to help her." The woman started crying again, babbling in Spanish about what a wonderful young girl Carmen was, how terrible it was that such a thing could happen.

Damn, Breidstein said to himself. *Who knows what could happen if Juana, in her grief, starts talking about what she and Carmen do for the Japanese consulate—and me, even if my one-time friend Agawa doesn't know about it. I could be hung as a spy if the Americans find out about the war plans information that Carmen regularly brings—or brought—to me.* "Who is with Carmen now," Breidstein asked the landlady.

"Juana, and the doctor from next door," the woman said between crying sniffles.

"Have the police been called?" Breidstein asked, hoping the woman would say no.

"Not yet. I'm going to do that after you hang up, " the woman answered.

Thank God, Breidstein thought. "No, No. Don't do that. Let me take care of everything. I'll notify everybody—the police will pay more attention to what I tell them. I know important people there. Don't call anyone—do you understand—no one? I will be there in a few minutes. You go back to the

Juana and tell her to wait for me. Tell her I will take care of everything—everything. Don't do anything until I get there. Do as I say. I'll make sure you get paid for any damage. Do you understand?" Breidstein demanded.

"Yes, yes. I will go now and tell her you are coming," the woman said.

"Yes, I will be there shortly. I will take care of everything," Breidstein said as he hung up the phone and wondered what he needed to do—to stop any type of investigation from occurring. He paused a moment, picked up the phone, called Enrique, and told him to bring the car around immediately.

Thirty minutes later Breidstein got out of the Mercedes in front of the small rented house that Juana—and once Carmen—called home. He told Enrique to park the car behind the modest but well kept building so the big car wouldn't draw attention in the neighborhood, which had few if any car owners. As Breidstein neared the front door, he could hear crying from inside.

Breidstein entered the house without knocking and went immediately to the room from where the crying was coming. Juana looked up from where she was sitting beside Carmen. Carmen lay on a bed, in a simple nightgown. Her hands lay beside her. Around each was a large pool of bright red blood, slowly seeping into the bed sheets from Carmen's slashed wrists. A kitchen knife lay beside one hand. Juana stood and came towards Breidstein, sobbing. "My Carmen is dead! *Herr* Breidstein, help me. I came to her room to wake her and found her like… this…. She wouldn't wake up. She was dead. The doctor couldn't wake her. What can I do? My Carmen is dead. What can I do?" Juana sobbed.

Breidstein put his arms around Juana, pretending to comfort her. He looked at the small Filipino man standing on the other side of the bed, dressed only in a white T-shirt and work pants, both now splattered with blood. Breidstein presumed the woman standing next to him was woman who had called him. "Are you the doctor?" Breidstein asked the man, still speaking in Spanish.

The man answered, "*Si.*"

"Are you the lady who called me?" Breidstein asked.

She answered yes as well.

"Why did Carmen do this, Juana," Breidstein asked as he removed his arms from Juana and gently pushed her away. "Do you know why?"

Juana looked at Breidstein, with downcast eyes. Slowly she reached into a pocket on her dress and drew out a letter. She silently handed it to Breidstein, as a flood of silent tears began streaming down her face.

Breidstein opened the letter and immediately realized it was Carmen's suicide letter. Carmen said that she had been betrayed by her lover, Ellington, the naval officer from whom she had been obtaining information for the Japanese and Breidstein. He was being sent back to the United States, and he wouldn't take Carmen with him because, he had finally admitted, he had a wife in the United States—that he had never intended to take her back to the United States. But even more startling, more devastating, to her was his refusal to even consider changing his mind when she told him she was pregnant with his child. Carmen blamed herself for what had happened—that it was God's punishment for her use of Ellington to obtain secret information. Carmen's final words asked for God's forgiveness, for what she had done and what she was going to do.

How innocently stupid Carmen must have been, Breidstein thought. *To think that the naval officer from whom she had been getting bits of secret information for nearly a year would be serious enough about her to take her back to the United States—even if she became pregnant. Who knows, she might not even have been pregnant—perhaps she just lied in a desperate attempt to make him take her with him. He must have really been quite a talker and lover—and liar. And to think that God wouldn't let Ellington take her to America because she had gotten information from him—how preposterous. Carmen probably wanted so desperately to go to the United States that she was ready to believe anything.* Breidstein wondered if some of the information she had gotten from him, whether she realized it or not, was really true or just things he said to impress Carmen.

Realizing he had to get things under control, Breidstein asked. "Doctor, about Carmen's death... how did you learn about it?"

"I live next door. Juana woke me early this morning, and brought me here to help. But it was too late. Now, I suppose, I will have to contact the police and fill out some reports. We need to contact them before we move the body," the doctor said.

No, no, I can't have that, Breidstein thought. "Doctor, won't Carmen have trouble being buried with a Catholic mass if she committed suicide?" Breidstein asked.

Juana looked up, and cried out. "Oh, no! That would be terrible. She has to have a proper burial. She must have a mass said for her, she must!"

"But, Juana, she committed suicide," Breidstein said as he baited Juana. "Isn't that a sin?"

Juana began to weep again, saying over and over how terrible it would be for Carmen not to have a burial mass said for her. Breidstein let his face show how stricken with concern he was that Carmen might not have a proper burial. "You're right, Juana, it would be a terrible, terrible thing if she could not have her mass."

Then Breidstein turned toward the doctor. "Doctor, isn't there anything we can do. The poor child deserves better than to be just thrown in some hole somewhere," Breidstein said as cruelly as he could. Juana howled with anguish. "Do the police really have to know about this? No foul play is involved here. It is just something between sweet Carmen, her poor mother, and her god," Breidstein said with feigned sorrow.

"Well, to do that, I would ... there is the matter of the death certificate... that is a legal document... if someone were to find out... I just don't know," the doctor answered hesitatingly.

The doctor's hesitation was all that Breidstein needed. "Doctor, I am in a position to assure you that the matter would go no further than this room. And your kind and most helpful services here this morning would be amply rewarded—very amply."

Breidstein saw the landlady look at the doctor and then at Breidstein. "And I certainly would be sure that the very helpful lady here," Breidstein said as he inclined his head toward the landlady, "would receive sufficient funds to redecorate this room, so that no one would ever be reminded—would ever know, would ever even need to know—what sad things occurred here today." The landlady nodded eagerly in agreement.

"Well, I suppose... that it might... be possible. There is no... harm... I suppose," the doctor said.

"Fine, doctor, fine. I will just take of it. You just fill out the death certificate and report how Carmen died of a... heart attack?" Breidstein asked.

"Yes, I suppose," the doctor replied, "Heart attacks can happen at any age, really."

IT WAS FIVE HOURS LATER—almost noon. Breidstein finally felt like things were about under control. Breidstein paid the doctor handsomely for his signature on the death notice certifying the cause of Carmen's death as a heart attack and assured him that it would be properly filed with the authorities. Breidstein felt confident that little or no official notice would be taken of the filing of the death certificate. Filipinos died right and left in Manila—and it was only the more affluent ones that received the attention of the authorities.

Finally, Breidstein arranged for an undertaker to come and take the body away, as Juana sobbed almost uncontrollably. Enrique recommended a particular undertaker who was quite adept at quietly and unobtrusively handling bodies and suitably preparing them, including removing any evidence of violent death, for burial—all for a very reasonable cost, all things considered. Assuring Juana that she could see Carmen the next day, Breidstein was finally able to calm Juana enough that he could tell her what she now had to do.

"Juana, you and I both want the same thing—a proper burial for Carmen. So we can't raise any suspicions about her death. You need to go to where she worked and tell them that she won't be coming back anymore—that she died. You take a copy of the death certificate and show them, just in case they wonder. Can you do that, Juana? Can you do that?" Breidstein asked, knowing that adequate proof of her death must be provided to forestall any questions on the part of the Americans or discreet inquiries from the Japanese consulate.

"I... think so, *Herr* Breidstein. I think so," Juana replied.

"You have to, Juana. You must do it tomorrow. I will have Enrique take you there. You come to my apartment and he will take you. Can you do that, Juana," Breidstein asked, hoping the woman would not make a mess of what she had to do.

"But, *Herr* Breidstein, what about her burial? You said she would have a proper mass said over her," Juana demanded.

"Of course, of course. I'll contact a church and arrange for her burial—and a burial mass," Breidstein answered, knowing a sizable contribution to some poor church would ensure that an elaborate mass would be said. He wondered what would be a good church to use—some nondescript one that was out of the way, that wouldn't attract attention giving a burial mass for a young girl who died of a heart attack. There were plenty of small churches scattered around Manila.

"No, *Herr* Breidstein, no. She must be buried beside her father... she must. It would not be right unless she is," Juana demanded.

Breidstein looked at Juana in surprise. Perhaps Juana was becoming a little too sure of herself. Maybe she thought all the things that he had been doing since the call this morning were because he felt beholden to her because of what Carmen had done for the Japanese consulate—and him. "Just where is her father buried, Juana?" Breidstein asked with feigned kindness.

"At *La Iglesia de San Fernando,* up the coast of Luzon near San Fernando, where I... we... where Carmen grew up. Do you know where it is?" Juana asked.

Breidstein looked at Juana in astonishment. Then he answered with words drawn deep from within his memory. "*La Iglesia de San Fernando del Mar y Hermanas del Convento de Luzon? Yes,* I know it well."

66

BREIDSTEIN LEFT for the church at San Fernando two days later, driving the Mercedes himself. Yesterday he had made the final arrangements with the undertaker for a coffin for Carmen that satisfied Juana, and made sure that Enrique got Juana to Carmen's supervisor at the Philippine military files offices to notify him of Carmen's death. By midafternoon Breidstein was nearing San Fernando on the west coast of Luzon, a little over a hundred and thirty kilometers northwest of Manila. As he got closer to the town, driving along the old coast road, he could not only see but also feel the familiarity of the sights along the winding roadway. It was the same route he—Willy Rosin, not Breidstein, but Willy—had traveled as a child when his mother, father, and he returned to the Villa San Fernando after they had reported to their American internment officer in Manila each month.

By midday, Breidstein reached *La Iglesia de San Fernando*, the church where Willy and his family had worshipped, where Willy had been baptized. Actually, it was more than a church. The church was really just an appendage to a convent. His mother had received much of her schooling there. Outwardly, it looked as he vaguely remembered it.

Parking the car and seeing no one in the church yard, Breidstein opened the tall wooden doors of the small church and entered the sanctuary. It took several moments for Breidstein's eyes to adjust to the darkness. He looked about. Seeing no one, he exited the sanctuary and returned to the bright sunlight. He walked around the side of the church building and soon saw the cemetery—surrounded by a high fence of vertical, rusting wrought iron bars. Inside the cemetery, behind the bars, was a nun in her habit, bent low on her knees tending to the flowers and grass covering the ground between the headstones and monuments.

Breidstein walked to cemetery gate. It gave off a shrill squeak as he pulled it open. The nun looked up, paused, then hoisted herself to her feet and began walking toward Breidstein.

"May I help you, *señor?*" she asked in Spanish as she raised her arm to wipe away the sweat running down her face.

"Yes, sister, perhaps you can. I am looking for the priest of the church," Breidstein answered in Spanish.

"That would be Father Vasquez. But he is away. He will not be back for several days. Perhaps Father Eduardo can help you? He assists Father Vasquez."

"Father Eduardo… I don't know…." Breidstein was in a quandary. He needed to get Carmen's burial settled—quickly. But, Eduardo—was it the same Eduardo who had ministered to his mother and might recognize him as Willy? Even if it were he, however, Eduardo might not recognize him after all these years—he was only ten years old when he left the Philippines. But still … .

"Isn't Father Eduardo rather old to be doing Father's Vasquez's work?" Breidstein asked, trying to determine whether it was *the* Edurado he had known as a child.

"Of course he's old. That's why Father Vasquez handles most things now. But Father Eduardo doesn't mind helping out when he can."

It must be him, Breidstein thought. "Let me get him. He may be in the clinic," the nun said.

"Clinic? What clinic? I thought this was a convent," Breidstein asked in surprise.

"Oh, it is a convent, but we also have a clinic for the parishioners. Father Vasquez started it soon after he arrived here—several rooms at the back of the convent have been enlarged to serve the needs of the clinic. But let me get Father Eduardo. I will bring him to you," the nun said as she walked through the open gate and started toward the rear of the church.

"Ah… perhaps… it is not really necessary…" Breidstein stammered indecisively. But the nun was already on her way.

Breidstein had two options: Either stay and face Eduardo, and possibly be recognized, or leave, without explanation, and not settle Carmen's burial. Breidstein decided to stay and bluff it out.

As Breidstein stood waiting for Father Eduardo, he glanced absentmindedly at the several graves the nun had been tending to. Suddenly, with shock, he realized at what he was looking: the headstones for his mother and her family. He had never seen her grave—after her death, his father had quickly taken him back to Germany without letting Willy see his mother's burial site, something he had never been able to understand. To see her grave now overwhelmed him. Memories of his young childhood in the Philippines ... and his beloved mother ... flooded his mind.

Willy leaned closer to the headstones to better read the ornate script chiseled deep into the white, seashell-hardened coquina. The first two were for his mother's parents:

Ignacio Miguel Hermosa
Conde de Cadiz de Espana
El Defensor del Trono Regio
El Mas Benevolo y Carinoso
El Mas Juicioso Consejero
Vicegobernar de Filipinas
Marzo 15, 1844 - Diciembre 26, 1905

Manuela Consaula Hermosa y Ortega
Condesa de Barcalona y de Luzon
La Esposa Mas Querida y Protegida
Protectriz de la Fe
Patrona de los Artes
Dador de Vida en Muerte
Enero 10, 1850 - Julio 6, 1892

The next was for her brother—the uncle who had died before Willy was born:

Raphael Ignacio Hermosa y Ortega
El Mas Valiente y Escalarecido
El Superior Capitan Armada Legos del Este de Espana
Hijo Esclarecido y Protector de Espana
Fiel Defensor a la Meuete
De Espana y Todo Sus Posesiones
Junio 2, 1871 - Mayo 1, 1898

And finally, the last headstone—Willy's mother:

Teresa Maragarita Consuala Rosin Hermosa y Ortega
Julio 6, 1882 - Diciembre 9, 1918

Willy looked at her headstone for a long while, the agony over her loss almost unbearable. And, he was puzzled. Why were there no accolades under her name, like there were for her parents' and brother's names. Nothing—just the dates of her birth and death. Then he heard the gate squeak.

Breidstein turned to see a priest walking slowly and unevenly toward him. He was bent and old. The nun was holding his arm to give him support.

"May I help you?" the priest asked with a weak voice as he neared Breidstein.

"Well, perhaps, you can, Father. My name is Werner Breidstein. I run a business in Manila. I am here on behalf of my maid, Juana Sanchez. *Senõra* Sanchez informs me that she was a parishioner here many years ago, before she went to Manila to live with her daughter."

"Juana Sanchez... Sanchez... ah... Sanchez, Juana Sanchez. Oh, yes, I remember her. She is a fine woman. I spent many hours with her daughter helping her learn to speak English well enough to obtain a well paying job in Manila. Juana left to join her daughter in Manila after her husband died quite a few years ago. How are Juana and her daughter—Carmen is her name, isn't it?" Eduardo asked.

"I am afraid, Father, that Carmen is dead—died of a heart attack two days ago. Very unusual at her age, but just as deadly," Breidstein said with faked sadness. *Good*, Breidstein thought, *the stupid old man doesn't seem to recognize me.*

"Oh no, how terrible. May God have mercy on her soul. I will pray for her tonight—and Juana. How is Juana?" Eduardo asked.

"Juana is fine—at least physically. She is, of course, very distraught, very saddened," Breidstein said. "That's why I volunteered to make the arrangements for Carmen's burial. It was just too much for Juana."

"Yes, I would imagine so, Carmen being so young. Why, she must have been only in her... ah... mid twenties, I suppose. I wish I could console Juana—if there were just something I could do," Eduardo said as tears came to his eyes. "Perhaps ... would Juana want Carmen buried here?" Eduardo asked.

"Yes, Father, she would," Breidstein answered. "Juana would like her daughter buried beside her father."

"Oh, yes, that would be wonderful. We could certainly do that. Let me see, where is *senõr* Sanchez's grave?" Eduardo said as he turned and began walking among the graves. In a few moments, he said, "Oh, here it is."

Breidstein walked to where Eduardo was standing.

"Yes, this will be fine," Father Eduardo said. "There are two remaining empty grave sites beside *senõr* Sanchez and Carmen's baby brother—he died when he was less than a year old—so everything will be perfect, the whole family can be together when Juana dies, someday, God bless her soul ... unless Carmen married and has members of a family to be concerned about. Did Carmen marry in Manila?"

"No, she didn't. So Juana and her husband had only one daughter—and the baby brother?" Breidstein asked, seeing a plan beginning to develop to control Juana—forever.

"That is correct. Only the four of them. Well, we will have to get everything prepared. Get legal proof of Carmen's cause of death, of course, for the church records, and arrange for the mass. When will Juana want the burial mass—and when will dear Carmen arrive?"

Breidstein smiled to himself as he pulled the phony death certificate from his pocket. "Here is the death certificate," Breidstein said as he handed it to Father Eduardo, who unfolded it and slowly read it with squinting eyes. "Carmen can arrive the day after tomorrow—the funeral home will bring her. My chauffeur, Enrique, will come too, just to be sure that there are no problems—that all is done properly. Juana would like the mass to be said the following day if possible."

"Yes, a mass in three days would be fine," Father Eduardo answered. "I will conduct the mass myself, and make arrangements for her burial here—beside her father."

"I know this will perhaps be a burden on the church here—what with Carmen coming from Manila and all. I thought that perhaps a contribution to *La Iglesia de San Fernando* would be in order. You could use it for the clinic if nothing else," Breidstein said as he opened his wallet and pulled a large stack of bills from it. He handed the money to Father Eduardo.

"Oh, my goodness. Such a large amount. This is not necessary ... but we can certainly make good use of it. The clinic has many needs. I will make certain Carmen has a beautiful mass said for her. Bless you, my son, bless you," Father Eduardo said as he made the sign of the cross.

"Thank you, Father. Now, I must say good afternoon. It is a long drive back to Manila," Breidstein said, trying to terminate the discussion now that the arrangements had been made, and now that he knew what he was going to do about Juana.

"Must you go so soon? Perhaps you might like to have confession... Father Vasquez usually listens to confession, but since he is not here... now... perhaps I could..." Father Eduardo asked.

"No, I am not of the Catholic faith," Breidstein answered with a lie, thinking, *the old man is almost begging to hear my confession. I hope he feels as useless as he looks. It would serve him right for all those years I had to listen to his dribble.*

"Oh. Well, shall I see you again ... at Carmen's mass?" Eduardo asked.

"Yes, I expect to attend the mass. Good afternoon, Father," Breidstein said as he turned and began to walk back to the Mercedes.

As he started driving south, Breidstein thought, *strange, why are there no accolades on my mother's headstone?* Breidstein pondered the question as he drove back to Manila, and as he thought through the details of his plan to deal with Juana.

IT WAS LATE in the afternoon, three days later. Carmen's burial had been completed almost three hours ago. Juana, dressed in black, sat in the back seat of the Mercedes as it moved south along the coast road toward Manila. Breidstein was driving, thankful that he was not in the back seat with the Juana, where she was still crying, though not as badly as she had on the drive up from Manila.

Finally Breidstein came to the bend in the road he had been looking for. He saw the side road and turned on to it. Juana, continuing to periodically wipe tears from her eyes and blow her nose, paid no attention to his driving. Breidstein came to the same deserted spot he had stopped at two days ago and where, about a half a kilometer off the side of the road, he had dug a deep hole. Breidstein brought the car to a stop, shut off the engine, and turned toward the back seat. "Juana, perhaps we should get out and stretch our legs some. I think it would do us both some good."

Juana looked up, and nodded. "Yes, I suppose so," Juana said as she pulled another handkerchief from her purse.

Breidstein got out of the car and went to the rear door to open it for Juana. As he opened it, he looked up and down the road. He saw no one. He reached in, as if to help Juana step from the car. She leaned forward, stretching out her hand. Breidstein took it and jerked her forward. Then he swung the fist of his other hand into her jaw as hard as he could. Her head snapped backward with a loud crack, striking the edge of the car roof. Blood gushed from her face. She fell limply to the ground, her body half in and half out of the car. Breidstein looked up and down the road again. Still no one. He pulled Juana from the car, grabbed her purse from the seat, hoisted her to his shoulder, and walked into the deep grass beside the road, toward the already prepared hole.

An hour later, Breidstein emerged from the grass, carrying the shovel he had used only two days ago—and then again only minutes before. He put the shovel in the trunk of the car and kicked some dirt over the now dried blood on the ground. Then he brushed himself off, got into the car, started the engine, and drove off. *All that remains*, Breidstein thought, *is for Enrique to tell Juana's landlady that Juana will not be returning, that she decided to remain in San Fernando—and to be sure that Enrique pays her well for her troubles in cleaning up Juana's little house before it is rented again.*

67

IT WAS ABOUT FOUR O'CLOCK when Shinako parked the blue convertible—the car Breidstein had given her to use after he got his Mercedes—behind the office. She had been gone almost a week, finally getting back today on the inter-island steamer from Taw Tawi in the Sulu Archipelago. She had interviewed a plantation owner, Derrick Hendrick, about the economic implications of the evolving international situation for his plantation. The United States' Neutrality Act restrictions, coupled with the British and Dutch embargoes, were causing many plantation operations in the Philippines and nearby islands to experience severe economic hardships.

Breidstein had suggested the interview, saying he could arrange it if she wanted to do it. She had checked via telegraph with Sorge in Tokyo and he agreed that it would be good background on changing economic conditions in the Orient.

Shinako had stayed two nights at Hendrick's plantation home. Louisa, Hendrick's wife, had made Shinako feel very welcome. And the interview itself had gone very well; she had brought back a copious set of carefully made notes.

But Hendrick himself was a different matter. Not that Hendrick had been unwilling to talk to her and answer her questions, but by the end of the day's interview, it was clear that he was viewing Shinako as more than just a journalist. As he had helped her out of the truck after their return from inspection of the plantation's packing operations, he had stood very close, uncomfortably close. Had it not been for Louisa coming back from town and arriving just at that moment, Shinako was not sure what Hendrick might have done next. Then, that night, her second and last at the plantation, she was sure that she had heard her bedroom doorknob jiggle after she had gotten into bed. Fortunately, she had had enough foresight to be sure the door was locked before she went to bed. In the morning, Hendrick acted as if nothing had happened, and so Shinako had said nothing. Immediately after breakfast she had started the long trip back to Manila.

Shinako started up the stairs to her office—well, not officially her office. It really was the "Manila Office - *Frankfurter Zeitung*"—all one room of it. She wanted to organize her notes this afternoon before she started her write-up tomorrow. She would see Werner later and let him know she was back.

As she turned into the hall to the office, she saw a small Filipino in dirty work clothes scraping the lettering off the glass window of the office door. She ran up to him, pulling his arm away from his scraping. "What are you doing? This is my office. You can't do that."

The startled little man looked at her. Then he smiled. "Mr. Breidstein say do this."

Shinako turned and started down the stairway to Werner's office. *What's happened?* she wondered with growing concern and anger.

She walked quickly past Luwani-ma, the receptionist, with barely a nod, but noticed a strange look on her face. She pulled open Breidstein's door, slamming it behind her. "What's going on? A man is scraping the lettering off my office door."

Breidstein rose from his chair. "I am afraid there is some bad news, Shinako. Sorge has been arrested for spying."

Shinako stopped dead in her tracks. "Arrested! Impossible. He is a journalist, not a spy."

"I'm afraid it's true," Breidstein continued, picking up two pale yellow pieces of paper from the corner of his desk.

Shinako read the first. It was a wireless from the German embassy in Tokyo:

OCT 18 1941
TO: CONSUL GENERAL BOGNER, CONSULATE, MANILA, PHILIPPINES

CORRESPONDENT RICHARD SORGE ARRESTED 16 OCT BY TOKKO FOR SPYING FOR SOVIETS/REPEAT/SOVIETS /HIS SITUATION NOW UNKNOWN/NOTIFY W BREIDSTEIN HAMBURG IMPORT-EXPORT COMPANY MANILA/TELL HIM TO DISTANCE HIMSELF FROM SORGE'S PAST ACTIVITIES/

(SIGNED)VON DIRKSEN, AMBASSADOR, TOKYO

Shinako was dumbfounded. Then she read the other message, a telegram from Germany.

OCT 19, 1941
TO:MISS SHINAKO FUJIMORI/MANILA OFFICE/FRANKFURTER ZEITUNG/MANILA/PHILIPPINES

WITH REGRET DUE TO CIRCUMSTANCES BEYOND OUR CONTROL CLOSING PHILIPPINE OFFICE FRANKFURTER ZEITUNG/ IMMEDIATELY DISCONTINUE ANY ACTIVITY WHICH COULD BE INTERPRETED AS DONE FOR US/CLOSE OFFICES IMMEDIATELY/ YOUR POSITION TERMINATED IMMEDIATELY/TURN OVER ALL PROPERTIES, FILES, EQUIPMENT & OTHER ZEITUNG MATERIALS IN PHILIPPINE OFFICE TO GERMAN CONSULATE OFFICERS/ OFFICERS WILL CONTACT YOU WITH INSTRUCTIONS/

(SIGNED) H. ZEISS, MANAGING EDITOR, FRANKFURTER ZEITUNG, FRANKFURT, GERMANY

Shinako was in shock.
"The consulate people came this morning and cleaned out the office. They took everything except the desks and chairs that I provided for the office."
Then the fear began to take hold of Shinako. What was going to happen now? Would loss of her job mean she could no longer stay in the Philippines? Her visa required that she be employed. Would she be deported? And what would happen if she returned to Tokyo? Would the *Tokko* arrest her also? Just knowing Sorge might be just the excuse they needed. And going back to Tokyo, just the thought of it now, made the painful memories of her father's death flood back into her mind. Knowing that Seiroku had not been brought to justice, that she had not gotten her revenge for his murderous act—and that she might now never obtain her revenge for what he did to her beloved father—was an agony that returning to Tokyo would only make unbearable.
"Werner, I'm afraid. I'm afraid of what might happen. What can I do?" Shinako asked.
Breidstein looked at Shinako with a reassuring smile as he spoke. "Shinako, I will let nothing happen to you. I will take care of you."

"But Werner, I cannot return to Tokyo. I don't think it would be safe for me, at least until Richard is cleared of these terrible accusations."

"Well, I am not sure he will be cleared, my dear. But as I said, I will let nothing happen to you. I will protect you."

"But Werner, how can I stay here—my visa... it says that I'm employed by the newspaper. I have to be able to support myself. Most of my salary came from the newspaper—now... what can I do?"

"My dear," said Breidstein softly, "the newspaper never paid any of your salary. I paid it, all of it. Sorge and I had an arrangement. In return for me paying your salary, he set up an office in Manila, so I could have you near me. All we need to do is to make official what has been in fact the case since you first arrived here—a mere formality."

Shinako looked at Breidstein in shock. Was this true—that Werner had done all this just to have her in Manila?

"Shinako, I still want you... to have you as my... ah... assistant, but now it can be full-time. The business continues to grow. My need... for assistance is growing. We can continue as before, except that now you can be officially employed by Hamburg Import-Export."

"Werner, do you mean I would be the receptionist? And... what would I have to do, what... more?" Shinako asked with apprehension. She liked Werner as a friend, but nothing more.

"No, no. Luwani-ma would still be here. Nothing will change. There is plenty for both of you to do."

Shinako was still unsure. *But surely Warner wouldn't do anything I don't want him to do. He has never even attempted anything like that. And besides, I really have no other options. Decent job opportunities for Japanese women in Manila are virtually nonexistent.*

"You can take on a more senior role, a more supportive role, now. You know, Shinako, how much I travel. I have to keep up with so many things. I need a personal secretary who can take care of things while I am gone. And the entertainment of my business associates is so taxing. Having you here to assist in entertaining them would be such a help."

"I... suppose so, Werner. Yes, Werner, that sounds good," Shinako said, sure that Breidstein meant what he said.

"Wonderful. You're hired," Breidstein said enthusiastically. A pause, then he continued. "You know, since you live so far out in the foothills, perhaps you should think about moving closer in, so that it wouldn't be so difficult when we have to entertain here in the city in the evening. You know how late some of these business dinners can go."

"But Werner, apartments are so expensive here in the downtown area. I don't think I could afford it."

"Perhaps... yes, I have an idea. The apartment next to mine here in town just became vacant. I am sure the building manager will reduce the rent as a favor to me." Breidstein paused, then spoke. "Better yet, I will have the company pick it up. I can handle the rent as a business expense—carry it on the books as an apartment for out-of-town business guests. You will not even have to worry about it."

Shinako looked at Breidstein, and smiled weakly.

SHINAKO SLIPPED OFF HER DRESS, slip, and stockings, put on a robe, got herself a drink, and then sank into the luxury of the soft couch by the window of her new apartment. Three weeks had passed since Shinako had moved her things into the apartment, and nothing had happened to make her concerned. Actually, the apartment was rather luxurious. And Werner was right; it was certainly more convenient, particularly on days like today.

Werner was out in the islands on another one of his trips, and she had spent much of the day dealing with his calls. Whenever he was out of town, she had to keep track of everything for him. Then there was the trouble with Luwani-ma. She had gotten sick in the morning, vomiting in the washroom and leaving a mess to clean up. She had wanted to send Luwani-ma to the doctor, but Luwani-ma said no. Luwani-ma said she knew what was wrong; she was pregnant. Shinako had told her to take the rest of the day off, to go home and rest. So it had been up to Shinako to not only get the mess in the washroom cleaned up and handle Werner's calls, but also act as receptionist.

And then about six-thirty, when things began to slow down as they usually did at that time of the day, a fist fight broke out on the dock behind the office, with knives being pulled. She had called the police, but it was too late when they got there. There was blood everywhere, or at least it seemed so to her. No one had been killed—there was more blood than real injury—and the police assured her that this type of thing happened all the time on the docks. The police took her statement right there, but by the time the police left, hauling both men away, it was well into the evening.

Shinako decided she deserved another drink. She got up and fixed it, then returned to the comfort of the couch. She took a large, long swallow of the amber liquid in the glass. She shouldn't have. It hit her like a ton of bricks.

BREIDSTEIN SHOOK Shinako's shoulder, trying to awaken her. She seemed to be in a stupor. He looked at the liquor glass on the table. Slowly he saw her become oriented.

Then Shinako asked, "Werner, what are you doing here? You weren't supposed to be back until Wednesday."

"Things worked out more quickly than expected—for the good I might add," Breidstein answered enthusiastically. "Jurgen agreed to ship exclusively with me. I took the evening ferry so I could get back tonight." *And*, Breidstein thought, *so I could spend a few hours in Marlene's bed before coming back to the apartment. I deserve some reward for closing the Jurgen deal. It was not easily done.* Unfortunately, he had arrived too late to see Marlene; he remained unsatisfied.

"I saw the light in your window when I drove up; I wondered what you might be doing up so late. Why are you asleep here on the couch? You know you left your door unlocked? It's one o'clock in the morning," Breidstein chided as he looked at Shinako's shapely legs uncovered by her partly open robe. He felt himself begin to harden.

"Oh, I was so tired I must have dozed off. It was a very long day at the office. The last thing I remember was thinking about all the confusion we had with Luwani-ma this morning and the fight this afternoon."

"Fight? What happened? Nothing wrong is there?" Breidstein asked.

Breidstein listened to Shinako describe the knife fight and Luwani-ma getting sick, wondering as Shinako described Luwani-ma's condition whether the child-to-be was his or her husband's. No matter, he thought, he would just give her some money, send her on her way, and get a new receptionist before the end of the month—and that would be the end of it.

His momentary distraction with Luwani-ma over, Breidstein looked more pointedly at Shinako's exposed legs as she continued to talk. His urgency began to grow. *It's about time to finally start getting some personal return on the considerable investment I have been making in Shinako, ever since her arrival in Manila*, Breidstein concluded.

"Well, perhaps I should be getting to bed, Werner. Thank you for coming by," Shinako said as she pulled her robe together.

"Let me sit down a moment. It's been a long day for me as well," Breidstein said as he sat down beside her, casually putting his hand on her now robe-covered knee. Shinako looked at Breidstein, a frown on her face.

"Werner, wouldn't you feel more comfortable in your apartment? You could go to bed and get some sleep," Shinako urged.

"In a moment, my dear, in a moment. Perhaps we could talk awhile. It might help me relax." Breidstein paused. "How long has it been, Shinako, since you came to Manila—nearly three years isn't it?"

"I think that is about right, Werner," Shinako answered.

"In all that time, we have had a very professional, business-like relationship, have we not?"

"Certainly, Werner, you have always been a perfect gentleman—someone I have always respected," Shinako answered.

"I often wondered if you felt like doing more for me than just assisting me in my business activities—things of a more personal nature?" Breidstein asked as he smiled.

"I just think the world of you. Werner. You have done such a magnificent job in building up Hamburg Imports-Exports here in Manila. It is so rewarding to work for you. And, Werner, you have been a wonderful friend—someone to whom I could always turn in time of need… almost like a father to me," Shinako said.

Being a father to Shinako was not what Breidstein had in mind.

"Yes, I have been pleased, Shinako, to be able to help you over the years, from that first time here in Manila. I've always hoped that you appreciated my help," Breidstein said, thinking, *it's about time you started appreciating me. I have needs to be satisfied—now!*

Breidstein moved his hand a little higher on her leg.

"Werner, I think we had better stop here. You need to go to your apartment, and I need to go to bed… alone." She began pushing his hand gently, but firmly away.

Breidstein looked at her. He removed his hand from her leg. "Certainly, my dear. It is getting late. I shall see you at work in the morning. Good night," he said in a cold, embarrassed monotone. He got up from the couch and walked to the door without looking back, humiliated.

Breidstein did not return to his apartment. He went downstairs and got into the lone taxi by the doorway. "Take me to Rose Maria's place, on Harbor Street. You know where I'm talking about?" Breidstein asked.

"Oh yes. But are you sure she will be taking customers this late?" the driver asked.

"She'll take me." *And,* Breidstein thought, *she will appreciate the money I pay her to fuck me like I want.*

68

SHINAKO AWOKE THINKING about what had happened the night before. All this time around Werner and nothing like that had ever happened. What was that going to do to her situation at work? She got up and looked out the window. Breidstein's car was already gone. She began to dress.

When Shinako arrived at the office, Breidstein cheerfully greeted Shinako. "Good morning, my dear Shinako. Sleep late?"

"Werner, about last night ... I just don't know what to say—"

"Shinako, please, you don't have to say anything. I hope you will forgive me. I just got carried away. It was late, I was tired—I was just not thinking. Please forgive me," Breidstein said.

"Please, Werner, do not apologize," Shinako said. "Sometimes things just happen. I am sure it will not happen again. Please, can we agree to not let last night get in the way of our friendship? I treasure that so much."

"Yes, as I do, Shinako. We're both adults. We won't let what happened get in the way of anything ... not anything." Breidstein paused, as if gathering his thoughts.

"Now, my dear secretary," Breidstein said with frivolity, "please call Karl Jahnel at the bank for me. I want to see if we can set up an outing on the bay for this weekend. I received a letter from Derrick Hendrick. Derrick and Louisa Hendrick have decided to come to Manila—Derrick was apparently quite impressed by your skills during your interview of him—and I think the time may be ripe for closing that deal between Derrick, the *Bank-Hamburg Geschäftlich*, and myself. Derrick and Karl need to meet. We'll do it up right—sailing on the bay and dinner at the Pacific Jade. That should soften up both of them enough to close the deal. And I am sure that you, Louisa, and Monika—that's Karl's wife—will get along fabulously."

Though Shinako did not particularly look forward to seeing Derrick Hendrick again—she was sure that Hendrick's interest in her was not because of her interviewing skills—she was not particularly concerned. His wife Louisa would be coming too. All Shinako had to do was avoid being alone with Derrick.

ON SUNDAY MORNING, Shinako rode with Breidstein to the Manila Palace Hotel to pick up the Hendricks, who had arrived the day before. On the way to the hotel, Shinako listened to Werner outline his plans: A relaxed day of sailing on the bay with Derrick, Louisa, Karl and Monika. Karl was not only Werner's banker, but also the owner of the eighteen-meter motor yacht they would be sailing on. Then later, a casual but elegant dinner, as Shinako knew, since she had made the arrangements.

Breidstein reiterated, for the tenth time it seemed to Shinako, that he wanted Karl and Derrick to meet informally, to get to know each other, before Breidstein got down to the hard business of securing a loan, a very sizable loan, to consummate a deal for purchase of a plantation on an island near Tawi Tawi. "I can't stress enough, Shinako, how important this get-together is. Absolutely nothing can go wrong—nothing. Nothing can be allowed to disrupt what must be an extremely pleasant day for both the Hendricks and the Jahnels. Do you understand that?" Breidstein asked.

"Certainly, Werner. I will do everything I can to make it an enjoyable time for all four of them," Shinako said, thinking, *Werner was such a gentleman last week, after that evening when he returned from the Jurgen plantation. He deserves every bit of my support to make the day successful.*

The Hendricks were in the lobby of the hotel when Breidstein and Shinako drove up. After cordial hellos, with Derrick's welcoming kiss on Shinako's cheek perhaps a bit too long, they drove to the dock. At the dock, Shinako, Louisa, and Derrick were introduced to Karl and Monika, who welcomed them onto the yacht. A short while later, the yacht cleared the docks and was moving into the channel. Shinako thought it looked as if it was going to be a wonderful outing.

Once well south of Cavite, they dropped anchor in the shallows to go swimming. Shinako took off her loose shirt and shorts to get down to her swimsuit, a modest but fashionable suit with an American flair to it. Louisa did the same. Her suit too was modest, but still did not hide her fat legs. Monika began taking off her outer outfit as well, but did a mock bump and grind as she did so, evoking playful whistles from the men. Looking at Derrick, she took off her shirt and pulled it up as far is it would go between her legs. She then proceeded to pull it slowly back and forth several times, finally throwing the shirt at him. Both laughed. Louisa smiled, but didn't laugh. Shinako was embarrassed and did not say anything.

The men began swimming, showing off by diving from the bow of the yacht. Their efforts became more grotesque as they downed more drinks and the day wore on. The women, for awhile, urged the men on from their perches on the deck, but tiring of this, they too jumped into the water. They splashed water at one another like children. In the midst of their shenanigans, Derrick came up under Shinako, grabbed her legs, and momentarily pulled her under. Shinako came up sputtering, not upset since she knew it was in fun, but as she did, Derrick's hand went, momentarily but firmly, between her legs, grasping her. Before she could say anything, he swam away—with a silly smirk on his face. Shinako was getting tired of having to deal with Derrick and was about to say something to him when Breidstein called from the deck, "Lunch everybody. Get it while you can."

Shinako got out of the water quickly, followed more slowly by the others. For the umpteenth time that day, Shinako thought, Monika made a show of pulling up her swimsuit from the low position to which it seemed to continually return.

Shinako helped Breidstein set out the picnic lunch they had brought. Then, as they relaxed after eating, Breidstein began talking about the plantation he wanted Derrick to buy and Karl to finance.

"You know the problem with most of these plantation operations here in the islands," Breidstein said authoritatively, "particularly those near Borneo, is that they are run by a bunch of damn natives. Not legally, of course. The owner is usually British or Dutch. But they are thoroughly, as I like to say, 'colorized'; they've lost all sense of ambition and their profits show it. Now Derrick, here, with his fine German upbringing, has done a masterful job of turning a profit on his plantation on Tawi Tawi."

Then—as if he had been coached, or so it seemed to Shinako—Derrick began talking smoothly about his plantation operation, frequently turning to Shinako and saying, "Isn't that right, Shinako, you've been there?"

Shinako would dutifully answer, "Oh, that's very true, Derrick. You have a wonderful plantation."

"HAVE ANOTHER DRINK, SHINAKO?" asked Jahnel as he looked at her sitting in the deck chair. It was late afternoon and the sun was low. Jahnel had turned them around about an hour ago and then given the helm to Breidstein. Shinako could see Manila's hills in the distance. Breidstein's prompting of Derrick had long since finished. Shinako was glad that Breidstein seemed pleased about how Jahnel had responded to Derrick.

"No, I think I've had enough," Shinako answered.

"Well, if you don't want it, Shinako, I do," said Derrick as he leaned over Shinako to take the drink from Jahnel. His arm rubbed across her shoulder.

Shinako winced with pain. She looked at herself. Red, fiery red.

"Sorry," Derrick said. "Ooh, look at you. You're going to hurt tomorrow."

"Oh dear, Shinako," Monika, Jahnel's wife, exclaimed, "we have to do something about that. Come down to the cabin with me. Karl and I always keep a supply of lotion on hand for occasions just like this."

Shinako followed Monika down to the small cabin, with Monika telling everyone, "I will take care of the lovely lady. Don't worry about a thing."

Once in the small cabin, Monika began rummaging through a cabinet. "Ah, here it is. Pull your suit down, Shinako, so I can rub this on your back and arms."

Shinako started to reach behind her to undo the zipper. "Oh, it hurts."

"Let me help," Monika suggested as she pulled down the zipper on the back of Shinako's swimsuit, folding open its edges. Shinako, with pain, undid the string around her neck, letting the string fall but keeping the front of the suit up with her hands to cover herself, even if only barely.

Shinako jumped a little as Monika began to gently spread the cool lotion on her back.

"How does it feel?" Monika asked.

"Very good. Just be gentle. I don't think I've ever been quite so tender," Shinako answered.

Monika continued to gently spread the lotion across Shinako's back and shoulders. As she did, Monika's breathing became deeper. Monika's hand made long, lingering motions across Shinako's back. Then, as Monika poured more lotion onto Shinako's shoulder, Monika's hand gently and slowly, but unmistakably, moved to Shinako's neck, then upper chest, and then downward toward Shinako's breasts, continuing to spread the cool lotion. "Doesn't that feel good, Shinako?" Monika asked in a low, tight voice.

Shinako didn't like what was happening. "I think that will be fine, Monika. I feel much better now." Shinako started to stand up quickly, moving herself away from Monica's exploring hand. As she did, Shinako hit her head, hard, on the beam overhead. "Oh, oh," Shinako cried.

Shinako, momentarily dazed, sat down again. Her suit fell from her grasp, fully exposing her breasts to Monika. Monika took a deep breath, and stared at Shinako.

"I think I had better put some lotion on, as well," said Monika as she looked at her arms. Then she pulled down the front zipper of her suit, letting her breasts emerge. "Sunburn can really creep up on you." She began rubbing lotion on herself, on her chest, then her fully tanned breasts. As she did so, her eyes narrowed, and her breathing became more rapid. Shinako frantically tried to pull her suit up so she could go back on deck, but couldn't get the zipper up. It was caught. Shinako wanted to call out to Breidstein, but she was afraid of how angry he would be if she created a scene.

Then Monika reached outward and grasped one of Shinako's breasts. Shinako jerked back, frightened. Shinako knew she had to get away from Monika. Shinako pulled the front of bathing suit up, leaving the back unzipped. Holding her head low, she scurried past Monika and back onto the deck, squinting her eyes against the bright sunlight as she emerged from the shadows of the cabin. She bumped into Derrick Hendrick.

"My goodness, Shinako, you look like you almost forgot to put your bathing suit on," Hendrick said with a leer.

Shinako tried to calm herself, tried to slow the pounding of her heart. In her nervousness and fright, she blurted out the first thing that came to her lips. "Oh, I wanted you to zip my suit up for me—the zipper is stuck."

"Gladly, Shinako, gladly," Hendrick said as he took the folds of the swimsuit in his hands, wiggled the zipper a few moments, and then slowly pulled the zipper up. "That better?" Derrick asked as he put both his hands firmly on her hips.

Shinako could feel Derrick's eyes trying to undress her. She couldn't stand the man—nor the woman from whom she had just escaped. She felt a wave of revulsion come over her. She pulled away from Derrick.

"I think I'll take that drink now—a double," she said to Jahnel. Jahnel smiled and poured her a drink. Shinako looked over at Breidstein standing at the helm, the wind ruffling his hair and his face beaming with enjoyment. He smiled at Shinako. She tried to smile back at him, wanting to tell him what Monika had tried to do to her—what she had done to her—but knowing she could not. When Jahnel handed her the drink, she quickly downed it.

69

SHINAKO HAD FINISHED dressing and was putting her things in her evening handbag when Breidstein knocked at the door of her apartment. She let him in, asking, "Are you about ready to leave?"

"Yes. The car is waiting for us downstairs. We'll drive over to the Manila Palace Hotel again and pick up the Hendricks. The Jahnels will meet us at the restaurant."

Shinako cringed. The afternoon's episode with Monika had been disgusting, degrading. Shinako didn't know whether she could stand to even be around Monika, much less have a meal with her. "Werner, is it really necessary that I go? I wouldn't want to get in the way of your business discussions," Shinako asked hopefully.

"Yes, it's essential. Absolutely no reason why you shouldn't be there. The Hendricks and Jahnels might be insulted if you didn't come. Why would you even think you shouldn't be coming along?" Breidstein asked sharply. Then, in a more conciliatory tone, he asked, "Will we have time to stop at the hotel bar for a few minutes before we have to go to the restaurant?"

"I believe so," Shinako said with a limp voice. "The reservation is for nine."

"Superb, my dear. Come, Enrique is waiting."

ARRIVING AT THE HOTEL a short while later, Breidstein called up to the Hendricks' room and said he and Shinako were waiting in the hotel bar. In about ten minutes, Derrick and Louisa came down. Breidstein suggested they have a drink before heading off to the restaurant. "Great idea, Werner," Derrick Hendrick said.

Shinako agreed silently with Hendrick; she needed something to steel herself against the rest of the evening. By the time the four of them left the bar, each had had two drinks; both of Shinako's had been doubles.

Arriving at the restaurant, the Jahnels waved as the four of them—Breidstein, Shinako, and the Hendricks—walked up the steps to the restaurant entrance, with Breidstein's hand firmly supporting Shinako's arm to keep her steady. Shinako merely nodded as the others all said hello.

The maitre d' led them directly to their table and took their drink orders. Shinako ordered a bourbon on the rocks. Shinako saw a frown come to Breidstein's face, but she didn't care anymore. She had to isolate herself from Derrick's leers and Monika's already pawing friendliness. She did, by consuming drink after drink.

Finally, after what seemed like hours to Shinako, the dinner came to an end as Shinako slowly emerged from her alcoholic refuge. They all walked out to portico covering the restaurant entrance, where the valet brought out the Jahnels' roadster and Enrique drove up with the Mercedes. With a reminder of the meeting time for the three men tomorrow, the Jahnels took off. Shinako saw Monika turn to look at her and smile as the roadster went down the street.

It took about twenty minutes to drive to the Manila Palace Hotel. As Enrique opened the door for the Hendricks, Breidstein snapped his fingers. "Damn. I forgot to bring the draft of the loan agreement, Derrick. I wanted you to review it before the meeting tomorrow. What if we drive over to my apartment right now and get it? My chauffeur can drive you both back."

Louisa gave a slight groan. "Werner, is that really necessary? It's been a wonderful evening, but I am absolutely worn out. Can't it wait until tomorrow?"

"Well ... if you insist," Breidstein answered with obvious reluctance.

"No, no, Werner. You're right," Derrick broke in. "I do need to look at that draft. Louisa, why don't you just go up to the room. I'll go with Werner and come back after awhile."

"Great idea," Louisa said as she stepped out of the car. "Good night, Shinako, Werner. Wonderful evening, wonderful."

AS THE THREE OF THEM came to the hallway leading to her apartment, Shinako had a great feeling of relief. The evening was almost over. "Good night, Derrick, Werner. I'll just go on to my apartment."

"Yes, fine, Shinako. Good night," Breidstein said.

"Yes, good night. I hope to see you again... soon... Shinako," Derrick said.

Not if I have anything to say about it, Shinako thought as she dug for her key in her purse. Finally finding it, she tried to fit it in the lock. She couldn't get it to go in. The drinks she had had, the lateness of the hour, the whole day, were all beginning to take their toll.

"Let me help you," Breidstein said as he took the key from her hand and opened the door for her.

"Thank you, Werner," Shinako said as she almost staggered into her apartment, exhaustion taking over.

As Breidstein closed the door behind Shinako and heard the door lock snap, he put Shinako's key in his pocket.

SHINAKO WASN'T SURE how much time had passed. After Breidstein had opened the door for her, she had turned on only one light in the living room before going into the bedroom, literally falling on the bed. Lying on the bed, she had somehow managed to pull off her dress, stockings, and shoes, in that order. But something had awakened her. Then she realized that someone had come into the apartment.

"Werner, is that you?" she called out as she struggled to get up and pull on her robe. "Werner?"

"No, my dear, it's me, Derrick."

My God, what is he doing here? How did he get in? "Derrick. I thought you left. Why are you here?" Shinako asked, afraid of the answer she knew she was almost sure to get.

"I thought it was time that you and I got to know each other better," he answered.

Shinako saw him take off his dinner jacket. She tried to close the bedroom door, but Hendrick stopped her. He pushed her back into the room, and onto the bed. "Oh, God, no. No, Derrick. Please, no."

Hendrick looked at her, and just smiled—and then reached out and slapped her. Shinako cried out.

"Don't say another word. Don't scream, or I'll do that again, only harder," he ordered.

Shinako pulled back toward the top of the bed, terrified.

Hendrick pulled off his bow tie. He undid his shirt but did not take it off. He kicked off his shoes and then undid his cummerbund. As he slipped his suspenders off, his pants fell. Next his underpants. Shinako could see he was ready.

Hendrick reached over to her and grabbed the top of her slip. He yanked it down, pulling her brassiere with it. Shinako gave a muffled cry of pain as the brassiere straps broke and slapped her sun-reddened shoulders. He pushed her slip up and pulled down her panties, throwing them down on the edge of the bed. Shinako tried to resist but could do little. A lethargy had fallen over her. *Today on the boat—and now this.*

Hendrick took her legs and spread them. He forced his way in.

Through the pain, Shinako could only think, *God, how has this happened? What has happened to my life?*

Derrick finished. He took Shinako's panties and wiped himself off. Then he put on his clothes, leaving his tie and cummerbund at the foot of Shinako's bed.

Shinako heard the door shut as Derrick left. She writhed in pain. Her head was pounding, her chest and neck burned, and, worst of all, there was the pain between her legs. God, it was terrible. She felt so degraded, so ashamed. She staggered into the shower and tried to wash the slimy feeling from herself. She took the shower head off the hook and sprayed the water directly into herself, trying to wipe out the memory of what had happened. She could not.

She collapsed on the bed, letting the protective cloak of sleep surround her.

70

WHEN SHINAKO WOKE the next morning, the painful memory of the night before was still with her. She had never felt such anger in her life. She dressed but did not even try to put on any makeup. She looked out the window. Breidstein's car was parked on the street; Enrique was still standing by its side, waiting for Breidstein.

She opened her apartment door, starting down the hall to Breidstein's apartment. At that moment Breidstein came out of the door, briefcase in hand.

"You don't look too good, Shinako. I think you need some makeup," Breidstein said.

"He raped me, Werner, he raped me! Derrick Hendrick raped me last night. It was terrible. What should I do? What are you going to do to him?" Shinako demanded.

"Why should I do anything, Shinako? Besides, I'm sure you're exaggerating. I'm sure that you and Derrick got along fine once you, shall we say, got loosened up," Breidstein said.

Shinako could not believe her ears. *What is he saying?* She didn't want to believe it.

"Werner, where is my apartment key?" Shinako asked.

"Why, my sweet Shinako, I gave it to Derrick. Didn't he leave it with you when he left?" Breidstein asked nonchalantly.

Shinako was stunned, realizing what he had just said. "Werner, how could you!"

"It was very simple, Shinako. I just took it out of my pocket and gave it to him," Breidstein answered.

Shinako stood motionless in betrayed silence.

Breidstein started walking to the elevator. "And, by the way, Shinako, don't forget to remind me tomorrow afternoon to write out the checks for the apartment rent and your salary." He got on the elevator, leaving Shinako by herself.

WHEN SHE FINALLY LIFTED her head from the tear-stained pillow, she realized what she was: a whore, nothing more, nothing less. Her life was a shambles again. Never had she felt her world so much at an end. But her spirit was not totally broken.

I must get away from Breidstein, she thought. *I'll get out from under him and his sick friends. I must return to my home, to Japan, where I belong.* She went to the desk and dug out the envelope with her small amount of savings. She counted the cash. Maybe a thousand pesos. Certainly not enough to get her out of Manila and back to Japan. She hadn't realized until now how much she depended upon Breidstein's salary.

I'll quit working for Breidstein; I'll get another job, she thought. *I'll make enough money to get out of this terrible place.* She grabbed yesterday's newspaper, still lying on the kitchen table. She turned to the want ads: secretaries, receptionist, office workers—lots of listings. Then she saw the heading at the top of the page: "Whites Only." She turned to the page marked "Non-Whites" and read below it: dishwasher, dockhand, maid, delivery boy, cook—and on it went. God, not only were they miserable jobs, but she knew she wouldn't be able to save any money on what those jobs paid.

My jewelry... I'll pawn my jewelry.

SHE PARKED HER CAR in front of a fruit stand near the pawn shop she regularly passed on the way to the docks—and the Philippine Transfer offices.

"I would like to pawn some jewelry," she said in English as she entered the pawn shop and took a cloth bag out of her handbag. The man behind the counter turned his head and called in Spanish to someone.

In a moment, a man with a bulging belly only partly covered by his shirt emerged from behind a curtain.

"What do you want," he asked in English, as he looked at Shinako.

"I would like to pawn some jewelry," Shinako said again.

"Let me see it," the man demanded gruffly, as he took the jewelry bag from Shinako's hand and dumped its contents on the counter. He looked at jewelry for only a brief moment. "This is all costume jewelry—worth nothing," he said.

"But... but, it must be worth something," Shinako said.

"Not enough for me to worry about—ah, what the hell. You're a pretty gal. I'll give you a hundred pesos for the lot—unless you got something else to sell?" the man said with a smirk.

A hundred pesos! Obviously, he is lying, Shinako thought. *And trying to proposition me too!* She scooped up the jewelry and quickly left. She looked up and down the street. There, on the next block, another pawn shop. She walked down the street toward it.

As Shinako entered the shop, an old man behind the counter looked up at her, seeming to study her for a moment.

"Good afternoon," the old man said in Japanese. "May I help you?"

Shinako felt much more reassured by him than by the crook she had just left.

"Yes, perhaps. I am considering pawning some jewelry. It is in here. Perhaps you might tell me how much it is worth," Shinako said as she opened her jewelry bag and slowly emptied its contents on a small felt pad spread on the top of the counter in front of old man.

"Certainly," he said as he looked at each piece of jewelry through his magnifying glass. He finally stopped. "I regret to tell you this has only limited value. It is only costume jewelry. Such items have little or no resale value… except for this one piece here, this bracelet, with the pearl and jade. It is very exquisite. I could give you nine hundred pesos for it."

He was pointing to the bracelet that her father had given her on her last birthday before she had left Japan for Hawaii. It was more precious to her than she could say. "No, I cannot sell that." She gathered up her jewelry and left.

71

AFTER PARKING THE CAR, Shinako walked rapidly to the door of the main office. She didn't know what she was going to do, but she knew she could not continue to work for Breidstein. She would get the salary money that was due her and get out. What she would do next, whether she even wanted to go on living, she didn't know.

She opened the door. Breidstein stood by the receptionist's desk. There was a new girl there.

Before Shinako could say anything, Breidstein spoke. "Shinako, this is Juliana. I hired her this morning. She will be replacing Luwani-ma. Should be a great help to you. Juliana, this is Shinako, my administrative assistant. Shinako will help you get oriented."

Shinako was flabbergasted. After all that had happened, and Werner acted as if it were just another day.

He continued. "And guess what, Shinako? I saw your naval officer friend today, at the docks. I was down there to check the arrival of some goods, and there he was, coming off a ship."

"Naval officer friend? Whom do you mean?" Shinako asked in surprise.

"Why that naval officer who is, I think, on Yamamoto's staff. Isn't his name Seiroku, Seiroku Takamatsu? Yes, that's right, that's his name," Breidstein said.

Shinako's body became cold. *Seiroku here, in Manila? The murderer of my father! Why is he here?*

"Yes, that's his name. Lieutenant Seiroku Takamatsu," Shinako answered coldly. "But he is no friend of mine."

"Is that right? Oh yes, that little spat in Tokyo. You never did tell me what that was all about—a lover's quarrel?" Breidstein asked, but went on before Shinako could answer. "Well anyway, he is not a lieutenant any more. He is apparently a commander now. He was met by a group of embassy personnel when he got off the ship—appeared to be quite the indispensable man. I tried to say hello but couldn't get close to him before he was whisked off in a consulate car."

I don't care how important he might be, she thought. *If I had the opportunity, and the courage, I would kill him on the spot.*

"Perhaps I might go see him—reintroduce myself," Breidstein said. "He must be quite an important man, don't you think, Shinako—what with being on Yamamoto's staff and apparently quite the world traveler."

Shinako knew what Breidstein was doing. She had seen it many times before—Breidstein manipulating someone to introduce him to someone important.

"He may not remember me. Perhaps you might introduce me again, Shinako. Indeed, you and he might want to become friends again—or whatever you might have been before," Breidstein said with a smirk.

Shinako was about to respond with an angry no, to scream at Breidstein how much she hated Seiroku for what he had done, but she stopped. "Perhaps I might," she said, her mind racing ahead. "I'm sure he doesn't even remember our little spat now." *But I remember what he did to my father and what he did to me. And now I can make him pay.*

THE NEXT MORNING Shinako returned to the pawn shop with the old man.

"You return, dear lady," the old man behind the counter said. "Have you reconsidered my offer?"

"Yes, I have," Shinako said, as she withdrew the beautiful pearl and jade bracelet from her purse.

"I will give you six hundred pesos," the old man said.

"But you said nine hundred," Shinako said accusingly.

"But that was yesterday, not today."

Shinako looked at the glass cabinet next to where she was standing. Several used pistols were spread out on a piece of long green felt under the glass counter top. "If you give me one of those guns, you can have the bracelet for five hundred pesos."

The man seemed to think about the offer for a moment, then smiled. "Yes, we have agreement." He reached under the counter, lifting an old, but shiny pistol from the green felt. He gave it to Shinako. "Please use this weapon wisely, only for good purpose."

Shinako felt the weight of the gun in her purse as she left the shop.

72

SHINAKO LOOKED at her watch, then out the car window toward the Japanese consulate entrance. She tried to carefully dampen the perspiration on her face without disturbing her makeup. She had to look as enchanting as possible. She had to make Seiroku fall in love with her again.

Then Enrique said, "Here he comes, I think."

Shinako looked toward the consulate gate. Yes, it was him. "All right, Enrique, drive up and stop there a short way from the gate—down the street from where he is walking."

Enrique pulled away from the curb, drove about half a block, and then pulled over to the curb. He got out and opened the door for Shinako.

Shinako got out and turned as if to walk toward the consulate gate. She saw Seiroku in his white naval officer's uniform walking jauntily, unknowingly, toward her. It was working out just as she, with Breidstein's help, had planned. She had been clever, drawing Breidstein into her little ruse by explaining to Breidstein that it would appear too forward on her part to just march right up to the consulate offices and ask to see Seiroku. She needed a reason for meeting him again, so Breidstein had Enrique do a little checking. Within a couple of days, Enrique was able to find out, by bribing some of the consulate maids, that Seiroku typically went out for a late morning walk. Seiroku's morning walk would become the moment of an "unexpected" meeting between him and Shinako.

Shinako had dressed very carefully that morning—an acceptable western outfit for Manila, but with a strong Japanese flavor to it. The dress accented her slim lines, more lush now than when she had last seen Seiroku. *This should stir up more than his heart*, she had thought as she left for the consulate.

Now, as Seiroku got closer, she stopped, as if recognizing him. Then she saw Seiroku slow his gait. She brought a smile to her face, and then started walking quickly toward him, as if anxious to see him. As she got close to him, she called in a lilting voice, "Seiroku, Seiroku. It is you. I can't believe it. How wonderful to see you—after so long."

"Shinako? Shinako, it is you! What are you doing here?" Seiroku asked.

"I'm on my way to the consulate—to get some papers signed," Shinako answered, knowing that she was not answering the question Seiroku was really asking.

"No, no. I mean here in Manila."

"Oh, Manila. I have been here for almost ... three years. I work for Werner Breidstein—didn't you meet him one time?"

"Well, yes, sort of—in Tokyo, when we had ... our ... argument," Seiroku answered sheepishly.

"Argument? Oh, that—that was no argument. I just didn't understand the situation. I have always wanted to apologize to you about that evening. But, now, I can. Forgive me for not understanding. And, to show you I mean it, I'll let you take me to lunch," Shinako said with a little laugh. "We have so much to talk about—you can take an early lunch, can't you? Your duties can't be that pressing," Shinako said as she reached out and put her hand on Seiroku's arm, drawing herself closer to him.

"Well ... I suppose not ... yes, let's go to lunch," Seiroku answered.

"Wonderful, Seiroku. It has been so long—much too long. There are so many things that we never got to do together. I hope we will have time for them—all of them, now," Shinako said as she looked tantalizingly at him.

"Shinako, do you mean that?" Seiroku asked.

"Every word, dear Seiroku," Shinako said as she tightened her grip on his arm. "We can use my car. Werner let me borrow it today," Shinako said as she waved her arm. The Mercedes moved quickly toward them. "We can talk about old times, Seiroku—and what the future may hold for us. Oh, Seiroku, it's so wonderful to see you again."

It was nearly one o'clock before Seiroku and Shinako finished their lunch at a quiet and elegant restaurant that Shinako suggested—and one with which Shinako had arranged the previous day for a table in the most intimate spot in the restaurant. Shinako made the lunch into a lovers' reuniting, letting Seiroku do most of the talking, letting him ask most of the questions, all of which Shinako had expected Seiroku to ask. How did she like it here in Manila? Had she been back home since coming to Manila? And just what did she do for this German newspaper?

"Until last month, I was a correspondent, as *Herr* Sorge calls it," Shinako said. "Unfortunately, the newspaper closed its Manila offices last month."

Shinako did not offer a reason for the closing; it was unlikely that Seiroku had any knowledge of Sorge's arrest.

"But how did you get your news?" Seiroku asked.

"Many ways. Sometimes I got it from local papers, sometimes I just talked to people. I traveled to many of the islands doing interviews. Of course, government activities here in Manila are a constant source of news. You can hear lots of gossip." Shinako laughed. "And Werner—*Herr* Breidstein—is very good at getting me on the invitation lists for many parties, at least when the English don't make up the invitation list."

"And what do you do now?" Seiroku asked.

"I work full time as Werner's administrative assistant, helping him carry out his business across the Philippines and the East Indies," Shinako answered.

"That is interesting. You must have to work very closely with *Herr* Breidstein. Is he ... ah ... what is your relationship ... is he your ... ," Seiroku asked without completing his question.

"Seiroku, please, it's not like that with him at all," she chided. "He has been very kind to me, almost like a father. But enough about me. What about you? The last time we saw each other," she paused and lowered her eyes in an appropriate fashion, "you were a mere lieutenant."

Seiroku needed no further coaxing. Seiroku described what he had been doing since Shinako had left Tokyo. In essence, it seemed that he had become more and more involved with naval planning on Yamamoto's staff. "I am one of his most important assistants. He often uses me as a sounding board for his thoughts and ideas," Seiroku boasted. Then, in almost a whisper, as if afraid others in the restaurant might hear, he added, "That's why I am here in Manila. I have come to relay and explain some important matters to Consul General Agawa, just as I did in Thailand two weeks ago before I came here—here where my life has blossomed because I have found you again."

Seiroku's voice became smooth and languorous. "When I saw you, Shinako, I couldn't believe my eyes. I had no idea you were here in Manila. After what happened ... at the embassy ... I was so worried—"

"Shh, shh," Shinako chided, as she placed her fingers delicately on Seiroku's lips. "Seiroku, that is past—forget about that. We are here now, together again." Shinako lower her hand and took Seiroku's hand in her's.

"You are so wonderful, Shinako. It is like when we were young, when I was still in pilot training. Our times together were so beautiful, Shinako. Do you remember ... that day ... in the garden?" Seiroku asked.

"It is a day I shall never forget, dear Seiroku—never forget," Shinako said as she smiled, and squeezed Seiroku's hand.

Seiroku's face beamed. He continued to speak of their years together in Tokyo, his words becoming more amorous. But finally he had to return to the embassy. "Until tomorrow," he said as he escorted her to the door of the Hamburg Import-Export offices. Shinako waved to him as he rode off in the Mercedes to be returned to the Japanese consulate by Enrique.

As the Mercedes swung around a corner and out of sight, Shinako turned and went inside to the office. She walked by the receptionist without saying a word and went quickly up the stairs to the washroom at the end of the hall—and threw up her lunch.

THE NEXT DAY, Seiroku arrived in the Mercedes that Shinako sent to pick him up. They went to another out-of-the way intimate restaurant that Shinako suggested. Another long lunch followed with Seiroku telling Shinako the many important responsibilities he had assisting Yamamoto. Shinako listened to him with pretended rapt attention. Again, when they parted, Shinako made their parting ever so sweet, even to the point of standing on her tiptoes and gently, and tantalizingly, kissing Seiroku on the lips. Again, they agreed to meet the next day.

BUT ON THE FOLLOWING DAY when the Mercedes drove up with Seiroku inside, Shinako was not alone. Breidstein, always the charmer, came out with Shinako and greeted Seiroku like an old friend. After a few moments, Breidstein invited Seiroku and Shinako to lunch. As they walked toward the car, Breidstein began to drop a few words about diplomatic life in Tokyo. Shinako watched with fascination—and disgust—at the way Breidstein was able to so obviously impress Seiroku with the names of the important people Breidstein knew on a first name-basis

XII

WAR!

73

SEIROKU SIGNED THE LOG with his name, noting the date and time of his leaving as required—December 5, '41, 1620—and walked out the side entrance of the Japanese consulate, briefcase in hand. He rotated his shoulders, trying to loosen his tense back muscles. It had been a long, tiring day. The coordination of required consulate activities with the time schedules established by the Imperial Staff had been difficult, particularly since the reasons for the various activities could not be disclosed to anyone but the consul general. Detailing the final steps for disruption of the city's telephone communications had been a very time consuming, very intense effort. The planning for severing telephone communications between Manila and Cavite had been particularly difficult, but it was essential they be disrupted to minimize the ability of the U.S. military in Manila to communicate with the naval forces at Cavite and Subic Bay. But even if only a tenth of the telephone lines were severed as planned, Seiroku was sure chaos would result in the critical first hours of the attack.

Seiroku wondered whether staff work was really worth it. When he had been flying on a regular basis, his days were always too short. Now, they sometimes seemed as if they would never end. But of course, working on Yamamoto's staff was the way to the top, particularly with assignments like the current one entrusted to him. And if he could continue to develop contacts like Breidstein, who could guess where he might go?

He missed terribly not having lunch with Shinako the last two days. The last week had been heaven for him. After all these years, after all the frivolous romances he had had, searching for someone, when all the time it was Shinako that he really wanted. But now it seemed to be working out so perfectly. Her father was only a distant memory, something he could forget all about. He was on Yamamoto's staff—one of his key aids. And now he was reunited with his real love, Shinako. The way she spoke to him left no doubt she loved him dearly too. Each word she uttered, each motion of her lovely body was like a god's splendor spilling over him, flowing about him, enfolding him in utter happiness. And with what was going to happen in the next few days—and the great things that would follow for Japan—he could not have imagined he could be so fortunate.

But there was still some final review he needed to complete in his quarters tonight. An extended day of work on Saturday might raise too many questions. He would finish his review tonight and spend much of Saturday with Shinako. Then he would return to the consulate on Sunday morning, have his final discussion with Agawa, and set sail on the *Azumasan Maru* on Sunday evening. The ship would be well into the South China Sea by Monday morning, so the events to come in Hawaii and the Philippines would pose no problem for his return to Japan. But he was still very concerned about Shinako—how to protect her and get her out of the reach of the Americans. If he could just get her to come to the consulate on Sunday, he could easily arrange for Shinako to leave Manila with him. But how to do that, unless he told her what was going to happen on Monday morning? But to do that would be a very dangerous breach of security, unless, perhaps, he waited until the final hours just before boarding the *Azumasan Maru*.

As Seiroku started walking up the street toward the quarters the consulate maintained for visiting military officers, Breidstein's Mercedes pulled to the curb. Shinako was sitting in the back, by a rolled-down window. "Seiroku. Seiroku," she called from the car, as she stuck her arm out and waved to him.

Seiroku stopped, surprised, and then hurried to the side of the car. "What are you doing here?" Seiroku asked.

"We came to get you," Shinako answered in English. "Werner," she said, as she inclined her head toward Breidstein siting in the front seat, "is having a small get-together at his villa on the peninsula, and you are invited," Seiroku said as she smiled.

"Yes, Captain. We'd certainly like you to come," Breidstein said. "Marlene, here," Breidstein turned and nodded toward the woman in the back seat with Shinako—the woman smiled—"and Mr. and Mrs. Jahnel and I will be there. The Jahnels are already at the villa, in fact. You haven't met the Jahnels, but you'll like them. They have a proper perspective on the world—an appreciation of who is best able to govern the rabble of the world. And, of course, Shinako will be there."

"Yes, Seiroku," said Shinako as she continued to talk in English. "It will be wonderful. The beach is beautiful. And the water is so much warmer than in Japan. The coast is gorgeous."

Seiroku wondered what to do. To be with Shinako, alone and away from the busy city, could be ecstasy. And if he didn't go, he wouldn't get to be with Shinako at all. But should he, with all that was going to happen? But the more he thought about it, the more he realized that everything was supposed to continue as normal. And what was more normal than a weekend outing at the beach? And he had the papers he needed to review in his briefcase, so he could do the review at Breidstein's villa—as well as get to know Breidstein better.

"We'll get you back on Sunday, as early as you like, if you're worried about your work, Seiroku. Enrique, my chauffeur here, can drive you and Shinako back together," Breidstein assured Seiroku.

A perfect way to get Shinako to the consulate on Sunday! Seiroku thought. *Leave the villa early and go directly to the consulate—and then only at the last minute tell Shinako why she has to leave Manila with me.*

"Please, Seiroku," Shinako said with a melodious voice. Seiroku looked at her lovely eyes and face, and then at her partially exposed breasts in the folds of the unbuttoned top of her blouse.

"Will I be able to call the embassy and let them know where I will be? I may need to speak to Consul General Agawa about a few things." Seiroku asked. *I need to tell Agawa to make arrangements for Shinako to be included on the* Azumasan Maru *passenger list. Shinako and I will not have a great deal of time when we return to Manila—but there will be enough. Yes, it will work out perfectly if I can call Agawa,* Seiroku thought to himself.

"Of course. You can make all the calls necessary," Breidstein said reassuringly, but failing to point out that the telephone connection to Manila was often inoperable.

"Well ... ah ... all right! Let me go get some clothes from my room," Seiroku said.

"No, you don't need a thing. We have to hurry. The ferry leaves in thirty minutes, and it is the last one for the day," Shinako said.

"Yes, Captain, Shinako's right. If we don't leave for the dock now, we'll miss the ferry, and it is more than a six-hour drive to the villa," Breidstein said

"But my clothes—" Seiroku started to object.

"Don't worry," Shinako said with a grin. "I bribed the maid at your quarters this morning to get some overnight things from your room. I even went shopping and bought you a swim suit!" Shinako said as she held up a shopping bag.

"I guess you have it all figured out," Seiroku said with a relaxed smile, as he climbed into the back seat.

"Yes, I do, Seiroku … yes, I do," Shinako said.

The Mercedes took off in a small cloud of dust, coughing up some smoke from the tailpipe. The Mercedes slowed at the end of the block and turned.

Across the street, a man stamped out his cigarette and waved his arm. A small car pulled up and he got in. As Breidstein's Mercedes disappeared around the corner, the small car accelerated and then turned the same corner as the Mercedes.

74

FRANCIS SAT HUNCHED over his desk reviewing the latest intercepts, trying to make some sense of them. He had been struggling with the intercepts all day long. Leftovers from the dinner plate brought back from the base cafeteria were still sitting on the corner of the desk, untouched. Radio traffic had been picking up noticeably the last couple of weeks. *Obviously*, Francis thought, *something is in the works, but what?* Francis continued to focus on the intercepts.

Ensign Louis Frankhill walked into the room with a small mailbag in one hand and a half-eaten sandwich in the other. He opened the mailbag and dumped its contents onto a table. Between bites of his sandwich, he began to sort the mail into small stacks. "Say, Francis," Louis said with garbled words as he took another big bite of the sandwich, "This one's for you. It's from the Navy Department—Office of Personnel in D.C."

"Put it on the desk," Francis grunted as he continued to look at the intercepts, laying them out side by side and underlining the key words in them that he had been able to decipher, seeing if he could see a pattern—any type of pattern which suggested a connection that would explain why so there was so much radio traffic, particularly from the Imperial Fleet in home waters along the Japanese coast. Why ... why so much traffic from the fleet, when they were in Japanese home waters, unless ... unless ... . *Damn*, Francis suddenly realized, *that could be it! Maybe they aren't in home waters— maybe it is all fake radio traffic to make everyone just think the Imperial Fleet is in home waters.*

The phone rang, breaking Francis' train of thought. "Marian, Communications, Post Y, Cavite."

"Francis, this is Jack Burkhart, at Army Intelligence."

"Hi, Jack. What can I do for you?" Francis said.

"It's not what you can do for me, but maybe what I can do for you—

something that may interest you," Burkhart responded.

"What's up, Jack?" Francis asked with interest, as he straightened in his seat.

"Well, you may or may not know, an apparently important mid-level Japanese naval staff officer came into town about three weeks ago from Bangkok on the *Azumasan Maru*—he was met at the dock by a Jap embassy car. He is a man I think you may know—Seiroku Takamatsu. Isn't he supposed to be on Yamamoto's staff in Tokyo?"

Darn right he's on Yamamoto's staff. And he always seems to turn up when big things are about to happen. Takamatsu—in Manila! Damn. Maybe he's connected to some of this increase in radio traffic. "Yes, Jack, he is. Go on. This is getting interesting."

"Well, of course, we have been keeping tabs on him, helping you Navy swabbies do your job," Jack said with a slight chuckle. Then he continued, his voice becoming serious. "A few days after he arrived, he started regularly meeting for lunch with some local Jap gal. Looked like a lover's meet, although we don't think they've had a roll in the hay yet. Now, if some Jap officer wants to get into some Jap gal's pants, that's okay with us. But we did some checking and found out that her name is Shinako Fujimori. Now that is interesting, because that gal used to work for that German newspaper *Frankfurter Zeitung*."

Shinako Fujimori! Shinako Fujimori meeting with Seiroku Takamatsu—what's going on here? Something big has to be in the works—right here in Manila, Francis thought.

"She works now as an administrative assistant, and maybe a little bit more on the side we figure, for a German guy named Werner Breidstein. I understand that you may have a special interest in Breidstein—according to my boss, head of G2 up here, we're supposed to keep you informed about him. Is that right?" Burkhart asked.

Francis could hardly contain his growing excitement. "Yes, Jack, that's what I understand too—and I sure do have an interest in Breidstein," Francis tried to say with an even voice. *Fujimori, now working for Breidstein—and meeting Takamatsu. Holy cow!*

"Well then, maybe this is right up your alley, as best I can figure what your alley is. A couple of hours ago, Breidstein, this Fujimori gal, and some other broad we don't know picked up Takamatsu outside the Japanese consulate— picked him up in Breidstein's car, that is—and drove to the harbor and took the car ferry to the peninsula. Now maybe this is just a little fun weekend—

Breidstein has a fancy villa on the ocean side of the peninsula, near Mauban—but there is something fishy about the whole meeting, beyond the fact that they were all together," Burkhart said.

"What's that, Jack?" Francis asked eagerly.

"Takamatsu didn't take any clothes with him, except the shirt on his back, so to speak. And he didn't leave his briefcase at the Japanese Embassy offices or the officer quarters there on Calla Maridana, where the out-of-town Jap brass usually stay. He took the briefcase with him. Now maybe it's an empty brief case, and … maybe it's not," Burkhart said with exaggerated slowness.

"Jack, how do I find Breidstein's villa?" Francis asked.

"I'll have a map ready by the time you get to my office."

Francis walked over to Louis Frankhill's desk. "I'm going up to Army G-2 in Manila. May be gone for awhile. Take a look at those intercepts on my desk while I'm gone. See if you might think the same thing I'm beginning to think—that they may be a ruse to try to make it look like the Imperial Fleet is in home waters, when maybe it isn't," Francis said.

Frankhill nodded as he continued to chew on the last piece of his sandwich. Francis turned to leave. Frankhill took a big gulp and said, "Don't forget that letter that came for you."

"Oh … yeah," Francis said as he grabbed the brown envelope—the kind used by the Navy for all its non-urgent messages—folded it in half, stuck it in his back pocket, and walked quickly by his desk and out the door to the jeep.

IT WOULD HAVE TAKEN about six or seven hours to drive around the bay to Mauban, and it was already six o'clock, so Francis pulled a few strings and located a Navy tug to take him across the bay to Limay. At Limay, he would pick up a jeep from the local constable's office. Burkhart arranged for the jeep by calling from Manila. The local constable had been reluctant to lend it—it was the only vehicle he had—but when Burkhart said General MacArthur would appreciate the assistance, the constable readily agreed. "MacArthur," Burkhart had said with a grin as he had hung up the phone, "might appreciate it, if he ever were to know about it. And I don't think this is going to be one particular bit of international cooperation he will hear about."

As the big tug plowed through the choppy waves on Manila Bay, Francis remembered the letter in his pocket. He pulled it out, unfolded it, and used his finger to tear it open. Inside was another envelope, clearly a non-Navy envelope. He held it up in the dim light of the pilothouse, trying to see who it was from. He saw that the letter had been addressed to him at the Navy Department in Washington, and had been forwarded from there. As he continued to squint at the letter, holding it upward toward the overhead light, he suddenly realized it was from Elaine—it had a return address in Fort Wayne. He tore open the envelope. He struggled to read it, barely able to make out its words in the weak light of the pilothouse.

September 12, 1941

Francis,
So many things have happened since I left you that night in Washington, I just felt I had to tell you what I have decided to do.
My son died three years ago, and Lewis and I separated shortly thereafter—I couldn't take his screwing around, literally, with his receptionist anymore. Not that, I suppose, I'm any better, considering what we did. But I couldn't bring myself to divorce Lewis—as long as Mom was alive. After the separation, I went to live with her in Colorado. I thought about contacting you then—actually tried to do it on the way out there, but lost my courage when I didn't get you at home in Chicago. When Mom died, I sold the ranch, filed for divorce, and moved back to Ft. Wayne. I have been living there with my sister. The divorce became final this last summer.
I feel so confused now, and I don't see anything getting better the way things are. I can't make up my mind—whether we should try to get together again, or whether it was just not meant for us to be together, that maybe it's just God's payback for what I did while I was still married to Lewis. So, I made a decision last week.
You know I'm a nurse. The church says qualified nurses are badly needed overseas. I have decided to volunteer to work for at least two years at clinics in the Philippines. I expect to leave the U.S. by the end of September. After a couple of years, maybe I can figure out what I want to do—about you, Francis, and about us. Maybe then, too, you will have come to know yourself better, and know whether or not you really love me—or were just infatuated by the first woman that you really had an affair with. Don't try to contact me—at least for awhile. I want to get my life in order again.

Elaine

Francis practically jumped for joy. The Philippines! Elaine was already here somewhere in the Philippines! If he contacted the Catholic archdiocese, he could probably find out where she was pretty easily. And even if she were having a hard time sorting things out, he would be damned if he would wait to find her. He knew what he wanted, and it wasn't just some roll in the hay. He loved Elaine—and he knew that more and more with each passing day.

"We're almost there, Lieutenant," the tugboat captain said, as he pointed to some lights on the shore. As the tug approached the dock, Francis could make out a man standing there beside a jeep.

75

IT WAS ABOUT ELEVEN O'CLOCK when Francis began to smell the sea's sweet odor of decay. He stopped the jeep and backed it into the edge of the high vegetation lining the dirt road. He got out of the jeep. He figured he was about half a mile from where the map showed the villa to be. He started jogging.

Several minutes later, Francis could see the line of dunes hugging the shore of the dark waters of the South China Sea along the Battan Peninsula. And there, below him, near the line of dunes, in the silvery light of the moon, he saw the villa. It was immersed in a manicured lawn and surrounded on three sides by a perimeter wall; the fourth side was open to the beach. Down the beach, farther to the right and outside the wall, there appeared to be some work shacks. Several lights were on in the main part of the house.

Francis moved toward the left to work his way down to the beach. Several minutes later, he reached the dunes and climbed over them so they were between him and the villa. He crouched low, making his way along the beach toward the villa to a point where he could get a close look at the villa.

Francis saw that the main section of the villa opened to a wide verandah. Two wings projected out at odd angles from the main section of the building. The one on the right was one story, but the one on the left had two levels. Individual balconies ran along the length of the two-level wing, each balcony framing French doors. Most of the doors were open to the night breeze. Some small lights were on in both wings, but the main section and verandah were well lighted. And there, sitting on the verandah engaged in animated conversation, were six people. Francis recognized three: Breidstein, Shinako, and Takamatsu. Francis edged his way along some bushes to get closer to the verandah and better hear what they were saying.

The conversation went on for about fifteen minutes. Francis couldn't hear much of it because of the breaking waves—just bits and pieces, small talk as best as he could tell. Then everyone began to get up. Francis realized that they were about to call it a night.

"KARL, MONIKA, do you remember the way to your room, down to the left?" Breidstein asked in German, glad to be rid of them—and Monika's continuing talk laced with sexual overtones—for the night.

"Of course we do, Werner," Monika replied with a slight slur. Breidstein had never seen a woman put so many drinks away with such limited effect.

Karl held Monika's arm as he guided her out of the room, although he wasn't much steadier than she. "Good night. Please, Werner, don't bother to call us for breakfast. We will sleep in," he said.

"Yes, don't call us—unless… you feel the need for some company," Monika said as she looked back at Shinako with a lewd smirk, "in the morning … that is. You're sure the commander will be able to keep you… occupied, Shinako?"

"Yes, Monika, I am sure," Shinako said with a disgusted frown.

Shinako turned her face from Monika to look at Seiroku. The frown was replaced with a smile.

"I don't know how they manage to do that and remain even halfway intelligible," remarked Marlene from across the room.

"Yes, I wonder too, my dear. But shall we also retire?" Breidstein asked leadingly.

Taking her cue, Marlene stood, swaying to keep her balance. She looked tentatively, invitingly, at Breidstein, saying in a whisper, "How long before you…?"

Turning his back slightly to Shinako and Seiroku sitting primly at opposite ends of the couch, Breidstein whispered to Marlene, "Yes, my dear, after awhile, after I put the two love birds into their nest and assure us of no interruption."

Marlene left the verandah, saying goodnight to Shinako and Seiroku.

"Well, my dear Shinako and my charming Commander Takamatsu, how about you? I intend to get you up bright and early, Commander, to show you my stables," said Breidstein as he returned to their common language of English.

"Yes, in a moment or two," Shinako answered.

"Well, don't diddle too long. We have a busy day tomorrow." *And,* thought Breidstein, *I want both of you to have a very enjoyable, very full night— together. And while you are screwing Shinako, Commander Takamatsu,*

I will have an opportunity to see what secrets you might have hidden in that briefcase you seem so careful of.

SEIROKU SAT QUIETLY for a moment after Breidstein said good night and left for his bedroom. Shinako shifted her position, letting the short slit of her skirt show a bit of her thigh. She looked at Seiroku, her tongue gently wetting her slightly parted lips.

Seiroku spoke. "Shinako, it is wonderful being here with you. I hope you know how much I care for you—how much I ... want you." He stood, moved close to Shinako, and then pulled her up. He put his arms around her. She did not resist his embrace. "Oh, Shinako, I have waited so long for a night like this."

"Yes, my darling, so have I," Shinako said as she pressed close to Seiroku.

He kissed Shinako; she returned his kiss. He became more amorous. Seiroku could feel himself harden as Shinako pressed against him. He felt her pushing her pelvis against him, twisting, grinding herself against him. This was the night for which he had been waiting, almost from the moment he had set eyes on her two weeks ago. But then she drew back.

"Not here, Seiroku. Werner may come back. Go to your room, while I get ready for you. Come to my room in about twenty minutes—I want it to be perfect for us, to please you more than any woman ever has." With that, she turned from him and walked hurriedly into the hallway and up the stairs.

In a few moments, after his arousal had subsided, Seiroku picked up his briefcase at the end of the couch and followed.

FRANCIS SAW ONE COUPLE leave the verandah and go to the single-level wing on the right. In a few moments, a light came on in one of the rooms, near the end of the wing. Then the other woman left, after making some remarks to Breidstein. She made her way to the right as well. As Breidstein started to leave, Francis saw another light come on about midway along the wing. Then, Shinako and Takamatsu were alone.

Francis saw Takamatsu get up, stand in front of Shinako, and pull her up from the couch. The ardor in their kisses was apparent. A light came on at the very end of the left wing, on the second level. He saw Shinako pull away from Takamatsu and leave the verandah. A short time later a light came on midway down the left wing, also on the second level. A few minutes later, after Takamatsu went up the stairs, taking a briefcase with him, Francis saw a light come on in what had to be Takamatsu's room, a room on the upper level next to the verandah. Francis knew he had to see what was in that briefcase.

Francis crossed the lawn to the edge of the verandah. He studied the setting for a few moments. *No*, he thought, *to go through the verandah is not the way to do it; too likely that someone might soon return. But the banyan tree growing beside the verandah might just do it—up the tree to the verandah roof and then across to the balcony.*

Francis climbed the tree, stepped across to the roof, and slowly walked toward the balcony. His feet began to slide on the roof tiles, his body teetering as he fought to regain his balance. Then his slide stopped. *Damn*, he thought angrily to himself, *these shoes were not made for walking on slippery tile shingles. Why didn't I think about something like this before I left Manila.* He moved more cautiously. Then he reached across the small, open space to the balcony, grabbed the railing, and climbed onto the balcony outside Takamatsu's room.

Francis peered into the room. Takamatsu, dressed in pajamas, was putting on a robe. A briefcase was on the chair beside a small writing desk, partially covered by his uniform hanging over the back of the chair. Francis watched Takamatsu step into his bathroom. In a moment, Francis heard the growl of the water closet and a faucet running. He watched Takamatsu step out of the bathroom, look at himself in the mirror, and then cautiously step through the bedroom door into the hallway.

This was his opportunity. Francis pulled the French doors open a bit wider and stepped into the room. He moved quickly to the bedroom door, listened for a moment, and then carefully opened the door. Seeing no one immediately near, Francis opened the door a tiny slit more and saw Takamatsu going into a room that had to be Shinako's room. *That should keep him busy for awhile*, Francis thought.

Francis stepped to the chair and picked up the briefcase. He undid the buckles on the straps and pulled out a small stack of papers, immediately recognizing them as Japanese naval documents. Francis placed them on the desk and focused on the first sheet, forcing the words into his mind, just words to be remembered later, only bits and pieces of understanding working through the intensity of his swiftly moving eyes. Bangkok... Luzon... coincident attack... Pearl Harbor. Then the second sheet, halfway through... more words to remember... naval landings with joint air attack... surprise dawn attack—

The bedroom door handle slowly twisted, with a squeak. Francis quickly scooped up the papers and briefcase and stepped into the bathroom. As he closed the door, he thought, *Jesus, I have everything in here with me. Takamatsu is sure to see it's gone.* Francis set the briefcase and papers carefully on the floor, getting ready to grasp Takamatsu's throat—to kill if necessary.

But the bathroom door didn't open. Francis heard someone walking around the room, opening drawers in the clothes cabinet and the writing desk. *What's going on?* Francis wondered.

Then, finally, the bathroom door opened. Francis stood behind the door, ready to grab Takamatsu.

Breidstein entered the bathroom, his back to Francis as he looked around the room.

Breidstein? What the hell?

Then a shot came from outside the bedroom. Then another. Breidstein turned back to the bedroom and then ran out into the hallway, slamming the bedroom door behind him.

AS THE DOOR SLAMMED, Francis looked into the bedroom and saw that he was alone. But he didn't have time to read any more. He had to get out of there! Something was happening outside the room and he dared not let himself get involved in it. He had to get word back to Manila about what he had read. He put the papers back into the briefcase, pulled the straps through the buckles, and carefully put the briefcase back under Takamatsu's clothes on the chair. He went to the French doors and quickly stepped out to the balcony. He stepped from the balcony onto the roof and started to reach for the banyan tree. His feet started to slide. He tried to grab a limb of the tree. He had one in his grasp, momentarily, but then his grip loosened and he fell awkwardly from the edge of the verandah roof. A sharp pain sliced through his left ankle as he hit the ground.

76

BREIDSTEIN YANKED THE GUN from Seiroku's hand as he shoved Seiroku into the bathroom. Seiroku did not resist. "Don't move," ordered Breidstein as he pushed Seiroku down onto the toilet seat. Seiroku didn't move, he couldn't. His arms and legs were limp. Breidstein turned back into the bedroom, closing the bathroom door. Seiroku remained immobile, his eyes glassy.

Breidstein looked at Shinako. She had not moved since Breidstein had forced her bedroom door open; nor would she ever move again. She lay on the floor in a widening pool of blood which contrasted sickeningly with the blue of the thin silk lace nightgown now spread about her, as if someone had taken special care to arrange it. Her petite, naked, and now dead body was clearly visible under the thin cloth of the gown. Breidstein could see where her tears had streaked her makeup; she must have been crying when she died. Why? What had happened here?

But first things first. Breidstein picked up the phone and rang the back bungalow where Enrique stayed. "Enrique… Breidstein. There has been some trouble. Get the car and drive it around immediately to the back entrance of the house. Then come to the middle guest room—on the second floor. Be as quiet as you can."

Breidstein returned to the bathroom. Seiroku had not moved. "What happened? Listen to me, you fool, what happened?" Breidstein demanded, speaking in English.

No answer. Breidstein shook Seiroku. Seiroku said nothing. Breidstein slapped Seiroku across the face. "What happened? Answer me!"

Seiroku seemed to come out of his daze. He started to speak in Japanese.

"English, you fool, English," Breidstein shouted.

"I… I… I came to her room, like she wanted me to. She told me to wait while she went into the bathroom. Then… then… she came out. She was crying. She had a gun in her hand. She said something about me and... and her... her father."

Breidstein broke in angrily. "You mean she knew that you killed her father?" *How did she know that*, Breidstein wondered. *Sorge said he had never told anyone what he had seen.*

"She shot at me... shot at me. Why did she do that? See, my arm, it is bleeding," Seiroku said as he pulled his robe off his shoulder to show Breidstein. Breidstein saw only a minor flesh wound; the blood was already beginning to clot. "If I had not grabbed the gun from her, she would have killed me."

"Did she say she knew that you killed her father?" Breidstein asked.

"No. No. She said nothing like that... why would she? I did not kill her father," Seiroku said.

You goddamn liar, Breidstein thought. *Somehow she knew. But it is too late now to do anything about it.* "How did she get shot?"

"I grabbed the gun... we fought... it went off," Seiroku answered weakly.

Breidstein did not know whether to believe him or not. Breidstein would probably never know. But it made no difference now; he had to take care of things. Then he heard the car drive up behind the house.

In a few moments, Enrique entered the bedroom. "¡*Dios mio!*" exclaimed Enrique.

"You just sit there. Do not go anywhere," Breidstein said to Seiroku. "I will be back in a few minutes."

BREIDSTEIN AND ENRIQUE picked up Shinako's body and started down the hallway, toward the stairway. Marlene, in her robe, was just coming up the stairs. "Werner, I thought I heard some noise, like shots." Then she saw Seiroku's limp body. "My God, Werner. What's happened?" Marlene said as her hand flew to her mouth.

"Just a little accident. Nothing for you to be concerned about. Go back to your room," Breidstein ordered.

"But Werner, she's dead—she dead!" Marlene screamed, as she picked up a corner of Shinako's blood-soaked nightgown and saw blood drip to the floor.

Breidstein knew he couldn't let Marlene become hysterical. He slapped her. Marlene staggered backward. Blood came to the corner of her mouth. "I said get back to your room. Now!"

Marlene shrank back down the stairs, and ran toward her room.

Breidstein and Enrique continued down the stairs, across the living room to the kitchen, and then out the back door to the car. Enrique dropped Shinako's feet and opened the trunk of the car. Breidstein rolled Shinako into the trunk, twisting her body to fit. Enrique slammed the trunk closed.

"What do you want me to do with her?"

Breidstein thought a moment. "Wait a minute."

Breidstein went back into the house to Marlene's room.

He opened Marlene's bedroom door, without knocking. Marlene was sitting on her bed, the phone in her hand, rapidly clicking the switch hook. Breidstein could only shake his head, as if scolding a child. *Such a pity,* he thought. *She is so imaginative in bed.*

Marlene looked at Breidstein, her eyes wide in fright. "No, Werner, no, please," Marlene pleaded as the phone dropped from her hand.

Breidstein approached her, putting his hands on her shoulders, as if to kiss her good night. "Why don't you lie down. We'll talk about everything in the morning. You'll understand then."

Marlene seemed to relax. Breidstein moved his hands quickly to her neck and squeezed.

Marlene tried to push him away. His weight bore down on her as he pushed her back onto the bed. "Werner, stop, please, stop!" She tried to pull his hands away from her neck, her fingers clawing at his hands and her legs kicking in the air. It was useless. "I won't say… anything… nothing…." Her voice turned to a gaggle; foamy red saliva ran from her mouth.

That's right, my dear, you won't say anything. Breidstein continued to tighten his grasp, twisting his hands until he heard the snap and Marlene resisted no more.

BREIDSTEIN CAME OUT the back door, carrying Marlene on his shoulder like a bag of potatoes. "Open the trunk."

Enrique said nothing as he pulled up the trunk lid.

Breidstein dropped Marlene on top of Shinako, shoving Shinako further back into the trunk. Enrique closed the lid, pushing down hard until he heard the lock click.

"Weigh them down with something. Then dump them off the end of the dock on the point. The current will take care of everything else. Then come back here," Breidstein ordered.

Enrique got into the car, started it, and drove slowly away.

Breidstein went back upstairs to deal with Seiroku.

77

FRANCIS TRIED TO RUN but could only hobble. His ankle was on fire. He knew it had been badly sprained if not broken. It felt just like that last parachute drop at Highstown. Well, he couldn't stop to try to wrap it right now. He had to get away from the villa! He struggled down to the beach and started dragging himself and his leg along, falling several times. Just about the time he was past the villa wall and ready to head back inland, he heard a car start up near the ranch shacks and saw headlights move toward the house. He hurt too much to try to guess what was going on.

Finally he was into the tall grass and bushes behind the dunes. He found a stick to use as a splint. He sat down on the sandy soil and got out his pocketknife. He cut off his pant leg and tore it into several long strips, winding them around his leg to hold the makeshift splint in place. He got up and tried to walk. It was slow and painful, but he could walk. He was breathing in big gulps, both from the exertion and the pain. He finally found a sturdy fallen limb that he could use as a cane. His speed increased somewhat.

Francis continued hobbling along, looking for the jeep. Then he saw it amongst the trees and bushes. He shuffled up to it and climbed in, letting his foot hang out over the side panel of the jeep. He started to push the starter button… then stopped. How could he shift gears and brake? He pulled his foot inside and used his hands to lift his leg and foot onto the clutch. He tried to push. God! The pain was unbearable. Wait—the cane… if he could push with the cane. He tried… it worked. He started the engine, then shifted into first gear. He tried to slowly let up the clutch with his makeshift cane, but the clutch suddenly engaged and the jeep lurched forward. Francis steadied the steering wheel as the jeep began to bounce down the rugged road.

FRANCIS HAD BEEN MOVING along in first gear for about an hour. The pain was making it difficult to focus his eyes. Then, suddenly, he saw the big pothole, but it was too late. The jeep wheel went into it and Francis' good foot accidentally pushed down on the accelerator, causing the jeep to jump forward. Then it was into the smelly muck beside the road, where the jeep came to a sudden stop. Francis' head banged against the steering wheel, knocking him unconscious.

78

BREIDSTEIN PUSHED SEIROKU into his bedroom and on to the edge of the bed. "All right, Commander. Calm down. It's all over now. I am going to take care of everything," Breidstein said.

Breidstein picked up Seiroku's uniform from the back of the chair and tossed it at him. "Get dressed." Then Breidstein saw the briefcase—*strange, he thought, I don't remember seeing it before.* He picked it up and opened it. He pulled a sheath of papers from it. He flipped through them, not knowing enough Japanese to really understand them, but recognizing enough to know that the papers dealt with military operations somehow. He turned to Seiroku, who was still sitting motionless on the bed.

"Nobody is going to know what happened here tonight except you and me, if you cooperate with me. Tell me what's in these papers of yours," Breidstein ordered, continuing to leaf through the stack of papers, his eyes latching onto the dates—dates that appeared to be only two, or in some cases, three days from now. Something was planned to occur soon. Breidstein had to know what the papers said so he could deal with what might be going to happen. He was not going to get caught unawares like he had been in September of thirty-nine when Poland was invaded.

"I cannot tell you that. You should not be looking at those papers. They are secret," Shinako said with a sullen voice.

"It is a little late to worry about that now, Commander. You listen to me. Unless you cooperate with me, I am going to call the police and tell them how you killed Shinako. And then what are you going to do?" Breidstein threatened. Breidstein was sure that Seiroku was still too dazed to realize that Breidstein would never think of calling the police. "And I just might let the Japanese authorities, maybe even your boss Yamamoto, know how the young, fanatical Lieutenant Takamatsu walked up the Foreign Ministry steps in nineteen-thirty-seven and shot the honored former Ambassador to Japan's ally,

Yukihiko Fujimori. How will that sit with the honorable Isoroku Yamamoto?" Breidstein threatened.

"No. You cannot do that. You must not," Seiroku pleaded.

"Well then, answer my questions," Breidstein ordered.

Seiroku's shoulders slumped. "December eighth will be the day for a major attack against American and British forces in the East Indies, the Philippines, and ... Pearl Harbor in the Hawaiian Islands."

"Pearl Harbor! You have to be mad. The whole Imperial Staff must be mad. An attack against the Hawaiian Islands will never succeed," Breidstein said in shock.

"But it will, it will... it will succeed... because it will be a surprise," Seiroku said.

"The Philippines—what about the Philippines?" Breidstein demanded.

"Preliminary attacks start on the eighth. Full-scale landings begin on the tenth. That is why I am here—to arrange for disruption of communications before the landing forces arrive. I will leave the Philippines tomorrow, before the attack starts. The consulate staff will remain—wait until our forces take Manila. They will be freed by Imperial troops if the Americans attempt to make prisoners of them."

Breidstein sat down, his mind a whirl. If Japan were going to attack Pearl Harbor—and the Philippines—the day after tomorrow, what should he do?

Obviously, he had to keep out of the reach of the Americans, at least until the Japanese landed and gained the upper hand. And he needed to warn Bogner at the consulate—get word to Berlin. But wait. Did he dare stay at the consulate once he told Bogner what was going to happen? Once the attack started, Germany would most assuredly declare war on the United States and then the Americans would take over the consulate—at least until the Japanese arrived, if they ever did. Bogner and the other consulate officials would be interned; they had diplomatic passports. But his own passport was not a diplomatic one, so he might be considered an ordinary prisoner of war. Then who knows what could happen? His real identity might be discovered—and then he would be considered a spy. No, he didn't dare go to the consulate. Besides, what could Berlin do about the Japanese attack? Knowing about the attack would change nothing. Indeed, they might already know about it and want it to happen.

And going to the Japanese consulate—he would be a fool to try that. Agawa would never welcome him into the consulate. And there was no guarantee that the Japanese plan would work. For the Japanese to think they could successfully attack the Hawaiian Islands was proof of how flawed their thinking might be.

No, his only safety lay in hiding, maybe changing his identify if the Japanese were not successful. He needed to get to Manila first, get all the cash out of the safe, and then go into hiding. But where?

Breidstein heard the car drive up to the back of the house. Enrique must have finished his task. Now, if he could only decide where to go. Then it came to him. The church—the church where his mother was buried. Now was the time to make some use of that old priest Eduardo. "Get dressed, Commander. Then wait here. I have to get something before we leave."

"Leave? Where are we going?"

"I'm taking you back to your consulate in Manila. You should be back in time to have Saturday dinner with some of your consulate friends, just like nothing ever happened."

Breidstein went downstairs to the back door. "Enrique, go around to the side of the house and cut the telephone line. Then come back here. We are returning to… Manila… for awhile."

"What about the Jahnels?" Enrique asked.

"Just leave them alone. I will leave a note saying we all went hunting for the day and not to expect us back before nighttime. By the time they figure out what to do, it won't make any difference," Breidstein said, and then paused, not sure if he wanted Enrique to know about the coming attack. "We will be back by then… be able to explain… about the… uh… hunting accident."

"The hunting accident? Oh… *si*, the hunting accident," Enrique said as he gave a smirk of understanding.

Then Breidstein returned to his bedroom. He opened a small wall safe and took out the several hundred American dollars in it, stuffing them in his leather travel bag. Next he pulled out a German passport, the one he had never destroyed as he had been directed to—the one for Franz Lundstrom. Finally, he pulled out the other passport. It still had the dried spots of blood of the man from whom he had taken it—after Breidstein had killed him that night in Balboa. An American passport might come in handy, if he could get the picture changed somehow.

He put all of it, the money and the passports, into the bag, along with the gun he had taken from Seiroku—the gun with which Shinako had tried and so miserably failed to obtain her revenge.

79

IT WAS LATE SATURDAY morning when Enrique turned the Mercedes inland toward Highway 7 on the road back to Manila after leaving the local doctor in Mauban. Breidstein and Enrique had spend the early morning hours trying to clean up the blood spots in the hallway, living room, and kitchen that had dropped from Shinako's body as they had carried her to the Mercedes. Cleaning up the blood in Shinako's bedroom had been impossible—there was just too much of it—so they had finally just rolled up the bedroom carpet and pushed it under the bed. By then it was late enough to give credence to Breidstein's story to the doctor about Takamatsu's wound and the hunting accident that had caused it. A generous payment to the doctor by Breidstein had kept the doctor from asking too many questions.

As they drove on toward Manila, Breidstein sat in the back seat with Takamatsu, trying to drill into him the story he would have to tell about what went on at the villa—about the accident and how he had gotten the gunshot wound. By the time they were approaching the outskirts of Manila in the afternoon hours, Breidstein had no qualms that Takamatsu knew what to say—but would he? *Maybe, just to assure Takamatsu's continued cooperation,* Breidstein thought, *I had best keep the papers from Takamatsu's briefcase—and besides, they just might become useful later.*

As they continued to drive on, Breidstein could tell Seiroku was finally getting his wits together. He was alert but agitated. He tracked the passing traffic and buildings with wide eyes, no longer slumping in the seat, but sweating profusely.

Then, as they sped through the slums of Manila's outskirts, Seiroku said, "Give me my papers. I must return them to the consulate files."

"I'm afraid not, Commander. I will have to keep them—I need to be sure that you won't have second thoughts about what to say to Agawa."

"I must have them—now," Seiroku demanded.

"No," Breidstein said, beginning to get worried. Had he pushed Takamatsu too far? Takamatsu was becoming more agitated, shifting in his seat, rocking back and forth. Breidstein picked up his travel bag and unzipped it. He reached into the bag, feeling the reassuring hardness of the gun there.

"I have to have them. I cannot return without them!" Seiroku said again in a hysterical voice.

"No, I'm telling you, no," Breidstein said as he put his hand around the gun in the bag.

"Yes, you must," Seiroku screamed as he threw himself on Breidstein, grabbing Breidstein's neck with one hand and trying to reach his briefcase beside Breidstein with the other.

Breidstein pulled the gun from the bag, shoved it into Seiroku's belly, and fired. The pistol made a muffled bang. Seiroku's hands loosened and his body slumped on top of Breidstein. From underneath Seiroku's body, Breidstein could feel Enrique putting on the brakes. "No, Enrique, no, don't stop. Keep going," Breidstein yelled. The car surged forward as Breidstein pushed Seiroku's body away and onto the floorboard of the car.

Breidstein looked out the back window to see if anybody was following. There seemed to be no one. "Do you think anybody saw anything, Enrique?" Breidstein yelled at Enrique.

Enrique twisted his neck, checking the rear view mirror. "No, it doesn't look like it. The shot wasn't too loud. Maybe nobody realized it was a gunshot," Enrique said as he continued to speed down the street.

"Get out of sight somewhere, Enrique—quick," Breidstein directed. "There, into that alley over there."

Enrique swerved the car to the right and into the squalid alley. He slowed as he reached the end of alley where it dead ended in dense undergrowth and piles of loose garbage. Enrique stopped the car.

"Get out and look around, Enrique. Make sure that no one's here."

Enrique climbed out of the car and looked around. Then he walked back down the alley, looking at the few old buildings along the sides of the alley. "Doesn't seem to be anybody," he told Breidstein as he came back to the car.

"All right. Help me get the commander out of the car—we'll put him in the trunk until we can find a safe place to get rid of him." Breidstein was unsure about what to do about the body; and until he was sure, he didn't want to leave it just anywhere. He had to be sure it wouldn't be found before he could go into hiding—it needed to be buried, not just dumped. But this alley was not the place to try to bury a body. After he and Enrique quickly put

Seiroku's body in the trunk, Breidstein removed his blood-splattered sports coat and put it in the trunk as well.

TWO HOURS LATER, as the sun was dipping low, the Mercedes reached Breidstein's apartment building. Breidstein told Enrique to go eat and be back at the rear door of the apartment building with the car in exactly three hours, making sure that one saw the bloody inside of the car. They would dispose of the body then, after Breidstein decided where to get rid of it. As Breidstein got out of the car at the front entrance of the building, with his travel bag and Seiroku's brief case, a man reading the evening paper in the café across the street looked at his watch and wrote something down on a pad of paper.

In his apartment, Breidstein had a cold dinner, showered, changed his clothes, and stuffed some clothes and toiletries into his travel bag, covering Shinako's pistol already there. Finally, he gathered up the limited money he had at the apartment and put it in his travel bag with the other money. Then, as he waited in the coolness of the darkening night for Enrique, Breidstein contemplated what to do about the dead commander and Enrique.

Enrique had not been privy to Breidstein's interrogation of Takamatsu; and the attack had not been discussed in the car coming back to Manila. *So, Breidstein thought, Enrique does not know about the coming attack. And I dare not tell him about it. He might want to hide with me at the convent at San Fernando, and that is impossible. I'm going to have a hard enough time trying to hide there myself. However, just having Enrique take me to San Fernando and leave me, without telling him why, is going to make him very suspicious—maybe suspicious enough to cause trouble by talking to someone, maybe even the police. But if I tell Enrique just to stay in Manila and then the attack does come, Enrique will probably figure it all out—that I got information from Seiroku about the attack—and may go to the Americans to make a deal to give them information about me to protect himself. No, there is only one thing to do: kill Enrique.*

Breidstein thought a few moments more about how he would do it. *I will tell him we are returning to the villa, to get the Jahnels like I said we would. I will kill him along the way, after I get him to bury Takamatsu along some back road well north of Manila—a perfect solution to today's messy events.* Breidstein looked at his watch. *Almost three hours.* He locked the apartment and went downstairs to the rear door of the building to wait for Enrique.

When Enrique returned, Breidstein ordered him to drive to the Hamburg Import-Export office at the dock. The man in the café across the street continued to read his paper.

By the time Breidstein and Enrique arrived at the Hamburg Import-Export office, night had come and a heavy fog was settling in. The dock was empty except for the tug that was normally berthed there. No one was on board tonight; the crew was sampling the flesh of the harbor nightspots. "Wait here, Enrique, while I get a few things from my office. Get a shovel from the garage and fill up the gas tank while I'm inside," Breidstein ordered as he got out of the car. "We have a long drive ahead of us."

"Where are we going?" Enrique asked.

"Back to the villa," Breidstein responded with his prepared answer. "We need to see the Jahnels and tell them about the hunting accident, so they don't get suspicious. Along the way up there, we will bury the commander's body back in some woods somewhere where it will never be found. We'll bring the Jahnels back here tomorrow. The Jahnels—no one—will never know what happened to Shinako and Seiroku."

"Oh," Enrique said.

Breidstein went to his private office and opened the safe. He pulled out the passport for Werner Breidstein and then all the cash, about three thousand in American dollars and several hundred more in yen and pesos—enough to get started again once he could come out of hiding. He stuffed the passport and money into the travel bag. He then slid Takamatsu's papers down into the inside compartment of the bag. Finally, he removed his own gun from the safe—a small pistol intended to be easily concealed, but very deadly at close range. He pulled the gun from its holster. He loosened his belt and slid the gun's small holster onto it, moving the holster around to his back to better conceal the gun. He checked the gun to see that it was fully loaded, and started to reach back to put it in the holster. But then he paused, thinking, *perhaps I had better keep it within easy reach.* He put the pistol in the travel bag, on the top of the clothes and money. He locked the office door and returned to the car.

"Is the car all gassed up, Enrique?" Breidstein asked as in he slid into the front seat of the car and set his travel bag on this lap. Enrique nodded his head.

"All right. Head back north on Highway One," Breidstein ordered.

"What about the German woman—what are you going to tell the Jahnels about her?" Enrique asked.

"That she... ah..." Breidstein fumbled. *Damn,* he thought, *I didn't think about Marlene.* "Ah... that she returned with us... that she decided to stay in Manila... that she was too tired to return," Breidstein said, hoping that satisfied Enrique.

Enrique turned to look at Breidstein. "How do we explain that we brought the navy officer back to Manila—why couldn't he come back to the villa?" Enrique asked.

"That's easy to explain. I just felt he needed to see a Japanese doctor at the consulate—as a precaution... and Shinako stayed with the commander," Breidstein answered reassuringly.

Enrique looked at Breidstein without saying anything for a moment.

"Let's go, Enrique, it's getting late," Breidstein ordered, hoping that Enrique was through asking questions.

"I don't think I want to go," Enrique said.

"What do you mean, Enrique?" Breidstein asked, getting worried.

"Just what I said. I don't think I want to go—too much killing has been going on. I think maybe I better take my pay, and just let you go on, by yourself, *Herr* Breidstein," Enrique said with a quiet voice.

"Well, if that's the way you feel, Enrique. I suppose I can trust you to keep your mouth shut, can't I?" Breidstein asked, trying to make Enrique less suspicious as Breidstein realized that things would have to be taken care of now, rather than later.

"*Si.* I'm not going to tell anybody what happened. Won't do me any good," Enrique said.

"Well, let me give you some money," Breidstein said as he started to reach into his travel bag. Enrique hesitated—just a moment too long—before trying to stop Breidstein's moving hand. Breidstein pulled the gun from the travel bag and fired point blank into Enrique's chest. Enrique's outwardly stretched hand went to his chest as he slammed against the car door, pushing it open. Enrique's body slid partly onto the pavement as the shot echoed along the dark streets of the warehouse district.

Breidstein looked up and down the dock, trying to peer through the fog. Seeing no one, he got out of the car. He thought a moment about what he should do—whether he should take the bodies in the car with him. But the more he though about it, the more he became convinced that he should get rid of the bodies as quickly as possible. Too much was happening too fast to chance being caught with the bodies in the car. He pulled Enrique the rest of the way out of the car and dragged him to the edge of the dock. He rolled the body over the edge; it fell into the water with a small splash. He returned to the car and pulled Takamatsu's body from the trunk. He dragged it to the edge of the dock. It too slid into the warm waters of the harbor with a small splash.

Breidstein returned to the car and looked again up and down the dock. No one. He got into the Mercedes, quickly started it, and drove away. As he did, a man stepped out of the shadows of one of the warehouse buildings and started running up the street.

80

THE RISING SUN was beginning to burn off the Sunday morning mist when Breidstein let the car slow to a stop at the side of the road about six kilometers from the convent. He looked up and down the road. Seeing no one, he drove the car off the road, gunning the engine hard so the car went deep into the bushes. He spent the next hour trying his best to cover up the car tracks and hide the car, although he was sure it would be only a matter of time before the car was discovered. But he needed only enough time for the Japanese to attack and capture Manila.

Breidstein's clothes were soiled with dirt from hiding the car—and blood from Enrique's murder. He changed into the clothes he had brought from his apartment. He spend a few more minutes making his way down to the beach where he washed his hands and face in the warm, salty waters of the South China Sea. He then worked his way back to the road, and started walking toward San Fernando with his travel bag in his hand.

About two hours later Breidstein came over the hill and saw the convent with the small church beside it. Parishioners were exiting the sanctuary. Two priests stood at the doors to the sanctuary, speaking to the departing people. Breidstein stepped into cool shade of a dense stand of trees and began to wait, and watch, hoping to see Father Eduardo appear somewhere in the churchyard—alone.

After an hour, Breidstein saw the priest who Breidstein knew had not to be Father Eduardo—because he walked quickly and erect—come to the front of the churchyard with two nuns, leading a mule-drawn cart. In a few minutes they got into the cart and started off down the road. They eventually passed from sight. Breidstein knew this was his opportunity. He walked quickly down the hill and toward the convent gate.

Breidstein pulled the bell chord. In a moment, a nun came to the gate. "May I help you," she asked in Spanish.

"Yes. I am in urgent need of confession. Is there someone who can hear my confession?" Breidstein asked.

"Must it be now, or can you wait for Father Vasquez to return?" the nun asked.

"It is extremely important that I give my confession now—I cannot explain more."

"Go to the confession booth in the sanctuary and wait. I will see if Father Eduardo will come," the nun said as she began to turn and walk away.

"Bless you, Sister, bless you," Breidstein said.

In a few moments, Breidstein sat in the confession booth, waiting. Twenty minutes passed. Then Father Eduardo entered the back of booth. Breidstein smiled to himself. *It worked. Now all I have to do is play on the sympathies of this old man to let me have sanctuary in the church—and I know how I can do that.*

"Forgive me, Father, for I have sinned," Breidstein intoned.

"How long has it been since you have confessed your sins, my son?" Father Eduardo asked.

"More years than I can say, Father," Breidstein answered.

"And how have you sinned, my son?"

"I have committed many sins. I have succumbed to the ways of the flesh outside of marriage, my Father," Breidstein answered.

"How often have you committed this sin?" Father Eduardo asked.

"Many, many times, my Father. And, my Father, I have denied my faith."

"And how many times have you done this terrible thing?" the priest asked.

"Once, my Father," Breidstein answered.

"When did you make this denial?" Father Eduardo asked.

"When you asked me if I was of the Catholic faith, my Father—when I told you I was Werner Breidstein." Breidstein heard the sharp intake of breath by the old priest.

"Why did you deny your faith?" Father Eduardo asked.

"Because, my Father, I am not Werner Breidstein. I am Willy Rosin. My mother is Teresa Margarita Consuela Hermosa Rosin Ortega." Breidstein heard the priest gasp.

"Father," Breidstein went on, knowing how much the priest had to be shocked by what Breidstein had said, "I wish to ponder my sinful ways and learn what I must do to receive forgiveness, for my many and most grievous sins, away from the influence of worldly things. I seek refuge in the church walls—inside these very walls, where my mother used to pray. I ask you, because of my mother's love for me and this church—and you, her confessor—to allow me to enter into the protection of this church," Breidstein said with all the piety he could muster.

"When... would you want... to withdraw yourself from the world?" Father Eduardo asked.

"Immediately," Breidstein responded.

"Your sins of the flesh are forgiven. Go, and sin no more."

Breidstein heard the priest step from the confessional. Breidstein stepped out as well. The priest looked at him.

"Yes, I see it is you again, the one who brought Juana to her daughter's burial mass. And now you say that the dear Teresa Margarita Consuela is your mother. How do I know you speak the truth? How do I know that it is you, Willy? It has been many, many years since I saw you, and you were then only a young boy."

"My Father, do you remember my mother's thirtieth-third birthday at Villa San Fernando?" Breidstein asked.

"I remember many things of that day," Father Eduardo answered.

"Yes. It was the day that my father gave my mother a horse, a beautiful animal. She named it *Hermosura Negro*."

"Yes, I remember the horse. Do you remember what happened to it?" Father Eduardo asked.

"Yes. My mother fell from it when it broke free from my father's hand. My mother broke her arm; you tended to her pain. My father had the horse killed the next day," Breidstein answered.

The priest looked at Breidstein, his eyes widening. "Willy, it is you! Why have you returned after all these years—why do you seek refuge here?" Father Eduardo asked.

"I have sinned so many ways. I seek refuge and asylum from the world—here near my beloved mother—to feel her strength, to find myself again. Will you help me, my Father?" Breidstein asked in a pleading voice.

The priest looked at Breidstein for a long time. Finally, he said, "You may stay. God will watch over you if you truly seek forgiveness. But first, I am compelled by the sacraments that I hold dear to tell you something which may change your mind. I know now that this was meant to be. It is God's test of your belief in Him."

"I will not change my mind," Breidstein said with confidence.

"We shall see. Wait here, while I get something." Breidstein wondered what the old priest was talking about.

Thirty minutes passed before Father Eduardo returned. He handed Breidstein three envelopes. Two, one large and one small, had originally been white but now were both well yellowed. The third was blue, or at least at one time had been blue. "I was given these letters by your mother's personal maid about two months after your mother's death when I returned from Rome. By that time, you and your father were already on your way back to Germany. The one letter addressed to me contained the other two," Father Eduardo said.

Breidstein took the three letters, wondering what they were all about.

"Read the blue one first," the priest said. "They will all make more sense if you do."

The blue envelope had been opened and a letter was in it. "I did not open that letter. When I received it, the envelope was already opened. I have read the letter, but only because of what your mother asked of me," Eduardo said.

Breidstein opened the letter. It was written in English.

February 16, 1915

My darling Teresa,
Our times together must end, for awhile. The conditions in Europe, what is happening all around us, require that I must leave our beloved island paradise. The world is breaking us apart. I shall miss you and our beloved Willy so very much. When I am able I shall return from America.

Love
Karl Albert

Willy was overwhelmed; his mind began to spin. *Did my mother have a lover, here in the Philippines? Is it possible*, Willy wondered, *that my father... is not my father?* Willy just did not want to believe it.

Willy looked at the small white envelope. It was covered with postmarks, chronicling its travels from the Philippines across the Pacific to San Francisco. At the bottom corner there was a smudged stamped message with, as best Willy could tell, a date of August 21, 1918 next to it: "No such addressee - return to sender." He opened the letter and read it. It was in the stilted English of Willy's mother.

April 2, 1918

My dearest Karl,
I not hear from you so long. I fear something happened. Will you return and bring your love to me again? We need you. I cannot live with you not here. You must come back. Life here is death without you.

My love forever,
Teresa Margarita

Finally, Willy opened the last envelope, and read it. The letter was in Spanish and dated December 7, 1918, two days before the death of his mother's. It read:

My Father Eduardo,
I write to you because I am not permitted to leave my home or communicate with others. I have sinned. I have had relations with another man, many years ago. The consequences of those relations have been beautiful, but they bring pain to others. I ask God for his forgiveness. Please pray for the understanding of my husband, whom I have dishonored. The enclosed letters were discovered by him two days ago. Please read them so you will understand. I do not know if he will ever forgive me, but I ask for your prayers to help me make it up to him, if only he will allow me to do so. Please pray to have God let me be the wife I should have been.

Teresa Margarita Consuela Hermosa Rosin Ortega

Willy looked at Father Eduardo. *What did this all imply?* He was afraid to really think it all out.

"Because of the uncertainties it raised about your dear mother's death, I was able to convince the bishop, the only other to whom I have shown these letters—until now—that she may not have sinned in her death. He allowed me to move her to where she is now—but without the accolades."

"Sinned in her death?" Willy asked.

"You do not know?" Father Eduardo said in a shocked voice. "It was initially believed your mother killed herself."

Willy felt as if a knife had been plunged into him—*my mother ... killed herself ... how could she have done that? It was unthinkable that she would do such a thing? But Father Eduardo said there was ... uncertainty.*

"What do you mean, uncertainty about her death?" Willy asked.

"The letters—they were found by your ... her husband. Then he, and you, left the Philippines so quickly after her death. There was no doctor's report, no mass was said for her. What was one to think?"

Willy didn't want to believe what the priest was implying. Willy's face became contorted, reflecting the bewilderment in him. His emotions were in turmoil—pain, sadness, resentment, hate—all mixed in a jumble. Then the anger exploded inside him as he looked at the priest. *My mother probably murdered by the man whom I thought all my life was my father, and the only thing you did was to move her burial place!*

"Was nothing done ... to confirm ... your suspicions ... something, anything?" Willy asked in disbelief.

"Things were in such turmoil back then—it just wasn't possible. But, of course, it doesn't make any difference now—it is matter now only for God," Father Eduardo answered.

"What do you mean—makes no difference now?" Willy asked in surprise.

"I don't understand your question," Father Eduardo said. "Documents came for the church records nearly three years ago. Your ... Count Rosin ... died of a heart attack in the spring of nineteen-thirty-seven."

Willy's shock was surpassed only by his hatred for the man who had called himself Willy Rosin's father—and the priest who suspected what he had done, but had done nothing about it. Willy remained silent for a long moment as he struggled with the things he had just learned—and how they explained so much. He finally looked at Father Eduardo.

"Are you ready to come with me, or do you wish to return to the world?" the priest asked.

There was a pause. "I am ready to come with you," Werner Breidstein finally answered, his voice cold and hollow.

81

FRANCIS WOKE THINKING he must be in heaven. He could hear church bells ringing and children singing. Then he felt the pain. He looked down at his leg. A large bandage was wound about a professional-looking splint on his ankle. And on his head, he could feel a bandage.

"Holy cow. Where the hell am I?" he said to no one in particular as he looked around the simple room he was in. It had one small table, a picture of Jesus hanging on the wall, and a chair—with a middle aged Filipino woman, in a nun's habit, sitting in it. The woman's eyes widened as she looked up from the bible she had been reading. She stood up and ran out the door, yelling, "*Padre Jose, Padre Jose.*"

A moment later, Francis had the shock of his life. Elaine Franklin, older and tanned, but still Elaine Franklin, rushed in. Behind her came a priest.

"Francis, how do you feel? God, Francis, I was so worried about you. Are you all right?"

"Elaine! Jesus Christ. Excuse me, Father," Francis said as he saw the eyes of the priest widen. "What are you doing here?" Francis asked. Then he remembered her letter, that she had volunteered to work in the Philippines—and that it wasn't Elaine Franklin anymore, it was Elaine Cotrall!

"Just relax, Francis," Elaine said as she reached down to put her hand on Francis' cheek. "You were brought here yesterday to the mission after some children found you. Father Jose tended to your ankle; he's a doctor too. He believes you have a severe sprain, but he's not sure. We tried to fix your head up as best we could. Father Jose thinks you may have suffered a mild concussion. He didn't want to move you more than necessary until you regained consciousness. We will need to get you into Manila tomorrow morning for a more thorough examination. You can have some soup and then go back to sleep—"

"What day is it? What time is it?" Francis asked as the details of his last night of consciousness flooded his mind.

"Why, it's about five o'clock on Sunday afternoon. Vespers are going to start soon," Elaine answered.

"Oh, my God. Elaine, get me some paper and pencil, quick," Francis demanded.

"Paper and pencil. Now just a minute," Elaine objected. "You need to rest—"

"I don't have time to explain. Get me some paper and pencil—now, damn it, now!" Francis bellowed at her.

Elaine turned to look at Father Jose. "If that is what he wants, my child, I see no harm in it. I think there should be some paper and pencil in the classroom. Sister Fernanda," he said, as he turned to the nun still standing at the door looking at all that had been going on, "please bring some paper and pencils from the school room."

Father Jose walked over to Francis and began to look into his eyes. "Watch my fingers," he told Francis. "How many?" Father Jose asked as he held up three fingers.

"Three," Francis answered.

Father Jose slowly moved his hand back and forth, watching Francis' eyes follow. "He appears to be lucid—he seems to be responding well," Father Jose said.

"Damn right I am. Where's that pencil and paper?" Francis demanded again.

"What is going on, Francis?" Elaine asked.

"I can't tell you right now. Don't talk to me until I've finished with the pencil and paper. Trust me, Elaine, just trust me."

After what seemed like ages to Francis, the nun returned. She clutched a stack of children's writing tablets and several pencils.

"Move that table close to me, Elaine, so I can put the paper on it. Help me sit up so I can write."

Elaine did as she was ordered.

Francis began to write, in Japanese. It strained his mind—literally hurt, like a hangover, as he furiously put characters on the paper, pausing every several seconds or so to stare toward the window, and then put more characters on the sheets of paper he tore from the tablets. Ever few moments he would put his hand to his head to massage his forehead.

Finally, he stopped. "That's the best I can do. Now what does it say?" he said, talking out loud. Neither Elaine nor Father Jose attempted to answer him.

Francis began moving his lips and jabbing his pencil at the paper, writing English words in the spaces between the rows of letters and symbols he had already written down. Then he began to talk, struggling to form intelligible English sentences from the words and phrases he had written.

"Orders for Special Military Envoys: Preparation of Local Resistance." Francis stopped. "No, Operatives," he said, correcting himself. "Develop and organize local operatives in… strike cities of Bangkok and Manila. Actions to… include destruction of telephone communications… false reports to local police to create confusion… no… create hysteria in general population. Plans to be completed by December 5… secrecy high… no… utmost importance. Initiation of plans no earlier than December 8, 0300 Imperial Time. Only phase one to be undertaken without … certain knowledge of actual air attack on Pearl Harbor. Embassy staff in Manila… go to consulate prior… to attack and wait for… release, no, liberation by advanced units of armed forces of Imperial Army."

"My God, Francis! Is that for real?" Elaine asked.

"It's from some Japanese navy documents I read—and they're for real," Francis answered.

"Oh, Lord, Francis. What are we going to do?" Elaine asked.

"Where is your telephone? I can call the base. It looks like an attack on Pearl Harbor is going to start tomorrow. Three o'clock Tokyo time… that would be… about nine in the morning in Hawaii. We still have time to warn Hawaii and MacArthur," Francis said.

"We don't have a phone here. The closest phone, when it's working, is at Balanga," Father Jose said.

"All right. We'll go there and make the call. Do you have a car?" Francis asked.

"Yes, but it's not in great shape," Elaine answered.

"Well, if it runs, it will have to do," Francis said.

82

AS THEY CHUGGED ALONG in the old Model T touring car, with Father Jose driving and Francis in the back of the car lying against Elaine's shoulder with his leg propped up on the seat, Francis learned how Elaine came to be at the mission as she filled in the details of the letter he had read only two days ago.

"So when did you get here?" Francis asked.

"I have been working at the Sacred Heart Mission Clinic for almost two months now," Elaine answered.

"Damn, and I have been writing half of the county clerks in Colorado trying to find you," Francis said with a laugh.

"County clerks?" Elaine asked.

"That was the only way I could think of figuring out where you might be, after you called me in Chicago," Francis answered.

"So, you know about that?" Elaine asked.

"Yes, and I know what you said in your letter—and I know what I want, Elaine. I'm not infatuated with you. I am in love with you."

Elaine just looked at Francis. "I don't know, Francis, I don't know. Too much is happening, too fast, right now. Let's just take things as they come—at least for awhile. Let me get used to you … again. Can you let me do that, Francis, just for awhile," Elaine asked.

Francis sighed. "For awhile—but you're not getting away from me again, Elaine Cotrall."

"Thank you, Francis," Elaine said. Then she began to wag her finger at Francis. "Now you tell *me* what's going on. How did you get to the Philippines?"

"Well, after D.C., I had some more language training in San Francisco, then Hawaii. Then I was assigned here to head up a communications group at Cavite. That's pretty much it," Francis answered.

"Pretty much it!" Elaine exploded. "Then how did you become an officer? How did you get to read those documents that you wrote down from memory? And how did you get hurt? What do you really do, Francis?"

Francis answered with less than full candor. "I have some special assignments from time to time. Nothing much."

They came around a curve. "Well, there's the town," Father Jose said over the noise of the car's engine. "I think we should go to the local constable's office. They know us there."

Father Jose stopped the car in front of the constable's office. He went inside and in a few minutes returned with a police officer who began helping Francis out of the car. "The chief is already trying to get through to Manila. I told him you have a very important call to make," Father Jose said.

"Chief Reynaldo will help us, Francis. Everything will be okay soon," Elaine said.

Francis leaned on Elaine as he hobbled into the constable's office.

Once inside, the chief stood up from his desk. "Hello, Miss Elaine," Chief Reynaldo said.

Elaine smiled. "Hello, Chief."

Then the chief spoke to Father Jose. "Father, I have the military police in Manila on the line. But I must ask you, Father, who is this man?"

Francis answered for Father Jose. "I am Lieutenant Francis Marian, U.S. Navy, in charge of Post Y Communications at the Cavite Naval Base. It is imperative that I make a call to General MacArthur's headquarters."

"I am afraid we have much difficulty here, Father," Reynaldo said. He looked at Francis. "Lieutenant, did you take a jeep from the constable's office at Limay Friday evening?"

"Yes I did, but it was with the permission of the constable there," Francis answered.

"But I am informed he was told it was requested as a favor to General MacArthur. General MacArthur's office does not seem to know of any such request. And the jeep has not been returned. I am afraid I must place you under arrest, at least until this matter is straightened out," Reynaldo said.

"But there is no time. There is going to be a Japanese attack on Pearl Harbor and here, the Philippines," Francis pleaded.

"I think he's telling the truth, Chief," Father Jose said.

"I am sorry, Father, but it is out of my hands. Perhaps, Lieutenant, you wish to speak to your military police," Reynaldo said as he held out the phone. Francis took it.

"This is Lieutenant Francis Marian. To whom am I speaking?" Francis asked.

"You are speaking, *Lieutenant*, to Captain Llewellyn, OD for the MP headquarters here in Manila. You have gotten yourself into a hell of a mess. What's going on?"

"I have obtained information that the Japanese are going to attack Hawaii tomorrow. General MacArthur needs to be notified immediately," Francis said.

"What? Hawaii! Bull shit. Are you drunk? You damn swabbies are all alike. Get off the damn line," Captain Llewellyn said.

"But, Captain, it's true. I was able to see some documents of a Japanese naval officer on Bataan," Francis said.

"Japanese naval officer, on Bataan? What kind of shit are you trying to feed me? I said get off the goddamn line," Llewellyn ordered.

"But—"

"Get off the goddamn line!" Llewellyn shouted over the telephone.

Francis handed the phone back to Chief Reynaldo. Francis looked at Elaine in disbelief. "He doesn't believe me… he doesn't believe me."

The chief put his ear to the receiver. "This is Chief Reynaldo again." Silence. "Well, he looks pretty beat up. He has bandages around his leg and his head. But he does have a naval officer's clothes on—at least what's left of them." Silence. Then, "If that is what you want, I will be glad to cooperate. We should have him there in about five hours."

The chief hung up the receiver. "Lieutenant, I regret that I must keep you under arrest. I am to take you to military police headquarters in Manila immediately," Reynaldo said.

"Chief, you have to believe him," Elaine implored.

"I am sorry, Miss Elaine. I wish you and Father Jose were not involved in this. All right, Lieutenant, let's get to my car. Ernesto, you will need to come too. Help the lieutenant to my car. We three have a long ride ahead of us."

"Francis, what's going to happen? What should I do?" Elaine asked.

"I don't know, Elaine. I just don't know," Francis answered in frustration.

Francis could see Elaine standing in front of the constable's office watching the car as it started up the beach road toward Highway 7 and Manila.

83

"BUT CAPTAIN, WHAT I AM TELLING YOU IS THE TRUTH. I work for Naval Intelligence. I was investigating a Japanese naval officer that arrived in Manila two weeks ago. I was able to look at some documents in his briefcase," Francis said to Captain Llewellyn, to whom the Chief Reynaldo had delivered Francis some five hours after leaving Balanga.

"And I suppose they were all written out in English so you could read them, real easy," Llewellyn said.

"Captain, I spent three years learning how to read Chinese and Japanese at considerable cost to the United States government," Francis said caustically.

"Don't get smart with me, Marian," Llewellyn said.

"Sorry, but what can I do to convince you?" Francis implored as he looked up at the clock on the wall. It read 11:56.

"Well, where are some of these papers," Llewellyn asked.

"I only looked at them, I didn't steal them. Look, is there somebody you could call to maybe vouch for me?" Francis asked.

"Well, who do you suggest? And don't get smart by saying MacArthur," Llewellyn said.

Francis thought for a moment. "Burkhart. Lieutenant Jack Burkhart, over at your G-2."

"You know Burkhart?" A pause. "He's a damn good tennis player, isn't he?" Llewellyn asked.

"No, Captain. He hates tennis. But he's a damn good poker player—and he's probably beat the socks off you plenty of times," Francis said as looked Llewellyn in the eye.

Llewellyn picked up the phone. "Ring G-2 for me, Sergeant."

Llewellyn looked at Francis as the connection was being made.

"This is Captain Llewellyn over at MP headquarters. We may have an emergency developing. Is Lieutenant Burkhart there?.... No? .... Yes, thanks."

Llewellyn pushed the receiver hook down for a moment, then clicked it several times. A moment's pause, then he requested a Manila number.

After a minute of silence, Llewellyn spoke. "Jack, this is Roger Llewellyn, over at MP headquarters.... No, I'm not calling about that... . Yeah, I know it's late, but this is business. I have a guy here—he looks in pretty bad shape—who says he knows you, that you can vouch for him. He has got some cock and bull story about seeing some documents that some Japanese naval officer had—says the documents say the Japs are going to attack Pearl Harbor," Llewellyn looked up at the clock on the wall, "today sometime."

Silence. Then, "Yes, that's him." A pause. "Here, he wants to talk to you," Llewellyn said as the handed the phone to Francis.

"Francis, is that you?" Burkhart asked over the phone.

"Yes, Jack, it is," Francis answered with relief.

"What's going on? Where have you been? I have been trying to find you. I have gotten some information about Breidstein," Burkhart said quickly.

"Jack, listen to me, listen. Takamatsu—he's here to set up some covert operations in advance of an attack on the Philippines. I got to look through his briefcase when he was out at the Breidstein villa. I got banged up trying to get back to Manila. Some of the documents say that Pearl Harbor and the Philippines—both—are going to be attacked sometime this morning! We have to raise the alarm," Francis said excitedly.

"Holy Jesus! You have to let MacArthur know. You get over to MacArthur's headquarters. I will call my boss, try to pave the way for you. You be ready to tell the whole story. They are going to have a hell of a time believing all this. Let me speak to Llewellyn," Burkhart said.

Francis handed the phone back to Llewellyn. "Yes?" Llewellyn said as he began to listen to Burkhart. A few moments later, Llewellyn said, "You got it." Then Llewellyn spoke to Francis. "Let's go, Lieutenant. Jack suggests I get you over to MacArthur's headquarters damn fast."

Chief Reynaldo helped Francis hobble to an MP jeep and watched as it Francis and Llewellyn took off down the street.

Twenty-five minutes later, Francis was standing with Llewellyn on the ground floor of the Marsman Building—where General MacArthur had his headquarters—and pleading again, this time with a Major Winston.

"I don't know about this, Captain," Winston said to Llewellyn. "I know I got a call from G-2, but this sounds pretty farfetched. Waking up General Willoughby at this time of night—Jesus Christ, that could get me canned."

"MacArthur has to be warned. Marian has to talk to him, sir," Llewellyn tried to explain.

"No, I am not going to wake up General MacArthur, particularly for some Navy guy. Maybe if Willoughby wants to do it—he's MacArthur's G-2 chief—that's his decision," Winston said.

"Listen, Major," Francis said. "I know you outrank me, but if you don't wake Willoughby, and the attack happens, you and I both will end up cleaning latrines for the rest of our lives. If I'm wrong, I'm the only one who is going to be in trouble. I'll take full blame for everything."

"Okay, okay," the Major said as he picked up the phone.

In a few seconds, a connection was made and the major began to speak. "Very, very sorry to disturb you, General, but this is Major Winston, the night OD, over at the Marsman Building... I know it's very late, sir. I really am sorry, sir, but we may have a developing problem.... Well, it seems a Lieutenant Marian, a navy officer from Cavite, says he has information about a Jap attack on Hawaii.... No, no, it hasn't happened. He just says it's going to happen... today.... Well, he says he read it in some secret Japanese documents.... Yes sir, I'll bring him over immediately."

The major called across the room, "Sergeant, take over the desk. I'm going across the street to the hotel to see Willoughby." Then he looked at Francis. "All right, let's go, Marian. I hope this is good."

Francis turned to Llewellyn. "Thanks for your help."

"Good luck. I think you're going to need it," Llewellyn said.

"I think we are all going to need it, Captain," Francis said.

WILLOUGHBY WAS IN A BATHROBE and pajamas when Major Winston brought Francis into the general's apartment. "You're Marian? You look like something the cat dragged in," Willoughby snarled. "What is this story all about—an attack on Hawaii, or whatever foolishness you're talking about?"

"I apologize, General, but it's been really quite... hectic the last several days. I am Lieutenant Francis Marian. I am in charge of the Post Y communication operations down at Cavite."

"Why the hell are you up here then?" Willoughby asked.

"Well, it's a long story, but time is running out. Let me explain." Francis told his story one more time, hoping against hope that Willoughby would believe him. But all Willoughby did was get angrier.

"Who in the hell gave you authority to break into this Breidstein's home and read some diplomatic papers. That could cause an international incident. Just who gave you orders to do that?" Willoughby demanded.

"Well, sir, no one specifically. It is … just the sort of work I do," Francis tried to explain.

"No orders—sort of work you do," Willoughby said, his voice rising. "You're going to get your ass court-martialed if you don't have a better explanation than that."

"But, General, the papers I read said that Pearl Harbor and the Philippines are going to be attacked!" Francis shouted.

"Hogwash! We know what the Japs are up to. And it isn't some mythical attack on Hawaii. You Navy people, always throwing a monkey wrench into everything. If you would just keep out of our way around here, we would be much better off. I ought to—"

The door to Willoughby's apartment opened. Douglas MacArthur walked in, also in robe and pajamas. "What's going on, Charley? Had a bit of trouble sleeping, thought I would take a short walk. Saw your light on—heard you … talking."

"Nothing to be worried about, General. This man has just been trying to feed me some cock and bull story about an attack on Hawaii—and here in the Philippines too—that the Japanese are supposed to make today. This man says he works for ONI down at Cavite."

MacArthur looked at Francis for a long moment. "Haven't we met before?"

"Yes sir, at a party given by President Quezon at his official residence in October of 1940."

Willoughby's face went pale.

"What's this about an attack?"

"General, the Japanese … they are going to attack Pearl Harbor and the Philippines—today! A Japanese officer on Yamamoto's staff came to Manila a couple of weeks ago. I followed him—"

There was a loud knock on the door and a young officer burst in. "General, we just monitored an alert message, in the clear, from Hawaii. They said, 'Air raid on Pearl Harbor. This is no drill.'" Francis looked at the clock hanging on a wall. It read 2:34 a.m., making it 8:04 a.m., December 7, in Hawaii.

84

AFTER FRANCIS TOLD MacArthur how he came to read Takamatsu's documents, and what few details about the attacks that Takamatsu's documents actually contained, MacArthur ordered Francis to see a doctor at the Army's Manila hospital. Delivered there by Major Winston, Francis dozed fitfully for several hours in a chair while waiting for a doctor. By the time Francis woke, rumors about Pearl Harbor were circulating around the hospital. And reports about Japanese sightings in the Philippines were rapidly growing.

After some hurried X-rays by an excited Army doctor, Father Jose's diagnosis was confirmed—a severe sprain but, fortunately, no break. And apparently there was no permanent damage to Francis' head. After hastily putting a light cast on Francis' ankle, the doctor told him to use a cane for a week or so and quickly sent Francis on his way.

Leaving the doctor's office, Francis decided he had better talk to Burkhart before he returned to Cavite, to fill him in on the details of what had transpired at Breidstein's villa. But Burkhart had surprising news for Francis.

"... and so on Saturday evening, while you were still unconscious in that mission hospital I guess, my surveillance people outside Breidstein's apartment saw him dropped off by his chauffeur. He goes into his apartment building with a small travel bag and a brief case. Then he shows up later at the dock where his office is located—he must have slipped out of the back of his apartment because we thought he was still inside. He goes into his office for awhile with the travel bag, but no brief case, comes out with the same bag—and then shoots his chauffeur, right there on the dock," Burkhart said.

"What! Are you sure?" Francis asked in surprise.

"Damn right. And that's not all! Not only does he throw the chauffeur's body into the harbor, he opens up the truck of his car and pulls out another body—Takamatsu—and dumps him into the harbor as well."

"Holy cow! Are you sure it was Takamatsu?" Francis asked.

"Damn sure. We fished the bodies out of the bay later that night—positive ID. Takamatsu had been shot in the stomach, the chauffeur in the chest," Burkhart answered. "We held up on telling the Jap embassy about Takamatsu, wondering how we were going to explain his murder to them without creating an international incident, but that won't be any problem now."

"Where's Breidstein now?" Francis asked.

"We don't know. He drove off. My man at the dock didn't have a car; we were only keeping the office under loose surveillance. We didn't expect anything like this to happen. All he was able to do was call in what he had seen," Burkhart said with a shrug.

"So, did you try to find Breidstein?" Francis asked.

"Yes—sort of. We thought for awhile he might be at his villa, so we sent some people out there to check on it Sunday morning—found two of Breidstein's friends there, half drunk. No trace of you, of course. The two people, a man—some big shot local banker—and his wife, had no idea where Breidstein or anybody else was. We brought the couple in for further questioning. There was a note that Breidstein apparently left that said that he and the rest of them had all gone hunting, but that was obviously a ruse. But the most important thing was the blood found on the floor in two of the bedrooms," Burkhart said as he raised two fingers.

"Blood!" Francis exclaimed.

"Yes. Has to be something to do with the shots you heard. A rolled up rug pushed under a bed had blood all over it. The other room looked like blood had been tracked in from the first. Some blood spots were also in the hallway by the rooms. Something really bad happened out there, but we don't know what, except that maybe Takamatsu got shot in the process. The police are still investigating—to the extent they can with all that's going on now. It may be quite awhile before we learn much."

"What about Shinako Fujimori—has she turned up?" Francis asked.

"No, nothing—and the other woman that was in the car that picked up Takamatsu on Friday, nothing about her either," Burkhart said. "Nobody has seen hide nor hair of either of them. I bet that one or both of them got knocked off with Takamatsu. Jesus, this is a real mess. But at least you're okay. Boy, when I first got the report about the blood, I thought you might have just bought the farm. I didn't know what to think. Nobody knew where you were. You really had me worried. Anyway, on Sunday afternoon, we got the police to issue a warrant for Breidstein's arrest on murder charges—so it's going to be jail for him," Burkhart said.

"Yeah—if we can ever find him," Francis said with disgust—and a deep feeling of sorrow that Shinako had gotten involved with Breidstein. When Shinako had tutored him in Hawaii, she seemed to be such a gentle person, not the type to get involved with someone like Breidstein—and in something like this. Her sweet innocence had, more than likely, gotten her murdered.

WHEN FRANCIS GOT BACK to Cavite, he found his gang already hard at work trying to pick up any information that might be immediately useful. They spent little time listening to Francis' explanation of where he had been, or why he had a cast on his ankle. They were too busy. The airwaves had never been so cluttered. Francis knew, however, that it was almost a hopeless task. By the time his gang could decipher a message, it would be too old to be of immediate use. But Francis knew of nothing else he could do. No change in standing orders for Post Y came down, so the group toiled on, hoping to gather something useful.

And Francis had another worry—Elaine. He presumed she had returned to the mission, but she needed to come back to Manila where it would be safe. But how could he contact her? There was no phone at the mission. Then Francis remembered Chief Reynaldo at Balanga. The chief just might be able to help.

After several hours off and on calling, Francis was finally able to get through to Chief Reynaldo.

"Chief, this is Lieutenant Francis Marian. Do you remember me?" Francis asked.

"Lieutenant Marian, remember you? How could I forget you? Did you finally get to see General MacArthur?" Reynaldo asked.

"Yes I did, but obviously it didn't do any good," Francis said. "Chief, I need your help."

"I will be most glad to help, if I can," Reynaldo offered.

"Miss Elaine and Father Jose—did they return to the mission?" Francis asked.

"When I got back to Balanga, they had already returned to the mission," Reynaldo answered.

"Could you go to the mission and have Miss Elaine call me? I have to find out when she is coming back to Manila," Francis said.

"Ah, Lieutenant, it will be very difficult to get to the mission right now. Things are very busy here," Reynaldo said.

"I know, Chief, but it's very important to me. Is there any way you can get a message to her—tell her to come to your office and call me here at Cavite?" Francis asked.

There was a moment of silence on the line. Then the chief answered, "I will send Ernesto to the mission with your message by tomorrow morning."

THE RINGING PHONE WOKE Francis. He lifted his head from his desk, trying to get himself oriented. He looked at the clock on the wall. It read 6:22. "Marian, Post Y, Cavite."

"Francis, oh, Francis. You're all right. Oh, Francis, I was so worried," Elaine said.

"Elaine! Are you all right?" Francis asked.

"Yes. Everybody is frightened, but nothing has actually happened. We are doing just what we always do, except trying to help everybody be calm," Elaine answered.

"Well, when are you leaving the mission and getting down here to Manila?" Francis asked.

There was a long silence. "Elaine, are you there?" Francis asked.

"Yes, Francis, I hear you," Elaine answered.

"I said, when are you going to leave—"

"I know what you said, Francis. I'm not going to leave the mission unless Father Jose decides to close it down," Elaine said.

"What do you mean you are not going to leave? You have to get out of there. The Japs might show up," Francis said with apprehension.

"Francis, my place is with the people here. Unless Father Jose decides to move everyone to someplace else, I will stay here with him," Elaine said.

"You can't be serious, Elaine. You're not a nun. You're just someone who is helping out. Nobody expects you to stay and maybe be captured by the Japs. You have to get out of there, Elaine," Francis said, trying to reason with her.

"Nobody expects me to be here, Francis—except myself. Nothing is going to change my mind about this," Elaine said.

"Elaine, don't be hardheaded like before—like the train, like D.C.," Francis pleaded.

"Francis, I made my decision. I love—"

The line went dead. "Elaine, Elaine!" There was no answer.

THE NEXT MORNING, the tenth, Francis and his Post Y gang monitored Philippine Army communications that said Japanese landings were taking place on the northern coast of Luzon. Then the bombing of Cavite started. It was almost totally unopposed by the Army Air Force. Francis could not believe how futile and inept the attempt to stop the raids was. *What was all this planning in War Plan Orange about?* he asked himself in frustration.

Admiral Hart began evacuating the remaining ships of his Asiatic Fleet still at Cavite as soon as the raids were over. By late afternoon, the two destroyers and several mine sweepers and tenders still in the harbor had departed, leaving only a few old patrol boats wallowing at the Cavite docks. Francis received no orders as part of Hart's departure. He and his gang were on their own. Francis decided to send a message directly to McDonald, asking for new orders.

Hours, then a day passed. Finally a message came, but from someone identified only as "Acting Commander, ONI, Hawaii." The message was short, terse, and, as Ensign Louis Frankhill described it, "not worth diddlely-squat": "MCDONALD UNAVAILABLE. FOLLOW STANDING ORDERS." Francis was beside himself. What had happened to McDonald? Francis could only think the worst. But without a change in orders, Francis and his gang could only do what they had been doing, despite the horrendous news of Japanese advances that continued to come in from across the Pacific.

Guam had fallen. The Japanese were apparently advancing southward through Malaya toward Singapore. The British Navy—the invincible British Navy—had suffered a humiliating loss with the sinking of the *Repulse* and the *Prince of Wales* off Singapore. Broadcasts were intercepted that said the Japanese had moved into Bangkok.

And Francis still had not heard anymore from Elaine. He had not been able to get through to Chief Reynaldo's headquarters at Balanga again for over a week. When he did finally get through, only the chief's deputy, Ernesto, was there. The chief was gone with the army to the northern end of Luzon, near Tuguegarao. That was all Ernesto knew. And no, he couldn't go to the mission. He had to stay at Balanga and be sure that order was maintained; that was the chief's last order to him. As Francis and his gang toiled on at Post Y, Francis' worry about Elaine continued to grow.

85

"ALL RIGHT, LIEUTENANT," the Navy doctor said. "You rewrap that bandage tightly every day when you get up in the morning. Sleep with it off and prop your leg up. Don't use the cane unless you feel it really necessary. Come back in a week for a checkup. Try to find some doctor to look at the leg—have him take some X-rays if possible, just as a precaution. If not by me, then by some other fool still here in Cavite. Now get out of here," the doctor ordered.

"Yes sir," Francis answered.

Francis left the doctor's office and started walking—with a limp, but no cane—toward the doorway when he heard someone calling his name. "Lieutenant Marian, Lieutenant Marian."

Turning, Francis saw a nurse at a desk holding up a phone.

Francis took the phone from the nurse. "Marian speaking."

"Francis, it's Jack. Boy, I'm been trying to track you down all morning. We've got some news on Breidstein—sort of," Jack Burkhart said. "It looks like Breidstein's car has been found—abandoned on the west coast of Luzon, up north, a few miles south of a place called San Fernando."

"You mean he's on foot somewhere up there?" Francis asked.

"I guess, unless he had got hold of another car somehow. Maybe he thinks he can join up with the Japs that landed up on the northern tip of Luzon," Burkhart suggested.

"What are you going to do, Jack?" Francis asked, sensing that Jack had a reason for calling.

"That's really why I'm calling you, Francis. My people are all tied up right now, checking reports on fifth column activities here in Manila—the brass is really worried about Jap sympathizers and the like. You know Breidstein, probably better than anybody. And I know you would like to catch up with him again," Burkhart said.

"You're right about that," Francis said.

"Can you get up to San Fernando—check with the local police there that found the car, and see if you can figure out where Breidstein might have gone to?" Burkhart asked.

"You bet I can! I'm on my way now." *And, now, thank God, I can find out if Elaine is okay. Going to the mission will add only a few hours to the ride to San Fernando.*

Francis told Jack he would be in contact after he got to San Fernando. Then he called Post Y and gave Louis a quick rundown on where he was going, telling him he would probably not be back until tomorrow.

Francis got into his jeep, his mind whirling—what was Breidstein up to, and was Elaine all right? He started driving, heading north through Manila and beyond, along Highway 3, and against the general exodus of frightened people converging on Manila. In about three hours, Francis reached the junction of Highway 3, which continued north, and Highway 7, which led to the south—and to the mission. Francis turned south. Another hour and he turned onto the bay road toward Balanga. He reached Balanga an hour later.

Ernesto was still there, alone. He had no news. Francis turned onto the dirt road to the mission.

The sun was well passed its zenith as Francis drove into the mission yard. He looked around. It appeared to be deserted. Then a nun stepped around the corner of the school building. After a moment, she spoke.

"It is you again. I see you well now," she said in stilted English.

"Where is everybody? Are you the only one here?"

"Only two other sisters here. Father Jose leave yesterday. He tell us our duty to care for mission until he return. He take other sisters in car to north to help wounded. He goes where he thinks he more needed."

"When will he be back?" Francis asked.

"He not give time. He said he return when God had no more need of him there."

Great, thought Francis, *that could be never.* "Did Miss Elaine go with him?"

"Yes, she go. She said I to give you something if you come looking for her. Wait. I get it."

In a few minutes, the nun returned. She handed Francis an envelope. Francis tore it open and began to read.

December 19, 1941

My Darling Francis,

Things have become clear in the days since the attack. I know now that I love you, and you love me. I know that I want to be with you forever, but I cannot turn my back on those in need. My son taught me that. I must go with Father Jose to help with the growing number of wounded. When the immediate crisis is over, if it ever is, I will try to get to you in Manila. If I cannot find you, I will try to contact you, as soon as I can, in Hawaii through the Navy.
Until we meet again, know that I love you—that I never stopped loving you.

Elaine

Francis' eyes got wet. "Where did Father Jose say he was going to go, Sister, where?" Francis asked.

"He said he go first to church at San Fernando to see if Father Eduardo and Father Vasquez there need help. Maybe, after finished there, go farther north—depend where he could help most," the nun answered.

"San Fernando? You mean the little town on the coast about a hundred miles north of here?" Francis asked.

"*Si,*" the nun answered.

As Francis got into his jeep and started to drive off, he yelled to the nun. "If Sister Elaine returns, tell her that I went to San Fernando to find her." *And,* Francis thought, *find Breidstein.*

IT WAS DARK by the time Francis approached the military roadblock near San Carlos a few miles from Lingayen Bay. San Fernando was about another thirty miles up the coast from the bay. The MP waved his flashlight and brought Francis to a halt. "Where do you think you're going, Lieutenant?"

"I'm going to San Fernando—to talk to the local police there about someone. And I'm trying to find some other people too. I think they may be near San Fernando, maybe at the church there in San Fernando—or maybe a little farther up the coast."

"Jesus, Lieutenant, that convent at San Fernando was bombed to kingdom come yesterday. Killed a bunch of people—the priest, nuns—almost everybody from what I heard."

"My God," Francis said in fear. *Is Elaine dead? Oh my God, no. It can't be—it just can't be!* "I have got to get to that church, Sergeant."

"I don't know about that, Lieutenant. Only reinforcements are supposed to go up that way."

"Sergeant, my fiancee may be one of the people at that church. I have to find out. I have to get up there."

The sergeant gave Francis a long look. "Okay," he said as he stepped back from the jeep. "Just be careful up there. Who knows what those Jap sons of bitches may try next."

86

ELAINE LOOKED DOWN at the young Filipino nurse, her white uniform splattered with a mixture of dried mud and blood, and her left arm and leg encased in makeshift bandages. The nurse was lying unconscious on the back seat, her head in Elaine's lap, as the car rumbled south. Elaine took a cloth and dipped it in the water sloshing back and forth in the small bucket at her feet on the floorboard of the car. She wrung out the dripping water and wiped the nurse's forehead and cheeks. The nurse did not look good; her skin was on fire.

Elaine still had not emotionally recovered from the carnage at the San Fernando convent she and Father Jose had found when they had arrived there in the afternoon shortly after the bombing. Elaine could not fathom why the Japanese had bombed the church. It should have been apparent that the building was a church—just no sense in the bombing. The church and convent—even the little clinic, where the crumbled, barely alive body of the nurse had been found—were a shambles. Elaine had counted eighteen dead, including a young priest that Father Jose said was Father Vasquez. Father Jose had cried openly as he saw the lifeless bodies. But three did survive: Father Eduardo, the young nurse, and the man.

Father Jose and the nuns had spent the rest of the day preparing the bodies for burial and then had held the funeral mass this morning. After the mass, Father Jose and the other sisters from the mission left to go north toward Luna and Candon to see what assistance they could provide there, leaving Elaine to care for the three survivors until Father Jose returned or she could get them transported to a hospital. He would return soon, he said, with an ambulance perhaps, to take the three to a hospital. When Father Jose left, Father Eduardo seemed in reasonably good shape, though he seemed to be still dazed—not in shock, just emotionally overwhelmed by what had happened—so Elaine could devote her attention to the other two, the man, who was going in and out of a dazed consciousness, and the nurse, who yet had to regain consciousness.

But by evening, Father Jose had not returned. And people going south were beginning to straggle by. Elaine quickly found out that the Japanese had finally broken out from the coastal landing areas near Vigan and Aparri along the northern shore of Luzon, north of Candon where Father Jose had gone. Elaine didn't know what to do, but she knew she had to leave before the Japanese came. But both the nurse and man needed her help. The young nurse's condition had gotten worse rather than better—Elaine surmised she had serious internal injuries, not surprising in view of her more obvious wounds. The man continued to go in and out of consciousnessness. Father Eduardo tried to be helpful, but there was little he could do; he was in no condition to walk far. Then, a godsend—Chief Reynaldo, in his police car.

Reynaldo had been ordered to return to Balanga to evacuate any remaining Filipino constabulary personnel in the area and get them working on the roads leading to Manila. The constabulary was going to be needed to help control the mass of humanity expected to move toward Manila in the days to come. He had stopped when he saw the church, or what was left of it, and found Elaine there.

They had loaded the nurse into the back seat and the man and Father Eduardo into the front, and started south.

"Chief, how long before you think we will get to Lingayen? There is a government hospital there," Elaine said.

"I do not know how long it will take, Miss Elaine. Maybe much of the night. There are so many people on the road—"

"We need to get these two some proper medical attention." Elaine leaned forward and looked toward the man slumped in the front seat by the car door, his head lying on Father Eduardo's shoulder. "Is he conscious, Father?"

Father Eduardo twisted his head to look at the man. "I don't think so, although he might have been conscious a little while ago. I am not sure." Then a low moan came from the man. "At least he is still alive."

Strange, Elaine thought, *Who is this man? Why was he at the convent?* He wasn't a man of the cloth, at least judging by his clothes. And those passports... all Father Eduardo would say about him was that he was a visitor at the church when the bombing occurred—just a visitor at an unfortunate time.

BREIDSTEIN WAS FINALLY BEGINNING to make some sense of what was going on around him. His head had never hurt so much in all his life—worse than any hangover he had ever had. He knew he was in a car with several other people, that they were talking—in English—about him and getting medical assistance. He remembered the bombing, or at least the last few moments before. He had been alone in his small room, looking over his three passports and trying to plan what to do next now that the Japanese had actually attacked the Philippines—and wondering whether he had to do something to guarantee Father Eduardo's silence should the Japanese attack fail and the Americans gained the upper hand. He had just put the passports back in his coat and stuck his gun into the holster still on his belt, when the bombing started—suddenly and without warning. He had heard a bomb falling, followed by an explosion, then the beginning of another, and then blackness. After that, only bits and pieces of awareness, until now.

Breidstein attempted to speak, but the result was not much more than a moan. He tried to get his dry throat to function.

"Where am I?" Breidstein was finally able to say. He spoke in English, to match the speaking he had been hearing.

"Oh, thank goodness, you're conscious. You're in a car going toward Lingayen. You were hurt in a bombing. We are trying to get you to the hospital at Lingayen," the woman's voice said.

"Oh yes, I remember the bombing. I feel terrible," Breidstein said.

"Just try to rest. We are going as quickly as we can—the roads are just clogged with people," the woman said.

Breidstein closed his eyes, beginning to get himself oriented and thinking about what the woman had said—and what might happen, when they got to Lingayen. Did he dare let himself be taken to Lingayen, where the American military post was? Breidstein slowly moved his hand to the inside of his tattered coat. He could feel the passports still there. And pressing against the small of his lower back, he felt the reassuring hardness of his gun.

87

FRANCIS WAS FINALLY ABLE to pick up speed. The crowd of people hurrying south had thinned now to only an occasionally encountered person or two. Then as he looked up the moonlit road, he saw the headlights of a car come around a curve in the road. He recognized the car—at least he thought he did. As it got closer, he was sure of it. It was Chief Reynaldo's police car. Francis braked sharply as he pulled onto the narrow dirt shoulder of the road. He stood up in the jeep, beeping the horn and waving his arms.

Chief Reynaldo pulled his car to the side of the road and stopped a short distance from the jeep, framing it in the bright headlights of the car. He got out of the car, leaving the motor running. As he did, Elaine emerged from the other side of the car, crying out, "Francis, oh, Francis."

Francis saw her and jumped from the jeep, almost stumbling as his weak leg hit the ground. He shouted, "Elaine, Elaine."

Elaine ran toward Francis. They met, their arms wrapping about each other.

"Oh God, Francis. I'm so glad you're here. It's been a nightmare," Elaine said.

"Elaine, thank God you're safe. I was afraid that you might have been hurt—that the church at San Fernando had been bombed," Francis said.

"Yes, it was, but I'm all right," Elaine answered. "We got there yesterday—Father Jose and four nuns, and me—just after the bombing. It was terrible. Father Vasquez, the priest at the church was killed… and all the others—nuns, clinic patients… dead too. It was ghastly. Father Jose held mass for all of them this morning. But three people did survive, the church's other priest, Father Eduardo—and a young nurse and some man who had been at the convent. I have been caring for them until we can get them to a hospital—they're all in the car," Elaine said as she titled her head toward the police car idling in the nighttime shadows cast by the moonlight slicing down through the clouds and onto the trees lining the road.

Chief Reynaldo came up. "It is good to see you again, Lieutenant."

"It's good to see you, Chief, although I wish it were under better circumstances," Francis said as he shook the chief's hand.

Turning to Elaine, Francis asked, "Where is Father Jose? I thought he was with you," Francis asked.

"He went north with his nuns, to see if he could help there. He was supposed to come back by the end of the day, but he didn't. I was really getting desperate—one of the survivors, the nurse, really started going sour after he left. She's in need of some real medical attention. Thank God Chief Reynaldo came along," Elaine said as she smiled and looked at the chief.

"Yes, Lieutenant, I was ordered to return to Balanga to assist in evacuating people to Manila. It was just luck—or God's will—that I found Miss Elaine at the church. We're on our way to Lingayen. There is a hospital there. Are you ready to go, Miss Elaine?" Chief Reynaldo asked.

"Yes, in just a few minutes, Chief. I need to talk to the Lieutenant... it has been ... so long since we have seen each other. Give us a few moments alone, if you don't mind, Chief," Elaine said.

"Of course, Miss Elaine," Chief Reynaldo said as he turned back toward the car.

"Elaine, we will have plenty of time to talk later. I'll go with you to Lingayen—" Francis said.

"No, Francis, I need to talk to you now," Elaine said with a stern voice.

"But Elaine—" Francis said, wondering why Elaine was so adamant.

"I said *now*, Francis," Elaine said with a fierce scowl as she took Francis' arm and led him to the backside of the jeep.

"What's gotten into you, Elaine?"

"Just act natural. I need to tell you about something—away from the car," Elaine said in a whispered voice. "Francis, there is something strange about the injured man in the car," Elaine said.

"What do you mean?" Francis asked.

"The priest, Father Eduardo, won't say anything about who the injured man is—very secretive. I know Edurado is still in a daze after what happened at the church, but it's more than that. He will only say the man is just a friend who was visiting the church when the bombing started. And earlier today, while the man was still unconscious, I looked for some identification for him. I found three passports in the man's inside coat pocket," Elaine said.

"Three?"

"Yes," Elaine answered. "One was a German passport for a man with the name of Franz Lundstrom. The picture looked pretty much like the injured man in the car. One of the other passports was German too, for a man named Werner Breidstein—"

"Breidstein! He's a German exporter in Manila—and probably a spy. He's wanted for murder. He killed two men this weekend before the attacks started—that's why I came up here, to look for him," Francis said excitedly.

"Oh, Lord, no. The passport picture looks just like the man. It must be him," Elaine said.

"But you said three passports?"

"Yes, Francis—the third … the third was American—for a person who didn't look like this Breidstein,"

"Damn, somebody else's passport, and an American one at that. Who knows how he got that. He was probably going to put his photo on it and try to use it later."

"But Francis," Elaine said, "the name on it—it was Harold Marian. Isn't that your brother's name?"

"Yes, but … what the hell is going on here—unless … ." Francis couldn't finish, unable to fathom how Breidstein might have been involved with Hal—if it were Hal's passport that Elaine had seen. "I don't know what's going on, but I sure am going to find out," Francis said with determination as he turned toward the car. *Did Breidstein—somehow—kill Hal?* Francis stared at the car but its highlights were too bright to see beyond them and into the dark interior of the car.

"Does Chief Reynaldo know about the passports?" Francis asked.

"No. I didn't know quite what to think, so I just kept it to myself," Elaine answered.

"Well, get him over here, so we can talk to him. We need to arrest Breidstein—and Breidstein might put up some resistance," Francis said.

Elaine turned from Francis, held up her hand to shield her eyes from the still shinning highlights of the chief's car, and then called, "Chief, could I talk to you a minute? Could you come over here a moment?"

Chief Reynaldo began walking toward the jeep.

BREIDSTEIN WAS NUDGED out of his stupor by the honking of a horn. He opened his eyes, but only barely, not saying a word. Then the car stopped and he saw a man in the starkness of the headlights limping toward the car—and recognized him. *It is that cursed Navy man, Marian—again.*

Why is he here? What is he up to now? It can't be anything but trouble. Every time I run into him, something seems to go wrong. But not this time. I'll kill him before I leave this spot!

Breidstein continued to watch what was going on through his only slightly opened eyes. He felt the priest next to him stir also, but said nothing.

Breidstein heard the woman, the policeman, and Marian talking, but the noise of the idling car motor made it difficult to understand their words. Then the woman said something about needing to talk to Marian alone. She walked with Marian to the back of the jeep. Then Breidstein saw Marian turn and look toward the car—toward him. The woman called the policeman over to her. As the policeman walked to the jeep, Breidstein's suspicions rose. Were they talking about him? Was Marian telling them who he was? Breidstein twisted in the seat and reached around to the small of his back, pulling the gun from its holster.

"I THINK WE NEED to make sure Breidstein doesn't cause trouble before we get to Lingayen, Chief. We probably need to tie him up," Francis said to Chief Reynaldo.

"But, Francis, he's injured," Elaine said.

"I don't care, Elaine. He's dangerous. He's a murderer," Francis said with barely controlled anger.

"I agree, Lieutenant. Let's go to the car. I have some rope and handcuffs in the trunk," Chief Reynaldo said.

The three of them turned and started toward the car. Chief Reynaldo started to draw his gun. Francis began to fumble with the canvas cover of his holster, trying to pull out his .45.

From the open window of the car, Francis saw an arm extend and point a gun at them. As Chief Reynaldo raised his gun, Elaine shrieked, "No, Chief, Father Eduardo ... in the car!"

Chief Reynaldo hesitated. Breidstein fired. The chief howled as he fell to the ground and blood began to gush from his thigh. Elaine screamed. Francis was finally able to get his gun out of its holster. He started to raise it to point it toward Breidstein as he also started to run toward the car. But his steps were slowed by his still weak ankle.

"Stop. Don't come any closer," Breidstein yelled as he opened the car door and staggered out, his gun pointed at Francis. Francis stopped.

"Throw the gun away, Marian."

Francis hesitated, not sure what to do.

"I said throw it away... or I shoot the woman," Breidstein said as he nodded his head toward Elaine.

Francis dropped his gun to the ground.

"Kick it away—hard. I assure you I won't hesitate to shoot her ... do it or I shoot."

Francis swung his leg and kicked the gun, sending it somewhere into the shadows of the grass beside the road.

"Get over here," Breidstein said to Elaine, motioning with the gun. "Get that woman out of the back."

"But she's injured," Elaine objected.

"I said to get her out—or do you want me to kill her?" Breidstein asked.

Elaine opened the rear door and leaned into the car. Breidstein moved toward the front of the car. "Help her," he said to Father Eduardo.

The priest got out of the car, staggering slightly. He leaned on the car, steadying himself. Elaine began to slide the nurse out of the back seat. Father Eduardo tried to help Elaine lift the nurse. They pulled her out and put her on the ground, propping her shoulders against the side of the car. The young girl gave a moan, and opened her eyes. Eduardo knelt down beside her. As he did, Francis said, "Maria!"

"Lieutenant Marian... is that you... it is time... for you medicine," Maria said in a delirious, wavering voice as her eyelids fluttered.

Elaine looked at Francis. "You know her?" she asked.

Francis started to answer. "Yes, she—"

"Shut up, Marian," Breidstein ordered.

Father Eduardo knelt down and began to pray over Maria, chanting, mumbling in Spanish.

"Shut up, Father. I don't want to listen to that dribble now," Breidstein said in English.

Father Eduardo looked at Breidstein.

"Marian—you go over to that jeep and let the air out of the tires." Francis didn't move. "Do what I say or I'll kill her," Breidstein said as he again pointed the gun toward Elaine.

Francis limped to the jeep and opened the valve stems on the tires. The jeep slumped as the air whistled out.

Francis stood and slowly started moving back toward Breidstein. Francis glanced at Chief Reynaldo; Reynaldo had risen to one knee. His gun lay somewhere nearby, deep in the tall grass beside the road.

"Stop. Don't come any closer," Breidstein ordered.

Francis stopped.

A cold smirk came to Breidstein's face. His hand tightened about his gun. As it did, the priest reached up to Breidstein. "No, Willy, you can't do this. You mustn't do this. Put the gun down," Father Eduardo pleaded.

"Leave me alone, old man," Breidstein said.

But the priest did not. He grabbed Breidstein's arm, trying to pull it down. Francis began edging closer toward the car.

"I said leave me alone." But the priest's hand continued to tug at Breidstein's arm. Francis moved nearer to the car and Breidstein.

Breidstein turned and looked at the priest, a look of rage on his face. He yanked his arm free of the priest's grasp. He hesitated a moment, and then swung the gun toward the priest and pulled its trigger. The muzzle flash cast a momentary, stark glow on Breidstein's face. Father Eduardo was flung back onto the ground. Elaine screamed. Breidstein started to turn back toward Francis, raising his gun.

Francis lunged the last several feet toward Breidstein, putting all the strength he could into his leap, but the weakness of his ankle caused the leap to be less than full force. He hit Breidstein hard, but not hard enough. They both fell to the ground, but Breidstein's hand still held the gun.

Elaine screamed, "Francis, look out!"

Reynaldo dropped to his hands and knees, trying to find his gun, swinging his hands in circles through the tall grass, frantically shoving it aside, unable to see in the dimness of the moonlight.

Francis gave a quick, loud shout, "Get back," as Breidstein turned his gun toward Francis. Francis swung his fist toward Breidstein's face, the blow only glancing off Breidstein's shoulder, but deflecting Breidstein's gun hand. Francis' arm when around Breidstein's shoulder as they rolled in the loose dirt at the side of the road, their legs kicking and flying. They twisted back and forth, but suddenly Breidstein was on top of Francis. Francis grabbed Breidstein's arm, trying to keep the gun in Breidstein's hand pointing away. But Breidstein used his other hand to unleash a tight fist into Francis' check. Blood spew from Francis' mouth.

Then Breidstein rammed his free hand down onto Francis' face, pushing his fingers into Francis' eyes. Francis flung his arm wildly towards Breidstein, momentarily knocking Breidstein's hand away, while clinging tenaciously onto Breidstein's other hand—with the gun. Francis' fingers tightened about Breidstein's wrist, trying to keep the gun turned away. But as his fingers squeezed around Breidstein's wrist, Breidstein quickly brought his other hand to Francis' throat. Francis could feel Breidstein's fingers tightening, squeezing. Francis began to choke on his own blood, but he knew he could not let go of Breidstein's other hand—and the gun it held. Breidstein thrust his knee sharply into Francis' stomach. Francis felt a stab of pain in his solar plexus. Francis' chest heaved as he tried to suck air into his lungs. In desperation, Francis brought his leg up, to kick Breidstein in the groin, but the kick was not strong. Breidstein grunted but his hand continued to tighten about Francis' throat. Francis couldn't breathe. He felt as if he were suffocating. He felt faint. He knew he was about to lose consciousness.

Francis did the only thing he could think of that he had the strength left to do. He yanked Breidstein's gun hand down to his mouth and sank his teeth into Breidstein hand. Breidstein howled and jerked his hand away, squeezing the trigger of the gun as a piece of skin was ripped away. Francis turned his head away from the flash of the exploding bullet leaving the gun. As he did, he saw the ghastly sight of blood suddenly erupt from Maria's chest as the bullet tore into her small body.

Francis' horror turned to rage as he saw Maria's head quickly sag to her chest. Francis looked back at Breidstein, and grabbed the gun in Breidstein's hand. Francis' strength began to grow—the rage in him taking hold—as he focused on Breidstein's gun and the hand that held it. Breidstein's other hand flailed uselessly at Francis. Francis lifted his knee and jabbed it as hard as he could into Breidstein groin—this time not missing the target! Breidstein mouth widened in silent pain. Francis could feel Breidstein beginning to weaken, and could sense Breidstein's growing fear. Slowly, agonizingly, Francis turned the gun back toward Breidstein, his hand grasping Breidstein's fingers. Francis could see a look of terror on Breidstein's face. Then, as the gun made a finally twist, a momentary look of acceptance came to Breidstein's face—and Breidstein's fingers relaxed as Francis' hand tightened. The gun when off. Breidstein stiffened momentarily, then went limp as his body collapsed on top of Francis.

"Francis, are you all right, are you all right?" Elaine shrieked as she ran to Maria, kneeling down to put her hand over Maria's wound—to stem the flow of blood. But it wasn't necessary—it was too late. Maria's small heart had already stopped.

Francis lay motionless for a moment, blood trickling from the side of his mouth. He worked to calm his breathing. Finally he said, "Yes … yes. It's okay," as he pushed Breidstein's body away. Breidstein rolled over onto his back, his eyes open in a vacant stare. Francis looked at Breidstein. Powder burns ringed the hole in the middle of his shirt. Francis put his hand to his Breidstein's throat. He felt nothing.

Werner Breidstein—Willy Rosin—was dead.

88

ELAINE TURNED to Father Eduardo, seeing from the corner of her eye Francis get to his feet and rush to the small woman now lying in the dirt. "She's gone, Francis. She's dead."

Francis knelt beside Maria's lifeless body, picked her up, and cradled her in his arms.

As Elaine knelt beside Father Eduardo, blood began running from his mouth. His eyes were glassy. It was apparent to Elaine that death was only moments away.

"Father, Father. Oh, God, Father. Francis, what can I do?" Elaine said in anguish as she lifted the priest's head in her arms. Francis did not answer.

"It… is… my time, my time… . I failed…. He tricked me. I believed… him," Father Eduardo said haltingly.

"Who, Father, who tricked you?" Elaine asked.

"Willy… the man… shot me," came the weak reply.

"Willy—who is Willy? Did Willy shoot you?" Elaine asked.

"Yes… Willy… Rosin. I baptized him… when he was… born… here, the Philippines. He went home… with his father… to Germany… his mother... " The priest's words became soft. Elaine put her ear close to the priest's mouth. "His real father… the letters… the letters." Father Eduardo gave a last cough of blood and his head sagged in Elaine's arms.

With a weary, sorrowful look, Elaine put Father Eduardo down gently, got up, and went to Maria—and Francis. Francis was still there with her, still holding her in his arms, tears steaming down his face. "She's gone, Francis," Elaine said again.

"I know, I know. She was just there at the church—just trying to help people, like she did me. She didn't deserve this," Francis said as he looked up at Elaine. "You know who she was, don't you," Francis said with a sorrowful voice.

Elaine raised one eyebrow. "A nurse named Maria. I don't understand ... who?" Elaine asked.

"Her uncle—President Quezon."

"Her uncle... president of the Philippines?" Elaine asked.

Francis nodded his head.

"Jesus, Lord," Elaine said. Then she looked over at Chief Reynaldo, who had been sitting in the grass, unnoticed and unspeaking, holding his hand to his leg.

Elaine hurried over to Chief Reynaldo. Reynaldo had already ripped his pant leg off and was pressing the cloth against the wound. The blood flow seemed to be slowing. "I think it is a clean wound. The bullet passed straight through. There is a first aid kit in the car trunk," Reynaldo said.

"Just be still while I get it," Elaine said, as she hurried to the car. She quickly returned to the chief and began wrapping the wound with a bandage from the first aid kit. As she finished, she saw Francis take off his jacket and gently cover Maria's face and shoulders. He then walked slowly over to Elaine and Chief Reynaldo.

"Did you hear him, Francis?" Elaine asked, "Father Eduardo said Breidstein is someone named Willy Rosin—born here in the Philippines. He whispered something about letters, but what letters?" Elaine asked.

"I don't know. I'll search Breidstein. Maybe he has them," Francis said.

Francis returned to Breidstein's body. He reached into one of Breidstein's inside coat pockets. His hand encountered the three passports. He pulled them from the pocket and then walked to the front of the chief's car.

In the light of the still burning headlights, Francis looked at the passport for Harold Marian. Francis began to feel weak. It was Hal, his brother, without a doubt. After a moment, he looked at the other two passports. The photos in them matched Breidstein's face. Then Francis looked more closely at Hal's passport—and the entries in it. They chronicled his travels in Mexico and Central America—and his last entry into Panama, from which he never returned. "Elaine, come here and help me look at the dates on these passports—the one for Hal and the one for this Lundstrom. Does that say Hal entered Panama in February of thirty-seven?"

Elaine stood and walked to Francis's side. Francis handed Hal's passport to Elaine. "And the one for Lundstrom or Breidstein, or whoever he is—doesn't it say he entered in March of the same year?" Francis asked as he handed her the second passport.

Elaine studied the passports. "I think you're right, Francis."

"Then that has to be what happened. Breidstein must have killed Hal and taken his passport. The timing is right. Hal's body was found in early April. That murdering bastard! We will probably never know how many people he has killed."

"I'm so sorry, Francis. You must have loved your brother very much," Elaine said in an attempt to comfort Francis.

"He was only a half brother… but, yes… I guess I did love him a lot." Francis stood silently for a moment, his head bowed. He finally let out a long, deep sigh.

"What about the letters, Francis?" Elaine asked

"Oh… yeah… the letters." Francis walked over to Breidstein's body again and put his hand into Breidstein's other inside coat pocket. Deep in the pocket, tightly folded, Francis found the three letters—each obviously very old. Francis wondered only a short moment whether he had a right to read them. He had an obligation to get the bottom of everything—if he could.

Returning to the front of the chief's car, Francis looked at the envelopes and saw that two had addresses written in English. He quickly opened the envelopes. He read the two letters, then handed them to Elaine to read. She did.

Then Francis had Chief Reynaldo, who had hobbled over to the car, read the one letter written in Spanish. As the chief finished speaking and handed the letter back to him, Francis realized what must have happened. "The Rosin-Ortega woman apparently had an affair—and Breidstein must have been the result. Apparently her husband found out too," Francis said to Elaine. "The real father must have left her to go to America, probably with promises to return—which he apparently never did."

"How extraordinary… and sad," Elaine said.

"Yes…." Suddenly something clicked in Francis' mind. *Wait a minute*, he thought. "Elaine, let me see those letters again. No… the envelopes," Francis said as Elaine started to hand Francis the opened letters.

Elaine handed Francis the envelopes. He looked carefully at the one sent by the Rosin-Ortega woman to the United States. He tilted the envelope back and forth in the beam of the headlight, trying to discern the smudged postal message on it. He finally made it out: "No such addressee - return to sender," with the date of what appeared to be August 21, 1918 next to it, and then, incredulously, the just barely visible name of the person to whom the letter had been sent in San Francisco: Karl Albert Marianninski. *My God*, Francis thought. *I don't believe it, but it has to be true.* The father—the father who left the Rosin-Ortega woman to go to America, was Karl Albert Marianninski, the same Karl Albert Marianninski—it couldn't be otherwise, all the pieces fit—that was Pa, Francis' stepfather! Francis looked at Elaine in shock. He didn't want to believe it, but he couldn't escape what was apparently the truth.

"What's wrong, Francis," Elaine asked.

"The name on the envelope is Karl Albert Marianninski... it's Pa... my stepfather... he's the father."

"What! How can that be?" Elaine asked.

"I don't know how it all happened, but it has to be true," Francis said in a still shocked voice. "Pa did business all over the Orient just before the World War. It has got to be him."

"But, Francis, I don't understand. You said the name is Marianninski," Elaine said in a confused voice.

"When Pa married Ma and became an American citizen, he changed his name to Marian. It was originally Marianninski. Ma always said he did it to make himself sound more American, so he could get along better in business. Maybe he had other reasons for changing his name; maybe he just wanted to forget his past," Francis said.

A bewildered look came to Elaine's face. "Francis," she asked, "if Breidstein's father is your stepfather, then... isn't ...he—?"

"Yes, Elaine, Breidstein was my... my step brother," Francis said, completing what she couldn't say. "And he killed Hal, his own—and my—half brother."

Francis slowly sat down on the running board of the car. He had never felt so tired, so drained in all his life. He didn't say a word for several long moments, his mind trying to adjust to all that had happened, tonight—and years ago: Pa, the father of this murderer, Breidstein—or Willy Rosin or whoever he was, the man who murder Hal—and now tonight, Maria's death, by a wild shot from same man who was, in a cruel, convoluted way, his brother—the man whom Francis had killed only minutes before as he fought for his own life.

Francis finally let out a big sigh. Then he took a deep breath and looked at Elaine. "We need to bury Father Eduardo and Maria... and... Breidstein. We better siphon the gas out of the jeep, too. Then we can get out of here. The Japanese may not be far away."

89

THEY HAD BEEN DRIVING for more than an hour, having finished the three burials shortly after the sun rose. People—men, women, children, whole families—were again crowding the road.

"Chief, I don't like what I am beginning to see," Francis said with concern. "Some of the people along the side of the road are going north rather than south. And look, some are turning around and starting back north, too. We better find out what's going on," Francis said as he slowed the car and brought it alongside a group of people carrying luggage on a cart.

Chief Reynaldo leaned his head out the window. "Where are you going? Why are you going north toward the Japanese?" he asked in Tagalog.

"Toward the Japanese?" one of them answered back. "They are to the south of us too. We are trying to get away."

"To the south? Are you sure?"

"Yes, they are there. They landed—many, many of them—at Bauang early this morning, as the sun came up. If you continue on toward Lingayen, you will be captured for sure."

The chief turned to Francis and Elaine. "The Japanese are to the south of us. They landed at Bauang—that's between here and Lingayen. We cannot go on."

"Shit," Francis said in exasperation.

"Oh Lord, Francis," Elaine said. "Can we go back north, Chief?"

"No, no. That is where I came from and the Japanese are there too. No, we cannot go that way."

"What can we do, Francis?" Elaine asked, a frightened look on her face.

Francis was quiet for a moment. Then he asked, "Chief, what's to the east? What about going east?"

"It is a possibility, but it is very mountainous. There are some villages well into the interior. The largest is Bayambong—my grandfather once lived there.

He would sometimes return there, taking me with him, so I know some of the area. The roads are poor, but it is possible we might get to Bayambong in the car. If I remember—it has been a long time since I went there—there is a road, maybe a mile back—that goes east toward Bayambong. If we got to Bayambong, we might then go south and go around the Japanese, and get to Manila that way."

Francis began turning the car around.

"But Francis, what if we can't get around the Japanese?" Elaine asked anxiously.

Francis turned to look at Elaine with a determined look on his face. "Then we'll hide in the mountains—for as long as necessary."

THEY REACHED THE VILLAGE of Bayambong about midday—tired and hungry, but safe. They soon learned from the mayor of the village that there was one—and only one—radio in the village, and its battery was dead. But when Francis and the chief found out it used an ordinary car battery, they quickly pulled the battery out of the car and hooked it up to the radio.

As Francis sat down in front of the radio, he gave the chief a hopeful smile. Elaine stood beside Francis with her fingers crossed. Francis flipped on the power switch and began to turn various dials, trying to find a channel he thought his Post Y gang might be monitoring.

"Marian calling U.S. Navy Post Y. Marian calling Post Y Cavite. Come in, come in, Post Y. Over."

Francis flipped the send-receive switch. He listened for a moment. All he heard was static.

He flipped the switch again. "U.S. Navy Lieutenant Marian calling Post Y, Cavite. Come in, Post Y. Lieutenant Marian calling Post Y, Cavite. Come in Cavite. Over."

He flipped the switch again. Static again. He looked at the chief in frustration, hopelessness beginning to well up in him. "Damn."

He tried again. "Marian calling Post Y. Come in, damn you. Come in!" Francis yelled into the microphone. He flipped the switch again.

Then, "Post Y calling Marian, Post Y calling Marian," crackled from the radio speaker. A look of elation came to Francis' face. "You're not supposed to swear over the airways, you know, Francis." Francis recognized Ensign Louis Frankhill's voice. "Where the heck are you, Francis? We had about given you up. Over."

"I am in the mountains in northern Luzon, trying to keep out of the way of the Japs. It's a long story. I need to know where the Japs are, so I can figure out how to get back to Manila. Over."

"That answer is easy, Francis. They are about everywhere. Besides, you're not supposed to come back to Manila. A message came from McDonald this morning. He's ordered you back to Pearl. Over."

"How the hell am I supposed to get back to Pearl? Over."

"Well, some special arrangements were to be made. I don't think I should talk about them in the clear—Japs are probably listening. With you not here, I'm not sure what to do. I need to get instructions from Pearl. Can you get back on line exactly twenty-four hours from now, on our secondary frequency—you know the one I mean? Over."

"Yes, I do. In exactly twenty-four hours from now. Over."

"Okay. We'll be in contact then. Over and out."

THE REST OF THE DAY passed quickly as Francis and Elaine rested, while Reynaldo spent much of the time telling the village people what had been happening over the last several weeks. Elaine also had Chief Reynaldo get in bed and prop his leg up to try to reduce the swelling, which had started in the hours driving to Bayambong. By next morning, however, the swelling was almost gone, and the leg didn't seem to be showing any signs of infection. Elaine concluded that the complete passage of the bullet through the leg was probably the reason the wound was healing so well.

Then the twenty-four hours were up.

"Marian calling Post Y, Cavite. Marian calling Post Y, Cavite. Come in, come in, Post Y. Over."

Francis flipped the send-receive switch. Elaine and the chief stood by anxiously.

"Post Y calling Marian, Post Y calling Marian," came the immediate reply. "Can you hear us? Over."

"Yes, five-by-five, Post Y. Over," Francis answered.

"Francis, are you ready to receive coded instructions? Over."

"Yes," Francis answered. Anticipating the need, he had already gotten some pencils and paper from the village school before initiating the call. "Over."

"Okay, Francis, here's McDonald's instructions. Quote. Use sequential numbering code with your emergency call signal. Message begins: 16, 11, 11, 21, break, 20, 10, 8, break, 17, 4, 9, 4, 10, 20, break, 17, 21, break, 11, 7 ... " Louis continued to read off a list of numbers. As he did Louis' voice began to get weaker. Static began to get louder. "…23-hundred, break, 1, 2, 19, 3, 20, 21, 16, 4, 20, break, 12, 4, 5. Message ends. Unquote. That's it, Francis. Did you…?" The static got louder. "… a repeat. Say if want…?" The message became lost in static. Then the static began to fade, but no voices replaced it.

"Well, I hope I got the message right—the battery is dead," Francis said.

Francis looked at the numbers in front of him. He understood a sequential code. It was one of the first that he had learned at HYPO. Francis picked up the pencil again and wrote in large letters across the top of the sheet of paper his emergency call signal—a signal which seemed to epitomize his travels and life in the U.S. Navy, from enlistment in Chicago, to his assignments in China and Japan, to his life in the Philippines—and his devotion to the U.S. Navy:

CHICAGO CHINA BLUE

He followed the call signal with the rest of the alphabet, and then sequentially numbered each letter, dropping spaces and duplicates, to build his code. Then he rapidly decoded McDonald's message. Both Elaine and Reynaldo watched as Francis went through his manipulations.

When he finished, he lifted his head and read McDonald's instructions:

MEET SUB PALAU PT, S END PALANAN BAY, E COAST LUZON 2300 CHRISTMAS DAY.

"Christmas day… when is—holy cow, that's only two days from now. Chief, do you know where Palau Point is?" Francis asked.

"Yes, it's on the east coast, across the mountains," Chief Reynaldo answered.

"How long to get there?" Francis asked as he bit his lips.

"By car? There is no passable road that goes the whole way," Chief Reynaldo answered.

"No, no—the battery is dead. Maybe by horse?" Francis asked hopefully.

"It is possible. Let me talk to the village mayor," Reynaldo said.

In a few minutes, the chief returned, with the mayor in tow.

"There are no horses, but we can use some mules—and the mayor's son will guide us," Reynaldo said. The mayor nodded with a smile. "But if we are to get there in time we must leave immediately," Reynaldo said emphatically.

IT WAS A FEW MINUTES before eleven o'clock at night on Christmas day. Francis stood anxiously in the edge of the trees lining the beach, looking intently out to sea, Chief Reynaldo's flashlight in his hand. He scanned his eyes back and forth across the dark waters, not really sure where to look. Elaine and the chief stood next to him, also looking into the darkness. The young guide remained farther back in the trees, holding the mules.

At precisely eleven o'clock, a light flashed in the darkness. Francis' eyes became riveted on the spot where he had seen the light. He flicked the flashlight twice. A return light began blinking, sending out a signal in standard Morse code: G-I-V-E--E-M-E-R-G-E-N-C-Y--C-A-L-L--S-I-G-N.

"What are they saying?" Elaine asked excitedly.

"They want me to blink my emergency call signal—to be sure, I guess." Francis began clicking the flashlight on and off, sending out his signal.

In a moment, Francis received a return message: O-K--C-O-M-I-N-G--I-N.

"They're coming in to get us," Francis announced.

After several long minutes, Francis could make out a rubber raft moving in toward shore. "I see them. Let's go."

Elaine looked at the chief. "Do you need some help, Chief?" The two days of mule riding had not been good for the chief's leg.

"I have decided to stay here. I belong here, in the Philippines, with my people. I can help them most if I remain here—to fight the Japanese," Reynaldo said.

Francis looked intently at the chief. "I understand."

"Are you sure, Chief?" Elaine asked.

"Yes, very sure," Reynaldo answered.

Francis spoke. "Chief, I can't tell you how much I appreciate what you have done, how much you have helped—more than you will ever know." He took the chief's hand and shook it.

"You don't have to thank me, Lieutenant. Just return and help drive the Japanese from my islands."

Elaine stepped toward the chief and put her arms around him, hugging him tightly. Tears were rolling down her face.

Then Francis and Elaine ran across the sandy beach toward the rubber raft as it rolled in on the waves and slid to a stop.

90

FRANCIS AND ELAINE stood on the conning tower with the captain of the submarine as it made its way toward the dock. As they got closer, Francis could see a familiar face—McDonald's. He had a wide grin. Francis gave a wave; McDonald returned it as the submarine began to tie up.

As Francis stepped to the dock, followed by Elaine, he gave a salute to McDonald.

"Good to have you back, my boy," McDonald said.

"It's awfully good to be back, sir." Looking at Elaine, Francis continued. "Captain, this is Elaine Cotrall. She was a nurse at a mission on Bataan. I met her when—"

"I know when you met her, Francis. Hello, Miss Cotrall. It's good to meet you after all these years," McDonald said.

"Thank you, Captain, but what do you mean, after all these years?" Elaine asked.

"Well, I first learned about you when you and Francis… when Francis was learning Chinese in D.C.," McDonald answered.

Elaine's face reddened. She turned a questioning face at Francis. Francis shrugged his shoulders. "This man continually surprises me with what he knows."

"Francis is a very valuable commodity, Elaine—may I call you that?" Elaine nodded. "I have to make sure he stays out of trouble, so to speak. And speaking of trouble, Francis, you gave us quite a scare there for awhile," McDonald said.

"Well, to tell you the truth, I was little scared myself, sir," Francis said.

"I would imagine so, from what little you said in your message from the sub. Let's get to my office. We have a lot of talking to do. Where can I take you, Miss Cotrall?" McDonald asked.

"Well, a hotel sounds like a good idea to me," Elaine said.

"I know just the place—secluded but not far from the base. I think it will do quite well until you can find a more permanent place," McDonald said.

LATER IN MCDONALD'S OFFICE, after getting Elaine checked into the hotel, Francis related what had gone on since the few days before the attack on Pearl Harbor—what had happened at Breidstein's villa, finding Elaine at the mission, the attempt to warn MacArthur, his search for Breidstein—and Elaine—the murders by Breidstein, Maria's death, the death of Breidstein—Willy Rosin, alias Franz Lundstrom—the escape to Bayambong, and the pickup by submarine—all of it. Well, most of it. It was difficult to put it all in words, so much of what had happened was so personal, so bound up with his emotions. It wasn't just a bunch of facts that Francis could recite from memory. And Francis couldn't bring himself to tell McDonald about... Hal... Pa... and... Willy... and himself; that was for Francis and Elaine to know.

"I really didn't realize, until now, Captain, how much has happened since that Friday afternoon when Jack Burkhart called," Francis said after several hours of discussion with McDonald.

"Yes, a hell of a lot sure did. It clears up a bunch of questions for me. I'm sorry that we sort of left you in limbo while we were trying to figure our what to do—how to get you and your gang out. Your request for new orders caught me in D.C.—that's where I was when the attack on Pearl came—in the middle of looking at possibilities, which were slim to none. With the situation deteriorating so fast, we couldn't see any way to get you out, at least any way we thought had any real chance of working. But ending up in the mountains like you did opened up the possibility of using a sub pickup on the east coast of Luzon—something that we couldn't have done if you still had been pinned up in Cavite. And it was damn important that the Japs didn't get their hands on you."

"But my gang, Captain—they're still there," Francis said.

"I know, Francis, but there is nothing we can do about it right now. I did, however, order them out of Cavite on the twenty-fourth, when MacArthur declared Manila an open city. They evacuated with MacArthur's forces to Corregidor. That's where they are now, helping in communications," McDonald said.

"Great. I am glad to know they are safe," Francis said.

"I am too, Francis. I'm sure the War Department's doing everything it can to relieve MacArthur. Which brings me back to you. Any more doubts about what you want to do—and what you have to do?" McDonald asked with a deliberate voice.

"No doubts, sir, none," Francis said with a firm voice.

"Good. So, are you ready to get back to work?" McDonald said with a wide smile.

"Yes sir!" Francis almost shouted.

"Good. First, I want you to get over to the base hospital and get that ankle fully checked out. Then it's back to work for you. You'll be assigned to work with Rochefort in the dungeon—that place is busy as a beehive over there. They need all the help they can get!"

THE END

Epilogue

MORE THAN A MONTH HAD PASSED since Francis' return to Pearl. He and Elaine had found a bungalow a few miles from the HYPO station, and Francis was back in the swing of things, working in the dungeon with Rochefort. Elaine was working too—at a civilian hospital not far from Pearl Harbor.

Francis was seated at his desk, concentrating on a recent intercept that had apparently originated from a Japanese warship east of Guam. The phone on Francis' desk rang.

"Lieutenant Marian speaking," Francis said as he picked up the phone.

"Francis—McDonald. Be at Admiral Nimitz's office at fourteen hundred, today."

"What? Why?"

"Just be there," McDonald said. A second later the phone clicked dead.

AS HE ENTERED NIMITZ'S OUTER OFFICE, Francis saw that both McDonald and Rochefort were already there. Looking at his watch, McDonald said, "I was wondering if you were going to get here on time."

"Well, what is going—" Francis started to ask, but was interrupted by Nimitz's aide, Captain Davis.

"The admiral will see you now. He has only a few minutes, so don't spend too much time on small talk. Since he has taken over command of CINCPAC, we have been going hell bent for leather around here. But the admiral made it quite clear that he did want to speak to all of you personally, together."

Captain Davis knocked on Nimitz's door. He was answered by a "Come."

"Sir," Captain Davis said as he opened the door, "Lieutenant Commander Rochefort and Lieutenant Marian are here with Captain McDonald."

Nimitz rose from his desk and greeted them. Speaking to Rochefort, Nimitz said, "Well, I see you managed to get our of your hole in the ground, Joe. Do your people over there ever see the light of day?" Nimitz asked with a slight Texas drawl as he shook Rochefort's hand.

"Well, sir, on special occasions—like this perhaps, when the boss calls."

"And Cam, I suppose this is your protégé, Marian," Nimitz said as he shook McDonald's hand.

"It certainly is, sir."

"Lieutenant Marian," said Nimitz in a firm voice of welcome, as he extended this hand to Marian. "First, I want to congratulate you. I have seen the report on what you did in Manila. If attention had been paid to you, we might have averted some of the damage and loss of life here. But that's in the past. What we are concerned about now is the future—and how we are going to win this war," Nimitz said with a determined look on his face. "Captain Davis, uncover the wall map."

The wide expanse of the Pacific spread out before Francis. Orange dots and lines spread across the South Pacific and the East Indies. Some green dots were located along the coast of Australia. Scattered here and there along the periphery of the mass of orange does were blue dots. It didn't take any effort for Francis to figure out who was orange and who was blue.

"This represents our latest information on disposition of Jap forces and strongholds. Captain McDonald," Nimitz said as he looked Francis in the eye, "has told me, Lieutenant, about your remarkable memory abilities. I imagine you are taking this all in right now," Nimitz said as he swung his hand toward the map. "And I want you to. I want you to remember it—because we need to change all that orange to blue. And you are going to help us."

"I need information—disposition of forces, enemy intent, what's really in the Japs' plans—indeed, what's in their minds. Captain McDonald says you're the man to get it for me. Rochefort and his people, as well as Cam and his ONI people back in D.C., need more direct information to supplement and clarify what we pick up through our listening operations."

"Yes," Rochefort jumped in, without invitation from Nimitz "One of the biggest problems we have, Francis, if you haven't figured it out already, is that we don't have enough independent information to verify what our deciphering tells us. If we had more reliable sources to provide such information, we could radically increase the value of our deciphering work. We need more accurate information—from someone who can read Japanese and remembers what he reads."

Nimitz spoke. "I want you to return to the South Pacific, Lieutenant Marian. You will fly to Australia to set up a base of operations there. From there—

well, we will see what are the best opportunities—pick the low hanging fruit, so to speak. My staff is looking at some options as we speak. And we will be working with MacArthur for an appropriate delineation of your responsibilities and authorities, but you will be responsible to Captain McDonald. You are to be my ears and eyes in the South Pacific, Lieutenant Marian—that is, if you think you are up to it. What do you say, Lieutenant?"

Francis looked intently at the map for a few moments, focusing upon the Philippines. "Yes sir, I think I can help you change the complexion of that map."